The Age of Decayed Futurity

The Age of Decayed Futurity

The Best of Mark Samuels

Hippocampus Press

New York

Published by Hippocampus Press
P.O. Box 641, New York, NY 10156.
www.hippocampuspress.com

Cover and interior art © 2020 by Aeron Alfrey.
Cover design by Kevin I. Slaughter.
Hippocampus Press logo designed by Anastasia Damianakos.

First Edition
1 3 5 7 9 8 6 4 2
ISBN 978-1-61498-303-3 paperback
ISBN 978-1-61498-307-1 ebook

This volume is dedicated to my old friend,
John "Jay" Mundy Jr.,
of Scranton, Pennsylvania.

CONTENTS

Introduction, *by Michael Dirda*..9

Mannequins in Aspects of Terror..13

The White Hands 29

Apartment 205 45

Vrolyck 59

Ghorla 73

Cesare Thodol: Some Lines Written on a Wall..93

Sentinels 105

A Gentleman from Mexico.. 121

The Black Mould 145

Thyxxolqu.. 149

Regina vs. Zoskia... 161

The Age of Decayed Futurity.. 175

My World Has No Memories... 189

Outside Interference 197

The Crimson Fog 215

Court of Midnight 245

In the Complex 255

Acknowledgments 267

INTRODUCTION

Mark Samuels's narrators nearly always address the reader with calm reasonableness, in prose that is quiet and unruffled. His protagonists tend to be writers, scholars, or business professionals, almost always male, without wives or children. I suspect the presence of families would risk causing his stories to grow unbearably painful. Instead, Samuels's hero-victims simply wander—haplessly, inexorably but often with philosophical detachment—into a Twilight Zone of the uncanny that usually climaxes with their death and transfiguration.

Transfiguration? In Samuels's work physical bodies may be ravaged by disease, or half-burned, or mutilated; they may suddenly disintegrate or calcify; they may even be taken over by an undead spirit or an alien life form. And yet this destruction or abuse of our corporeal shell often leads to revelation. More often than not, Samuels's protagonists disturbingly end up accepting, even embracing, that which they initially feared and fought against. His final, kicker-like sentences announce, often quite abruptly, that a new reality awaits when one surrenders to the Otherness. In fact, his stories are always about the triumph of that Otherness, though the consequence may be awe and wonder as much as horror. Even with a face half-eaten away by some unseen entity one character shows an expression of "insane ecstasy." He is not alone. Samuels's fiction could readily supply myriad examples for a latter-day Longinus's "On the Monstrous Sublime."

That phrase—it derives from critic S. T. Joshi—doesn't describe merely the effect of Samuels's writing, it also suggests something of its philosophical tenor. Throughout the pages of *The Age of Decayed Futurity*, the narrators reflect on metaphysical and epistemological questions. One madman's particular brand of horror is actually grounded in an esthetic principle:

"Remember that there is always an end to suffering in life: pain, disease, and madness lead either to recovery or extinction, but such is not necessarily the case in art. In art a moment may be fixed for all eternity."

In another tale, the unnamed narrator reflects:

"There were hints that the revelations experienced were based on the concept that it is the dead that sustain the structure of the waking world through their dreams and that all living existence is illusory."

In the context of their stories, neither of these observations is made gratuitously.

As is well known, Samuels laces his fiction with allusions to the classics of supernatural literature, notably the works of Arthur Machen, Algernon Blackwood, M. R. James, H. P. Lovecraft, and Thomas Ligotti. Take one small instance from what is still his best-known story, "The White Hands": In appearance the former Oxford don Alfred Muswell closely resembles a composite of Arthur Machen (note the initials) and the occult scholar Montague Summers. That same story's beautiful Lilith Blake—some of whose weird tales she may have written after her death—calls to mind Poe's Ligeia even as she also possesses something of the post-mortem influence of Medea da Carpi, the femme fatale of Vernon Lee's "Amour Dure."

Given his literariness, Samuels may be viewed, from some angles, as a metafictionist, constantly reworking or amplifying the classics of the supernatural tradition. Throughout the pages of *The Age of Decayed Futurity* attentive readers may detect variations on John Collier's "Evening Primrose," the film *Apocalypse Now,* Poe's "Conversation of Eiros and Charmion," M. P. Shiel's *The Purple Cloud,* Borges's metaphysical fables, the myth of Medusa, Fred Chappell's "The Adder," Richard Matheson's *I Am Legend,* and the gruesome Grand Guignol of both the theater of cruelty and modern splatter cinema. This doesn't mean that Samuels actually knows all these earlier works, though I suspect he does.

Overall, Samuels likes to play with notions typically associated with the science fiction of Philip K. Dick: How can we distinguish between what is real and what isn't? Who is human or alive and who isn't? Might everything around us be a Potemkin Village, masking cosmic nothingness or some horrific truth? Samuel's "The Crimson Fog" opens, "How far does reality extend? That's the question I keep asking myself." According to another story, the world of screens and electronic signals "actually is the real world and the one outside, *our one,* is fake." One character discovers that "everything human is a sham: a façade for something else entirely. And what lies behind the façade cannot be understood." In several stories, the protagonist uncovers what amounts to—in Thomas Ligotti's phrase—a conspiracy against the human race.

Samuels's favorite tropes include dreams, derelict or labyrinthine buildings, run-down European cities, subtle infection and contamination, mandalas, the dead alive, a pervasive sense of alienation, and the quiet desperation of the corporate world. Some stories approach the Kafkaesque or go beyond the darker fabulations of the contemporary writers Steven Millhauser and Zoran Živković. Above all, though, Samuels's prose remains engagingly seductive— when his narrators begin to speak one cannot choose but hear:

"I had been wandering aimlessly for months around the dark corners of conquered Europe seeking respite from the tyranny of dreams when I finally found myself a resident of the Court of Midnight."

Naturally, we never find out who or what conquered Europe, but we do learn more about the tyranny of dreams, the Court of Midnight and the leprosy-like disease called lunar fever. In one powerful story, "In the Complex," we follow the course of a human being's psychological and physical degradation. Like Winston Smith in *Nineteen Eighty-Four,* the narrator comes to believe that all the mutilations visited upon him are justified responses to his trivial acts of free will. In an instance of Orwellian double-thought, he parrots some official propaganda: "Communicable disease of my type is a form of violence when those afflicted by it refuse treatment. It is even more dangerous because it manifests itself unseen, with no physical symptoms."

Reader, you won't regret buying this volume of "the best of Mark Samuels": these are wonderful stories that will leave you shaken and stirred. Unreliable narration, Lovecraftian nightmare, psychological dislocation, pervasive unease, monstrous entities, numinous climaxes and, throughout, elegant prose—what more could one want from modern urban horror? Start reading *The Age of Decayed Futurity* and you will understand why Ramsey Campbell called Mark Samuels "the contemporary British master of visionary weirdness."

—MICHAEL DIRDA

MANNEQUINS IN ASPECTS OF TERROR

"Your eyes did see my unformed substance."

—Psalm 139

The office tower had long fascinated me.

The building dominated the skyline in the Euston area of London and consisted of twenty-seven floors with an exterior of green, dark glass. I would gaze at this structure from the window of Barlow and Barlow Associates, the architectural firm at which I had been employed for the past five years. During this period of time, I had observed a process of gradual abandonment taking place in which company after company deserted the edifice. Commercial success seemed to elude any business located there. An increasing number of its windows stayed dark at night. From what information I could gather, those working within its confines complained of a general malaise and progressive worsening of staff morale. I learnt that various health and safety checks were made in order to try and determine the nature of the problem but that these proved inconclusive. There were rumours that the air-conditioning carried some form of Legionnaires' disease, but extensive tests showed no trace of its presence. Blame was officially attached to a psychosomatic tendency that indiscriminately affected all those who worked in the tower. This conclusion satisfied no one and was not favoured as the reason for the nebulous degeneration amongst the staff and management, with both sides preferring to cling tenaciously to their own theories as to the true cause of the problem.

Finally, I saw that the last of the companies had seemingly relocated and the single floor that had been lit during the hours of darkness now possessed windows as black and as much a part of the night as the others. In my mind's eye I saw the building's abandoned and silent spaces, empty offices, and labyrinth of chill corridors. The vacancy of the tower stood in stark contrast to the teeming metropolis surrounding it, whose streets were filled with men who swarmed like a colony of insects.

I came to believe that the structure had a profound effect upon my work. My past architectural designs, created on behalf of the firm, brought me little satisfaction. My realised projects had only consisted of nondescript homes, public utilities, and an unremarkable bus depot in the north of the country. I longed for the opportunity to work on a larger scale, on some construct that could be seen for miles around: my own pinnacle amongst the others scattered across the city. It was my ambition to be the designer of another tower that might have the same stark prominence: rising high above the teeming hordes, framed only by the sky and whose very existence provoked awe. In idle moments I would draw plans of my own proposals and, invariably, their lineaments carried some recollection of the structure that was in my view for most of the day.

I told myself that it was solely for the purposes of my pet architectural project that I so badly wished to wander freely around inside the office tower. Yet perhaps it was also my desire for isolation that drew me to it.

Certainly I was conscious of its appeal becoming stronger as more and more of the windows were unlit at evening. Thus, now completely abandoned, it seemed to me a consummation of terrible beauty amidst the maddening whirl of asinine human activity. I viewed it as a vertical desert, closed off from the outside world, a region without any distractions. Whenever I thought of finally examining its interior, the prospect was combined with a sense of my being in an abandoned structure, without the trappings of human occupancy. It would be like entering a desolate cathedral and paying homage to a cryptically absent god.

A few days after the lights on that last occupied floor were extinguished I tried to gain entry to the deserted edifice. I had done my work for the day at the architects' firm and tramped through the series of streets that lay between my place of employment and my destination. Even though I knew that my expedition was likely to end in failure, I felt that an attempt to gain entrance to the office tower had to be made. If I encountered a night-watchman patrolling outside, I hoped that I might even be able to bribe him into allowing me access to the interior of the building.

As I drew near to that gigantic monolith it gradually blotted out much of the night sky. Up close I was forced to accept the fact that gaining entry was next to impossible. The foyer had been boarded over and padlocked and the first two floors were protected by corrugated iron sheets. Looking up again at the darkened windows beyond these iron sheets, I fancied that I saw briefly a pale white face at one of them. But the sight was momentary and I told myself that it must have been only an illusion. The whole building was almost certainly deserted and there was no reason for anyone to be in there.

For a time I wandered aimlessly around the building's perimeter and across the abandoned square of concrete loggias and unused parking facilities in which it stood. In the end, however, I gave up on my hopeless task and made my way home to my apartment on the other side of the city.

For weeks thereafter I would think of the edifice during the day. While at night I would dream of treading those lost corridors and empty offices, canteens, stairways, storage rooms, and bathrooms. During my lunch hours at the company where I worked I would make studies of the tower, charting its angles and lines in great detail. My fascination with it made my colleagues curious, and some of them even asked to view the structure through my field glasses. These I had purchased so that I could examine it in more detail from a distance. I felt resentment at any interest my fellow workers displayed and believed that I alone could truly appreciate the splendid starkness of its design and the desolation that it housed within.

Doubtless this behaviour added to my already strange reputation. Those who knew me had long regarded me with a certain suspicion. This attitude seemed to stem primarily from knowledge of the amnesia that had afflicted me five years ago.

They found me wandering aimlessly in the streets of the city, unable to tell anyone who I was or whence I came. Personal memories of my past life did not return, and my new identity had been constructed piecemeal ever since. Consequently, I felt like a character that disappeared in the interval between the first and second act of a play, only to re-emerge in the second act of an entirely different play. For the first year after my amnesia I was an object of unwelcome attention by the police, for it was obvious that my features had been radically changed. Evidence of plastic surgery was apparent from the scars I bore; however, my blank fingerprints denied the authorities the means of linking me to any criminal or suspect whose details they had on file. DNA tests were maddeningly inconsistent. That I had been a victim of some assault or accident was obvious, for both my hair and teeth were absent and I was forced to resort to artificial substitutes. Even dental records were useless in helping to establish my former identity.

Eventually the police had to concede that there were insufficient grounds for keeping me under surveillance. It was then that I began to try and start my life all over again. Every job vacancy for which I had applied had been with firms of architects, and I felt an unaccountable compulsion to take up this type of employment. After months of fruitless interviews, the architects Barlow and Barlow Associates agreed to take me on as a trainee for a trial period, at a very low rate of pay. However, it was soon apparent that I was already familiar with the requirements that the position demanded. Indeed, as I worked, a feeling of déjà vu was my almost constant companion, and specialised knowledge that I was not aware of possessing came back to me. Consequently, I rose through the firm's ranks with great rapidity and was soon entrusted with senior projects, though their limited scope gave me no real sense of satisfaction. Barlow and Barlow realised that they had gained an employee whose abilities were of a high order and yet who was without the usual architectural qualifications that accompany them.

One afternoon, whilst I was making my way back from a café where I had purchased a sandwich for my lunch, I was handed a flyer. I had just turned a busy corner close to the local underground station, and from amongst the crowds of people an individual had stepped forward and thrust a piece of paper into my hand. I had taken it automatically. But when I glanced at it I was astonished to find that it was an advertising leaflet with the name "Eleazer Golmi" printed in bold letters across the top. It was a name of great interest to me, no less than the name of a man I considered a genius. I looked back over my shoulder to try and locate the man who was handing out these flyers, but he was lost in the crowd.

I turned back towards the direction from which I'd just come, pushing past the people in my way, until I was at the spot where the flyer had been handed to me, just outside the station. I could see no one handing out leaflets. There was a homeless man wrapped in a blanket asking for spare change, a woman giving away free lifestyle magazines, but no sign of my quarry. Then, out of the corner of my eye, I caught sight of a stiff-backed person walking awkwardly towards the ticket barriers in the station, and he half turned to regard me from behind dark glasses. Our gazes met and, though I could make out nothing of his shielded eyes, I was struck by the strangeness of his skin, which possessed an almost plastic sheen.

Once I was back in my office I examined the flyer more closely. It was an invitation to an art installation that had long been housed on the uppermost floors of the tower, and whose existence I had not suspected. This installation, conceived by the artist Eleazer Golmi, had apparently been exhibited there for an indefinite period. It was entitled *Mannequins in Aspects of Terror,* and the leaflet claimed that the participant would enjoy an audio and visual art-experience of "infinite claustrophobia." Golmi's output was well known to me, though not in the context of the art world. He had also been the architect who had designed the very building that was to house this installation.

Due to my interest in his structure, I had tried on several occasions to track down Golmi and express my appreciation for his designs, but had been advised that he no longer worked in the profession and had, effectively, "gone underground" after a severe personal crisis ten years ago. Those persons I spoke to regarding Golmi had said that some sort of nervous breakdown was to blame for his disappearance. But now it seemed that he had returned and completely reinvented himself as a conceptual artist.

The flyer told me that the installation had been temporarily closed for new additions to be incorporated into the work, but that it was due to reopen on the last day of the following week. Admission was at the door, spontaneous, and with no prior booking.

*

When I arrived at the office tower on the designated night, I found that the padlocks had been removed, the boards covering its windows had been taken away, and the foyer had been opened. The installation was advertised by means of a hastily erected poster on a small hoarding next to the entrance. This poster had a gaudy yellow background and black lettering in a Gothic script. At its centre was a grainy photograph of Golmi. He was in his fifties with brylcreemed grey hair. He possessed a high forehead and dark eyes. One of them, the right, seemed considerably larger than the other, giving him a strange, almost lopsided appearance. Even aside from this outlandish feature, the face in the photograph was bizarre. Its expression had that rigid look that was common in daguerreotypes from the mid-nineteenth century, where the subject had to be perfectly still for four or five minutes due to the time the camera shutter had to be open for the exposure.

I again gazed up at the monolith whose presence signified the vacancy in which I longed to immerse myself. The fact that Golmi had designed the very building that he had chosen as the backdrop to his art installation offered the possibility that he, too, had realised the spectral potential of the tower. Perhaps he was also one of those who relished desolate spaces in the teeming metropolis. Might this not be indicated by the fact that he had kept his installation intact as the edifice became utterly deserted? I wondered if it were the case that some dim intimation had come to him during his architect days as to the final destiny of his project: to house his own personal nightmare, to create a zone where human beings could not live. Could the blueprint of elaborate angles and lines that went to make up the structure have been designed to cause the very malaise from which those that worked there had suffered? Might not the mannequins in his latest project, the art installation, be metaphors for those assimilated within the interior vacuum of the building? I thought of plastic imitations of the human body: unthinking, blank; form without content, eyes that stare but do not see, hands that reach but do not grasp, mouths shaped for noise but unable to speak.

I entered the foyer and made my way to an unmanned desk with a sign declaring that the installation began on floor twenty-five and that payment was to be made after the "art-experience." Next to the sign was a list of entry times. I saw by my watch that the next vacant slot was in some twenty minutes. The last visitor had signed the register five minutes ago and marked the entry time clearly. It seemed that admittance was staggered to ensure that each visitor was sufficiently isolated.

At the time allocated I accordingly signed in my name in the register, then wandered over to one of several lifts. A sign indicated that this only was to be used in order to visit the art installation, the others being out of order. I watched the numbers on the indicator board above the entrance flash from twenty-five downwards as the lift descended. While I waited I looked over at the blank spaces where once there had been brass plaques advertising the companies that had traded in the tower.

When the lift arrived I opened the outer door and then pulled back the inner trellis door that separated me from the panelled wooden cage within. The interior was not large, having a capacity for a maximum of four persons. The back wall was comprised of a full-length mirror. Gazing into it, I was somewhat startled by my anxious-looking appearance. My eyes seemed to stare wildly from behind my glasses and my cheeks were pale and drawn with tension. The business suit that I was obliged to wear to work seemed apt, as did the briefcase I carried, since I had come directly from my office and had not had the opportunity to change my clothes.

I still harboured unease at the idea of the sterility and emptiness of the edifice being compromised by its now housing an art installation. I hoped that my only consolation would not simply lie in the fact that it alone would provide the access I craved to the building itself. At worst, I thought that I might be able to bypass the installation and explore those regions unaffected by it. Doubtless it was this internal conflict that had given rise to the feeling of tension that welled up inside of me.

The cage rumbled upward through the lift shaft, and floor after floor passed me by before I reached the twenty-fifth, where the installation began. I pulled back the trellis door, opened the outer one, and entered a long, deserted corridor that was dimly lit and silent. The floor was covered in tiled green linoleum. It curled upwards with old age where it met the walls. In certain places it had come away altogether, revealing the stained concrete underneath. I also saw holes in the false ceiling, where panels of polystyrene had fallen down. Teeming cables and wires spilled out of these gaps. There was an opening to my left and, impelled by sheer curiosity, I went through it into an abandoned bathroom that was thick with dust. The cubicle doors hung ajar and the toilet bowls were broken, with fragments of porcelain scattered everywhere. I left and went back to the corridor, where I saw a notice indicating the direction I was to follow.

I turned right. Up to this point I could discern no evidence of the art installation, for this new corridor seemed to be nearly identical to the first one. I was, however, beginning to feel a sense of emptiness creep over me, deadening my spirits and replacing the tension I'd previously felt. The isolation was complete. I felt utterly alone, and as I walked through the confines of this artificial void its atmosphere of neglect and decay steadily numbed my mind.

And then, as if from a great distance, I believed that I heard a sound, much like the white noise found on frequencies between radio stations. It grew no louder as I proceeded and I could not detect its source, though I suspected that it must have been piped through concealed speakers. Looking through the windows to my left, I saw the vast panorama of the city below, its glittering sodium-orange lights appearing to be so very far removed from this enclave of desolation. Within the building it was eternal twilight, grey and shadowy.

There was a large office to my right and I entered into it. The room was completely empty and there were marks on the thin carpet where tables, chairs, and filing cabinets must have once stood. I moved on. By now, it was only through a conscious effort that I could detect the continuous hiss of background static, familiarity having rendered it subliminal. But when I made the effort I realised that it served as no distraction, but was like whispering in a void, unintelligible yet charged with an awful significance, some cryptic nothingness behind surface reality.

I saw another notice as I passed along the next corridor. It was a ragged thing, with letters scrawled as if in a child's handwriting and made of cardboard. Written upon it were the words: *Mannequins in Aspects of Terror.*

Then I encountered the first of the mannequins. In the twilight of that corridor, and from a distance, I initially thought that it was an attendant, but the object's perfect stillness suggested otherwise.

As I drew nearer to the mannequin I noticed that the background hiss contained a new element. This change in its nature alerted me again to its presence. There were definite words amongst the static, though broken and garbled, like speech distorted by poor radio reception. I could not make out the words, but the voice seemed to speak as if in terrible pain, as if it were incoherent with that pain. I thought that one of the words might be "alive" croaked out over and over again, but could not be sure.

I had drawn close enough to see the face of the mannequin. The artist had indeed wrought a thing of terror. Its face was rigid and frozen in stark panic, as if it were confronted by an unbearably horrific sight. The arms were raised, warding off some approaching menace. As I stared at the dummy, I felt contaminated by its aspect and could not help imagining that my own features were mimicking its expression. And I thought of that gaping, lifeless mouth actually forming the broken words that mingled with the low, background noise of the static, driving my mind towards the infinite moment of fear in which the mannequin itself had been frozen.

This noise began to fade as I continued to walk across the length of the corridor and was gradually replaced by another sound, like that of people muttering in low tones to one another whilst engaged in office work in some part of the building very close by. The voices were just audible, and I could not shake off the feeling that those speaking were conscious of my presence and discussing my imminent arrival, even though the idea was patently absurd.

I even began to mutter to myself involuntarily, and the sound of my own voice offered no comfort, for its low and enfeebled tone only mimicked that of those ahead.

At the next turning was a room that appeared, at first glance, to be still in use, for it was brightly lit, unlike the rest of the twenty-fifth floor. I paused for a moment, taken in by the illusion, until I perceived that the figures therein were absolutely motionless. I entered and had the unsettling idea that they had stopped their activities once I had first caught sight of them. I told myself that a hidden motion sensor had detected me and must have simply turned off a tape recording that was part of the installation, but the irrational part of my mind still insisted that I was being observed and, even worse, possibly *controlled* in some indefinable fashion.

Four mannequins occupied this office, all of which, except one, were hunched in front of dead computer screens. Their hands were at the keyboards, as if they had just been interrupted in the act of typing. The dummies were dressed in business suits that showed signs of old age and wear. The elbows and cuffs of their pinstriped suits were frayed, with patches of ugly discoloration in the fabric. The mannequins seemed to be smiling. But as I drew closer for a better look at them, I saw that those smiles were not pleasant, but were crafted so as to resemble the grins of lunatics, without humour or warmth.

The only dummy standing had been clad in one of the same shoddy suits as the others, but its expression was entirely different. The thing's eyes bulged and its mouth was open in a grimace of agony much wider than any possible in a mouth of flesh and bone—a grimace that reached literally across the whole width of its plastic face. Its body was twisted over to one side as if in contorted agony. This thing of profound deformity seemed to have been designed wholly in order to convey repellence to its observer.

When I had left the place and carried on walking along the corridor outside, the sounds of activity started up again behind me—furtively at first, but with increasing boldness as each step that I took drew me further away from the source. I could not help looking back as I moved away, for I had an irrational dread that the standing mannequin would start into spasmodic life and come after me. I could not rid my mind of the image.

This whole experience had not been quite what I had anticipated. The mannequins did not seem to symbolise the void that I had imagined. They seemed rather to stand for some greater abyss that lay beyond it, a wasteland, not where thoughts die away, but are endlessly repeated, where madness is continuous and without cessation.

I had by this time reached the stairwell up to the next floor, and a notice indicated that I was to ascend. The walls here were in a state of advanced decay, being riddled with cracks and spaces where the sepia paint had flaked off. A draught of air coming from above bore with it the unmistakable odour of mould. The noise of movement ahead became louder, and I could hardly bring myself to make the climb up the stairwell. The echoes filtered through a door directly at the top, and now that the sound was clearer I detected what I thought were more voices. These were not like the low mutterings that I had heard previously. They were much clearer and made no attempt at concealment. They filled me with dread. These voices possessed a breathless and hollow quality as if the unintelligible words they uttered were formed by some imperfect replica of the human model, speaking in accents that betrayed their attempt at imitation. I thought of lips not designed for speech, croaking out anguished words, trying vainly to communicate but hampered by their own rigidity.

I stood there on the stairwell for what seemed like hours. Whether it was the awful atmosphere that worked on my brain or whether the sound was real I couldn't tell, but I heard from the floor below awkward footsteps coming closer. Whatever it was seemed to stagger forward, dragging its limbs awkwardly like a drunk. The sound made me panic, and I raced towards the door ahead, bolting through it with no other thought save flight.

When I was through the door the sound of the broken voices ceased. I stood shaking with my back to it, listening for signs of movement. There was none. And I wondered (if I dared open it): would there be a form slumped on the stairs, a form horribly familiar, now again inanimate, or would a dummy be standing there with a look of triumph, its impossibly wide mouth framed in a grimace that reached from ear to ear and with arms outstretched as if to clutch me in a deathly embrace? Yet I heard nothing further and so I pressed on, knowing that I could not bear to go retrace my steps.

Although all was now quiet, the smell of the mould was overpowering. It grew everywhere in this new corridor. There were great patches of it on bare walls and even underfoot on the worn linoleum. A notice told me to bear left, and I found myself in another abandoned office. On a table were several duplicate sheets of paper, filled with handwritten words. The strip lighting here was as poor as elsewhere in the building and this, coupled with the awkward script, made the writing difficult to decipher. But I carried the papers to the dusty window where the faint illumination from outside made reading a little easier. The manuscript was some sort of manifesto, or statement, written by the artist Golmi:

Mannequins in Aspects of Terror: An Art Installation by Eleazer Golmi

> Many have ruminated on the attraction of horror in art and in literature, and have drawn erroneous conclusions. The art of false horror seeks not to engender actual fear, but to distance those experiencing it and allow them a pleasurable frisson—the sensation that one might approach without arrival. But this art installation is an immersion into terror. It is designed to generate a situation wherein the individual is subject to that terror and participates di-

rectly. In this installation one does not play a character, as does an actor in a play: one is that character. Nor must the artist himself be exempt from this necessary immersion. In order for the work of art to be authentic he also must become a component of it. He must feel the terror that he creates.

Remember that there is always an end to suffering in life: pain, disease, and madness lead either to recovery or to extinction, but such is not necessarily the case in art. In art a moment of suffering may be fixed for all eternity.

Imagine, if you will, simulacra whose existence is such a state. This is the purpose of my installation. The desolate spaces are my own enclosed universe of terror. And the mannequins are my children, playing in the wilderness of torment, in the misery of one moment of supreme terror. And I, too, play with them, having been allowed this privilege by deciphering the secret of the alphabet of the 221 gates.

The greatest fear of which I can conceive is not that of murder or torture or any of the outrages that man inflicts upon his fellow man. The greatest fear is the prolongation of life indefinitely, to a point where all thoughts are endlessly revisited, where every memory loses its meaning by repetition, where concepts finally blend into one: consciousness doomed to immortality—a mind filled with the nightmare of its own being, a mind that is dying in perpetuity without final release.

Our flesh and blood perishes and with it perishes the mind. But imagine a mind in a body that cannot die: a body of plastic and paint carefully crafted in an aspect of pain, terror, disease, madness, or decay. The form mirrors the inner torment. And then further imagine what it might be like to be a mind imprisoned forever within that artificial body. What distinction is there between mind and matter? Imprisoned within a mannequin in an aspect of terror, the two become one.

The mind, now riddled with the continuous agony of its new body, built expressly for suffering, believes it to be the only existence it has ever known. Plastic and paint seem more real than flesh and blood. Who then is to say which of them is artificial? And should these new bodies start into motion, should those glass eyes turn in their sockets, who then would deny their occupants the right to welcome visitors to this cryptic universe of terror I have wrought? To welcome them in the only way they know how, so that the same visitors might also participate in their haunted cavalcade throughout all eternity? Let me then conclude by thanking you for choosing to experience my installation, for choosing to contribute to my pretty little vision, where henceforth you will see only through my eyes.

YHVH Elohim Met.

As I finished reading those words I was overwhelmed by the sensation that I was trapped in another man's nightmare. I felt as if I no longer possessed an independent existence and that, like the dummies I had encountered, I was some mental construction wrought by Eleazer Golmi. The idea was ridiculous, of course. I had not been dreamed into existence. And yet in this "enclosed universe of terror," as he termed it, the identity I had forged over the past five years seemed under assault. What was I, after all, but a man with no past, an amnesiac whose own life had been partially obliterated by an unknown accident?

I left the room feeling shaken and drained and made my way again along the grimy corridor covered with mould. All the doors that I passed were locked, although many had glass panels and beyond them I could see more of the mannequins. Some had their faces turned to the walls and were set in crouching positions, whilst others were curled up in a ball on the concrete floors, surrounded by debris. There was one dummy, however, which had been positioned in front of one of the windows in the doors. It was more horrifying than any I had thus far seen.

The dummy's face, if such a corroded and incomplete thing could be called a face, was close to the glass panel. Its head was thrown back and the eyes had been rolled up in their sockets. All that remained of its artificial hair were a few charred strands hanging from a mutilated scalp. The paint covering that terrifying visage had been clawed away and the plastic beneath was scarred and pitted as if burnt by acid. Yet in what remained of its features it was still possible to recognise a hint of awareness of the creative destruction the artist had exercised upon it. This awareness, frozen in time, was that it had been shaped to suffer and that it existed for no other purpose. That I knew this to be the case was not simply a matter of seeing. It was more a chilling feeling of *kinship* with the object. The longer I was in its presence, the more this feeling gained upon me. And a horrible idea came to me that my own flesh was merely a temporary reprieve, an interlude between escape and recapture.

I finally turned away in dismay. But I had come far and reasoned that I had almost reached the end of this "art installation." I turned left into a further corridor. At the far end there was a handwritten sign reading "Exit."

There was no way to go but forward in order to end the experience. As I began to walk towards a set of double doors where the passageway terminated, I felt stiffness in my limbs, like the onset of cramp, and my movements became awkward. I told myself that it was only exhaustion that slowed me down, that the horrible sensations I was experiencing were a consequence of shock. At the same time I was aware that the command I had over my movements seemed to slip away, as if I were a mere automaton. Even my gaze seemed to be controlled by another will.

By the time I reached the end of the corridor the pain I suffered in my limbs was unbearable. I pushed open the doors, drawn forward as if by invisible strings, and beyond was a large room that had once served as a canteen. The tables and plastic chairs were still there, though some were broken and others had been tipped over. Rubbish, mostly polystyrene cups and empty cartons, was strewn all around the canteen's linoleum floor and the tiled walls were smeared with grease. Scattered amongst all this debris were dozens and dozens of mannequin parts. There were no doors leading off of this room, only windows letting in a sickly sodium glow cast by the city lights outside.

The dummies here had been torn to pieces. There were heads, torsos, and limbs scattered around. It seemed that someone had crafted these things and then deliberately wrecked them. My own agony was so awful that I could hardly register the enormity of the scene before me. Despite having no control over my motion or gaze, I was still directed to walk amongst those last horrors.

The closest mannequin to me had the appearance of the victim of a car crash. Its face and trunk had been smashed in and one of its arms was ripped away. Only the eyes were whole, the glass eyes, and peering into them I knew, with awful clarity, that consciousness was present in what remained. There was a mind imprisoned in this broken form that was experiencing an agony that no living thing could bear, that flesh and blood could not possibly tolerate.

The artist, the maker of these mannequins, had reached beyond the boundaries of pain and terror in his work, had taken them to an extreme that no human form was designed to experience. The very word agony could not begin to describe their state: to be endlessly dying and never to be released.

But I moved on, screaming soundlessly in my mind, as my stiff limbs were willed into motion by another mind, each step being the action of that which was not made to move. And all around me were those dismembered dummies in their eternal death throes, each separate part riddled with pain. As my legs jerked forwards, one of my feet caught the arm of a mannequin, sending it clattering across the floor.

My eyes involuntarily rolled back in their sockets. I saw the re-flected lights shifting and changing on the ceiling as my knees buckled under me and with a clatter my body slumped forward to the floor amongst the mounds of mutilated plastic remains.

I heard the sound of footsteps approaching and then felt my-self being turned over onto my back. Looming above me was a man whose skin seemed more like plastic than flesh. His right eye was much larger than his left, and this gave his features a lopsided appearance. He made a low, grinding noise like broken machine gears, trying to gain control of a mouth that should not be able to utter sounds. Although the words were indistinct, he seemed to be saying *"good to have you back."*

He delved into a leather tool-bag that he carried with him, drew out a blowtorch, and ignited the hissing gas flow. The blue jet of flame glittered in his dead, cold eyes. And I knew that the agony I had experienced up to now was only a foretaste of that eternal agony to come once the artist Golmi set to work on my helpless, immobile body.

THE WHITE HANDS

You may remember Alfred Muswell, whom devotees of the weird tale will know as the author of numerous articles on the subject of literary ghost stories. He died in obscurity just over a year ago.

Muswell had been an Oxford don for a time, but left the cloisters of the university after an academic scandal. A former student (now a journalist) wrote of him in a privately published memoir:

> Muswell attempted single-handedly to alter the academic criteria of excellence in literature. He sought to eradicate what he termed the "tyranny of materialism and realism" from his teaching. He would loom over us in his black robes at lectures and tutorials, tearing prescribed and classic books to shreds with his gloved hands, urging us to read instead work by the likes of Sheridan Le Fanu, Vernon Lee, M. R. James and Lilith Blake. Muswell was a familiar sight amongst the squares and courtyards of the colleges at night and would stalk abroad like some bookish revenant. He had a very plump face and a pair of circular spectacles. His eyes peered into the darkness with an indefinable expression that could be somewhat disturbing.

You will recall that Muswell's eccentric theories about literature enjoyed a brief but notorious vogue in the 1950s. In a series of essays in the short-lived American fantasy magazine *The Necrophile,* he championed the supernatural tale. This was at a time when other academics and critics were turning away from the genre in disgust, following the illiterate excesses of pulp magazines such as *Weird Tales.* Muswell argued that the anthropocentric concerns of realism had the effect of stifling the much more profound study of infinity. Contemplation of the infinite, he contended, was the faculty that separated man from beast. Realism, in his view, was the literature of the prosaic. It was the quest for the hidden mysteries, he contended, that formed the proper subject of all great literature. Muswell also believed that literature, in its highest form, should unravel the secrets of life and death. He never fully explained this latter concept,

but he hinted that its attainment would involve some actual alteration in the structure of reality itself. This, perhaps inevitably, led to
his being dismissed in academic circles as a foolish mystic.

After his quiet expulsion from Oxford, Muswell retreated to the
lofty heights of Highgate. From here, in the London village that had
harboured Samuel Taylor Coleridge during the final phase of his
struggle against opium addiction, Muswell continued his literary cru-
sade. A series of photographs reproduced in the fourth issue of *The
Necrophile* show Muswell wandering through the leafy streets of
Highgate clad in his black three-piece suit, plump and bespectacled,
cigarette jammed between his lips. In one of his gloved hands is a
book of ghost stories by the writer he most admired, Lilith Blake.
This Victorian author is perhaps best known for her collection of
short stories, *The Reunion and Others*. Then, as now, fabulously rare,
this book was printed in an edition of only one hundred copies.
Amongst the cognoscenti it has acquired legendary status. Muswell
was undoubtedly the greatest authority on her life and works. He
alone possessed the little that remained of her extant correspondence, as well as diaries, photographs, and other personal effects.

In moving to Highgate, Muswell was perhaps most influenced
by the fact that Blake had been resident in the village for the entire
twenty-two years of her brief life. Her mortal remains were interred
in the old West Cemetery in Swains Lane.

I first met Alfred Muswell after writing a letter to him requesting
information about Lilith Blake for an article I was planning on supernatural writers of the late nineteenth and early twentieth centuries.
After an exchange of correspondence he suggested that we should
meet one afternoon in the reading room of the Highgate Literary and
Scientific Institution. From there he would escort me to his rooms,
which, apparently, were difficult to find without help, being hidden in
the maze of narrow brick passageways beyond Pond Square.

It was a very cold, clear winter afternoon when I alighted at the
Underground station in Highgate and made my way up Southwood
Lane towards its village. Snow had fallen since the night before,
and the lane was almost deserted. Only the sound of my footsteps
crunching in the brittle snow broke the silence. When I reached the
village I paused for a while to take in my surroundings. The Georgian houses were cloaked in white and glittered in the freezing sunshine. A sharp wind blew chilly gusts across the sagging roofs and

chimney pots. One or two residents, clad in greatcoats and well muffled, plodded warily along.

I accosted one of these pedestrians and was directed by him towards the Institute. This was a whitewashed structure, two storeys high, facing the square on the corner of Swains Lane. I could see the glow of a coal fire within and a plump man reading in an easy chair through one of the ground floor windows. It was Alfred Muswell.

After dusting the snowflakes from my clothes, I made my way inside and introduced myself to him. He struggled out of his chair, stood upright like a hermit crab quitting its shell, and threw out a gloved hand for me to grasp. He was dressed in his habitual black suit, a cigarette drooping from his bottom lip. His eyes peered at me intensely from behind those round glasses. His hair had thinned and grown white since the photographs in *The Necrophile*. The loss of hair was mainly around the crown, giving him a some-what monkish appearance.

I hung up my duffel coat and scarf and sat down in the chair facing him.

"We can sit here undisturbed for a few more minutes at least," he said. "The other members are in the library attending some lecture about that charlatan, James Joyce."

I nodded as if in agreement, but my attention was fixed on Muswell's leather gloves. He seemed always to wear them. He had worn a similar pair in *The Necrophile* photographs. I noticed the apparent emaciation of the hands and long fingers that the gloves concealed. His right hand fidgeted constantly with his cigarette while the fingers of his left coiled and uncoiled repeatedly. It was almost as if he were uncomfortable with the appendages.

"I'm very pleased to talk with a fellow devotee of Lilith Blake's tales," he said, in his odd, strained voice.

"Oh, I wouldn't describe myself as a devotee. Her work is striking, of course, but my own preferences are for Blackwood and Machen. Blake seems to me to lack balance. Her world is one of unremitting gloom and decay."

Muswell snorted at my comment. He exhaled a great breath of cigarette smoke in my direction and said:

"Unremitting gloom and decay? Rather say that she makes desolation glorious! I believe that De Quincey once wrote, 'Holy was the grave. Saintly its darkness. Pure its corruption.' Words that describe Lilith Blake's work perfectly. Machen indeed! That red-faced old coot with his deluded Anglo-Catholic rubbish! The man was a drunken clown obsessed by sin. And Blackwood? Pantheistic rot that belongs to the Stone Age. The man wrote mainly for money and he wrote too much. No, no. Believe me, if you want the truth beyond the frontier of appearances it is to Lilith Blake you must turn. She never compromises. Her stories are infinitely more than mere accounts of supernatural phenomena . . ."

His voice had reached a peak of shrillness, and it was all I could do not to squirm in my chair. Then he seemed to regain his composure and drew a handkerchief across his brow.

"You must excuse me; I have allowed my convictions to ruin my manners. I so seldom engage in debate these days that when I do I become overexcited." He allowed himself to calm down and was about to speak again when a side door opened and a group of people bustled into the room. They were chatting about the Joyce lecture that had evidently just finished. Muswell got to his feet and made for his hat and overcoat. I followed him.

Outside, in the cold afternoon air, he looked back over his shoulder and crumpled up his face in a gesture of disgust.

"How I detest those fools," he intoned.

We trudged through the snow, across the square and into a series of passageways. Tall buildings with dusty windows pressed upon us from both sides and, after a number of twists and turns, we reached the building that contained Muswell's rooms. They were in the basement, and we walked down some well-worn steps outside, leaving the daylight above us.

He opened the front door and I followed him inside.

Muswell flicked on the light switch, and a single bulb suspended from the ceiling and reaching halfway towards the bare floor revealed the meagre room. On each of the walls were long bookcases stuffed with volumes. There was an armchair and footstool in one corner along with a small circular table on which a pile of books teetered precariously. A dangerous-looking Calor gas fire stood in the opposite corner. Muswell brought another chair (with a canvas back and seat) from an adjoining room and invited me to sit down. Soon afterwards he hauled a large trunk from the same room. It was extremely old and bore the monogram "L. B." on its side. He unlocked the trunk with some ceremony and then sat down, lighting yet another cigarette, his eyes fixed on my face.

I took a notebook from my pocket and, drawing sheaves of manuscripts from the trunk, began to scan them. It seemed dark stuff, and rather strange, but just what I needed for the article. And there was a mountain of it to get through. Muswell, meanwhile, made a melancholy remark, apropos of nothing, the significance of which I did not appreciate until much later.

"Loneliness," he said, "can drive a man into mental regions of extreme strangeness."

I nodded absently. I had found a small box and, on opening it, my excitement mounted. It contained a sepia-coloured photographic portrait of Lilith Blake, dated 1896. It was the first I had seen of her, and it must have been taken in the year of her death. Her beauty was quite astonishing.

Muswell leaned forward. He seemed to be watching my reaction with redoubled interest.

Lilith Blake's raven-black and luxuriant hair curled down to her shoulders. Her face was oval, finished with a small pointed chin. The eyes, wide apart and piercing, seemed to gaze across the vastness of the time that separated us. Her throat was long and pale, her forehead rounded, and stray curls of hair framed the temples. The fleshy lips were slightly parted and her small, sharp teeth gleamed whitely. Around her neck hung a string of pearls and she wore a jet-black, velvet dress. The most delicate and lovely white hands I had ever seen were folded across her bosom. Although the alabaster skin of her face and neck was extremely pale, her hands were paler. They were whiter than the purest snow. It was as if daylight had never touched them. The length of her graceful fingers astonished me.

I must have sat there for some time in silent contemplation of that intoxicating image. Muswell, becoming impatient, finally broke my reverie in a most violent and unnecessary manner. He snatched the photograph from me and held it in the air while he spoke, his voice rising to a feverish pitch:

"Here is the hopeless despair of one haunted by the night. One who had gone down willingly into the grave with a black ecstasy in her heart instead of fear!"

I could only sit there in stunned silence. To me, Muswell seemed close to a complete nervous breakdown.

*

Later, Muswell must have helped me sort through the various papers in the trunk. I remember few of the details. I do know that by the time I finally left his rooms and found my way back to the square through the snow, I had realised that my research into Blake's work would be of the utmost importance to my academic career. Muswell had treasure in his keeping, a literary gold mine, and, given the right handling, it could make my name.

After that, my days were not my own. Try as I might, I could not expunge the vision of Blake from my mind. Her face haunted my thoughts, beckoning me onwards in my quest to discover the true meaning of her work. The correspondence between Muswell and myself grew voluminous as I sought to arrange a time when I would be enabled to draw further on his collection. For a while he seemed to distrust my mounting interest, but at last he accepted my enthusiasm as genuine. He welcomed me as a kindred spirit. By a happy chance, I even managed to rent a room in his building.

And so, during the course of the winter months, I shut myself away with Muswell, poring over Blake's letters and personal effects. I cannot deny that the handling of those things began to feel almost sacrilegious. But as I read the letters, diaries, and notebooks I could see that Muswell had spoken only the truth when he described Blake as supreme in the field of supernatural literature.

He would scuttle around his library like a spider, climbing stepladders and hauling out volumes from the shelves, passing them down through the gloomy space to me. He would mark certain passages that he believed furthered a greater understanding of Blake's life and work. Outside, the frequent snow showers filled the gap between his basement window and the pavement above with icy whiteness. My research was progressing well, my notebook filling up with useful quotations and annotations, but somehow I felt that I was failing to reach the essence of Lilith; the most potent aspect of her vision was eluding my understanding. It was becoming agonising to be so close to her, and yet to feel that her most secret and beautiful mysteries were buried from my view.

"I believe," Muswell once said, "that mental isolation is the essence of weird fiction. Isolation when confronted with disease, with madness, with horror, and with death. These are the reverberations of the infinity that torments us. It is Blake who delineates these echoes of doom for us. She alone exposes our inescapable, blind stumbling towards eternal annihilation. She alone shows our souls screaming in the darkness with none to heed our cries. Ironic, isn't it, that such a beautiful young woman should possess an imagination so dark and riddled with nightmare?"

Muswell took a deep drag of his cigarette and, in contemplating his words, seemed to gaze through everything into a limitless void.

Sometimes, when Muswell was away, I would have the collection to myself. Blake's personal letters became as sacred relics to me. Her framed photograph attained a special significance, and I was often unable to prevent myself from running my fingers around the outline of her lovely face.

As time passed and my research into Lilith Blake's oeuvre began to yield ever more fascinating results, I felt that I was now ready to afford her the posthumous attention she so richly deserved. Whereas previously I had merely planned to include references to her work in my lengthy article on supernatural fiction during the late nineteenth and early twentieth centuries, I now realised that she had to be accorded a complete critical book of her own, such was the importance of the literary legacy I had stumbled across by associating with Muswell. It seemed obvious to me that the man had little real idea of the prime importance of the materials in his possession and that his reclusive lifestyle had led him to regard anything relating to this dead and beautiful creature as his own personal property. His understanding was hopelessly confused by the unsubstantiated assertion that he made of the importance of the "work behind the works," which I took to mean some obscure mystical interpretation he had formulated from his own muddled, ageing brain.

One afternoon he came across me working on my proposed book and took an apparently polite interest in my writing, but mingled with that interest was an infuriating sarcasm. I voiced my contention that Blake deserved a much higher place in the literary pantheon. The only reasonable explanation for the failure of her work to achieve that place was, I had discovered, the almost total lack of contemporary interest in it. I could trace neither extant reviews of *The Reunion and Others* in any of the literary journals nor mention of her in society columns of the time. At this statement he actually laughed out loud. Holding one of his cigarettes between those thin, gloved fingers he waved it in the air dismissively and said:

"I should have thought that you would have found the silence surrounding her person and work suggestive, as I did. Do not mistake silence for indifference. Any imbecile might make that erroneous conclusion, and indeed many have done so in the past. Lilith Blake was no Count Stenbock, merely awaiting rediscovery. She was *deliberately* not mentioned; her work was specifically excluded from consideration. How much do you think was paid simply to ensure she had a fitting tomb in Highgate Cemetery?! But pray continue, tell me more of your article, and I shall try to take into consideration your youthful naiveté."

As I continued to expand on my theories I saw clearly that he began to smirk in a most offensive fashion. Why, it was as if he were humouring me! My face flushed and I stood up, my back rigid with tension. I was close to the breaking point and could not tolerate this old fool's patronising attitude any longer. Muswell took a step backwards and bowed, rather ornately, in some idiotic gentlemanly gesture. But as he did so, he almost lost his footing, as if a bout of dizziness had overcome him. I was momentarily startled by the action, and he took the opportunity to make his exit. But before he did so he uttered some departing words:

"If you knew what I know, my friend, and perhaps you soon will, then you would find this literary criticism as horribly amusing as I do. But I am extremely tired and will leave you to your work."

It seemed obvious to me at that point that Muswell was simply not fit to act as the trustee for Lilith Blake's estate. Moreover, his theatrics and lack of appreciation for my insights indicated progressive mental deterioration. I would somehow have to wrest control over the estate from his enfeebled grasp, for the sake of Blake's reputation.

The opportunity came more quickly than I could have dared hope.

One evening in February Muswell returned from one of his infrequent appointments looking particularly exhausted. I had noticed the creeping fatigue in his movements for a number of weeks. In addition to an almost constant sense of distraction, he had also lost a considerable amount of weight. His subsequent confession did not, in any case, come as a shock.

"The game is up for me," he said. "I am wasting away. The doctor says I will not last much longer. I am glad that the moment

of my assignation with Blake draws near. You must ensure that I
am buried with her."

Muswell contemplated me from across the room, the light of
the dim electric bulb reflected off the lenses of his spectacles, veil-
ing the eyes behind. He continued:

"There are secrets which I have hidden from you, but I will reveal them now. I have come to learn that there are those who,
though dead, lie in their coffins beyond the grip of decay. The
power of eternal visions preserves them: there they lie, softly dead
and dreaming. Lilith Blake is one of these, and I shall be another.
You will be our guardian in this world. You will ensure that our bodies are not disturbed. Once dead, we must not be awakened from
the eternal dream. It is for the protection of Lilith and myself that I
have allowed you to share in my thoughts and her literary legacy.
Everything will make sense once you have read her final works."

He climbed up the steepest stepladder to the twilight of the
room's ceiling and took a metal box from the top of one of the
bookcases. He unlocked it and drew out an old writing book
bound in crumpled black leather. The title page was written in Lilith Blake's distinctive longhand style. I could see that it bore the
title *The White Hands and Other Tales*.

"This volume," he said, handing it to me, "contains the final
stories. They establish the truth of all I have told you. The book
must now be published. I want to be vindicated after I die. This
book will prove, in the most shocking way, the supremacy of the
horror tale over all other forms of literature. As I intimated to you
once before, these stories are not accounts of supernatural phenomena but are supernatural phenomena in themselves.

"Understand this: Blake was dead when these stories were
conceived. But she still dreams and transmitted these images from
her tomb to me so that I might transcribe them for her. When you
read them you will know that I am not insane. All will become
clear to you. You will understand how, at the point of death, the
eternal dream is begun. It allows dissolution of the body to be held
at bay for as long as one continues the dreaming."

I realised that Muswell's illness had deeply affected his mind.
In order to bring him back to some awareness of reality I said:

"You say that Blake telepathically dictated the stories and you
transcribed them? Then how is it that the handwriting is hers and

not your own?"

Muswell smiled painfully, paused, and then, for the first and last time, took off his gloves. The hands were Lilith Blake's, the same pale, attenuated forms I recognised from her photograph.

"I asked for a sign that I was not mad," said Muswell, "and it was given to me."

*

Four weeks later Muswell died.

The doctor's certificate listed the cause of death as heart failure. I had been careful, and as he was already ill, there was little reason for the authorities to suspect anything.

Frankly, I had never countenanced the idea of fulfilling any of Muswell's requests, and I arranged for his body to be cremated and interred at Marylebone and St. Pancras Cemetery, amongst a plain of small, indistinguishable graves and headstones. He would not rest at Highgate Cemetery alongside Lilith Blake.

The ceremony was a simple one, and aside from myself there were no other mourners in attendance. Muswell's expulsion from Oxford had ensured that his old colleagues were wary of keeping in touch with him, and there were no surviving members of his family who chose to pay their last respects. The urn containing his ashes was interred in an unmarked plot, and the priest who presided over the affair muttered his way through the rites in a mechanical, indifferent fashion. As the ceremony concluded and I made my way across that dull sepulchral plain, under a grey and miserable sky, I had a sense of finality. Muswell was gone forever and had found that oblivion he seemed so anxious to avoid.

It was a few days later that I made my first visit to Lilith Blake's vault. She had been interred in the old west section of Highgate Cemetery, and I was unable to gain access alone. There were only official tours of the place available and I attended one, but afterwards I paid the guide to conduct me privately to Blake's vault. We had to negotiate our way through a tangle of overgrown pathways and crumbling gravestones. The vault was located in a near-inaccessible portion of the hillside cemetery, and as we proceeded through the undergrowth, with thick brambles catching on our trousers, the guide told me that he had only once before visited this vault. This was in the company of another man whose description led me to conclude that it had been Muswell himself. The guide mentioned that this particular area was a source of some curiosity to the various guides, volunteers, and conservationists who worked here. Although wildlife flourished in other parts of the cemetery, here it was conspicuous by its absence. Even the birds seemed to avoid the place.

I remember distinctly that the sun had just set and that we reached the tomb in the twilight. The sycamores around us only added to the gloom. Then I caught sight of an arched roof covered with ivy just ahead, and the guide told me that we had reached our destination. As we approached it and the structure came fully into view I felt a mounting sense of anticipation. Some of the masonry had crumbled away, but it was still an impressive example of High Victorian Gothic architecture. The corners of its square exterior were adorned with towers, and each side boasted a miniature portico. On one of the sides, almost obliterated by neglect and decay, was a memorial stone, bearing the epitaph: LILITH BLAKE. BORN 25 DECEMBER 1874. DIED 1 NOVEMBER 1896.

"It is getting late," the guide whispered to me. "We must get back."

I saw his face in the gloom, and he had a restless expression. His words had broken in on the strange silence that enveloped the area. I nodded absently but made my way around to the front of the vault and the rusty trellis gates blocking the entrance to a stairway that led down to her coffin. Peering through the gates, I could see the flight of stairs, covered by lichen, but darkness obscured its lower depths. The guide was at my elbow now and tugging my jacket sleeve.

"Come on, come on," he moaned. "I could get in real trouble for doing this."

There was something down there. I had the unnerving sensation that I was, in turn, being scrutinised by some presence in that perpetual darkness. It was almost as if it were trying to communicate with me. Images began to form in my mind, flashes of distorted scenes, of corpses that did not rot, of dreams that things no longer human might dream.

Then the guide got a grip of my arm and began forcibly dragging me away. I stumbled along with him as if in a trance, but the hallucinations seemed to fade the further away we got from the

vault; by the time we reached the main gate, I had regained my
mental faculties. Thereafter the guide refused any request I made
for him to take me again to the vault, and my attempts to persuade
his colleagues were met with the same response. In the end I was
no longer even granted access to the cemetery on official tours. I
later learned that my connection with Muswell had been discovered and that he had caused much trouble to the cemetery authorities in the past with his demands for unsupervised access. On one
occasion there were even threats of legal action for trespassing.

As indicated, Muswell had informed me that I was to be his literary executor, and thus his collection of Blakeiana was left in my
control. I also gained possession of his rooms. So I turned again to
the study of Blake's work, hoping therein to further my understanding of the enigma that had taken control of my life. I had still
to read *The White Hands and Other Tales* and had been put off doing
so by Muswell's insistence that this would enlighten me. I still held
to the view that his mystical interpretation was fallacious, and the
thought that this book might actually be what he claimed it to be
was almost detestable to me. I wanted desperately to believe that
Muswell had written the book himself, rather than as a conduit for
Blake. And yet, even if I dismissed the fact of his peculiar hands,
so like Blake's own, even if I put that down to some self-inflicted
mutilation due to his long-disordered mental state, not to mention
the book's comparatively recent age, still there remained the experience at the vault to undermine my certainty. And so it was to *The
White Hands and Other Tales* I turned, hoping there to determine
matters once and for all.

I had only managed to read the title story. Frankly, the book
was too hideous for anyone but a lunatic to read in its entirety. The
tale was like an incantation. The further one progressed the more
incomprehensible and sinister the words became. They were sometimes reversed and increasingly obscene. The words in that book
conjured visions of eternal desolation. The little that I had read had
already damaged my own mind. I became obsessed with the idea of
her lying in her coffin, dreaming and waiting for me to liberate her.

During the nights of sleeplessness her voice would call across
the dark. When I was able to sleep, strange dreams came to me. I
would be walking among pale shades in an overgrown and crumbling necropolis. The moonlight seemed abnormally bright and

even filtered down to the catacombs where I would follow the shrouded form of Lilith Blake. The world of the dead seemed to be replacing my own.

For weeks I drew down the blinds in Muswell's library, shutting out the daylight, lost in my speculations.

As time passed I began to wonder just why Muswell had been so insistent that he must be interred with Blake at all costs. My experiences at her vault and the strange hallucinations I had suffered—might they not have been authentic after all? Could it be that Muswell had actually divined some other mode of existence beyond death, which I too had gleaned only dimly? I did not reach this conclusion lightly. I had explored many avenues of philosophical enquiry before coming back again and again to the conclusion that I might have to rely on Muswell's own interpretation. The critical book on Blake that I proposed to write floundered, lost in its own limitations. For, incredible as it seemed, the only explanation that lay before me was that the corpse itself did harbour some form of unnatural sentience, and that close contact with it brought final understanding of the mystery.

I sought to solve a riddle beyond life and death yet feared the answer. The image that held the solution to the enigma that tormented me was the corpse of Lilith Blake. I had to see it in the flesh.

I decided that I would arrange for the body to be exhumed and brought to me here in Muswell's—*my*—rooms. It took me weeks to make the necessary contacts and raise the money required. How difficult it can be to get something done, even something so seemingly simple! How tedious the search for the sordid haunts of the necessary types, the hints dropped in endless conversations with untrustworthy strangers in dirty public houses! How venal, how mercenary is the world at large! During the nights of sleeplessness Lilith Blake's voice would sometimes seem to call to me across the darkness. When I was able to sleep I encountered beautiful dreams, where I would be walking among pale shades in an overgrown and crumbling necropolis. The moonlight seemed abnormally bright and even filtered down to the catacombs where I would find Lilith's shrouded form.

At last terms were agreed upon. Two labourers were hired to undertake the job, and on the appointed night I waited in my rooms. Outside, the rain was falling heavily and in my mind's eye, as I sat anxiously in the armchair smoking cigarette after cigarette, I saw the deed done: the two simpletons, clad in their raincoats and with crowbars and pickaxes, climbing over the high wall that ran along Swains Lane, stumbling through the storm and the over-grown grounds past stone angels and ruined monuments, down worn steps to the circular avenue, deep in the earth, but open to the mottled grey-and-black sky. Wet leaves must have choked the passageways. I could see the rain sweeping over the hillside ceme-tery as they levered open the door to her vault, their coats flutter-ing in the wind. The memory of Lilith Blake's face rose before me through the hours that passed. I seemed to see it in every object that caught my gaze. I had left the blind up and watched the rain beating at the window above me, the water streaming down the small Georgian panes. I began to feel like an outcast of the universe.

As I waited, I thought I saw a pair of eyes staring back at me in the clock on the mantelpiece. I thought too that I saw two huge and thin white spiders crawling across the books on the shelves.

At last there were three loud knocks on the door. I came to in my chair, my heart pounding in my chest. I opened the door to the still-pouring rain, and there at last, shadowy in the night, were my two graverobbers. They were smiling unpleasantly, their hair plas-tered down over their worm-white faces. I pulled the wad of bank-notes from my pocket and stuffed them into the nearest one's grasp.

They lugged the coffin inside and set it down in the middle of the room.

And then they left me alone with the thing. For a while, the sodden coffin dripped silently onto the rug, the dark pools forming at its foot spreading slowly outwards, sinking gradually into the worn and faded pile. Although its wooden boards were decrepit and dis-figured with dank patches of greenish mould, the lid remained se-curely battened down by a phalanx of rusty nails. I had prepared for this moment carefully; I had all the tools I needed ready in the adjoining room, but something, a sudden sense of foreboding, made me hesitate foolishly. At last, with a massive effort of will, I fetched the claw hammer and chisel, and knelt beside the coffin. Once I had prised the lid upwards and then down again, leaving the rusted nail-tops proud, I drew them out one by one. It seemed to take forever—levering each one up and out and dropping it on-to the slowly growing pile at my feet. My lips were dry and I could barely grip the tools in my slippery hands. The shadows of the rain still trickling down the window were thrown over the room and across the coffin by the orange glow of the street lamp outside.

Very slowly, I lifted the lid.

Resting in the coffin was a figure clothed in a muslin shroud that was discoloured with age. Those long hands and attenuated fingers were folded across its bosom. Lilith Blake's raven-black hair seemed to have grown whilst she had slept in the vault, and it reached down to her waist. Her head was lost in shadow, so I bent closer to examine it. There was no trace of decay in the features, which were of those in the photograph, and yet it now had a horrible aspect, quite unlike the decomposition I might have anticipated. The skin was puffy and white, resembling paint applied on a tailor's dummy. Those fleshy lips that so attracted me in the photograph were now repulsive. They were lustreless and drew back from her yellowed, sharp little teeth. The eyes were closed and even the lashes seemed longer, as if they too had grown, and they reminded me of the limbs of a spider. As I gazed at the face and fought back my repulsion, I had again the sensation that I had experienced at the vault.

Consciousness seemed to mingle with dreams. The two states were becoming one, and I saw visions of some hellish ecstasy. At first I again glimpsed corpses that did not rot, as if a million graves had been opened, illuminated by the phosphoric radiance of suspended decay. But these gave way to wilder nightmares that I could glimpse only dimly, as if through a billowing vapour; nightmares that to see clearly would destroy my mind. And I could not help being reminded of the notion that what we term sanity is only a measure of success in concealing underlying madness.

Then I came back to myself and saw Lilith Blake appearing to awaken. As she slowly opened her eyes the spell was broken, and I looked into them with mounting horror. They were blank and repugnant, no longer belonging in a human face—the eyes of a thing that had seen sights no living creature could see. Then one of her hands reached up and her long fingers clutched feebly against my throat as if trying to scratch, or perhaps caress, me.

With the touch of those clammy hands I managed to summon up enough self-control to close the lid and begin replacing the coffin nails, fighting against the impulses that were driving me to gaze again upon the awakened apparition. Then, during a lull in the rain, I burned the coffin and its deathly contents in the back yard. As I watched the fire build I thought that I heard a shrieking, like a curse being invoked in the sinister and incomprehensible language of Blake's tale. But the noise was soon lost in the roar of the flames.

It was only after many days that I discovered that the touch of Lilith Blake's long white fingers had produced marks that, once visible, remained permanently impressed upon my throat.

*

I travelled abroad for some months afterwards, seeking southern climes bathed in warm sunshine and blessed with short nights. But my thoughts gradually returned to *The White Hands and Other Tales*. I wondered if it might be possible to achieve control over it, to read it in its entirety and use it to attain my goal. Finally its lure proved decisive. I convinced myself that I had already borne the darkest horrors, that this would have proved a meet preparation for its mysteries, however obscenely they were clothed. And so, returning once more to Highgate, I began the task of transcribing and interpreting the occult language of the book, delving far into its deep mysteries. Surely I could mould the dreams to my own will and overcome the nightmare. Once achieved, I would dwell forever, in Paradise . . .

*

Text of a letter written by John Harrington whilst under confinement in Maudsley Psychiatric Hospital:

> My dearest wife Lilith,
> I do not know why you have not written or come to see me.
> The gentlemen looking after me here are very kind but will not allow any mirrors. I know there is something awful about my face. Everyone is scared to look at it.
> They have taken your book away. They say it is gibberish. But I know all the secrets now.
> Sometimes I laugh and laugh.
> But I like the white hands that crawl around my bed at night like two spiders. They laugh with me.
> Please write or come.
> With all my heart, John.

APARTMENT 205

Pieter Slokker awoke from a dream in which he was trapped in a dark, windowless room. It was three o'clock in the morning, and it sounded as if someone were hammering at the door of his flat.

Slokker had not lived long in Paris. He had moved from Bruges to this cramped apartment close to the Gare du Nord station only a few months before, in order to finish his studies in medicine. He knew no one in the mouldering old building save the garrulous concierge, and had seldom even passed a fellow tenant as he made his way up and down the torturous spiral staircase that led to his rooms on the fourth floor.

As he became more fully awake, Slokker felt a mounting sense of apprehension. The blows continued to strike the door; he had no idea who it could be, but ignoring the summons was no longer possible. Slokker got out of bed, threw on a dressing gown, and made his way to the hall. Peering through the spy-hole, he could at first see only the dim outline of a man.

As his eyes grew more accustomed to the dark Slokker was able to make out more of the man's features. Such was the person's appearance that he hesitated before unlocking the door. He had encountered a few patients badly disfigured by their illnesses during the course of his medical training, but his insistent visitor looked worse than most. He was cadaverously thin, with an angular white face and a shaved head. But it was the man's sunken, black-rimmed eyes and hollowed cheeks that chiefly disturbed Slokker. He was reminded of the time when he had been on a tour of the hospital morgue with his fellow students. A pathologist had shown them the corpse of a man who had starved to death after being locked in a lightless cellar by his mad wife. The memory of this man's appearance had long haunted Slokker's dreams, and so similar was this night-visitor that he could almost believe that the self-same corpse stood outside. Was it possible, he wondered, that he was still dreaming?

Slokker's state of full consciousness was, however, soon confirmed by another volley of blows against the wood, so loud this time that echoes pulsed back and forth along the empty corridor. Slokker began to draw back the bolts, though he was awake enough to remember to keep the chain on, allowing just enough space to speak to the caller. Thinking more clearly now, he had begun to formulate a diagnosis. Surely this man was a drug addict and had found out that a medical student lived in the building. Perhaps he had come in search of supplies?

Although the door was open only a fraction, the outsider thrust his emaciated face into the aperture. His wild eyes searched frantically for the occupant and in a desperate voice he cried out:

"Please! You must assist me, Monsieur. I cannot bear to be alone any longer! If you have any human feeling at all you will open the door!"

Slokker took a step back; the sight of that awful face close up, and the pathetic urgency of the request, had unnerved him. He reminded himself that as a medical student it was his duty to offer any help he could. After all, the man seemed coherent enough, if rather disturbed. Drawing his dressing gown closer around himself, Slokker took the chain off the door and gestured at the man to enter.

The visitor staggered across the room without a word and slumped into a chair. Perhaps he was trying to compose himself, but his eyes darted restlessly towards the shadows. He appeared to be averting his gaze from the windows; whenever he turned inadvertently in their direction, he would put his head in his hands. After observing the man in silence for a few minutes, Slokker reappraised his initial diagnosis; he was beginning to suspect that drugs were probably not the cause of his visitor's obviously dire condition. His sleeves were rolled up to the elbow, and the deathly white skin betrayed no telltale track-marks. Perhaps, then, the man was simply unhinged and wasting away through self-neglect.

"Please, it's late. Tell me how I may be of assistance. Perhaps some brandy might calm you?" Slokker used his most soothing bedside manner.

The man turned his gaze towards Slokker and tried very hard to keep it level. Then he laughed, a mocking chuckle, as if enjoying a private joke.

"You are kind. Yes, I will drink with you."

He swallowed the brandy as if suffering from a terrible thirst, but the alcohol had little visible effect on him. Despite Slokker's questions, the man seemed disinclined to speak. The medical student could do little but sit and watch his silent guest, though he was filled with unease at his presence. There was something truly unearthly about the man.

Occasionally, as the night wore on, he seemed on the verge of revealing something about himself, but would then lapse back to staring into space, occasionally laughing as if at the same sick joke. Any suggestion Slokker made to the effect that the visitor should leave was accompanied by renewed pleas of a piteous nature, and he was forced to resign himself to the strange companionship.

Finally, just as dawn was breaking, the visitor made to depart and Slokker watched him as he staggered back along the corridor. To his surprise and interest, the man entered an apartment only four doors away. Had he tried the three doors separating them before hammering on Slokker's?

As he wearily relocked his door and returned to bed Slokker resolved to discuss the matter with the concierge later in the morning. His strange neighbour required prompt attention, and possibly commitment to a psychiatric hospital. And Slokker would be very glad to do without any further nocturnal visits.

*

The concierge, who was an elderly man with a dislike of Flemish Belgians, ran his fingers over the white stubble on his chin. An unlit Gauloise hung from his lower lip.

"He came from Apartment 205, you say?"

"Yes. I don't know his name. The man's in need of treatment. I think he could be dangerous—to himself, if not to others."

"I find that hard to believe. The gentleman who occupies that room is Monsieur Deschamps. A little odd, I'll grant you, but he's careful about his appearance and always gives me a good tip. I haven't seen him for a few weeks, but then he's always liked his privacy. Lately he's even taken to having his food delivered." He scratched his chin. "Though I haven't seen the delivery boy for a while. . . . But I wouldn't—"

Slokker interrupted the old man's monologue.

"Well, I am not leaving until you come upstairs with me and see for yourself. If you won't I'll complain to the landlord."

The old man got to his feet with a long-suffering expression and took down from its hook the duplicate key for Apartment 205.

A few moments later the two were climbing the spiral staircase to the fourth floor, the concierge grumbling as they made their way upwards. He paused several times to draw on the now lit cigarette. It seemed to Slokker that he took as long as he possibly could.

"You're a medical student, you say? Well, let me tell you, Monsieur, that I haven't much time for doctors. One of you scoundrels gave me six months to live and that was more than twenty years ago! What do you think of that, eh?"

"What I'd like to know is what you meant when you said that this Deschamps was a little odd."

"Odd, eh, odd? Well, isn't everyone a bit odd in their own way? When you're as old as I am, perhaps you'll realise that too. Odd? I meant nothing by it. Only that when I helped Monsieur Deschamps move his belongings upstairs, oh, when was it?" He had stopped again. "Yes, when I helped him I happened to glance at his books."

"And?"

"Well, they were unusual books. Things about premonitions, fortune telling, magic, and the like. He seemed ashamed of them. Oh, and some on black magic! So what do you make of that, eh, my young Flemish friend! Eh? Black magic!"

At which statement the concierge laughed. This set off a violent coughing fit. He threw his cigarette to the floor and insisted they wait a while for him to recover.

When they finally reached 205 the concierge at first tapped gently on the door, calling out to Deschamps in a regretful tone, glancing disapprovingly at Slokker all the while. But there was no answer, even when the medical student shouted through the keyhole and they had both banged uninhibitedly on the door. The commotion had attracted a small crowd of people in the hallway.

"Don't you have a key?" Slokker asked the concierge.

"But he might just be out." The old man replied grumpily.

"Open the door and don't be such a fool! Something might have happened to him!" said a large, powdered lady cradling a white fluffy cat. She seemed to have more influence over the concierge than Slokker, because to the medical student's annoyance he bowed obsequiously and mumbled "Of course, of course, as you wish, Madame," before drawing the key from his pocket and inserting it in the lock.

The concierge had some difficulty in dissuading the crowd from following them into the apartment, especially the powdered woman with the cat, but once they had been shooed away, he and Slokker made their way cautiously down the uncarpeted hall and into the main living room. The floor was littered with papers and discarded food cartons. Thick dust lay over everything. Clothes, old newspapers, and books were heaped on the floor, and Slokker and the concierge had to navigate between them carefully. The curtains were half-drawn and a stale, sickly odour permeated the room. Behind the curtains, newspapers had been stuck to the windowpanes, creating a permanent yellow twilight. A brief further inspection revealed that the other rooms were in a similar state of chaos and neglect. There was no sign of Deschamps.

And then they came across a tiny, windowless room. Its walls had been draped with black velvet curtains. There was a large mirror on the wall, on either side of which the curtains were parted, and a single chair with an electric lamp positioned just behind it. The bulb was of a very low wattage, and the legs of the chair had been sawn off so that it tilted backwards. If you sat on the chair you found yourself gazing directly into the mirror, only, judging from its height, it would not be possible to see one's own reflection, only the mirror image of the darkness of the room.

"Eh, my friend? What do you make of it?" asked the concierge.

Slokker found himself completely lost for words.

*

Whatever had happened to Deschamps remained a mystery. It seemed that he had abandoned his rooms and Pieter Slokker was the last person to have seen him. The concierge reported Deschamps's disappearance to the police, and his name was added to their list of missing persons.

As the days passed, no more information was forthcoming. Deschamps had paid his rent for the month ahead and the landlord decided that the rooms would remain unlet for this period, just in case his tenant should return. However, at the end of the month, the apartment would be re-advertised.

Shortly after his neighbour's disappearance, Slokker, who when not being awoken by deranged neighbours usually enjoyed a good night's sleep, found himself experiencing a bout of sleepwalking. One night he woke to discover that he had left his rooms, wandered along the corridor, and was trying the door of Apartment 205. This pattern of sleepwalking repeated itself two or three times every night of the following week, and finally Slokker was forced to resort to keeping himself in bed by means of an elaborate system of cords with which he bound his ankles to the bedstead. He tied the knots in so complicated a fashion that any attempt to unravel them in his sleep usually resulted in failure. He often awoke in pain, his fingertips sore and bleeding from picking at the unyielding rope.

Perhaps inevitably, Slokker's studies began to suffer. After two weeks of exhaustion, he began to feel that the only way to put a stop to his unconscious compulsion was to find a way to re-enter Deschamps's apartment. The next day, while a deliveryman was usefully distracting the concierge with a disputed receipt, Slokker managed to "borrow" the duplicate key from the hall office. He pressed it carefully into a tablet of wax he had prepared by melting a couple of candles.

As it turned out, having a copy key made was an easy matter. The key cutter in the booth on the Boulevard asked no awkward questions, and he made the key there and then, while the medical student waited on the street. Later that evening, when the building was quiet, Slokker made his way along the corridor. He carried with him a torch so that he would not risk attracting any unwelcome attention by switching on the lights.

The interior of the apartment was even more desolate by night. Nothing had been touched, and the only change was that a thicker layer of dust now covered the debris littering the floorboards.

Slokker flashed the torch around, making shadows start out from the peeling walls. Once in the windowless room he switched on the low-wattage lamp behind the chair and extinguished his torch. He sat down on the angled seat and directed his gaze to the mirror. The reflection showed only the velvet curtains behind him. He was looking into a rectangular slab of perfect blackness.

At first he focused on the surface of the mirror, but because there was nothing of any interest to look at, he allowed his gaze gradually to relax. For some time nothing happened, but then the focus of his eyes altered and he seemed to be staring beyond the mirror at a distant object hidden in its depths. Slokker's very gaze seemed to be bringing forth something from the darkness. Whatever it was, and he could not be sure there was really anything there, it was surrounded by a silvery-white glare. The object seemed to come closer the more he concentrated on it, and for a moment he had the feeling that something or someone was looking back at him, albeit from far away. Slokker could not be sure whether the distant vision was merely a product of his own imagination. The whole process was exhausting, and he found that he was developing a throbbing headache. Finally he gave up the exercise and, as quietly as he could, made his way out of the rooms into the corridor.

Once back in his own apartment Slokker was astonished to discover that four hours had passed. He slumped gratefully onto his bed and for once fell immediately into a deep, untroubled sleep.

*

For the first few nights after this experience Slokker suffered no further episodes of sleepwalking. It seemed that his plan had worked and that his strange need to visit the windowless room had been sated. He gave up the practice of binding himself to the bed with cords, but on the fourth night he awoke to find himself crawling on his hands and knees along the corridor towards 205.

Although he had discovered the cure for his somnambulism, Slokker was loath to resort to it again. His visit to the room with the mirror had been troubling and unpleasant; and although he was inclined to regard the far-off face in the mirror as a delusion brought on by tiredness, he retained a fear of it that he found hard to dismiss. However, he needed uninterrupted sleep if he were to continue his studies successfully, so the following morning he let himself into the abandoned apartment. This time he began a search of Deschamps's rooms in the hope of discovering something to help him understand the purpose of the windowless room.

Deschamps's books did not seem to have been arranged in any particular order. They were piled in corners and scattered randomly across the floor of the living room. However, as he examined them more closely, it appeared to Slokker that those most recently read had been piled around the base of a folding canvas chair. Deschamps seemed to have made notes about these on pieces of scrap paper, which he had then inserted into the volumes. He had also scrawled notes directly in the margins of some texts.

Contrary to the concierge's assertion, very few of the books dealt with black magic, and these were riddled with dismissive remarks in pencil: *"in other words an excuse for sexual self-gratification," "the desire for power over others by means of a system of obfuscation," "drug-related hallucinations," "auto-suggestion and hypnosis,"* etc. The texts that appeared to have held the most fascination for Deschamps were those stacked closest to the chair. Here Slokker found a series of privately printed pamphlets dating from the early 1890s. He noticed that the pamphlets were all stamped with the official seal of the Bibliothèque Nationale: no doubt Deschamps had furthered his occult researches by stealing from a public library. Slokker sat down in the canvas chair to read them.

It seemed that they concerned the use of a chamber called a "psychomantium." The pamphlets had been issued by an obscure sect of psychic researchers, and they were illustrated with photographic records of experiments conducted in rooms much like the one that Deschamps had fashioned in his apartment. The photographs were evidently of long exposure and showed blurred and distorted images of a series of faces apparently reflected in a mirror. The pamphlets claimed these to be "the faces of the dead." In truth, the quality of the reproduction was so poor that they rather resembled crudely fashioned dolls' heads in various states of disrepair. Nevertheless, the accompanying texts stated that these were authentic visitations and that the mirror served as a doorway to the afterlife.

Once more, Slokker felt compelled to enter the windowless room. He turned on the feeble lamp, sat down before the mirror, and attempted to clear his mind. He stared into the void.

For the first few minutes he saw nothing. He began to relax, and then felt a prickling sensation at the back of his neck; he shivered as he realised that once again he could see the silvery-white glare within the depths of reflected darkness. Then he saw that within the glare was a face. The longer Slokker stared, the closer it seemed to approach, and the brighter became the glare, as if a camera lens were zooming in inexorably. He did not know how long he stared; his senses were becoming confused. That the face was that of a dead man Slokker had no doubt. The yellowish tinge of the bloodless skin betrayed that much, and the eyes of the apparition did not blink. But what caused him to overturn the chair and stagger out of the psychomantium in a blind panic was that the face he saw in the mirror was his own.

*

It was not difficult for Slokker to obtain the drugs he needed to calm his nerves, but he did it as discreetly as he could, for his medical studies were in a state close to chaos and his failure to attend seminars and lectures was attracting comment. There was really no alternative, however, because the strain was becoming unbearable.

In one of the pamphlets that he had not read the previous night, and which he seemed to have had the presence of mind to bring with him to his rooms, Slokker found a short history of the group calling themselves "La Société des âmes mortes." They had made their first investigations into the afterlife by means of séances but had dismissed this line of enquiry after a series of encounters with fraudulent mediums. They had then explored the "science" of ouija boards and claimed that their subsequent use of psychomantic chambers was a consequence of a spirit message thereby received. The first experiments had been uneventful and the techniques they had borrowed from the psychic literature of the time, involving the sitter concentrating on photographs and handling the effects of the deceased, produced results that were easy to dismiss as mere fancy.

Just after the Society proposed the abandoning of this new line of research, one of the sitters began to make extraordinary claims about having communicated with the dead. He insisted that a horrible secret had been revealed to him. Investigation of the transcripts he had made whilst experiencing the visitations revealed disturbing hints about the nature of consciousness after death. But the most extraordinary claim of all was that he had begun to communicate with his own dead spirit. However, he would not be drawn on the exact nature of these exchanges. What was apparent was that his mental state had suffered a dramatic collapse and, only a few weeks later, he was found to have committed suicide. There were those in the Society who followed in his wake, unable to resist the lure of the forbidden knowledge that their dead selves might impart to them. Those who did not succumb to the temptation abandoned all association with psychic research. There were hints that the revelations experienced were based on the concept that it is the dead that sustain the structure of the waking world through their dreams and that all living existence is illusory.

When Slokker came to a part of the pamphlet featuring a sepia photograph, one hundred years old, of the members of the "Société des âmes mortes," he nearly dropped the thing in fright. Even had there not been a list of names beneath the photograph, he would have recognised the face of the man in the second row at the extreme right. It was that of Deschamps, or some identical ancestor. But this was not the worst of it. The other faces also seemed familiar, though they were blurred. One had a curious resemblance to the old concierge. And sitting next to him was someone whose identity could scarcely be mistaken. It was Slokker's own face that stared back at him from the photograph.

*

Although Slokker tried to dismiss these strange events and revelations from his mind, he found that his nightly compulsion to return and gaze into the mirror of the psychomantium was overwhelming. The drugs helped him to sleep and he still had recourse to binding his feet to the bed, but events soon overtook him, despite all his precautions.

One morning, just as he had finished shaving, the mirror above the sink filled with the silvery-white glare. Slokker's normal bleary-eyed reflection was replaced with an image of his leering corpse-face. Its eyes had sunk deep into black-rimmed sockets and the yellowish skin stretched tight over the skull, drawing the lips back from teeth made prominent by the flesh's decay. Hair was plastered down horribly across its mottled forehead. The face was close enough to touch, and though it materialised for only a moment Slokker could trace each lineament of decay. It seemed to lean forward towards him, confidentially, and whispered:

"You are simply a dream . . . and I am tired of dreaming."
Then it was gone.

*

After that, Slokker could not bear to be alone. For hours he tramped the streets of the city, seeking people, crowds. He sat in cafés during the afternoon and mingled with revellers in the evenings, but despite all his efforts to join in he was gripped by the idea that all this was merely scenery, abandoned backstage.

While he was out drinking himself into a state of oblivion in a bar close to Sacre Coeur, a group of his fellow medical students came across him, slumped over a corner table. They pressed their company upon him, enquiring after his health with real concern. Slokker was glad of their attentions and lost himself in evasion and claims that he would soon return to the university and complete his studies. But as his drunken elation reached its height, when even he half believed that his fears were caused by nothing more than nervous exhaustion that would be overcome with time, he happened to glance at a mirror hanging on the wall behind one of his friend's heads. There again was the silvery brightness and his dead, decaying face twisted into an expression of malign contempt. But this time it was not a momentary visitation; the image remained. And he thought that within the laughter around him he could hear a mocking quality, as if it were at his own expense. The dead face, too, seemed to be laughing, and Slokker's friends exchanged anxious glances as his own laughter turned to screams of horror. He got to his feet and pushed through the throng, shoving them roughly aside, until he was out into the streets and the Parisian night.

From then on all mirrors seemed to have become contaminated. In the darkness even shop windows glowed with the silver-white glare. When he got back to his apartment he smashed the mirrors in his rooms and covered the windows with newspaper to mask any reflections.

*

Shortly after Slokker had begun to retreat from the world he received some startling information from the concierge. Coming across him in his office after a trip out to buy some bread, the old man had beckoned Slokker over. It seemed that Deschamps's body had finally been discovered. A police boat had found it floating miles downstream in the Seine, weeks of decomposition having brought the corpse to the surface. It seemed that the man had drowned himself. Apartment 205 was to be let out again, after extensive redecoration, of course.

*

Slokker's mental condition continued to deteriorate. Some of the medical students who had heard about the encounter in the bar attempted to visit him, but he refused to let them in. Even his old lecturer came to the apartment once, but his initial sympathy soon turned to threats of calling in the authorities when faced with Slokker's stubborn refusal to communicate. But Slokker viewed all these visitors as he would a series of shadows. He was afraid that the dead face in the mirror was now really set on his shoulders, despite the fact that his sense of touch told him otherwise. It had been days since he'd looked in a mirror. Mornings and afternoons were taken up with sitting in the corner of his living room, watching the flies circling around the centre of the ceiling. And when it was night he would sit in the darkness and stare into space, hoping to lose himself in it. He no longer dared sleep. Even after binding himself to the bed he found that the once laborious process of disentanglement no longer woke him. He had learned to untie the most complex knots whilst still asleep.

Exhausted, emaciated, Slokker gradually lost the strength to resist the silent summons that drew him to the psychomantium. Soon, he knew, he would give himself over to the compulsion to see again the dead face and to listen to anything it might care to tell him.

Late one night, as he struggled to resist, Slokker remembered the landlord's intention to have Apartment 205 redecorated. Suddenly panic-stricken, he hurried from his rooms and down the short corridor. He could barely turn the key in the lock for fear that the psychomantium might not be there, but as he entered he saw that, although the painters' ladders and buckets had been stacked in the living room, work had yet to begin. He entered the windowless room and the dead face, appearing more decomposed than ever, was visible at once, as if it had been waiting for him. In the background was the familiar glare, like a continuous burst of lightning that reached only as far as the mirror's surface. Slokker sat in the darkness for hours as the rotting face with the whispering, hollow voice spoke to him. It urged him to cast aside his life, this mirage, this dream in the decaying brains of the dead. It told of the grey, insensible void where the hopes and miseries of living existence have no meaning. "The world you move in is not real," the voice told Slokker. "The thoughts you think are not your own. Down in their mouldy graves, where the worms creep, the dead sustain the illusion you call life, waiting for you living beings to awaken in your narrow houses for all eternity. You will not die," said the voice, "for you have never been alive."

And as Slokker gazed into the mirror he saw the revenant smile malignantly.

*

Some days later the old concierge made his way up the stairs to Slokker's apartment. He had not seen the young man during this period, and although he didn't particularly care for him, he was obliged to investigate, as the owners of the building had complained that the rent had not been paid. Up until now the concierge had ignored the various entreaties that Slokker's medical friends had made; his distaste for their profession made him dismiss them as do-gooders. The old man had his own theory: Slokker had simply absconded in the last few days without a word to anyone in order to escape his debts. It had happened before. What else would you expect from foreign students?

No one answered his knocking, so he entered, using the duplicate key. He had knocked quietly, as he had no desire to attract the usual crowd of neighbours. Inside, the apartment looked much as it had before. The old concierge shuffled about, looking through Slokker's personal effects. His clothes were still hanging in the wardrobe, and even his watch lay on the bedside table, next to the unmade bed. The mirror on the wardrobe door had been smashed and likewise the one above the sink in the bathroom. There were newspapers stuck to the windows, and he recognised the pile of pamphlets that Slokker must have taken from Deschamps's apartment.

The concierge closed the door quietly and walked softly down the corridor to 205. He was doing his best not to feel jumpy, but he had to admit that the whole thing was odd. Once inside, he too noticed that although the painters' equipment was there, they had yet to begin work. Nevertheless, it looked to him as if someone else, probably Slokker, had been there before him. Things had been moved around. When he checked the windowless room he had to leave the door open so that he could see more clearly into the unlit chamber. There was an odd shadow in the gloom, and so he switched on the dim lamp.

The light revealed Slokker's starved body hanging in mid-air. The face was fixed in a grimace of pain and the lips were drawn back from clenched teeth. The sightless eyes were staring downwards at his reflection in the mirror. Slokker must have taken the belt from his trousers, fastened it around his neck, climbed up onto the chair, and then attached the buckle to the obsolete light fitting on the ceiling. He had then kicked away the chair.

The concierge made himself turn away from the sight, and his first thought was of the nasty reputation another suicide might lend the building. First Monsieur Deschamps (though he had at least had the decency to end his life elsewhere) and now this young idiot! He closed the door behind him, ensured that it was securely locked once more, and made his way back to his office downstairs. As he sat waiting for the gendarmes' arrival, he realised that he must have picked up some of the pamphlets from Slokker's rooms. They lay in front of him, on the desk. He must have put them down there before he'd telephoned the authorities.

That night, after they had taken Slokker's body away, the concierge was troubled by a dream about being trapped in a dark, windowless room.

Vrolyck

I had been living in a cramped apartment out in the suburbs to the south of the city. The apartment overlooked a dingy street, invariably strewn with rubbish due to the preponderance of fast food outlets. Amongst these was a café that remained open for twenty-four hours a day, seven days a week.

The café was useful to me. After 1 A.M. it was usually deserted, and I often spent time there, sipping a greasy coffee and reading. My insomnia made sleep impossible most nights, and the owners were uncommunicative foreigners who took no interest in their customers. The décor (moulded plastic seats and formica tables) seemed not to have changed since the 1970s. Overhead, neon strip lighting gave the place a gleaming white sanitary air, like a hospital canteen.

One night, as I sat in the café drinking a lukewarm coffee in my usual corner, a woman in her early thirties, wearing a fur-trimmed black coat, came over to my table.

"May I join you?" she asked. "It's okay if you'd prefer to be alone."

My first reaction was one of alarm; I was surprised that she should take it upon herself to invade my privacy. But her manner was apologetic and inoffensive, and I had no wish to cause a scene by being rude.

She bought me another coffee. I had been sipping at the dregs of the last one for the past half-hour. The woman told me that her name was Emily Curtis.

"Excuse my curiosity," she said, "but you look very tired. Do you suffer from insomnia too?"

We had a conversation about sleepless nights and the various forms of medication prescribed to alleviate the condition. She had tried many of the same drugs as I, and had similarly found that the side effects had led her to abandon their use.

"Did you try the latest," she asked, "the supposedly extremely powerful one that's just come on the market?"

"Triaxopol?" I asked. "It worked for the first few weeks with me. But the stomach cramps became unbearable. The only way I could fend off the pain was with stimulants, which defeated the purpose of the soporific! In the end I found that I preferred to live with the exhaustion."

"I think my condition is hereditary," she said. "My mother suffers from the same problem. One or other of us is awake during the small hours. Still, we keep each other company."

"I live alone. I don't find I have much in common with other people," I replied.

I learned that she and her mother lived on the north side of the city and that she had been visiting some friends in this quarter. She had come into the café in order to while away the hours until dawn. I suppose that I envied her ability to approach a stranger without betraying any self-consciousness, for my own temperament is acutely solitary.

After half an hour or so, she asked me about the "white makeup" that entirely covered my face and hands. I suppose that the question was inevitable, and I was surprised that it had taken her so long to broach the subject.

"Please excuse my saying so," she said, "but it gives you a ghoulish appearance. I thought that you might wear the makeup deliberately, as some Goths do, to appear morbid."

"Hardly," I replied. "I don't have a choice. It masks the worst signs of chronic psoriasis. It's one of the crosses I bear along with insomnia. I'm told that it's psychosomatic and was brought on by the stress of an accident I suffered recently."

"You're really in a pretty bad way, aren't you?"

"Isn't everyone?"

Although our conversation flowed naturally and I found her more congenial than anyone with whom I had spoken in many weeks, I soon began to resent the intrusion and was longing to return to my apartment.

The woman noticed the book that I had set aside in order to talk with her. It was a battered old copy of *The Noctuary of Tine*, and she picked it up, turning the pages with curiosity.

I was gratified she did not, with liberal ignorance, insist "tine" was a misprint for "time."

"I love this stuff," she said. "I have done for as long as I can remember. When I was, oh, around four years old I found a copy of *Struwwelpeter* amongst the books in the local library. The pictures started off my obsession with weird horror."

"And now that you're older?" I asked.

"I read the European writers, the ones whose work deals with cruelty and pain: the likes of Hanns Heinz Ewers, Stefan Grabinski, and Leonid Andreyev. Are you familiar with their fiction?"

"I am indeed."

She laughed. "I think my reading habits have contributed to my insomnia, you know. When I do sleep, some of the dreams I have are quite awful!"

"Mine too. But at least I can use them; I write."

"Really? Have you had anything published?"

"Just a couple of slim books of weird tales. They weren't very successful, but they did bring me some little recognition amongst those who read such works. Just lately I haven't written a great deal. I've been trying to finish something that I began just after my accident."

"What is it called?"

"The working title is 'The Dybbuk Pyramid.'"

"I'd love to read it," she offered.

"I don't know. It needs more work, though I can't quite see what to do with it at the moment."

"Perhaps I could make a few suggestions?"

I thought for a moment, then nodded my assent.

By now it was past four in the morning and I could no longer resist the urge to be alone. As I stood up and pulled on my black overcoat, she thanked me for the conversation and told me that she would be back in the café in forty-eight hours' time and hoped that we might talk again. I promised to bring along the manuscript of "The Dybbuk Pyramid."

The fact that she'd admitted suffering from literary-inspired nightmares fascinated me, and I resolved to keep the appointment.

*

Our next meeting was rather perfunctory. We only spoke for a short time, since she was somewhat inebriated, but I gave her the manuscript of my story and called for a taxi to take her home. We did, however, arrange another appointment at the café, and she insisted on giving me her telephone number. Before I put her in the taxi she squeezed my hand in an affectionate manner. I noticed with embarrassment that traces of my masking lotion were left behind on her fingers.

*

Our third meeting proved to be the most interesting to date, as it revealed the degree to which my influence on her had grown.

She was in the café before I arrived, nursing a coffee and smoking the same brand of cigarettes that I myself bought. I noticed a certain change in her features; the naïve quality seemed to have been repressed, and in its place was an unusual expression, almost of dislocation, which I knew very well indeed. She had the copy of "The Dybbuk Pyramid" laid out on the plastic-coated table before her.

I sat down and accepted the cigarette she offered. Without preamble, she uttered the following:

"This story is without doubt the strangest thing I've ever read. It is as if the text is a reflection of my own thoughts. No—that's wrong. It is as if my thoughts are only a reflection of the story. While I read I couldn't tear my eyes away from the page, and I forgot all about the outside world. It seemed as if my mind was becoming a part of the text. It was horrible and irresistible at the same time. And the really bizarre thing is that, on the surface, it appeared only to be a confused jumble of disconnected words!"

"It's an experiment," I told her, "a new technique I'm trying to perfect."

"It's kind of like Joyce's stream-of-consciousness or Burroughs's cut-ups?"

"Kind of," I agreed warily. I suppose that the majority of writers would be pleased and flattered by such remarks. It was after all a sign that the story had had precisely the desired effect. However, personal satisfaction as a writer was no longer any use to me.

"What inspired you to write it?" she asked.

"I have some notes here that I made in an attempt to sort things out in my own mind, when it all began. They're very short. You're welcome to read them."

I passed her a sheet of paper I had torn from my notebook:

"The Dybbuk Pyramid" is an attempt to delineate an utterly alien consciousness that comes into contact with this world and interacts with it. It is not the case that the creature is evil—such an interpretation is solely of the human paradigm—but that its very existence is inimical to mankind.

The first draft attempted to present the tale from the viewpoint of the alien creature itself: its thought processes were to be markedly different from those of humans, and naturally it would not do to utilise vocabulary common to the experience of mankind.

I soon realised that the first draft could not possibly succeed. It read as total gibberish. Ninety-nine percent of the experiences of an alien entity would have no meaning for us. Even had the tale been confined to a simple encounter with the human race, the tremendous distortion in narrative technique meant that it would most resemble the aimless scrawling produced by some schizophrenics.

Then I realised that it might be possible to write such a tale in a first-person narrative, were the alien consciousness fused with that of a man or woman, perhaps as a prelude to an invasion by outside forces. Thereby the alien aspect might be filtered through human perception, giving the narrative a cohesion and familiarity that would enable it to be communicable to its human readership.

Curtis had finished reading and seemed to be considering what I'd written. During her silence I lit one of my own cigarettes, offered her one, and watched the smoke curling up towards the neon light strips on the ceiling.

"You succeeded," she said finally. "The story's like an incantation. There's some mysterious power in it that words can't explain. Perhaps the closest analogy I can make is that one feels as if everything human is a sham—a façade for something else entirely. And what lies behind the façade cannot be understood."

I nodded and flicked ash into the saucer of my coffee cup.

"You're as close as anyone can get to the truth," I said.

The word "contamination" rose unbidden in my mind. I stubbed out my cigarette in the saucer, drank the last dregs of my coffee, and told her that it was late and I really must go. "I am a person," I said, "who requires separation from other people." I had found that too much contact with them invariably disturbed the state of withdrawal that allowed me to function. Also, I knew that my work here was practically done.

She smiled, as if she understood my dilemma, and then put one of her gloved hands over my own, stroking it with her fingertips.

"One thing I've not mentioned," she said, "is the sense of isolation that comes across in the story. It's as if the author is utterly at a loss in this world, utterly alone. Perhaps it's a cry for help?"

I removed my hand from beneath hers, stood up with finality, and thanked her. Wrapping myself in my heavy winter overcoat, I made my way towards the door. There was no need for us to meet again, unless further personal intervention was required to accelerate the process.

*

The walk back to my apartment was only a matter of minutes. I invariably found pleasure in the sight of the deserted streets at this time of night. During the day the main thoroughfare was busy with traffic and pedestrians, but after midnight it had an air of pleasing desolation.

I let myself into the nondescript block and made my way up the stairs towards my rooms. As far as I knew there were only three other tenants, and this suited me very well, for at night the whole place was deathly quiet.

Once inside, I sat down in the armchair adjacent to the window. The familiarity of my surroundings allowed me to relax after the encounter with Emily Curtis. I looked across the room at the low bookcase filled with the three dozen or so battered books that I had read and re-read. I knew the volumes by heart, from the blemishes and tears on the dust-wrappers through to the dark horror of their contents. I had used them as exemplars in perfecting my method.

From the armchair I reached across to the window and opened the curtains so that I could gaze up at the stars. As usual, I felt the delicious sensation of falling upwards in a rush of cosmic vertigo, as if the sky were below me rather than above. I opened the window and leant out for a clearer view. For some time I allowed the pleasurable nausea to overwhelm me, but finally I had to return my gaze to the street. I was afraid that I might overbalance and plummet to the pavement below, as had happened to me once before.

There, beneath a streetlamp, I saw the pale face of Emily Curtis, watching me with a concentrated stare. I drew the curtains against the sight, and when I opened them again half an hour later she had gone.

*

I managed to sleep for a few hours. Later that morning, after I'd bathed and applied the masking lotion to my skin, the phone rang. It was Emily. I cradled the receiver between my shoulder and ear and listened, lighting a cigarette, as she apologised for her intrusion.

"Vrolyck, I can't shake off the effects of that story," she explained. "It keeps racing through my mind, day and night. The thing's become a part of me. Whatever I do I can't stop thinking of it. Even as I'm speaking to you now I see the words on the pages."

"Ah," I said, between puffs on my cigarette.

"I have to see you. We have to talk about this. It's not right. I'm worried that I'm losing my—"

"I would prefer not to discuss the story any further," I cut in. "Just now I require total isolation."

"For how long?" she asked desperately.

"For an indefinite period."

As I put the receiver down, I recalled that she not only knew my telephone number but also where I lived. I hoped that she would heed my request to stay away. It was imperative that I discover whether or not my own physical presence was a factor in any developments.

*

Weeks passed and I settled back into my nightly routine of haunting the café opposite and watching the stars whirl above me from the window. What had happened to Emily Curtis had been, I feared, merely an isolated incident, a consequence of brief exposure that would fade without any permanent effects. Such incidents had occurred before and had been a grave disappointment to me. All my previous contacts had been with subjects of little imagination, and although a few had suffered weird and horrible dreams after reading "The Dybbuk Pyramid," the effects were not long-lasting. I wondered whether, if I rendered it into plainer English, permanent contamination would be achievable.

I had no great interest in the fate of Emily Curtis at this point, despite the fact that one of my correspondents, who also lived in the city, wrote to tell me that he had encountered her on the streets. This was possibly on the same night that I had spotted her looking up at my window. Apparently she had been wandering as if in a daze, and when he approached her she had fled in terror. She seemed not to have recognised him, although they had met on several occasions since our meeting to discuss my published short story collections.

Two weeks later I received a manuscript posted to me by Emily Curtis. It appeared that she had written a tale of her own, which she had called "The Communication." There was an accompanying letter. One glance was enough to confirm that the contamination was a progressive rather than temporary condition. It was a very short letter and the salient portion ran as follows:

I am in a confused state of mind. I quite forget my own name, or even where I am, for much of the time. I watch the shadows from the window during the day as they creep towards me. And I watch the men who work by night. The enclosed story, which I began a week ago, belongs to you. I may not have time to finish it. Before what I have been is lost for good, best that you should see it.

It was as I expected: the manuscript appeared incomprehensible. Written on foolscap, it consisted of seemingly random words. These were not written in horizontal lines, but at varying angles to one another, in spirals and around the edges of the paper. Some of the words were in English, others in various other languages, and a number were *outré* characters that would have been mere gibberish to anyone but myself. Those portions that were in English I have quoted below, having first arranged them in a linear fashion and incorporated translation where required. They mirror almost exactly my own story "The Dybbuk Pyramid."

In the dream she had found herself in a strange and unknown city. Her body was unfamiliar to her and appeared to be that of an almost hairless biped covered by dark fabrics. This body was a source of repulsion; being an upright mass of tissue filled with water, fæces, and mucus. Its senses were overwhelming; disparate but consecutive images of vivid colour and puzzling airborne perceptions seemed to enter through holes in its head, vibrations that made no sense entered through other holes on each side and pressures that varied with a maddening intensity rippled across the biped's outer layer. As this creature stumbled across the deserted and dark city of monoliths and past black vertical columns that fanned out into rustling limbs, it sucked air into itself repeatedly, with a horrible sense of uneven rhythm. The dream did not seem to last very long and was terminated when the creature came across another of its kind. Seeing this other and knowing that this was the form in which she also was trapped, Curtis found the horror too much to bear. The creature staggered towards her, clad in similar fabrics, but these did not hide the monstrosity of its awful face, like that of some deranged white ape. When it made an expression that was utterly alien, she fled, to be awoken by her own screams, fully clothed on the bed in the apartment she shared with her elderly mother. Whether it was the dream itself that had awakened her, or the memory of the dream whilst in a state of semi-consciousness, she could not tell.

I realised that what had been set in motion now required my own intervention: it was time that Emily met with an accident of her own. Doubtless she would do so anyway, in due course, but such had been the corruption of my own physical form in the interim that in order for me to gauge the success of my plan my timetable had to be brought forward. My psoriasis had worsened into something more akin to leprosy, and I was unsure how long my health would hold out.

*

The journey on the bus to Curtis's part of the city took just under an hour. Apart from the driver and myself, the bus was empty. One of the small windows that provided ventilation was jammed open and freezing air blew into the deck. I had telephoned ahead and Curtis's mother had answered.

"Hello?" She had sounded strained and tense.

"Mrs Curtis? This is Trefusis Vrolyck. I'm a friend of your daughter. Excuse my calling, but I understand she's ill and I'm concerned about her."

"Oh, Mr Vrolyck, thank you for calling. Emily's mentioned you to me several times."

"How is she?"

"The doctor thinks it's a nervous breakdown. She's not left her bed for days. She doesn't speak or eat, only lies there, staring."

"Perhaps I could see her? It might help."

"Oh, yes, please. I'm at my wits' end. She often told me how much she admired you, and unless her condition changes the doctor says she'll have to be taken into some horrible psychiatric unit. I couldn't bear that to happen."

"I can be there in an hour or so. Would that be convenient?"

"Oh, yes, it'd be wonderful. Thank you so much, Mr Vrolyck."

"I'll see you shortly, then."

And so I alighted onto the pavement next to a very busy dual carriageway flanked by 1950s council estates. The buildings were blocks seven storeys high, each of identical plain grey concrete with flat roofs and exterior walkways. The Curtis apartment was situated in one of the blocks on the eastern edge.

All the walls were covered with graffiti, most of it simply the names of those who had turned their spray cans upon them, but there were some symbols indicating an origin that was familiar to me. These were the symbols that I had attempted to communicate in English via "The Dybbuk Pyramid."

I had to climb a vandalised stairway to reach the second floor. On the way up I passed a vagrant who seemed to be lost in some private ritual of his own. He was muttering to himself and arranging the rubbish strewn on the stairs into a little pile. He eyed me curiously as I passed, and there was something in his expression that made me hesitate. On closer inspection, he seemed unused to the flesh and muscles that covered his skull and continually screwed his face up in a contorted manner as if unsure of the appropriate impression it should convey to others. I had myself experienced such a dilemma after my accident.

When I reached the Curtis apartment I had to ring the bell several times before I heard shuffling footsteps. The door was opened a few inches, though held by a safety chain. An old woman peered out at me.

"Mr Vrolyck?" she asked.

Initially I thought that she was perturbed by my appearance, for in truth, the masking lotion I employed no longer disguised the ravages time had wrought upon my skin. However, it was obvious that her eyesight was not keen and she was simply squinting at me myopically, too vain or stupid to wear spectacles.

"That's right. You must be Emily's mother."

"Yes. Oh, please come inside, won't you?" the woman said.

She unchained the door and beckoned me to follow her as she shuffled back down the hallway in her carpet slippers. She said:

"I've just had a telephone call from Dr Phelps telling me that he felt I really should sign the papers. You know, the ones authorising him to arrange for Emily to be taken into care? It's all so distressing."

"I can imagine that it must be terrible for you. But I think you're wise to try every option before agreeing to that course of action," I replied.

"Do you know what I think caused all this?" she asked.

"Please tell me."

"It's the vandals on this estate. They're all into drugs, you know. For some reason she took an interest in their graffiti and they took advantage of her."

"Really?"

"Some of the neighbours told me that she'd paid them to spray-paint her own designs on the walls. But why should she do that? I don't believe them. They're gossips. Nasty people. And since those vandals were found dead, you'll have read about it in the papers, they've been spreading the rumour that my Emily was somehow to blame!"

"How so?"

"I've no idea. Everyone knows they killed themselves. It was probably the drugs, and my daughter's never taken drugs. Can you believe what they're saying? My daughter! Can you believe it, Mr Vrolyck?"

"It's ridiculous, of course—"

"Of course it is. And anyway, I saw a gang of them just the other night spraying the walls again, the same ones that Emily used to meet. So how do they explain that, eh? I think newspapers make these stories up."

"That's probably the answer."

"It's an absolute disgrace . . ."

"I understand how you feel."

We stood outside Emily's room. Her mother opened the door and, although it was dark within and the curtains were drawn, I could just make out a figure in the bed propped up with several pillows.

As I drew closer I could see that Emily Curtis's face was blank and her eyes stared straight ahead without blinking. But I thought I detected a flicker of movement as I came into her view.

"Do you think that I could be alone with her for a short while?" I asked her mother.

"Oh, yes. I'll make us some tea and bring it in. You sit down next to her."

Left alone with Emily, I sat down on the edge of the bed. I softly spoke her name. Her eyes rotated in the direction of my voice and a vague, unnatural smile distorted her previously placid features. There were two forces at war within her brain, and the pressure upon it could only be relieved when one of them gained control.

The sound of her mother making tea filtered along the hallway. I heard cups clinking and a kettle being filled. I would not have long. Removing one of the pillows from beneath Emily's head, I gripped it tightly in both hands and pressed it down over her face as hard as I was able. There was a gurgling, and then her body thrashed around for what seemed a long time. Finally she slumped back and I took the pillow away from her face. Her mouth was open and her eyes wide with death. I gently closed them and turned her head to one side. I replaced the pillow in its original position, making it look as if she were asleep.

A few seconds later the mother entered bearing a tray. Before she could find anywhere to set it down I motioned that we should leave the room.

"Was there any response?" she asked in a hushed voice as we walked back down the hall.

"I think so, yes. She seemed to recognise my voice before she drifted off to sleep. She even smiled."

The mother poured out the tea in the kitchen. I sat and sipped the weak liquid, explaining that it would be wise if we let Emily rest. I suggested that perhaps the response I had witnessed might be the first sign of a pleasing amelioration in her condition.

When I left there were tears of gratitude in the eyes of the old woman.

"Perhaps you could come again soon?"

But I pretended not to hear.

*

As I made my way back down the vandalised stairway the vagrant was still there. He had been busy in my absence and had completed the arrangement he was fashioning from crumpled wrappers, ash, and cigarette butts. It looked like a rubbish heap, but on examining it more closely I could see that it had been fashioned into a crudely shaped pyramid. His face was still struggling with its expressions, and from time to time one of his grimy hands traced a path along the graffiti upon the walls. But it was when he spoke that I knew the contamination had not been confined to my own contacts. For the tramp, with his pale dead face, mouthed the words:

"It is the time of the black radiance from the stars."

Although the words were English, it was in my own language that I received his telepathic transmissions.

It was brilliant. The city was covered with such graffiti, the symbols reproducing like bacteria. How much more effective than my own attempts to disseminate them under the guise of my writing! As you may have guessed, the symbols were a sign, a sort of cosmic homing-beacon, calling down others of my kind to enter the bodies of human beings. And I thought how ironic it was that, after all my efforts, it was vandals, those self-styled popular artists contaminated by Curtis, who had proved the more effective communicators.

*

My last sight of Emily Curtis was in the café where we first met.

Some days after the incident I have just described, I was out on the streets, seeking further signs of the contamination. There was indeed ample evidence of its unchecked spread. The symbols had been plastered on bridges, railway carriages, buses, and any wall that would show them clearly. I am not sure that the people were particularly aware, except for Curtis, the unknown vagrant, the vandals, and, of course, myself. I had been one of the very first— the pathfinder, so to speak. There were twelve billion of us waiting out there, so only around half our number would be able to find shelter in the human race on this planet. In order for a successful transfer to take place, all human thoughts had to be extinguished from the individual for a long enough period to allow our own to take hold, so the prior death of the brain was entirely necessary.

Emily Curtis was sitting in the window, gazing out through the misty, condensation-soaked glass of the café at nothing in particular. Her skin was even paler than it had been in life and was caked in the same white foundation that I wore. As I passed by, her eyes met mine for a brief moment. There lurked within them a black radiance, filtered from the stars.

She knew now, as did I, that we are here only temporarily, until these physical shells rotted away. Then we would have to move on again, fleeing the death that pursued us. But for now, like me, she was trapped within the human carcass, suffering the horrifying existence of the biped simian, the maddening trace-memories lingering within the fabric of their brains: a dead person's memories, names drawn in the sand just beyond the reach of the waves breaking from the black ocean before it.

GHORLA

My contention is that high-level sentience collapses in on itself near death in a manner akin to the demise of a massive star and that dying thoughts approach infinite duration. Post-mortem, these thoughts, if driven by a will of sufficient power, can tumble over a synaptic event horizon and subsequently appear in another body with an almost exact genetic identity. Such "heirs" are subject to the invasion of their minds by ideas and emotions that originate with the dead. The living are simply vehicles for a series of disturbing and broken alien responses that we take to be our own personalities. I now believe that the majority of thoughts we think actually come from the "ghost shells" of ancestors in varying states of psychical decay. They are the products of disintegrating remains, frightful masks that have not been shed. Afterlife geography is seen in the UHF frequencies between TV channels, consisting of immense steppes of static. It is a projection in time, comprised of anti-matter and populated by the dead.

—Julius Ghorla, *Black Holes* (1983)

The bus approached Crawborough railway station. It was a wet, miserable morning in late October. The rain had not ceased for three days and the weather forecasts predicted another week more of it. All the holidaymakers were long gone from this stretch of the Yorkshire coast; no more backpackers, elderly couples, or dirty weekenders used the bus service to ferry them north. Most of the time, except during school-run hours, the vehicle was empty save for one or two lone shoppers ferrying their heavy bags back from the supermarket to home. Even they usually travelled only as far as four or five stops.

The driver of the bus, one Bill Jones, was confident he would not have to take on any passengers for this service from Crawborough to Banwick. The incessant rain seemed to have forced everyone off the streets. This pleased him quite a bit because it meant he could enjoy the luxury of smoking whilst he drove, instead of waiting until he reached the depot at Banwick, well over an hour away. There would be no one to comment on his flouting the bus company's regulations.

But as he pulled into the turn near the railway station he was disgruntled to see a lone figure waiting underneath the bus-shelter ahead. The prospective passenger had a large suitcase with him, two plastic carrier-bags, and a wicker-basket for carrying a small dog or large cat.

When he pulled up alongside the shelter and opened the doors Jones saw that the man was glancing accusingly at a fob watch he'd produced from the left pocket of his shabby beige mackintosh.

The man immediately struck Jones as being a difficult passenger. He tut-tutted loudly as he put away the fob watch, as if to insinuate that the bus was running late. Moreover, his appearance and demeanour gave the overall impression that he fancied himself an eccentric. This did not endear him to Jones, who regarded any person even remotely out of the ordinary as highly suspicious; perhaps even of having come up from London. The passenger wore a black pork pie hat and sported a polka-dotted bow tie. He looked to be in his middle fifties. His thin face was a network of worry lines, as if he had analysed all the problems of the world and come to no solution for them. His complexion was sallow, like candle-wax, particularly around his cheeks. He had a long, aquiline nose, beady little eyes, and a small chin as smooth as a billiard ball.

The passenger began to haul his luggage up into the bus and crammed it in the storage space just in front of the seats on the left-hand side of the aisle. Jones noticed that the two carrier bags were stuffed full of paperback books. They smelt musty with age. When the passenger turned back to collect the wicker basket, which had been left until last, Jones called out in a flash of spiteful inspiration:

"Hurry along there, you're holding up the bus."

The man glared back coolly and then, with an air of studied irony, began to look around him, making it perfectly aware that he knew he was the only passenger boarding at this stop.

"My good fellow," he replied in a wearied tone, "kindly refrain from being objectionable." His accent was very Received Pronunciation, the type of voice passed down by generations of BBC broadcasters until regional accents were finally ushered in.

After he'd paid his fare, the passenger, whose name was Arthur Staines, carried the wicker basket with him to a seat close to the back of the bus. He wanted to be as far away as possible from the oafish driver. From inside the basket there came a long meowing noise, and Staines lifted the lid to allow his cat Edgar to examine their surroundings. The creature, a fat and bad-tempered beast with mangy black fur, poked its head out and looked around with evident distaste. The cat leant one paw against the edge of the basket and dug its claws into the side. Staines feared that it might, at any moment, waddle forward and attempt to attack the driver, so he persuaded Edgar to settle down again before it was too late.

Edgar was Staines's sole companion. The two had been together for over ten years. Once the cat had reached maturity it decided not only that it preferred never to be left alone but also that it was no longer prepared to walk anywhere at all. Occasionally it would drag itself from one side of a room to another in order to eat or defecate, but its great bulk now meant that even this concession was haphazard.

Outside, the rain lashed across the landscape of rolling fields and hills. Staines gazed absently at the deluge, more interested in the streams of water coursing down the glass of the bus windows than in the vistas cloaked by the low grey clouds. The vehicle crept along narrow roads between towns and along the sides of valleys, throwing up gigantic splashes as it motored through puddles and pools that had formed on the route.

He took a map from the breast pocket of his shabby mackintosh, unfolded it, and spread it out across his knees. His destination was an old fishing village called Scarsdale Bay, not far south from Banwick. Staines had carefully circled the coastal town on the map.

For some time he had been engaged upon research concerning an obscure author who had made the village his home during his latter years. This writer, Julius Ghorla (1930–1985), had scraped a living writing pulp novels. Staines planned to make Ghorla the exclusive subject of the next instalment (the third) of his limited-circulation periodical *Proceedings of the Dead Authors Society*.

Staines was one of those obsessive bibliophiles who were unable to take any interest in fiction unless its creator had long been in the tomb. Had Ghorla been alive and still writing today it was certain that Staines would have thought his work insignificant. Moreover, Staines even ignored prestigious dead authors, reserving his praise for those sufficiently obscure to have escaped critical attention almost altogether. It was as if by championing those writers who had been unfairly overlooked, and who were safely dead, he might thereby obtain for himself some measure of the reputation they had been denied. Vanity had turned him into a ghoul of letters. Ghorla's books had appeared only during the boom in cheap glue-bound paperbacks, never seeing print in hardcover, and issued solely by Eclipse Publications Ltd, an imprint of a disreputable firm whose catalogue otherwise consisted of risqué or "spicy" novels.

Staines calculated that it could not be more than a 45-minute journey from Crawborough to Scarsdale Bay, despite the tortuous route that this particular local bus service followed. He had travelled all over the country in search of recondite literary discoveries, indulging his own predilections, although he made his actual, meagre living from what little freelance journalism he could sell to local newspapers and the likes of specialist glossy monthly magazines such as the *Paranormal* and *UFO Times.*

Julius Ghorla had been a favourite writer of his ever since he'd stumbled across a tattered paperback copy of the author's best-known (inasmuch as "best-known" is applicable) and final work back in 1984. The book was Ghorla's episodic novel *Black Holes,* a series of short stories joined together to form a reasonably lengthy opus of some 50,000 words. These stories were concerned with the interior experiences of the dying brains of several characters. Ghorla had come up with the intriguing idea that consciousness slows down at the point of death to a degree whereby interior time bears no relation to the passage of time in external reality.

Edgar began to meow again. The cat was in state of some agitation and showed his displeasure by rocking back and forth inside his wicker basket. Staines was momentarily at a loss to account for the cause, until he caught a faint whiff of what appeared to be cigarette smoke. He looked up towards the front of the bus and there saw a wispy curl of blue tobacco vapour float out of the driver's cabin.

Staines was not especially puritanical himself when it came to smoking, but the effect it had on Edgar was not to be ignored. He got up from his seat and wandered forwards, hoping to catch the driver in the act. However, by the time he was staring through the glass partition at him there was no trace of the offending cigarette. The driver's window was slightly open and it looked as if he had managed to flick the butt outside moments before Staines's investigation.

"Have you been smoking in here?" Staines said, whilst tapping on the partition.

"What?" Jones responded, as if he didn't understand the question. There were telltale traces of ash on the sleeve of his uniform.

"I shall report you," Staines continued. "You have greatly upset my cat with your thoughtlessness."

"If you don't get back in your seat and shut up," the driver replied, raising his voice, "I'll throw you and your bloody cat off the bus."

Staines took a quick look at the still-raging downpour outside. It really would not do to have to walk the seven or so miles remaining before they reached Scarsdale Bay, especially in this foul weather. He doubted that Edgar would survive such a trauma. Loud caterwauling emanated from within the wicker basket. Doubtless Edgar wondered where Staines had gone.

*

At the top of Scarsdale Bay, Staines stepped down from the bus and joined the luggage he'd deposited on the pavement. He heard the driver mutter something obscene as the doors closed.

The rain had eased and was now no more than persistent drizzle. Staines looked back and forth along the deserted lane until he spotted a sign indicating that Scarsdale Bay town centre was to his right, down a turning. As yet he could not see his destination but supposed it could only be a few minutes' walk downhill. He tied the carrier bags of books around the outside of his suitcase. It had a retractable handle and little wheels at the base so that he could haul it along after him relatively easily. In his other hand he carried the basket containing Edgar. Mercifully, the cat seemed to have fallen asleep after the excitement of the bus journey.

Once he'd turned the corner he had his first sight of Scarsdale Bay. It was situated on the side of a steep cliff, and he saw a jumbled panorama of red-tiled rooftops and chimney-stacks. Cottages jostled one another over the warren of tiny and narrow stairways and lanes. It had doubtless been a haven for smugglers a few centuries ago. Staines made his way down the central street, Ormsley Parade, passing a series of overhanging upper storeys, dilapidated arches, and little flights of steps for pedestrians that were designed to break up the extremely steep gradient. Really, thought Staines, this curious little place might have been designed by an admirer of the artist Piranesi. It was certainly a fitting town for Julius Ghorla to have chosen as a retreat in order to pen his outré series of tales.

A sea wall had been erected in the 1950s near the bottom of the village to prevent any more of the fishermen's cottages being washed away by waves during storms. Only Ormsley Parade wound all the way to the very bottom of the cliff. During high tide the waves lapped halfway up the cobbled and seaweed-coated steps leading to the beach. When the sea was rough Staines could easily imagine that it spilled over the steps and into the Parade in a foaming torrent.

The hotel in which Staines had booked a room loomed large to his left. It was the sole guest house in Scarsdale Bay. Although most of the cottages here were let out to tourists during the summer season, such an expense was beyond his limited means. This hotel, called Shadwell Vistas, was very cheap, especially at this time of year, and he anticipated that he was unlikely to be bothered by any other guests. He paused outside the building, looking up at the timbered mock-Tudor structure with its bull's-eye windows, and then made his way inside to the reception area via a set of panelled double doors.

He crossed a threadbare carpet. The room had a sofa, a few chairs, and some black-and-white photographs in frames by way of decoration. They depicted scenes of Scarsdale Bay taken during Victorian times. From another room close by he heard a discordant conversation punctuated by bursts of static that sounded as if it were coming from a television set. There was no one manning the reception desk, and so Staines rang the bell to signal his presence. A miserable-looking man in his early sixties emerged from a back office. He had doubtless been engrossed in watching the television that Staines had heard. He was bald with a thin Orwellian moustache, and wore an undone waistcoat with check trousers. Staines noticed that he wasn't wearing any shoes, or even socks.

"Can I help you, sir?" the man said without enthusiasm.

"I made a reservation by telephone. The name's Arthur Staines."

The man appeared to consult a list that he kept beneath the desk.

"Single room, staying for a week? Non-smoking?"

"Yes, that's it. Thirty-five pounds a night was the figure I was quoted."

"I have the booking here, Mr Staines. Quite correct. By the way, I'm Charles Browning, the acting manager here during the off-season. Anything I can do for you, please don't hesitate to ask."

Staines signed the register, was told breakfast was served between seven and nine in the morning, and then was given a key with the number seven tagged onto it. Just as he began to climb the stairs with his luggage, the man came around the desk and caught him up.

"Oh. Forgot to tell you, Mr Staines," Browning said. "There's a letter here for you. It was delivered yesterday."

Staines looked bewildered. He wasn't expecting any letter. Perhaps it was from a correspondent, one of those who shared his enthusiasm for Julius Ghorla's work, with late information concerning the village. He stuffed the envelope into his pocket, nodded at Browning and continued up the stairs. When he reached the landing on the first floor he noticed that all the doors had bolts on the outside in addition to the standard inside locks.

*

Edgar was peering out of the basket and refused to leave it; he seemed decidedly unhappy about his surroundings. The hotel room was shabby and tiny. The mattress on the bed had been thinned by the weight of hundreds of guests. Staines imagined that someone deranged had chosen the wallpaper; it was a confused jumble of red whorls and spirals on a garish yellow background. He was glad it was so old that the colours had faded. When new it would have driven anyone mad.

He'd unpacked his belongings and now turned his attention to the letter. His name and the address of the hotel had been typed on the envelope, so he had no clue as to the sender. Even the post-mark was smudged, so its point of origin could not be determined.

He tore open the envelope and recognised the handwriting at once; a numbing sense of dread rose up from his guts as he read the abrupt missive:

> Heard about your good fortune in discovering that Ghorla's hitherto unknown sister is living in Scarsdale Bay. Will join you as quickly as possible. Do nothing until my arrival!
> Yours etc., Eric

Staines crumpled the letter into a ball and threw it across the room. That blasted Eric Cooper! Always dogging his footsteps! Cooper, like Staines, was obsessed with Julius Ghorla and was conducting his own research into the writer's life and work. By the weekend he too would be in Scarsdale Bay, pestering Staines to share what information he had gathered and then taking credit himself for what discoveries were previously made. Well, thought Staines, this particular act of treachery would not succeed. He had the head-start and resolved to press his advantage. By tomorrow he was determined to find and interview Ghorla's sister. Moreover, he would warn her in no uncertain terms to have nothing to do with Eric Cooper. By the time his adversary arrived he would be too late.

Edgar purred from his basket. It seemed that he'd finally be-come accustomed to his surroundings and it was time to feed him his evening meal: three tins of Swedish meatballs in tomato sauce. He opened the cans with the Swiss Army knife that he always car-ried with him. The cat shied away at first sight of the implement, and became calm only when it was returned to Staines's jacket pocket.

*

Breakfast at the hotel consisted of a plateful of fried sausages, bacon, mushrooms, eggs, and bread. Staines managed to eat around a quarter of it, washed down with greasy tea, and fed the rest to Edgar, who was lurking in his basket underneath the table.

The dining room was deserted except for Staines. He'd been right in assuming that there would be few, if any, other guests stay-ing at the hotel. Mr. Browning appeared periodically to see whether Staines required anything further. Staines wondered whether the man did all the work in the hotel during the off-season. It seemed plausible.

When Browning returned to take away the crockery and cutlery, Staines asked him whether he knew anything of a "Miss Ghorla" and where she lived. The town was so small and had so few permanent residents that it seemed inconceivable he would not know of her.

"Oh, yes," Browning said, responding to Staines's query with a wry smile. "I know about her. Everyone here does. She's quite a local celebrity."

He said nothing more on the subject but wrote down her address and directions to the place on a table napkin. Her cottage was located about three-quarters of the way up the cliff in a cul-de-sac.

"One more thing," Staines said. "Why the bolts on the outside of the guest-room doors?"

"Oh, that," Browning replied, "was just a mistake. We never use them. They should have been fitted on the inside—you know how it is. We just haven't got around to removing them yet."

Within twenty minutes of Staines finishing breakfast he was traversing the labyrinthine series of stairways, raised pavements, and house-to-house archways in search of the cottage. He finally found a cobbled little turning, terminating in a high brick wall, where her home was located.

Staines knocked on the door three times and waited. In one hand he had a carrier-bag of books by her late brother, so as to prove his credentials as a scholar of his work, and in the other he carried the ubiquitous basket containing his cat. He'd covered the top of the basket with a sheet of plastic so that Edgar wouldn't get wet. The rain, though less ferocious at times than yesterday, was nevertheless still persistent.

The door finally swung open, and the sight of one of the strangest women he had ever seen confronted Staines. The thing that struck him at first was the uncanny Ghorla family resemblance. He recalled a photograph he'd once seen of Franz Kafka with his younger sister Ottla; the two might have been twins. The case of Julius and Claudia Ghorla was much the same. Yet the appearance of the woman was remarkable in itself; and this was the judgement of a man who prided himself on being regarded by others as an eccentric in his own dress. Claudia Ghorla wore a blond wig with a long fringe, a carefully sculpted coiffure in the 1950s beehive style. She could not have been any younger than seventy years of age. Her face was pinched and withered, and she wore an obscene amount of foundation, rouge, and lipstick. Her blue eyes, almost hooded by false lashes, peered at Staines with a contemptuous lack of interest. The woman was emaciated. The off-black velvet dress she wore hung from her skeletal body as if displayed on a clothes hanger in the window display of a run-down charity shop.

She looked him up and down.

"I don't want to buy anything," she said in a throaty voice. "Now go away, you awful little man."

Staines was taken aback at the idea anyone might mistake him for a travelling salesman or hawker of any description.

"Madam," he said, raising the cultivation of his accent several degrees by way of emphasis, "you misunderstand my motives in coming here."

"Nor," she replied, adopting a tone of hauteur even more cutting than her last effort, "do I wish to be bothered by—ugh—journalists."

This second assault was harder to bear, since it possessed an element of truth. Nevertheless, Staines tried to shrug it off. He had not come this far to fall at the last. Not with Eric Cooper coming up along the rails close behind him.

Edgar let out a loud meow from inside the basket. He had endured quite enough of being outside in the damp air and alerted Staines to the fact.

"What's that you've got in there?" she said, her expression changing from one of stony hostility to one of interest.

"It's my cat Edgar. I take him with me wherever I go."

"You drag a poor animal around in this foul weather? Bring him inside where it's dry, you wretched man, before you kill the helpless creature!"

*

Staines had been trying unsuccessfully for over three hours to elicit information from Claudia Ghorla about her brother. The stick-like woman fussed around Edgar, making the cat the centre of her attention and practically ignoring whatever questions Staines asked that related directly to the author's life and work. It was as if she'd forgotten all about the existence of her late brother.

Staines sat in an armchair in her small drawing room, sipping at a cup of lukewarm tea. On the carpet were piled the paperback editions of Julius Ghorla's fiction. They failed to arouse any curiosity in her. When advised that Staines was planning a special issue of his little periodical *Proceedings of the Dead Authors Society* in her brother's honour she'd taken the news with no more than a noncommittal shrug. She was fanatically neutral about it all. He mentioned how unscrupulous his rival, Eric Cooper, could be, but she took the news calmly. Even Staines's claim that Cooper would rifle through drawers and cupboards in search of papers the moment her back was turned was met with nothing more than raised eyebrows.

He'd managed, at least, to convince her that he was not a journalist in search of a story, simply an amateur scholar engaged on private research for a small group of devotees. If he had not achieved this immediate aim he had no doubt that Claudia Ghorla would have taken no notice of him at all, except perhaps to contact the nearest branch of the RSPCA and have him reported for possible cruelty to his cat.

It had finally stopped raining and Staines suggested by way of a diversion that they might take a short walk while the weather was good.

Although Staines was still anxious to turn the subject around to Claudia Ghorla's brother, she persisted in instead discussing whatever came into her mind.

They were sat upon an old bench overlooking the bay. It commanded a magnificent view of the jumbled house and cottage rooftops, the tangled alleyways and bridges. The turbulent waves crashed up against the sea-wall far below. It was high tide now, and no trace of the weed-choked beach below could be seen. Behind the bench was the former cemetery, overrun by the expanse of woodland, its boundary walls mere ruins where exposed roots and twisted trunks had pushed their way through. The wind swept up from the bay and whistled past them.

"Quite a pleasant spot. The beauty of nature, errm . . . and all that sort of thing," Staines remarked, looking behind and then in front of him, comparing the two aspects of the scene around them. He said it to be polite. Frankly, he was very much of the view that the countryside was something green-coloured that you travelled across in order to get from one city to another.

"The modern world . . ." Miss Ghorla responded. "I find its sentimentality for Nature pathetic. Mother Nature! As if it concerns itself with the welfare of human beings! Or, for that matter, with any other creatures. Nature is an idiot, a mindless force that fumbles across this black planet. And yet the stupid people worship it!"

"It's very inconvenient sometimes. Perhaps a little too wild," Staines mumbled.

"When Nature acts in a way that is inimical to mankind, then we hear cries that hurricanes, floods, and droughts are somehow unnatural! During one decade society claims we are on the brink of a new Ice Age, during the next that global warming will finish us all off! All this is the consequence of our worshipping Nature! We think of it as a mother and cannot bear the idea that it has no regard whatsoever for us. We fret and wail looking for signs of her displeasure, convincing ourselves that we have wronged her, as if she ever cared—or even noticed—our existence in the first place."

"I wonder if your brother shared your—" Staines said, before he was interrupted yet again.

"Plagues and cancer," she spat. "Aren't these too a part of Nature? Yet we do not hesitate to try and eradicate them! Mother Nature is riddled with venereal disease!"

Edgar began to meow from inside the large wicker basket that Staines had put down carefully next to the bench. The cat had also reached through the grille at the front and was clawing at the air in order to catch Staines's attention. The feline appeared to have had enough of Miss Ghorla's theories on humanity's attitude to the natural world.

The whole thing was a dead loss, thought Staines. The woman was useless to him. Let Eric Cooper see what he could do with her. Staines had endured enough of the old crone's nonsense.

"I really must be getting back to my hotel," he said. "They serve dinner at six and I'm famished."

"For a journalist, you've been quite entertaining," she replied. "Here, take this. Look it over and I'll visit you this evening at your hotel around nine, once you've eaten. We can talk privately about my brother's theories then. Perhaps even try some of them out in practice."

The old lady took a loose-leaf notebook from her handbag and passed it to the astonished Staines. He rifled through it as she got up, spoke a few more words, and then turned away to vanish into the warren of streets below them.

"I've underlined some passages for your convenience that I think you'll find of particular interest."

The notes related to Julius Ghorla's episodic novel *Black Holes.*

*

Long after Claudia Ghorla had departed, Staines could still be found sitting on the bench. He was poring over the notebook in a state of total fascination. It was only once it had got dark and become difficult to read that he noticed night had come. Edgar had fallen asleep; he'd given up trying to attract Staines's attention. Luckily, the advent of a rising moon provided Staines with sufficient light to carry on reading the handwritten text without interruption. This might be his only chance to do so. The old lady was capricious and could well change her mind about providing him with further information later on.

Staines was surprised to find that Claudia Ghorla had added the following entries of her own towards the end of the notebook, having scored out her brother's own pages with a black marker pen.

12th July 1985

Well, it's done. Last night I followed the instructions left by my late brother and drilled a hole in the front of my skull. It was an incredibly messy business. I really had no idea that there would be so much blood. The thick strip of bandage that I had wrapped around my head (just above my eyebrows) was soon soaked lipstick-red.

I had to cover the carpet in the bathroom with plastic sheeting. Mirrors were placed at precisely the correct angles around my head so that I could see the progress of the operation clearly. An injection of 2ccs of lidocaine in my forehead served as an anaesthetic. I cut a V-shaped flap of skin, drew it back to expose the skull beneath, and proceeded to drill through bone and marrow. The noise and the vibration were terrible. The drilling went on for an hour. Often I had to stop in order to wash away the blood running down my face and into my eyes. I felt as if my head would split apart before I reached the surface of the brain and finally created the socket for my Third Eye.

I knew the consequences of the operation going wrong; possible brain damage causing paralysis, idiocy, or blindness. But I had sworn to carry out my brother's last wishes—even though his attempt to do the same thing had ended in his destruction.

My thighs are dotted with cigarette burns. Often, when I am smoking, I turn up my skirt and press the burning tip of my cigarette onto the cold white flesh there. The pain temporarily distracts me from the mental anguish I feel at my own helplessness. I am setting down this cheap autobiographical episode to prove to myself that any good liar can write convincingly. Now to await the changes that Julius predicted.

14th July 1985

What I still saw was the same thin, not unattractive woman with silvery, shoulder-length hair: a female version of my dead brother. Her body is almost emaciated and possessed of an awkward gait. Her skin is pale and unblemished, and her cheekbones elegantly distinct. Perhaps the lips are a trifle too thin, but the perfect regularity of the tiny teeth that they reveal more than makes up for any slight imperfection. Curved eyebrows arch above dazzling, glacial-blue eyes.

This morning that face is almost the same, except for the ugly, sutured wound in the middle of my forehead. I am somewhat afraid of what lies beneath that stitched flap of skin—and of what it will be able to see if I remove that freshly made eyelid.

20th July 1985

Summertime in England: warm rain and leaden skies. A seaside town in the middle of July. Mercifully, it is off the tourist routes and has nothing that would attract a holidaymaker. The beach is all shingles and pebbles, not sand, and miles from the nearest railway station or main road. The people here are unspeakably ordinary, and they blur into the background of the grey cliffs and the North Sea. There are no churches, piers, ancient monuments, or amusement arcades.

In the afternoon I walked along the beach in the uncomfortable humidity. I wore my green silk headscarf to cover the V-shaped wound, and a half-length mackintosh. I expect that I should have also taken an umbrella. The skies, as usual, threatened rain. Despite the rubber grip of my plimsolls, I once or twice slipped on the stones underfoot. They were still slippery, for the tide had only just turned, leaving foam and kelp in its wake. Mother often told me that my feet were too small in relation to my height, so it was scarcely surprising that I was destined to stumble through life (metaphorically as well as literally) rather than advance boldly.

I wanted to find a deserted spot some ways outside the town where the sea-spray crashed up across the rocks, where I could be alone. Then and only then would I unveil my new Third Eye, gaze out across the ocean, and see as I had never seen before.

Doubtless I must have been an odd sight to any observer: a grinning middle-aged woman with thin limbs, scrambling wildly along the shoreline. The fact is that I did not care. I was in the grip of a wild exultation. Part of me was unsure whether I was simply overcome with a sense of relief at having survived operating on myself.

There was a natural ledge set in the cliff face ahead of me. It was easily reached by clambering over some boulders and proved to be the perfect vantage point. I settled down on the rough surface, using my raincoat as a cushion on which to sit. I fairly tore the headscarf off me and my fingers worked on the sutures. I cut them away with tiny scissors and eagerly unpicked the strands with my long, painted fingernails. Then I pulled back the V-shaped flap of skin. As I did so I closed my old eyes in order to see the world purely through my new one.

The light was so intense, so white, and yet so cold, that I screamed with shock. It seemed that the surface of my brain was freezing over.

A moment before, the sea was a foaming expanse of gently rolling waves. The next it was a solid white mass of ice stretching to the horizon, like that of the Arctic wastes or the surface of some frozen moon at the edge of the solar system. I now opened my old eyes too, but my overall sight remained unaffected as if, with the dominant contribution of my Third Eye to the other two, I saw a new dimension for the first time. Only when I covered my forehead with my palm did the sea again become liquid and its waves break upon the shore beneath me.

And the sky! Before it had been dull, cloaked with low grey clouds, oppressive, and trapping the sticky heat beneath its leaden folds. Now it was crystalline blue, clear and vivid, a sheen of gaseous frost beneath abysmal outer space. Starlight shone straight through the chill and thin atmosphere, even now in the daytime.

Far away, at the limit of my vision, there was a great wall of ice. It looked like a frozen continent visible at the horizon's edge. Was it just my imagination or did it advance closer, albeit almost imperceptibly, as I gazed across the expanse separating it from the shoreline? Its motion was like that of the minute hand of a clock—so gradual that it exists on the borderland of optical illusion and reality.

I pulled down the V-shaped flap of skin, closing my Third Eye and covering the self-inflicted wound from view with my headscarf. The world was no longer encased in ice. It was once again a typical miserable English summer's day, but I could feel the presence of my Third Eye in the socket I had created. The orb turned and rolled wildly beneath the thin layer of flesh on my forehead that covered it.

It was suddenly vital that I return to my dwelling and gather together my thoughts. They were racing through my brain with such rapidity as to be maddening. Ideas jostled for precedence in my mind, but I could scarcely make sense of them. They were haphazard and dreamlike, beyond the scope of my ability to render into words. These concepts were more like patterns or designs than a linear sequence of fictional events. In one of these flashes of inspiration I had the notion I might delineate the horror of an ice-crystal in the decay of its symmetry or participate in the madness of a reflection produced by a shattered mirror.

Snow flakes continuously dance around me, like the static between TV channels. This is the beginning of a new Ice Age.

The dying sun casts shadows across the frozen beach as it sets behind the seafront trees and buildings. The ice is streaked with darkness. I think of the reflection of my own face I'd once seen in a shop window: an empty shell of a face, like that of a mannequin left out in the rain, cheap mascara dribbling from its lifeless eyes.

My Third Eye is invariably uncovered. I wonder if my two original eyes might atrophy in response to the dominance of my third eye. Perhaps they will begin to wither away, dissolving in the sockets, like molluscs that have had salt sprinkled on them. Eyes are the windows of the soul, but the Third Eye is a doorway, through which my brother's thoughts come and go. It is his eye. It is green; mine are both blue. What other physical features possessed by Julius might transfer to me?

*

Staines looked up from the notes resting on his lap. He felt a sense of dull sickness in the pit of his stomach. The old woman must have gone mad immediately after the death of her brother. Their relationship seemed to have been abnormal, possibly even incestuous. He wondered if they'd made some bizarre suicide pact that Claudia had failed to honour.

The sea rolled back and forth in the near distance beyond the muddle of moon-drenched rooftops. Above the waves, across the night sky, thousands of stars stood out in the blackness. He wondered if he might see one of them suddenly blink out of existence as he watched, collapsing in itself like one of the dying minds Ghorla had described. He had no idea how long stars took to perish but suspected that their life span dwarfed that of a human being into insignificance. The thought of time reminded him that he'd no idea how late it was now, and he took his fob-watch out of his mackintosh pocket. It was eight-thirty precisely.

He'd missed dinner at the hotel and realised he'd have to make a meal of Swedish meatballs from a can. But if it was good enough for Edgar it was good enough for him too. He picked up the basket (containing the still-slumbering cat) plus his bag of paperbacks and hurriedly made his way to the hotel through the crazily angled passageways of Scarsdale Bay. He didn't wish to be late for his appointment with Claudia Ghorla at nine.

*

Only upon opening the basket when back in the hotel room did Staines discover that Edgar was dead. The cat was curled up; its body rigid and cold, its eyes open and staring sightlessly up at him. He couldn't bear to remove the dead animal and sat down on the edge of the bed, trying to decide just what to do next. Eventually, Staines resolved to go downstairs into the hotel's lounge bar and drink himself into a stupor. He could deal with the disposal of Edgar's body in the morning. He had quite forgotten about his appointment with Miss Ghorla.

Just then someone knocked at the door to Staines's room. He opened the door: standing on the threshold was Miss Ghorla. She was clad in a ratty blouse and skirt. At this precise moment she was the very last person Staines wanted to see. He was incapable of questioning her closely or paying much attention to her responses, even should they reveal some insights into the life and work of her brother.

"Mr. Browning directed me to your room," she said. "I thought it best if we talked in private rather than downstairs where we might be overheard."

"I'm sorry, Miss Ghorla, but I've had a shock. It's my cat, you see . . ."

Waving aside his faltering objections, the old lady wandered into the room and cast a glance over at the basket containing Edgar's corpse.

"I warned you to take better care of that poor creature," she said in a low menacing voice.

Staines felt a wave of annoyance rising up inside him at the sheer bloody cheek and lack of tact that the woman displayed. He was about to let loose with a stream of abuse when he noticed a trickle of blood making its way down the centre of her forehead from her beehive wig.

"I think you must have hit your head . . ." Staines said.

She ignored his remark and picked up the notebook jointly written by her and Julius that Staines had left on the bed.

"Well," she said, "now you know some of it. But not, as yet, of the process akin to hypnosis whereby a mind in a healthy body might also be induced to collapse in on itself . . . but I can show you. I've sometimes wondered whether transfer between radically dissimilar genetic material is possible."

Another trickle of blood ran down her forehead and around her nose, dribbling along her right, foundation-caked cheek. She raised an attenuated, veined hand and dipped her long fingers into the coiled mass of hair covering her forehead, unpicked some sutures and parted her fringe.

*

Eric Cooper set down his carpetbag in front of the reception desk in the Shadwell Vistas Hotel. He rang the bell in order to attract someone's attention. Eventually the temporary manager saw fit to drag himself away from the static between channels that he'd been watching on television in the back room and attend to the visitor.

"Do you require a room, sir?" Browning said. "We've plenty available."

Eric Cooper looked around disdainfully at the sorry-looking foyer and curled his lip at the thought. After he'd caught up with Staines he intended to have a wash and brush up at the luxury cottage (with full mod-cons) that was to be his base during his visit to Scarsdale Bay. It might suit Staines to stay here in this godforsaken flea-pit, but not Cooper.

"No," he said. "I believe a friend—ah—colleague of mine is a guest here. His name's Arthur Staines. I want to surprise him. Can you show me up to his room?"

Browning smiled at the well-dressed visitor. Cooper was a tall man with round eyeglasses, immaculately dressed in a navy double-breasted pinstripe suit with a striped tie done up in a Windsor knot. The only blemish in his appearance was an ill-fitting wig that was a slightly different shade of grey-brown from the natural hair left on his head.

"Very popular tonight," said Browning, "is our Mr. Staines. He's with a lady friend at this moment, one of our local celebrities."

"What?" Cooper responded. He had a sinking feeling of dread at what might be coming next.

"Yes, Miss Ghorla. She went upstairs to see him about a half hour ago."

Cooper passed a ten-pound note across the desk.

"Can you show me up straightaway? I'd like to see them both if it's possible. Presumably you have a pass-key."

If I can gain the element of surprise, thought Cooper, all might not yet be lost. Were he to arrive unannounced he might interrupt some conversation of import relating to Julius Ghorla that he might otherwise not hear.

Browning covered the banknote with the palm of his hand, slid it towards himself, and nodded.

"Right away, sir. Please follow me. It's only on the first floor, not far."

When the two arrived at the door to Staines's room, Browning knocked once perfunctorily and immediately unlocked it. He let Cooper enter by stepping aside and discreetly moving back just outside the doorway.

The shabby little room was in semi-darkness. Moreover, it was like walking into a huge freezer. The temperature within was some twenty or so degrees below zero. Cooper saw a dingy bed that looked fit only for the rubbish dump and was appalled by the sight of the most garish wallpaper he'd seen since the mid-1970s. It could even have been an authentic relic from that era. Then his attention was drawn to an armchair in the corner of the room, back amongst the shadows. A peculiar gurgling noise came from its occupant. At first Cooper thought it was a life-size dummy dressed in charity clothes, something left over from a stage show.

But he realised it was actually a very old woman—or something much like one. For although it was clad in a blouse and skirt, the skirt was pulled back over its withered navel, its stockings and knickers were around its ankles, and it was stubbing out a cigarette on a burn-dotted left thigh. Just above the score of burns rested a flaccid penis. Its beehive wig was askew and in the centre of its forehead was a bloody third eye that stared unblinkingly.

Just before Cooper backed away in shock, a hitherto unseen figure crept out from around the side of the bed. It was Arthur Staines, and the demented man was crawling on all fours like an animal, his breath steaming in the frigid air. A grotesque mewing bubbled in his throat.

"Did the bad man hurt poor kitty? Now all's well, now all's made well again," said the croaking voice of the figure in the chair.

Cooper took a long backwards stride in the direction of the door behind him, but Mr Browning had already taken the opportunity to quietly close it and draw shut the bolt on the outside.

"We don't like to see Miss Ghorla distressed, sir," said Browning through the panelling. "So if you'd be kind enough to accommodate her it would be easier all round. It's only what we've all had to get used to, here in Scarsdale Bay."

CESARE THODOL:
SOME LINES WRITTEN ON A WALL

Of this one thing I am, at least, absolutely certain: no one is now more qualified than myself to write of the facts concerning Cesare Thodol.

It may be the case that they choose to ignore the findings I have recently made available for scrutiny. However, none of them are aware of the information known to me alone. Doubtless they will continue to dismiss what I have to say as a consequence of an over-active imagination, of a brain too deeply immersed in the outré minutiae of Thodoliana, to be objective. I can only retort by insisting that they consider the evidence. If they would take the time to examine this account and remember that I have previously expressed my doubts as to the claims of parapsychology, then they might realise that I came to my conclusions from an initial basis as sceptical then as is their own now.

Let me begin by restating the biographical information concerning Cesare Thodol that is accepted by everyone. He was born in Düsseldorf in 1870, one of two twins, brother and sister. His parents were Gerhard Thodol and Eva Thodol (née Hess), the former a lawyer and the latter the daughter of the wealthy industrialist Johann Hess. Eva Thodol died giving birth to the twins, Cesare and Elsa. They were sickly children, confined for much of their adolescence to the gloomy chambers of the family home. Cesare's fevered imagination found succour in the fairy tales of the Brothers Grimm and in the *Struwwelpeter* of Dr. Heinrich Hoffman.

Educated privately by tutors, he had reached twenty-three years of age before he showed any signs of wishing to leave the family home. His intense attachment to his twin sister made the suspicion of an incestuous relationship having developed between them all the more credible given that later correspondence showed Cesare's fanatical hatred for his detail-obsessed and drunken father.

The old widower had died after a mysterious fall in the family home in 1885, and neither Cesare nor his sister showed the least sign of remorse at his passing. Indeed, the two's virtually total seclusion between the years 1885 and 1893 and the horrible intimacy that existed between brother and sister were remarked upon by all those private tutors who had attended to Cesare's schooling.

Only after his sister's death via consumption did the young Thodol venture forth into the world. An inheritance passed to Cesare, and he took the opportunity to emigrate from Germany to England, settling in London during 1894 and leaving the scandal that had by then attached itself to the Thodol name in his wake.

By this time already the author of several weird metaphysical essays in German, Thodol's love of the strange and horrible led him to the works of Edgar Allan Poe, Charles Baudelaire, Joris-Karl Huysmans, and Ambrose Bierce. Poe's "The Fall of the House of Usher" exerted an influence on his mind that Thodol himself described as "forming the single most important impetus to my writing, nay, my life, that I have ever experienced."

During the year before the trial of Oscar Wilde brought down the curtain on all things decadent in the Victorian era, Thodol, as if sensing its end was close, threw himself into the lifestyle with a fervour to rival even that of Count Stenbock. Thodol's descent into drug-fuelled excess and sexual debauchery continued for a period of nearly ten years, taking a terrible physical and psychological toll on him. The fact that Thodol locked himself away with his perversions, keeping them out of the public gaze, doubtless spared him any outside interference.

But it was his eventual refusal to admit anyone at all into his London home that drew comments from the society papers of the day and led to his downfall. There were rumours that his only companion in his chambers was a waxwork dummy that he had commissioned from Madame Tussaud's. The thing had been formed according to Thodol's own specifications. It was said that the simulacrum was an exact representation of his dead sister and that he spoke to it as if it were alive.

When finally the alienists were called to see for themselves the degree to which Thodol had succumbed to madness, they were at once set upon by the German refugee, who believed that they, and not the waxwork dummy he entertained, were imitations of humanity.

Apparently this wax mannequin was in a shocking state, though Thodol pleaded with his captors that he might be allowed to take it with him. Its mottled face was infested by a fine webwork of tiny fungi. The German had been unable to arrest its deterioration himself and refused to call upon outside help. He could not bear the thought of anyone else seeing, let alone touching, what he thought to be his dead twin sister.

When his financial status was examined it was found that Thodol was effectively a pauper. He had exhausted his inheritance on drugs and on incredibly naïve investments that brought no return, and spent what remained on dresses, flowers, and gaudy trinkets for the fantastically elaborate waxwork of his sister. At this time, in London, the principal terminus for the destitute insane was Colney Hatch Asylum, and it was there, in 1905, that Thodol was taken in a horse-drawn carriage with barred windows. And there he remained until his death in 1938.

The above are the bare facts commonly known to history. What happened to Cesare Thodol during the thirty-three years of his incarceration in Colney Hatch has remained untold. For most Thodolian scholars the story of his life is over by 1905, and they have contented themselves with just a paragraph or two of speculation relating to his existence amongst the deranged in that huge citadel on the outskirts of the city. One or two have mentioned that Thodol believed that all the inmates and staff of the asylum were wax dummies come to life, and that he screamed at the sight of any person, but of the bizarre writings he produced whilst incarcerated there is no account. However, during that time he wrote—not on paper, but on the walls of his cell, until he had covered much of them with his tiny, crabbed handwriting.

One of the psychiatric doctors at Colney Hatch, Sidney Rhodes, took photographs of the writing on the walls after Thodol's death, transcribing them for possible use in a monograph that he was preparing on the creative impulses of the mentally disturbed. It is by thorough analysis of the phantasmal imaginings Thodol sought to preserve in this most desperate of fashions that we can separate truth from fiction. Since I alone now have access to the Rhodes papers, I alone am able to speak with authority on the subject.

The diagnosis of Thodol's mental illness in 1905 was "acute

hallucinatory disorder," but this is vague, unsatisfactory, and more
suited to the time when the insane were treated by those terming
themselves "alienists" rather than by psychiatrists. However, I believe that even the psychiatry of today would produce a diagnosis
just as useless. One can, with some legitimacy, point to the organic
degeneration in Thodol's body caused by his habitual abuse of intox-
icants, but this is little more than a side issue: the reality is terrifying.

The psychiatrist's fascination with the cell in which Thodol had
been kept seems to have developed over quite a length of time.
During Thodol's incarceration Rhodes, although intrigued by the
patient, had very little direct contact with him. Thodol was only
calm when left alone, since, as I have already remarked, he was
driven into hysterics by the approach of any human being. Treatment of the patient was actually counterproductive, since it was
personal interaction and face-to-face contact itself that resulted in
phobic reactions. When sedatives were used (these were hidden in
the food left for him outside the small hatch at the foot of his cell
door) they proved of little benefit. Although physically docile,
Thodol's eyes still had in them a crazed fear, and he would reveal
nothing to the doctors except that he earnestly desired total solitude.

Finally it was decided that an extreme shock was the last recourse left by way of treatment. Since Thodol had been absented
from the waxwork dummy of his sister there had been no improvement whatsoever in his case. Perhaps, it was argued, contact
with what appeared to be the cause of his dementia might jolt his
mind back into a state where communication was possible. Certainly the doctors had nothing to lose.

Tracing the whereabouts of the simulacrum was not easy, since
most of Thodol's former belongings were sold at auction in order
to pay creditors. It transpired that the owner of a small waxworks
exhibition that toured the country had purchased this particular lot
number. He had made a tidy sum displaying the thing and telling
the story of Thodol's disgrace and morbid fascination with it.
However, since the scandal had been a number of years ago, interest in the matter had inevitably waned and the owner was prepared
to turn it over for a pittance in the interests of good publicity. For
several months he had, in any case, kept the dummy locked away in
a trunk. It was by now in an even worse state than when it had last
been in Thodol's possession. Indeed, the more ghastly it was, the

more horrible a fascination it exerted over the paying public, so the waxwork exhibitor had reported.

It is very easy, in hindsight, to state that reuniting Thodol with the object was bound to result in tragedy. And yet, it was genuinely felt that nothing but the most desperate measures remained. What occurred when two orderlies carried the dummy down the corridor accompanied by the psychiatrist in charge of the case, unlocked Thodol's cell, and entered is clearly recorded.

The German stared at the thing, got to his feet, and, ignoring all those around him for once, flattened himself against the wall at his back. The orderlies and the doctor withdrew, leaving him alone with it, though watching the proceedings through the observation hole in the door. Thodol spasmodically tottered forward, as if with great effort. His features twisted into a loathsome smirk of welcome. His eyes were riveted on the fungi-ridden and corroded parody of the female form. He took it in his arms, brushed away the mass of straggly hair covering one side of its mottled face, and began to whisper into its ear.

The men outside withdrew altogether for several minutes, satisfied that no damage had been done. Complete privacy seemed the next logical step. But when they returned to the cell there was no trace of the dummy. Thodol himself was not in any state to give an account of what had transpired. Yet the thing that repelled all three was that he had undergone some horrible physical alteration. His hair actually appeared to be much longer, and his gait stiff-backed and awkward. Moreover, his skin was riddled with a widespread dermatitis that had erupted only during the three men's short absence.

No one could explain what had happened to the waxwork of his sister Elsa. However, psychosomatic trauma was finally listed as the cause of his physical symptoms. Evidently allowing Thodol to be reunited with the dummy had not produced the beneficial mental jolt, but something even worse.

*

Rhodes has pointed out that the fungus did not appear elsewhere in the Colney Hatch asylum; that, for some reason, it was confined, like Thodol, to one cell. The German had no means of nurturing it, and the reappearance of the growth on the cell walls, mere hours after apparent eradication by carbolic acid, was unaccountable. Moreover, it was evident that the fungus multiplied only whilst Thodol was present. When he was not in close proximity it remained dormant, neither expanding nor contracting over the area it had come to occupy.

The fungus had a peculiar hue. No one could identify its actual colour, saying that it seemed to be both monochrome and ultraviolet. Staring at it for longer than a half a minute induced severe nausea, although Thodol himself appeared unaffected by the sight of the morbid growth. Its propensity to spread over the written characters that he scrawled on the walls, as if tracing their design, led Rhodes to speculate that it sprang from some rogue toxin in the India ink Thodol used. Later he came to a quite different conclusion.

There was also the matter of the stench. Again, this seemed not to bother Thodol himself, and all attempts by nurses to approach his cell and rid the place of the infestation were met with frenzy. It was an unfortunate set of circumstances, and one that lent itself to Thodol's being abandoned for longer and longer periods of time.

His genuine, unshakable belief was that he himself was not mad; rather, it was the world around him that had gone insane. Although this is not an uncommon delusion amongst mental patients, and they can often be very thorough in creating elaborate conspiracy theories that they use to self-validate their delusions, in Thodol's case we cannot rely upon the common interpretation.

The end was of course predictable. Whether by design or not, Thodol was left alone and unattended for a period of well over two weeks. The short corridor in which his cell was located contained no other inmates, since even the noise of footsteps drove Thodol crazy with fear at the thought that the waxworks were closing in on him. Rhodes was one of the few honest enough to admit that Thodol's German nationality created a great deal of resentment towards him, and he overheard at least one other doctor say that it would be no great shame if "that Kraut was ignored and left to rot." This remark caused the doctor who uttered it a great deal of satisfaction once the Nazi policy of exterminating the mentally ill was fully documented after World War II. I doubt that he saw the irony of it.

When the cell was finally opened the stench that emanated from within was unbearable. The fungus had completely overrun the interior, covering the walls, the ceiling, and the sparse furniture. Thodol himself had been dead for more than a week. He had been forced to resort to eating the growth, scraping it away from a corner of the room with his fingers and consuming it as a substitute for food. But it was not hunger that had killed him. His corpse lay curled up in a contorted foetal position. The shocking grimace upon his face indicated the effects of poisoning and a slow, agonising death. His features were covered by a webwork of the fungi.

Thodol was buried in a plot in the asylum's graveyard marked only with a metal plate bearing his case number. Like the other inmates who had died whilst in confinement in the institution, his name was not even recorded on the meagre memorial. There was no scandal.

The cell was thoroughly cleaned, and all trace of the writings that he had scrawled on the walls disappeared along with the fungus that covered it. Rhodes, however, without official permission, managed to take numerous photographs of the growth before the fungicidal chemicals did their work and then while the demented text they had obscured was briefly revealed. Where the markings were too faint to be photographed he reproduced them (as best he could) in a notebook. He even managed to salvage a small piece of the fungus, storing it in a jar of formaldehyde for subsequent examination. Alas, none of these are extant.

*

It is not necessary for me to go into any great detail as to the circumstances that led to my seeking out what information I could about Sidney Rhodes. If I say that I noted a curious parallel between his derided 1942 speculative-medical treatise *On Brain Fungus* and Cesare Thodol's 1899 tale entitled "Inside the Fungi Mind," doubtless readers familiar with the latter will understand my determination to interview Dr. Rhodes. I could not help but speculate that the one owed much to the other. At the time I had no idea that Rhodes had come into direct contact with Thodol at the Colney Hatch asylum.

I attempted to trace further details concerning Rhodes through the usual channels—the BMA register, telephone directories, and via the offices of the specialist publishing house that had issued *On Brain Fungus*. However, these were in vain. Rhodes seemed to have disappeared after 1943. It was a chance remark over the telephone by one of his long-lived relatives that put me on the right track. A cousin whom I had traced, Frank Sutton, although not willing to be interviewed, had told me before he hung up that lunacy is contagious and I was wasting my time.

On a hunch I went back to the Colney Hatch records in order to try and determine who had occupied Thodol's cell after his death. The answer was shrouded in evasive, patchy hospital records, and yet I half knew what it would be. Dr. Rhodes had never left Colney Hatch. By 1943 he had instead become a patient there.

The transition from doctor to inmate must have occurred gradually, and I cannot help but imagine that the German's neglect had preyed upon Rhodes's mind. Although his contact with Thodol was of the slightest, somehow he had allowed himself to become too emotionally involved with the fate of the patient, a pitfall against which those working in the psychiatric profession are warned. The reason why he was treated at Colney Hatch (it was after all an institution designed specifically for the treatment of the poorest in society) is easy to explain. It would have led to a scandal had one of their doctors succumbed to insanity. That was hardly the type of publicity the asylum sought. Incredibly, the committee there agreed to shut Rhodes away and deal with the matter internally, though on a semi-official basis.

It appears that Rhodes even acquiesced in the outcome, for he is listed as a voluntary admission. Moreover, it seems that the suggestion that he be domiciled in Thodol's old cell came directly from Rhodes himself (though whether in a lucid or deranged moment I cannot say). Perhaps it was felt that such occupancy might allow the psychiatrist to come to terms with what formed the source of his neurosis.

The most incredible aspect of Rhodes's case is that his delusions exactly duplicated those of Cesare Thodol. He too believed himself to be surrounded by waxworks masquerading as the living. Moreover, he was convinced that the German had been right all along and that the whole process of psychiatric treatment had nothing to do with curing the patient but with forcing a false model of reality upon his perception of the world. The best that could be achieved was that the individual was sufficiently indoctrinated so that he might function in outside society; Rhodes therefore implied that his mental state was a consequence of a verifiable ontological nightmare. He laid particular emphasis on the hitherto unsuspected sentience of fungi growing within the skulls of human simulacra.

Rhodes believed that Thodol had attempted to communicate the truth by writing it on the walls of his cell. But the fungus had obscured his account, tracing a pattern over his words, covering them with its noxious presence. At some point the growth had emerged from its hosts' skulls, after usurping the brains within and shaping new waxen forms from the old tissue and flesh of their bodies. But no one had realised that the change had taken place. It was all a bizarre, incomprehensible joke that the fungi played upon each other—a game of charades whereby they pretended to act as human beings for their own amusement.

The revulsion that the animate waxworks had displayed at the fungus was just one aspect of their horrible antics, another jest they used to further torment those unfortunates under their supervision. The Electro-Convulsive Therapy that Thodol had undergone over a period of years was not designed to shock his brain into functioning normally; in fact, it was an attempt to accelerate the production of spores inside the skull by the layer of fungus that already coated the cerebral hemispheres.

Now here it must be admitted that it is difficult to accept the idea of Rhodes submitting voluntarily to the custodianship of the Colney Hatch Asylum if he really believed in Thodol's morbidly fantastic interpretation of events. However, I suggest that there was still enough doubt in his mind, even at that stage, for him to fall back on his training as a psychiatrist and hope that the terrifying ideas racing uncontrollably through his mind might have their origin in some nervous or organic disorder. To be incarcerated in the very institution where he had treated others was awful, but remember that he may have thought he could more easily escape outside publicity and that he was used to being there.

Rhodes did not ultimately benefit from what treatment he received in the asylum. How could he have done so? For a good number of years he was very much the focus of attention amongst the other psychiatrists who, one might imagine, would be fascinated and appalled at the psychological deterioration of one of their own. This was in spite, or perhaps because, of the fact that Rhodes experienced the selfsame horror Cesare Thodol had felt when becoming aware of other persons in his vicinity. But as time passed no improvement in his condition was evident. His case was increasingly like that of Thodol, even to the extent that, despite having no previous knowledge of the language, he was often overheard muttering to himself in German, as if the dead madman's personality had transferred itself to Rhodes's body.

But if even this aspect might be explained in terms of a guilt-complex connected with Thodol's death, then what remained inexplicable (except if one maintains the view that Rhodes was the victim of a malign conspiracy) was the reappearance of the fungus in the cell. And although it was certain that Rhodes had no writing apparatus available, when the fungus was destroyed script was discovered beneath and not in the former psychiatrist's handwriting at all. True, it seemed to be that of Thodol. And indeed, when compared it was found to be in the exact style of the script that had appeared previously when the German author had occupied the cell. But one of the more inquisitive of the doctors had discovered another twist to the puzzle.

No one had thought to check at the time of the first infestation whether Thodol's own handwriting tallied with the scribbling on the walls. It did not. Even if Rhodes had copied it, thinking it was in Thodol's style, who was the true begetter? Why was the pathologist's autopsy file on Rhodes destroyed within days of his death in October 1959? And why was it an unwritten rule in the institution that the cell must not be occupied in the future?

*

Colney Hatch Asylum was finally shut down in 1994. Even renaming the institution "Friern Barnet Hospital" could not dispel its notoriety. By then the vogue was for "Care in the Community" rather than confinement. It cost the Tory government less money. The grounds, which had formerly been extensive, and boasting gardens, courtyards, and outbuildings, were redeveloped shortly afterwards. A warren of cul-de-sacs with ugly modern houses was built there. Only the main building now stands intact. Its lofty

domed tower and cupola can be seen for miles around and domi-
nates the view in the area, rising above the dreary North Circular
Road and the American-style Retail Park. The main building bears
no indication of its former purpose and has become an exclusive
housing community for the wealthy. Where the reception area and
hall used to be, there is a gym and health club for residents and fit-
ness fanatics from outside.

Ironically though, the place is still surrounded by walls and
fences. They yet serve their original purpose: to separate residents
from society. However, their function has now been reversed.
They keep the public out rather than keep the inmates inside.
Moreover, in a cabin-office at the main gates is a uniformed security guard, the grounds are patrolled, and every section is under
twenty-four-hour CCTV surveillance. Approaching from these
main gates one might not notice any significant change. That familiar façade is as impressive as ever, with its terraced portico sheltering five archways, the twin pillared towers flanking the domed
central tower set further back, and its bow windows reflecting the
mood of the sky. The ornate fountain in the driveway is still there;
so too the pagoda, Victorian lampposts, and the willow trees on
the front lawn. It is only behind the imposing length of the main
building, at the back where the clock tower stands, that one encounters the ugly housing estate that has replaced the remains of
the institution.

I came to see what remained of the structure and found myself
unaccountably drawn to it. A few of the flats in the main building
were unoccupied, and I resolved to explore the possibility of my
moving into one. I think it no coincidence—in fact, I now know it
was no coincidence—that still currently on the market was an
apartment in precisely the location where once had been Thodol's
and then Rhodes's own fungi-ridden cell.

*

In order to dwell in what remained of the asylum it was necessary for me to draw heavily on my savings. The rent I paid was ridiculously expensive, and yet I was in the grip of an obsession that
made all other considerations insignificant. I felt certain that my de-

sire to understand what had happened to the two men was intimately connected with the very walls at which they had stared day after day.

Consulting blueprints of the original building in the archives of the local council, I determined that the cell had formerly been where my bedroom was now situated. Its dimensions had not altered, although a connecting door had been added through which access was gained to the other rooms in the flat. I furnished the place with the cheapest items I could find, and a small library of dog-eared paperbacks formed my only source of diversion.

I think that, from the first hour of my tenancy, I was waiting for its reappearance. My gaze roved the walls, the ceiling, and the corners of the bedroom seeking evidence of the slightest discoloured stain or tiny blemish on the recently painted white surfaces.

While I made my minute observations of my surroundings, my thoughts keep returning to the idea that both Thodol and Rhodes had harboured about animate waxworks whose skulls housed not brains but a mass of sentient fungi. I could not account for it, but found that despite my resolution not to succumb to the same irrational phobia I too shunned contact with society. It seemed to me that what faces I saw beyond the windows *were* somewhat like waxen masks, rigid and dehumanised. And in their eyes did I not now detect the hint of an eerie glow, as if a phosphorescent fungus lurked within?

The first growth sprouted in the top left corner of the room, a single toadstool of violet-grey. It looked diseased, but within a matter of a few hours a cluster of them had grown and formed a line along the edge of the corner, following the angle of the wall inwards. From the fungi there wafted a musty, nauseous odour.

When I scraped some of it away, I found the following words beneath:

"Of this one thing I am, at least, absolutely certain: no one is now more qualified than myself to write of the facts concerning my dear brother Cesare Thodol."

And so I sit and watch the inexorable spread of the fungi across the walls and the ceiling. Soon I will have to eat something. My food ran out yesterday and I am quite tormented by hunger.

SENTINELS

Inspector Gray's involvement in the affair was due to a combination of ill fortune and the photographic cover of a London "urban legends" paperback called *The Secret Underground*. He should not really have been in that part of London at the time, but had been forced to stay late in the office and complete a batch of gruelling paperwork required by his superior the following morning. Had he driven past a matter of seconds before, he would have seen nothing. After all, he was off-duty and his main concern was to get back to his dingy flat in Tufnell Park, sink a few glasses of whiskey, and forget about that day.

He planned to lose himself in some cheap and trashy horror paperback from his little collection. The TV had broken down months ago, and instead of replacing it he found that he had got into the habit of reading musty book relics from the 1960s and '70s, with their yellowing, brittle pages and lurid covers. Gray fancied himself something of a connoisseur when it came to the covers; in fact, he felt himself in opposition to the old maxim about never judging a book by them. He harboured the conviction that those featuring a weird photographic composition were invariably superior to those that had artwork depicting the tired cliché-symbols of horror—skulls, snakes, or Gothic castles, for example.

In fact, he had come in for some jokes at his expense back at the Yard over his choice of reading matter. Most of his colleagues talked about little except what they watched on TV the night before, often sleazy porn videos that they'd "borrowed" from the Obscene Publications division. They'd taken to calling him "The Weird Detective" behind his back, and on one occasion he'd turned around sharply to find a group of constables miming having vampire fangs by putting their index fingers at the corners of their mouths. Gray made sure thereafter that he wasn't seen reading any of his books during the little time he had for lunch. Instead, he read one of the broadsheet papers as he consumed his sandwiches at his desk. His alienation from his colleagues caused him pain, and he suspected that the department would run more smoothly were he not there.

What Gray saw as he passed by in his car appeared to be some sort of stunted, emaciated creature peering through the trellis gates of Kentish Town Underground Station. The thing was only around four or five feet tall and dressed in black ragged overalls. Its face was obscured by a mass of dusty shoulder-length hair.

It was gone 1 A.M. when Gray passed the Underground Station, and it had been closed for only a short time. He had pulled over to the side of the road and looked back in order to see whether the apparition was still there, but there was no sign of it at all. Doubtless, he thought, his colleagues back at the Yard would have laughed at what he thought he saw: too many of those damn books he read. But Gray felt his heart racing in his chest. He could not dismiss the thing that easily from his mind. What he'd seen was no product of the imagination; it had really been there.

Although the station was closed, it might not yet be deserted. Once the train service finished there were still staff working on the platforms and in the tunnels. An army of cleaners called "Fluffers" made their way along the lines and scoured them for debris. All manner of litter had to be cleared away—beer-cans, half-eaten junk food, newspapers, even tumbleweeds composed of skin and human hair. There were also the "Gangers": the engineers who checked track safety. Perhaps Gray had simply glimpsed one of those overnight workers having a break, one whose similarity to the uncanny thing on the front cover of *The Secret Underground* was nothing more than a trick of the light.

Nevertheless, what he had observed remained in his thoughts, causing uneasy dreams when he finally slept: dreams of endless subterranean tunnels and of a gaunt silence punctuated by a distant rustling or whispering noise. Had he not seen whatever it was at the station (or whatever he *thought* it was) the case that came to his attention afterwards might not have seemed significant and worth pursuit.

*

As he sat at his desk the next morning, sipping at a cup of vile instant coffee, Gray flicked through the case files in his in-box. He had a feeling that had become increasingly commonplace during the course of the last few months: that the investigations to which he had been assigned were effectively a waste of effort. The assault that he'd suffered months ago during the arrest of Montrose the serial rapist had left him hospitalised for weeks and resulted in internal ruptures that would, he had been advised by the surgeon, require a much more sedate lifestyle. The Yard had done the best it could under the circumstances and found him a role, albeit desk-bound; but although his initial assignments had been current, Gray discovered that as time passed he was being asked to examine cases that had little chance of being solved. The bulk of these were missing persons.

Scarcely sociable before, Gray had turned further inwards after the beating. It had affected his mind just as much as his body. Somehow he had allowed his old friends to drift away and found excuses not to keep in touch with them. He felt himself to be little more than an empty shell, and contact with others only served to reinforce the impression. The Yard offered Gray counselling to help him come to terms with the trauma caused by the Montrose incident, but he found the idea even more repellent than his doctor's suggestion that he take a course of antidepressants. When fate worked upon him he intended to adapt to it and not resist. Even so, he felt like a missing person who had himself been assigned to trace other missing persons.

Gray ran his tongue over his scalded lips, again cursing the too-hot and foul-tasting coffee, when his attention was taken up by a communiqué that had come in only a few hours earlier. Although a missing persons report is not usually filed until some days after a disappearance (except where children are involved), this one had been "fast-tracked" because there was no question of the subject having absented himself deliberately. The missing individual was a tube train driver (or "operator," as they were now called). His name was Adam Drayton. The curious thing was this: he had abandoned his train between the Camden Town and Kentish Town stations on the Northern Line. It had been the very last service of the night, due to terminate at High Barnet at 1.30 A.M. Moreover, if there had been any passengers in the carriages then they too had vanished.

Early in the morning a replacement driver had shunted the train into a siding. On the front of the case file a joker in the office had scrawled the words "Mary Celeste Tube? A Case for the Weird Detective?" with a marker pen.

But Inspector Gray, through some bizarre coincidence, was one of the few people who would recognise the name "Adam Drayton" in another connection. For it was also the name of the author/editor of that outré book of urban legends published under the title *The Secret Underground,* whose cover preyed upon his mind.

*

Gray spent the afternoon interviewing Drayton's colleagues in the staff mess room of the train depot just outside Finchley Central Station. This was where the tube drivers spent their time between shifts, sitting around drinking coffee, smoking their cigarettes, and reading newspapers. They were a talkative bunch, although the inspector could not help noticing their mistrust and fear of him as a representative from an outside authority. Some of them even seemed to believe that Drayton's disappearance was an internal matter and should be left to the union to investigate. Outside interference, whether from the law or elsewhere, was certainly not welcome. Still, there were one or two who retained a sense of individuality and were able to realise that Gray had not come in order to apportion any blame, merely to discover what may have led Drayton to act in the manner that he did.

One of the drivers, Carlos Miguel, a Castilian, was particularly communicative. He had settled in this country after leaving Madrid in the early 1990s. He had been almost alone in befriending Drayton, who had been regarded by the others as an oddball whose political views were not sufficiently radical. Miguel was a tall, distinguished man in his forties with a shock of jet-black hair and a neatly trimmed moustache. He had shared Drayton's enthusiasm for the recondite, and whilst the others talked of union activities or the football results, the two men had retreated to a corner and held their own discussions.

Had Gray not been aware of Drayton's editorship of that paperback *The Secret Underground* he doubted he would have achieved quite the same rapport with Carlos Miguel.

"So," the Spaniard declared, "you know of *el libro de Drayton?*"

"Yes," Gray replied. "I think it's a bit garish but the cover's particularly—"

Miguel cut in.

"*Señor,* you know that Drayton only applied to become a train operator so that he could travel the tunnels of the Northern Line and examine their mysteries?"

Gray looked blank and shook his head.

"Well," Miguel went on, "you must understand that it would not be mistaken to say that he was obsessed with them. Drayton told me that the Northern Line has the longest continuous Yerkes tunnel on the network, over seventeen miles long. The stretch between East Finchley and Morden. Also it has the deepest. At Hampstead nine hundred feet below ground. He had numerous theories about what was down there; *fantástico, ¿no?*"

"Speculations, rumour, hearsay," Gray responded. "Amounting to nothing more than fiction. He was just an editor of a horrible series of urban legends. I confess that the parallel between his disappearance and obsession is striking but—"

"*Perdón, señor,* but it is more than that simple fact. Drayton was my friend; it was in me that he felt he could confide. *Las estaciones fantasmas,* you know of them? In English: the ghost stations? North End, City Road, South Kentish Town, and King William Street? These were what obsessed Drayton."

"The abandoned stations?"

"*Sí,* abandoned. *Pero* in Drayton's eyes, *no.* Taken over he would have replied. No longer safe to use. *Señor,* if you are operating the last train on the line it is easier to slow down when you wish, no? Perhaps while travelling through one of those stations and even bringing trains to a complete stop. There are not so many passengers, and they are too drunk or sleepy to complain at that time of night, *¿tú comprendes?*"

"Are you suggesting that Adam Drayton stopped his train and got out at one of these ghost stations?"

"*Como una palomilla atraída por la llama . . .*"

"I don't understand."

". . . like a moth drawn to a flame."

*

That evening, once Gray had got back to his cramped flat in Tufnell Park, he sat down in his easy chair with his copy of *The Secret Underground*. He flicked back and forth through its yellowed, brittle pages, glancing at them over and over again. The book was divided into several chapters, each specialising in a subterranean urban legend: (1) Cases of Posthumous Mutation in London Cemeteries; (2) Derelict Reverse Skyscrapers 1936–1957; (3) Mass Disappearance of Persons Sheltering in the Underground during the Blitz; (4) Graffiti or Occult Symbolism?; (5) Suppressed Eyewitness Accounts during the Construction of the Underground Railways 1860–1976; (6) The Fleet Line Extension to Fenchurch Street Must Be Halted; (7) Secret Bunkers or Extermination Centres?; (8) The Deep-Level Platforms of the Proposed Express Tube: Why They Caused Insanity; (9) The Hidden Shafts That Connect Subterranean London.

There was one paragraph in the final chapter that seemed to be the inspiration for the uneasy dreams Gray had experienced. It ran as follows:

> Most of the city is now underground and not above the surface, and I scarcely need list its innumerable tunnels, subterranean car parks, cellars, crypts, bunkers, basements, vaults, passageways, and sewers. Every building in London has an underside buried deep in the earth. Beneath our feet are the ruins of Anglo-Saxon Lundenwic and of Roman Londinium. The contemporary city will, in time, be swallowed up. This neon and concrete labyrinth will become an Atlantis of catacombs. The higher we build up, the deeper it is necessary to build down in order to support the structures above. All the nightmare sewage that we pump into the depths, all the foulness and corruption, the abortions, the faeces and scum, the blood and diseased mucus, but mostly the hair: what a feast for those underground beings that exist in darkness and shun the sunlight! Those things below hate us and have every reason to do so.

His attention kept jumping from the text to the series of bizarre black-and-white photographs throughout the book. Quite where Drayton had obtained them was not made clear; they were not credited. They may even have come from his personal collection and consisted of the following:

(Front cover) A blurred humanoid figure seen from a passing tube train whose face is almost completely covered by its hair. Between the strands there seems to be a mouth lined with shark-like fangs. The haggard creature is backing into a siding, away from the light.

(p. 18) A photographic record of a series of exhumed graves with empty coffins whose bases had been torn apart.

(p. 33) A blueprint of a subterranean reverse-tower with forty-five storeys and access shafts radiating from it in all directions, some leading to burial grounds, others to sewers, etc., bearing the legend "North End (Hampstead)."

(p. 49) What appears to be a series of bloody, smeared handprints on the white wall tiles of British Museum Station during its use as an air-raid shelter circa 1941.

(p. 87) Human bones, including a skull, photographed lying alongside the tracks of an Underground tunnel.

(p. 102) Graffiti scrawled (in charcoal?) on the side of 1972 Mk. 1 train stock that reads "THE HUNGRY CANNOT SLEEP," "WE CRAWL THROUGH GRAVES," "THE DARKNESS BEHIND YOUR EYES," and "BELOW THERE IS ONLY PAIN."

(p. 126) A sewer chamber choked by vast quantities of hair hanging from a curved ceiling of Victorian brickwork.

*

It was relatively easy for Gray to obtain a search warrant to enter the disused South Kentish Town station. Although above ground the building was now occupied by a massage parlour where once the ticket hall had been, all the subterranean shafts, corridors, and other passageways were still owned by the London Underground. Since their abandonment there had been no reason to maintain them, and parts of the former station were unsafe. In order to gain access Gray had to agree to be accompanied by a track maintenance engineer who worked on that stretch of the Northern Line and who was familiar with the site.

This engineer, John Heath, arranged to meet Gray outside the massage parlour at the corner of Kentish Town Road and Castle Place. The inspector parked his car directly in front of the building and was struck by the fact that its exterior still had the appearance of an Underground Station, lacking only the familiar sign displayed outside. Hanging around in front of the entrance to the newsagents was a small man in a yellow safety helmet and boiler suit. He carried a heavy bag with a sub-contractor's logo on it. His hands were entirely covered with a thick layer of soot. Doubtless it was the man who had been assigned to assist Gray.

Heath looked just like a throwback to the 1960s. His hippie-length hair was brittle and grey as dust. Over his mouth and nose he wore a loose protective mask. He also wore a pair of John Lennon–style glasses with thick lenses that made the eyes behind them look liquid. He was really quite horribly ridiculous.

After Gray had produced his police ID, the two went inside, and the inspector explained his purpose to the owners of the massage parlour (who seemed relieved that the search was not connected with what went on at their premises). Then Heath, consulting a map of the structure, led Gray down into a storage cellar at the back of the establishment where access to the emergency stairs could be gained.

The old lift shafts were useless. Their cages and all the workings had been removed back when the station was closed in 1924, but the stairway to the upper lift landing and the emergency staircase to the lower lift landing were passable. The entry doors were padlocked, and Heath sought and tried several keys drawn from his bag before he found the correct ones to use.

"They told me," Heath said, his voice muffled by the baggy mask covering his mouth and nose, "why you want to get down here. Anyway, it's pointless. We already looked for Drayton. All you're doing is putting yourself in danger."

"I'll be the judge of that," replied Gray. "Just get on with it. You do your job and I'll do mine, OK?"

"Watch your step as we go. These old passageways are treacherous. Even if you don't wind up falling into a ventilation shaft, you might stumble in front of a passing train. Hear the noise?"

As he unlocked the door there came from far below in the depths the sound of carriages rumbling along distant tracks, followed moments later by a powerful draught of musty air.

Heath chuckled. He turned on a powerful torch and aimed its beam along the stairway and around to the dark-green tiled walls at the turn ahead. The steps were littered with debris.

Gray was amazed at how familiar and yet how strange their surroundings appeared. Like any Londoner, he had used the tube system on innumerable occasions and had passed through the subterranean mazes of many stations, though always when they were illuminated by overhead strip lighting, with hurried passengers making their way to or from a platform. But here the darkness was in control, and every echoing footfall reinforced the grim feeling of total isolation. And yet, it was only the withdrawal of light and of other people that created this feeling; actually it was just the same as any other tube station would be after the services had stopped running. Except that this was no temporary interruption to be resumed in the morning. This really was what Carlos Miguel called *Una estación fantasma*.

"Did you know Adam Drayton?" Gray asked in order to break the grim silence between the sound of passing trains.

He could only see the back of Heath. The engineer's slightly hunched form crept downwards along the steps, apparently intent solely upon what he was doing. But he finally responded after what seemed to be a considered pause.

"Oh, yes," Heath said. "I knew *of* him all right. He was legendary on the Northern Line. Kept stopping his train at odd places and holding up the services. Only worked at night, when it didn't matter so much. The union stepped in to stop him getting the sack, said he was worried about safety."

"Safety?"

"The union said it was faulty signals that were to blame. And strange noises on the track. Made him cautious. Better to be safe than sorry. Go slow is preferable to taking chances. That's what the union said."

They had reached the bottom of the stairway and emerged onto the upper lift landing. The tiles here were a grimy cream-and-red colour. In the circle of light cast by Heath's torch, he caught glimpses of advertising posters from the early 1920s that had been left up on the tiled walls of the corridor ahead; "Lifebuoy," "Bovril," "Oxo," "Wrigley's," and "Guinness." Another tube train roared through one of the tunnels below, and the accompanying blast of air flapped the torn parts of the posters.

"What do you know about the disused stations here on the

Northern Line? Have you seen the others for yourself?" Gray asked.

"I know something," Heath responded. "I've been in them all at one time or another. They have a bad reputation. The most significant is North End or the 'Bull & Bush,' as the train operators like to call it."

"Why significant?"

"The floodgates, y'know. Instead of the tube station that was going to be there in 1906, they developed it into a central command centre. Certain stations on the network have the gates, but they're all controlled from North End. Reckon the building goes down more than a thousand feet, though only the higher levels were initially used. It was started in the 1940s so they could stop the entire Underground system being flooded. Most of the gates were individually controlled before then."

"How could the whole system be flooded?"

"If the Nazis had dropped a bomb in the Thames the tunnels under the river could have collapsed. Within ten minutes the Underground system would have been completely filled with water and submerged, y'know. Well, that's what they said. Later on, in the early 1970s, they built a second zone of gates just outside stations like Shepherds Bush, Aldgate East, and Bounds Green, before where the tracks emerge overground."

"What have they got to do with flooding?"

"Nothing. But they thought people would go mental when the three-minute warnings went off and try to run along the tracks into the train tunnels to escape from Soviet atom bombs. Well, you get the idea . . ."

By now they'd reached the emergency spiral stairway, which led much further downward to the lower lift landing. It was considerably steeper than the previous stairway, and Gray kept a hand against the wall as the two men descended. Their footfalls echoed as if ghosts were following close behind.

"Talking of weird stuff like that, you know about the Sentinel Train?" Heath asked. He didn't wait for an answer before continuing with his topic. "First stop, King William Street Station along the abandoned spur, runs down to Borough without halting, then reverses up the Bank branch of the Northern Line. Only stops at the ghost stations along the route, nowhere else; goes on to City

Road, right here to South Kentish Town, then back via Camden, before terminating at the deepest of all: North End, under Hampstead Heath. Anyway, I told you about that one, didn't I? The Sentinel lets the inspection crews examine the stuff the public never sees. Company doesn't leave the traction current to the rails on overnight, so a diesel locomotive pulls the old F Stock carriages. The train has a free run on the deserted tracks. Happens once a week or thereabouts. Every tube line has its own Sentinel."

"Are you pulling my leg?" Gray replied testily. "That's straight out of Drayton's book. It seems to me you must have read it."

They'd reached the lower lift landing.

"This passageway leads to the north and southbound platforms," Heath said, "but they're long gone."

Were the idea not totally ridiculous, Gray could have mistaken his companion for something dressed up in a boiler suit in order to pass as human. His colleagues at the Yard would have laughed at his suspicion. But he could not shake off the impression that, in the darkness, Heath's appearance was genuinely similar to the figure that Gray had glimpsed peering out of the trellised gates of Kentish Town Station. That was only a few nights ago and one stop along the Northern Line from this ghost station. He'd seen it with his own eyes, and the experience was not drawn from the pages of a crazy book like *The Secret Underground*. Gray could easily believe that this character Heath had not just read the volume but had stepped out from its pages into life.

"You didn't answer my question," Gray said. From his coat pocket he drew a packet of Benson & Hedges cigarettes.

"What one was that again?" Heath snuffled.

"The one about having read *The Secret Underground*," Gray responded as he jammed one of the smokes between his lips and touched the end with the flame from a battered old Zippo. A faint smell of petrol wafted from the lighter. He drew on the cigarette and exhaled, sending curling blue smoke across the beam of Heath's torch.

"Oh that . . . look, you can't smoke down here. It's dangerous."

"Do you see any 'No Smoking' signs around? Anyway, I'm sure your mask will protect you."

Heath paused and regarded the glowing tip of Gray's cigarette. He finally came back to the point.

"Yeah, I've read that book. I know it off by heart. It's a favourite of mine."

From further back along the passageways Gray thought he detected a rustling noise, like a pile of leaves dispersed by the wind. But before he was able to tell from which direction it came, the racket of a passing northbound train drowned them out. Gray thought he heard Heath muttering.

It sounded like ". . . bigmouth . . . Miguel . . . he's sorted . . ." but most of these words were also lost in the roar.

It was obvious that Heath knew something about Drayton's disappearance and may even have had a hand in it. Perhaps he was also dangerously obsessed with all those ghost stations and had come to regard Drayton as his rival. In any case, the place to interview Heath was back at the Yard, not here and now. Gray's back and stomach ached; the old ruptures were acting up again. It was time to get back to the surface. There was nothing down here that was of any use to his investigation. Besides, although Heath was small, Gray feared that he was dealing with a lunatic.

There was that damn rustling again! It sounded closer this time. Heath seemed not to notice it, though, and coldly regarded Gray smoking his cigarette, glaring through narrowed eyes that swam behind the thick lenses of his glasses.

"Well," said Gray, "I've seen everything I want to see here. Let's get back to the surface."

"All right," Heath replied. "But you ain't looked yet. To come all this way and not look at it would be a waste of my time and yours."

"Look at what exactly?"

"Over there in the corner. Thirty yards, right up against the wall." Heath flashed the torch's beam onto what appeared to be a large pile of rags. "Go and see. I already know what it is. I'll stay where I am. In case you're worried, like."

As he got nearer, Gray glanced back to make sure that Heath made no attempt to creep up on him. What he believed was a pile of rags was in fact a body slumped in the angle between wall and floor, its face turned towards the tiles. The back of its skull was smashed in. Dried blood caked the matted hair. As he turned the body over, Gray guessed that its face would be unfamiliar; he expected it to be Drayton, whom he'd never seen. But it was the

Spaniard, Carlos Miguel. Heath had not moved an inch whilst Gray examined the corpse, but something living dropped from the darkness of the ceiling onto him, and the impact drove the police inspector crashing to the floor.

His head struck the concrete and he blacked out.

*

Gray awoke in a tube train carriage. He felt nauseous with pain as consciousness returned. He ran his fingers over his head and found half a dozen scratches and wounds around his face and on the back of his skull. There was a stabbing pain in his stomach, and he was aware of feeling wet around the seat of his trousers. The fall had reopened some of his old internal ruptures, and blood was leaking out of his lower intestine.

Although wracked with pain, he forced himself to take in the details of his surroundings. He was on a moving train, one that hurtled through the tunnels at breakneck speed.

The floor was littered with prostrate bodies. Some were hanging by their necks from knotted leather straps attached to the ceiling rails. All had been recently murdered and bore signs of mutilation. There were dozens of the corpses packed into the carriage. Their limbs protruded at misshapen angles from the humps of flesh and clothing. Extreme terror and pain marked their facial expressions. The body of Carlos Miguel lay amongst the charnel crowds. Like the Castilian, Gray had been left for dead.

Somehow he'd come to be a passenger in a carriage that appeared to date from, he guessed, the 1920s. The carriage lights were single bulbs housed in Art-Deco glass oysters with a very wide aisle running between the longitudinal seating. It must have been antiquated rolling stock, for there were advertisements from that far-off decade above the windows and the Underground map showed routes such as the Hampstead and Highgate Line, the City and South London Railway and the Central London Railway. Back then the Victoria and Jubilee lines had not even been thought of, let alone built. Moreover, the map was like a complicated tangle of spaghetti and not modelled on the famous Beck circuit-board design.

Struggling to his feet and clutching the pole at the end of the seats, Gray stood in a daze for a moment, rocking with the motion

of the train. His wristwatch showed 1.20 A.M. He'd been out cold
for well over eight hours. His left trouser leg stuck to the inside of
his thigh, where the stream of blood oozing from his rectum had
partially dried. He picked his way through the corpses and found
that he was trapped in the last carriage of the train; the connecting
door to the penultimate carriage had been welded shut.

Gray crept back to a seat and peered through the window to
the tunnels outside. Suddenly the train entered a platform, without
slowing, and he pressed his face to the glass in order to try and
make out the station name as it flashed past. The light from the interior of the carriages projected enough illumination for him to see
a faded sign reading "North End." It also just made visible the
stunted, faceless forms that haunted the shadows of passageways
further back—forms that shunned the light, but which welcomed
the arrival of the Sentinel with malefic glee, chattering deafeningly
in the semi-darkness.

Gray had no doubt that the inner and outer gates were closed
right the way across the Underground network, now that the Sentinel had completed its journey. He harboured the notion that
these gates served a purpose quite different from the official one
and were used to prevent escape along the tracks to the surface.
Drayton had described many pieces of the jigsaw in his book *The
Secret Underground*. Gray had not fitted them together until it was
too late and would finally solve the mystery in the labyrinthine
reaches of an industrial Sheol.

In his mind's eye he saw a vision in which the disparate chapters of Drayton's book merged to form a coherent explanation of
what was happening. It was an explanation involving a series of
derelict reverse skyscrapers, one of which was beneath North End,
whose ultimate depth was probably over a thousand feet; a structure populated by beings who were sometimes bored with the re-
past foraged by using the smaller tunnels that led to the cemeteries
and burial grounds across London. Could it be possible that the
feasters had absorbed some of the characteristics of the corpses
upon which they preyed, as in cannibalistic folklore?

He thought of an abandoned train and its driver . . . *Como una
palomilla* . . . of a man called Heath with thick eyeglasses, his face
obscured, and who knew as much as Drayton himself . . .

As he thought about the ghost stations on the Piccadilly Line, the Central Line, the Metropolitan Line, and all the others, he guessed that each doubtless had its own Sentinel operating that night as well.

Suddenly the lights in all the carriages went out.

Acting on the signal, as they had done so many times in the past, they surged up from the edifice's black abyss of corridors and debris-choked rooms in a ravenous tide.

As the stunted forms eagerly scrambled across the divide between them and the train, he finally realised that, in order to keep them down there in the dark, to prevent them overrunning London altogether, it was necessary for them to be fed.

Gray only had time to scream once in the darkness.

A GENTLEMAN FROM MEXICO

"Barlow, I imagine, can tell you even more about the Old Ones."

—Clark Ashton Smith to August Derleth (13 April 1937)

Victor Armstrong was running late for his appointment and so had hailed a taxi rather than trusting to the Metro. Bathed in cruel noon sunlight, the green-liveried Volkswagen Beetle taxi cruised down Avenida Reforma. In the back of the vehicle, Armstrong rummaged around in his jacket pocket for the pack of Faros cigarettes he'd bought before setting off on his rendezvous.

"Es OK para mí a fumar en tu taxi?" Armstrong said, managing to cobble together the request in his iffy Spanish.

He saw the eyes of the driver reflected in the rearview mirror, and they displayed total indifference. It was as if he'd made a request to fold his arms.

"Seguro," the driver replied, turning the wheel sharply, weaving his way across four lines of traffic. Armstrong was jolted over to the left and clutched at the leather handle hanging from the front passenger door. The right-hand seat at the front had been removed, as was the case with all the green taxis, giving plenty of legroom and an easy entrance and exit.

Like most of the taxi drivers in Mexico City, this one handled his vehicle with savage intent, determined to get from A to B in the minimum possible time. In this almost permanently gridlocked megalopolis, the survival of the fastest was the rule. Armstrong lit up one of his untipped cigarettes and gazed out the window. Brilliant sunshine illuminated in excruciating detail the chaos and decay of the urban rubbish dump that is the Ciudad de México, Distrito Federal, or "D.F." for short. A great melting pot of the criminal, the insane, the beautiful and the macho, 25 million people constantly living in a mire of institutionalised corruption, poverty, and crime. But despite all this, Mexico City's soul seems untouched, defiant, and no other great city of the world is so vividly alive, dwelling as it does always in the shadow of death. Another earthquake might be just around the corner, the Popocatéptl volcano might blow at any hour, the brown haze of man-made pollution might finally suffocate the populace. Who knows? What is certain is that D.F. would rise again, as filthy, crazed, and glorious as before.

They were approaching La Condesa, a fashionable area to the north of the centre that had attracted impoverished artists and writers ten years ago, but which had recently been overrun with expensive restaurants and cafés. Armstrong had arranged to meet with an English-speaking acquaintance at the bookshop café El Torre on the corner of Avenida Nuevo León. This acquaintance, Juan San Isidro, was a so-called underground poet specialising in sinister verse written in the Náhuatl language. A notorious drunk, San Isidro had enjoyed a modicum of celebrity in his youth but had burnt out by his mid-twenties. Now in his mid-thirties, he was scarcely ever sober and looked twice his actual age. His bitterness and tendency to enter into the kind of vicious quarrels that seem endemic in Latin American literary circles had alienated him from most of his contemporaries. Armstrong suspected that San Isidro had requested a meeting for one of two reasons; either to tap him for money or else to seek his assistance in recommending a translator for a reissue of his poetical work in an English-language edition in the United States. It was highly unlikely that San Isidro was going to offer him a work of fiction for one of his upcoming anthologies of short stories. The taxi pulled up alongside the bookshop.

"¿Cuánto es?" Armstrong asked.

"Veintiún pesos," the driver responded. Armstrong handed over some coins and exited the vehicle.

Standing on the corner outside the bookshop was a stall selling tortas, tacos, and other fast food. The smell of the sizzling meat and chicken, frying smokily on the hob, made Armstrong's mouth water. Despite the call of ¡Pásele, señor! Armstrong passed by, knowing that, as a foreigner, his stomach wouldn't have lasted ten minutes against the native bacteria. Having experienced what they called "Montezuma's Revenge" on his first trip to D.F. a year ago, there was no question of him taking a chance like that again. Across the street an argument was taking place between two drivers, who'd got out of their battered and dirty cars to trade insults.

Since their abandoned vehicles were holding up the traffic, the rather half-hearted battle (consisting entirely of feints and shouting) was accompanied by a cacophony of angry car-horns.

El Torre was something of a landmark in the area, its exterior covered with tiles and windows with external ornate grilles. A three-storey building with a peaked roof, and erected in the colonial era, it had been a haunt for literati of all stripes—novelists, poets and assorted hangers-on—since the 1950s. During the period in which La Condesa had been gentrified some of El Torre's former seedy charm had diminished and, as well as selling books, it had diversified into stocking DVDs and compact discs upstairs. Part of the ground floor had been converted into an expensive eatery, whilst the first floor now half occupied a café-bar from where drinkers could peer over the centre of the storey down into the level below, watching diners pick at their food and browsers lingering over the books on shelves and on the display tables. As a consequence of these improvements, the space for poetry readings upstairs had been entirely done away with, and Juan San Isidro haunted its former confines as if in eternal protest at the loss of his own personal stage.

As Armstrong entered he glanced up at the floor above and saw the poet already waiting for him, slumped over a table and tracing a circle on its surface with an empty bottle of Sol beer. His lank black hair hung down to his shoulders, obscuring his face, but even so his immense bulk made him unmistakable.

Armstrong's gaze roved around and sought out the stairway entrance. He caught sight of the only other customer in El Torre, besides himself and San Isidro. This other person was dressed in a dark grey linen suit, quite crumpled, with threadbare patches at the elbows and frayed cuffs. The necktie he wore was a plain navy blue and quite unremarkable. His shoes were badly scuffed and he must have repeatedly refused the services of D.F.'s innumerable *boleros*. They keenly polished shoes on their portable footstands for anyone who had a mere dozen pesos to spare. The man had an olive complexion, was perfectly clean-shaven, and about forty years old. His short black hair was parted neatly on the left-hand side. He had the features of a *mestizo*, a typical Mexican of mingled European and Native Indian blood. There was something in the way he carried himself that told of a gentleman down on his luck, perhaps even an impoverished scholar given his slight stoop, an attribute often acquired by those who pore over books or manuscripts year after year.

He was browsing through the books on display that were published by the likes of Ediciones Valdemar and Ediciones Siruela that had been specially imported from Spain. These were mostly supernatural fiction titles, for which many Mexican readers had a discerning fondness. Armstrong was glad, for his own anthologies invariably were comprised of tales depicting the weird and uncanny—a market that, at least in the Anglophone countries, seemed to have self-destructed after a glut of trashy horror paperbacks in the 1980s. But these were not junk; they were works by the recognised masters, and a quick glance over the classics available for sale here in mass-market form would have drawn the admiration of any English or American devotee. Here were books by Arthur Machen, Algernon Blackwood, M. R. James, and Ambrose Bierce, amongst dozens of others. Most striking, however, was the vast range of collections available written by H. P. Lovecraft. The browsing man in the dark suit picked up one after the other, almost reluctant to return each to its proper place, although if his down-at-heels appearance were an indication, their price was surely beyond his limited means. New books in Mexico are scarcely ever cheap.

Armstrong looked away. He could not understand why this rather ordinary gentleman had stirred his imagination. He was, after all, merely typical of the sort of book-addict found anywhere and at any time. Meanwhile, Juan San Isidro had noticed Victor's arrival and called down to him.

"¡Ay, Víctor, quiero más chela! Lo siento, pero no tengo dinero."

Armstrong sighed and made his way up the stairs.

When they were eventually sitting opposite one another, Armstrong with a bottle of Indio and San Isidro with a fresh bottle of Sol, the Mexican switched from Spanish to English. He was always keen to take whatever opportunity he could to converse in the language. A huge bear of a man, he'd recently grown a shaggy goatee beard, and the T-shirt he wore bore the logo of some outlandish band called "Control Machete," whose music Armstrong did not know and did not want to know. Years ago Armstrong had foolishly mentioned San Isidro's literary efforts to the publisher of a small-press imprint in California that was looking for cosmic or outré verse. The result had been a chapbook with a selection of San Isidro's Aztec-influenced work translated into English, and thereafter Armstrong had never been able to entirely shake off his "discovery."

"So," San Isidro said, "how are things with you? Still editing those *antologías*?"

"There's scarcely any money in them, Juan," Armstrong replied. "Unless I've managed to wrangle something original out of Steve King, the publishers want to nail my balls to the wall."

"You know him? King? Do you think he'd give me a loan? He's very rich, no? Help out a struggling brother artist?"

Armstrong tried not to smile inappropriately. He could only imagine how quickly San Isidro would piss away any handouts he'd receive on booze. No one other than their agents, accountants, lawyers, or publishers milks cash-cow authors.

"He's a busy man. I don't think he'd appreciate my—"

"You mean he's a *pinche cabrón*. Keeps his money up his *culo* where no one else can get at it. That's why *todos los gringos* walk around with their legs apart, like cowboys, no? All those dollar bills stuffed in there."

Armstrong was relieved to be British. Even liberal Americans who came south, seeking to atone for the recent sins of NAFTA and a long history of land grabbing, were objects of ridicule here. They might get away with such conscience-posturing in the North, in cities like Monterrey that were closer to the border and which looked to rich U.S. states like Texas for inspiration; but in D.F. *gringos* are only ever *pinches gringos,* and no amount of self-loathing or atonement on their part could ever erase the fact. The British, on the other hand, despite their imperial past, were redeemed by virtue of having given the Beatles and association football to the world.

"Why did you want to see me, Juan?" Armstrong asked, taking out his packet of Faros and putting them on the table. His companion looked at the cheap brand with amused contempt. Nevertheless, this attitude did not stop him from smoking them.

"I want you to take a look at some *cuentos*," San Isidro replied, puffing away on the cigarette he'd taken. "Read them and make me an offer. They're in your line of work."

He delved into a shoulder bag lying underneath the table and took out a pile of papers, individuated into sections by rubber bands, and handed them over.

"I thought you didn't write short stories," Armstrong said.

"I didn't write them," San Isidro replied. "I'm acting as the exclusive agent. They're in English, as you see, and they're the type of horror stories you like. I handle all his stuff."

"Who's this author?" Armstrong said, looking at the top sheet. "Felipe López? I can't say I've heard of him."

"*El señor López* has only been writing for a couple of years. He's my personal discovery, as you discovered me, no? *Es un autor auténtico,* not some hack. *Mira al cabellero* down there, the one who's looking through the books. That's *el señor López.* He doesn't want to meet you until you've read his stuff. I told him I knew you, and that you weren't the same as all those other *culeros* who'd rejected him."

So that man in the crumpled grey suit was San Isidro's first client, Armstrong thought. He hesitated for a moment but then relented. At least this man López had the appearance of being literate.

"All right," Armstrong said. "I'll take them away with me and call you once I've read them. I can't promise anything, though."

"Why not sit here and read them now, *compañero?* I tell you, these things are a goldmine. We can have a few more *chelas* while I wait for you to finish. He also does his own proofreading, so you won't need to *trabajar mucho* yourself."

"Short stories," Armstrong riposted, "are fool's gold, Juan. I told you, there's no real money in them anymore. Have another on me if you like, but I've got to go. I'll be in touch."

With that closing remark Armstrong stood up, left a hundred pesos note on the table, and made his exit. He didn't notice whether or not *el Señor López* saw him leave.

*

Over the next few days Armstrong almost forgot about the stories by Felipe López. He hated being asked to read fiction by an unknown author who had been praised by one of his friends. All too often he had to prick their enthusiasm, usually fired by beer and comradeship rather than by an objective assessment of literary merit. And San Isidro had never acted as an agent for anybody before; he was far too consumed by his own literary ambitions. So it appeared obvious to Armstrong that San Isidro was paying back a favour of some sort. That, however, seemed unlikely given the down-at-heels appearance of López, but perhaps it was a case of San Isidro owing him money.

Armstrong was staying close to Cuauhtémoc Metro station in an apartment owned by Mexican friends of his, a couple, Enrique and María, who were in London for a few weeks, staying in his flat there in an exchange holiday. It was something they did every other year to save on hotel bills. There were only three days left before they were due to cross each other high over the Atlantic in flights going in the opposite direction. Enrique and María were both involved in publishing themselves, and he'd struck up a friendship with them in 1995 whilst attending a fantasy and horror convention held in San Francisco.

Since he was staying in an apartment belonging to friends, Armstrong paid little attention to the telephone, as he knew he'd just be taking messages for his absent hosts. Anything desperately important that needed to be passed on to them would be left on the answering machine. When he got around to checking it, there were three messages, two for Enrique and María and one for him. It was left by Juan San Isidro:

"*Oye,¿qué onda?* Man, don't fuck me over. Have you read *los cuentos?* I think not. Otherwise you'd be chasing my ass like a *puto.* You don't leave Mexico until I hear from you, *¿te queda claro?*"

Despite his reluctance, Armstrong didn't see any alternative but to look the stories over. He took them out onto the little balcony overlooking the *privada* in which the apartment was situated. It was pleasantly warm outside in the evening, being October, and since the only traffic passing below consisted of pedestrians it was easy to concentrate. He sat down on the chair he'd moved out there, put the papers that he'd retrieved from his suitcase on his lap, and looked them over.

San Isidro had given him four stories, the longest of which was the third at around forty thousand words.

Armstrong had seen this type of story on dozens of occasions in the past, usually sent for his consideration by "fan authors" who were obsessed with the life and works of H. P. Lovecraft. Most of these pastiches contained long lists of clichéd forbidden books and names of unpronounceable entities to be incorporated into the so-called Cthulhu Mythos. As he turned the pages of the first of López's tales, though, he was surprised to discover that they did not also contain the other feature associated with Lovecraft fan pastiches: there were no obvious grammatical, spelling, or common textual errors. The work had already been gone over by an author with a keen eye for copyediting. Additionally, it had to be the case that Felipe López was fluent in English to the degree of being able to pass completely for a native. The text contained no trace of any Spanish-language idioms indicating his Mexican nationality. Indeed, López even favoured the British spelling of certain words, rather than that used in the United States, in exactly the same fashion as Lovecraft had done himself.

Despite his disdain for pastiche, Armstrong kept reading. Eventually, to his surprise, he found that López's mimetic skills were so expert that he could almost believe that he was reading a previously undiscovered work written by Lovecraft himself. The story had the exact same sense of nightmarish authenticity as the best of the Providence author's tales. By the time he'd finished reading the first story, Armstrong was in a state of dazed wonder. Of course he realised, on a professional level, that the thing had no commercial potential. It smacked far too much of an in-joke or a hoax, but it was nevertheless profoundly impressive in its own right. He began to wonder what this López person might be able to achieve were he to wean himself from the Lovecraft influence and produce fiction utilising a distinct authorial voice. It might result in another modern-day writer of the order of Thomas Ligotti.

Armstrong was dimly aware of the telephone ringing in the background. He ignored the sound, allowing the answering machine to deal with whoever it was. He supposed that it could be San Isidro again and that it might have been better to pick up, but he was too eager to discover whether the story he'd just read was a fluke or not. Since the mosquitoes were now busy in the night air, he took the manuscripts inside and carried on reading.

*

Whoever had left the weird message on Enrique and María's answering machine was obviously some crank, thought Armstrong.

He played it back again the morning after it was recorded.

There was a click on the line and the sound of unintelligible voices conferring amongst themselves, and then a jarring, discordant muttering in English. The voice had a Mexican accent but was unknown to Armstrong. It said:

"He belongs to us. His products belong to us. No one will take him from us."

That was all.

After listening to the message one more time, Armstrong wondered if it were not simply San Isidro playing a joke on him, pretending to be another rival party involved with the works of Felipe López. Perhaps he thought the idea of some competition might spur Armstrong to a quick decision. If so, it was an unnecessary ploy.

After having read the second of López's tales he was convinced that the author had unmatched imagination and ability, despite being almost ruinously handicapped by his slavish mimicry of Lovecraft's style and themes. However, there was more than enough pure genius in there to convince Armstrong to take the matter further. If he could meet with López in person, he was determined to press upon him the necessity of a last revision of the texts—one that removed entirely the Cthulhu Mythos elements and replaced the florid, adjective-ridden prose with a minimalist approach.

When he telephoned Juan San Isidro it was no surprise that the poet-turned-agent was deeply suspicious about Armstrong's insistence that he must meet López alone.

"You want to cut me out of the deal, *¡estás loco!* Forget it, man. Now you know *que es un maestro, lo quieres todo para ti.*"

"I only want to suggest a few changes to the texts, Juan. Nothing sinister in that, really. You'll get your commission, I'll not cheat you, believe me."

Their conversation went round in circles for ten minutes before Armstrong eventually convinced San Isidro that he had no underhanded motive with regards to López's work. Even so, Armstrong realised that there was something more going on between the two of them than the usual protective relationship between an agent and his client. Nevertheless he successfully elicited a promise from San Isidro that he would ensure López met with him alone in the Café la Habana on La Calle de Bucareli at 2 P.M. that same afternoon.

*

The Café la Habana was a haunt for distinguished old men who came to play chess, smoke their pipes or cigars, and spend the better part of the afternoon dreaming over coffee or beer. It had a high ceiling and was decorated with framed photographs of Havana from the time before Castro's revolution. Many communist exiles from Batista Cuba came here, having fled persecution, and its fame dated from that period. The number of exiles had dwindled as the years passed, but it still had a reputation amongst all those who championed leftist defiance. The place had a long pedigree, having been a favourite meeting place, in even earlier decades, of those Spanish Republican refugees who'd settled in D.F. after escaping the wrath of General Franco's regime.

Armstrong sat in a corner, lingering over a glass of tequila with lime, when López walked in. He was half an hour late. His lean form was framed in the doorway by the brilliant sunshine outside. López cast his glance around the place before spotting Armstrong and making for the table at which he sat.

López had changed his dark grey suit for a cream-coloured one, and this time he was wearing a matching panama hat. He gave a nod of recognition towards Armstrong as he approached.

Before he sat down he shook Armstrong's hand and apologised in English:

"I hope that you will excuse my tardiness, Mr. Armstrong, but the truth is that I was distracted by a particularly fascinating example of eighteenth-century colonial architecture whilst making my way over here."

Armstrong did not reply at once. He was taken aback by López's accent. Unless he was mistaken, it was pure, authentic New England Yankee. There was not a trace of Mexican in it.

"No need to apologise," Armstrong finally said. "Can I get you a drink—some beer or tequila perhaps?"

"Thank you but no. I never partake of alcoholic beverages, even for the purposes of refreshment. However, a cup of coffee, perhaps a double espresso, would be most welcome."

Armstrong ordered López's coffee and asked for another tequila with lime to be brought to their table.

"I liked your tales very much; it was quite an experience read-

ing through them, I can tell you. Of course they're overly deriva-
tive, but I imagine that you easily could tone down all the Lovecraft elements—"

"I'm afraid, Mr. Armstrong," López said, with a chill tone entering his voice, "that alterations of any sort are completely out of
the question. The stories must be printed as written, down to the
last detail, otherwise this conversation is simply a waste of my time
and your own."

The drinks arrived. López calmly began to shovel spoonful after spoonful of sugar into his cup, turning the coffee into treacly,
caffeine-rich syrup. Armstrong looked at him incredulously. Now
he understood what was going on. San Isidro was definitely having a
joke at his expense. He must have coached this López character, telling him all about H. P. Lovecraft's mannerisms and . . . to what end?

"Why are you persisting with this absurd Lovecraft impersona-
tion?" Armstrong blurted out. "It's ridiculous. San Isidro put you
up to it, I suppose. But what I can't figure out is why, so let me in
on the joke."

López looked up from his coffee, and his eyes were deadly serious. And here it comes, boys and girls, thought Armstrong; here
comes the line we've all been waiting for:

*This is no joke, Mr. Armstrong, far from it, for I am in reality Howard
Phillips Lovecraft of Providence, Rhode Island.*

"Surely the only rational answer has already suggested itself,"
López replied, very calmly and without any melodrama. "You are
in fact sitting across the table from a certifiable lunatic."

Armstrong leaned back in his seat and carefully considered the
man opposite. His manner betrayed no sign of humour, and he
spoke as if what he'd suggested was an established truism.

"Then despite your behaviour, you know that you're not really
Lovecraft?" Armstrong said.

"Howard Phillips Lovecraft died in agony on the morning of
Monday, the fifteenth of March, 1937, in Providence's Jane Brown
Memorial Hospital. I cannot be him. However, since Tuesday, the
fifteenth of March, 2003, I have been subject to a delusion whereby the identity of Lovecraft has completely supplanted my own. I
currently have no memories whatsoever of having once been Felipe López of Mexico City. His family and friends are complete
strangers to me. Meanwhile, everyone Lovecraft knew is dead. I

have become an outsider in this country and in this time. Unless one accepts the existence of the supernatural, which I emphatically do not, then only the explanation I have advanced has any credence."

Armstrong was taken aback by these remarks. This was like no madman he'd heard of: one who was not only able to recognise his derangement, but who also was totally a slave to it. It was more like some bizarre variant of a multiple personality disorder.

"What did the doctors here have to say?" Armstrong asked.

"They did their best," López said, after taking a sip of his coffee, "but with no appreciable effect, let alone any amelioration, upon my malady. They tended to agree with my analysis of the situation."

"What about López before this happened? Did he have any interest in Lovecraft prior to your—um—alteration? I can't believe something like that would come out of nowhere."

It was annoying, but Armstrong found himself questioning López as if he were actually addressing Lovecraft inhabiting another body.

"Quite so. I have discovered that López was a fanatical devotee of Lovecraft's life and work. Moreover, he was one of that rather contemptible breed of freaks who adhere to the outlandish belief that, rather than writing fiction, Lovecraft had unconscious access to ultramundane dimensions. The group to which he belonged, who styled themselves 'The Sodality of the Black Sun,' advocated the piteous theory that Lovecraft was an occult prophet instead of a mere scribbler. This indicates to me a brain already on the brink of a potential collapse into total chaos. You see before you the inevitable consequence."

There are a lot of sad crazies out there, thought Armstrong, who believe in nothing except the power of their own imaginations to create whatever they want to create from a supposedly malleable reality. A whole bunch of them had doubtless fastened upon Lovecraft's mythos for inspiration, but he doubted that any others had wound up like Felipe López.

"Well," Armstrong said, "I don't know what to make of all this. But surely one consideration has occurred to you already? If you really were Lovecraft, you'd know certain things that only he could possibly have known."

"An ingenious point," said López, "but with all his contemporaries in the grave, how then to verify that information? Mr. Armstrong, I must remind you that the idea of Lovecraft's consciousness not only surviving the death of his physical form, but also transferring itself to another body, is patently ridiculous. I make no such claim."

López stared at him wordlessly and then, having finished the dregs of his coffee, got up and left.

*

When Armstrong arrived back at Enrique and María's apartment, he found the door already ajar. Someone had broken in, forcing the entrance with a crowbar or similar tool judging by the splintered wound in the side of the door's frame. He was relieved to find that the intruders had not torn the place apart and seemed to have scarcely disturbed anything. When he examined his own room, however, he noted at once that the López manuscripts were missing. He unmistakably remembered having left them on his bedside table. But in their place was a note left behind by whoever had stolen them. It read: "Do not meddle in our affairs again, lest the darkness seek you out."

Obviously, this was a targeted burglary by the people who'd left that message on the answering machine warning him against having dealings with López. They must have wanted to get hold of the López stories extremely badly and, whoever they were, must have also known that San Isidro had passed them on to him, as well as knowing that Armstrong had an appointment with López, thus giving them the perfect moment to strike while he was gone.

It was difficult to figure out what to do next. Everyone in Mexico City realises that to call the police regarding a burglary has two possible outcomes. The first is that they will turn up, treat it as a waste of their time, and do nothing. The second is that things will turn surreal very quickly, because they will casually mention how poorly paid police officers are and, in return for a "donation," they are able to arrange for the swift return of your goods with no questions asked. Given that the burglary was not the work of organised crime but some nutty underground cult, Armstrong thought better of involving the police.

Great, thought Armstrong, now I'm in trouble not only with the local branch of occult loonies, but with San Isidro and López for having lost the manuscripts. The first thing to do was give San Isidro the bad news. Since a matter of this delicate nature was best dealt with face-to-face, Armstrong decided to make his way over to the poet's apartment, after he'd arranged for someone to come over and fix the door.

*

A cardinal, though unspoken, rule of travelling by Metro in Mexico City is not to carry anything of value. If you're a tourist, look like a tourist with little money. The security guards who hover around the ticket barriers are not there just for show. They carry guns for a reason. D.F. is the kidnapping capital of the world. Armstrong had always followed the dress-down rule and, although he stood out anyway because he was a pale-skinned *güerito*, he'd encountered no problems on his travels. The stations themselves were grimy, functionalist, and depressing. Architecturally they resembled prison camps, but located underground. Nevertheless Armstrong enjoyed travelling by Metro; it was unbelievably cheap, the gap between trains was less than a minute, and it was like being on a mobile marketplace. Passengers selling homemade CDs would wander up and down the carriages, with samples of music playing on ghetto blasters slung over their shoulders. Others sold tonics for afflictions from back pain to impotence. Whether these worked or not, there was certainly a market for them, as the sellers did a brisk trade.

One of the carriages on the train that Armstrong took must have been defective. All its lights were out and, curiously, he noticed that those who thought to board it anyway changed their minds at once and preferred to either remain on the platform or else rush over into one of the adjacent carriages instead.

Armstrong alighted at Chapultepec station, found his way through the convoluted tunnels up to the surface, and turned left alongside the eight-lane road outside. The noise of the traffic blocked out most other sounds, and the vehicle fumes were like a low-level grey nebula held down by the force of the brilliant afternoon sunshine. People scurried to and fro along the pavement, their gazes fixed straight ahead, particularly those of any lone women for whom eye-contact with a *chilango* carried the risk of inviting a lewd suggestion.

A long footbridge flanked the motorway and was the only means of crossing for pedestrians for a couple of miles or so. At night it was a notorious crime spot, and only the foolhardy would cross it unaccompanied. However, at this time of the day everyone safely used it and a constant stream of people went back and forth.

Juan San Isidro's apartment was only five minutes' walk from the bridge and was housed in a decaying brownstone building just on the fringes of La Condesa. Sometimes Armstrong wondered whether the poet was the structure's only occupant, for the windows of all the other apartments were either blackened by soot or else broken and hanging open day and night to the elements.

He pushed the intercom button for San Isidro and, after a minute, heard a half-awake voice say:

"*¿Quién es?*"

"It's me, Victor. Come down and let me in, will you?" Armstrong replied, holding his mouth close to the intercom.

"Stand in front where I can see you," he said, "and I'll give you *mis llaves.*"

Armstrong left the porch, went onto the pavement and looked up. San Isidro leant out of one of the third-floor windows, his lank black hair making a cowl over his face. He tossed a plastic bag containing the keys over the ledge, and Armstrong retrieved it after it hit the ground.

The building had got even worse since the last time he'd paid a visit. If it was run-down before, now it was positively unfit for human habitation and should have been condemned. The lobby was filled with debris, half the tiles had fallen from the walls, and a dripping waterpipe was poking out from a huge hole in the ceiling. Vermin scurried around back in the shadows. The building's staircase was practically a deathtrap, for if a step had not already collapsed, those that remained seemed likely to do so in the near future. As Armstrong climbed he clutched at the shaky banister with both hands, his knuckles white with the fierce grip, advancing up sideways like a crab.

San Isidro was standing in the doorway to his apartment, smoking a fat joint with one hand and swigging from a half-bottle of Cuervo with the other. The smell of marijuana greeted Armstrong as he finally made it to the fourth floor. Being continually stoned, he thought, was about the only way to make the surroundings bearable.

"*Hola, compañero,* good to see you, come on inside."

His half-glazed eyes, wide fixed smile, and unsteady gait indicated that he'd been going at the weed and tequila already for most of the day.

"This is a celebration, no? You've come to bring me *mucho dinero,* I hope. I'm honoured that you come here to see me. *Siéntate, por favor.*"

San Isidro cleared a space on a sofa that was littered with porn magazines and empty packets of Delicados cigarettes. Armstrong sat down while San Isidro picked up an empty glass from the floor, poured some tequila in it, and put it in his hand.

"*Salud,*" he said, "to our friend and saviour Felipe López, *el mejor escritor de cuentos macabros del mundo, ahora y siempre.*"

"I want you to tell me, Juan, as a friend and in confidence, what happened to López and how he came to think and act exactly like H. P. Lovecraft. And I want to know about the people who are after him. Were they people he knew before his—um—breakdown?" Armstrong looked at the glass and tried to find a clean part of the rim from which to drink. At this stage he was reluctant to reveal that the López manuscripts had been stolen. San Isidro was volatile, and Armstrong wasn't sure how he might react to the news.

San Isidro appeared to start momentarily at the mention of "H. P. Lovecraft," but whether it was the effect of the name or the cumulative effect of the booze and weed, it was difficult to tell.

"So he told you, eh? Well, not all of it. *No recuerda nada de antes,* when he was just Felipe López. *No importa qué pasó antes,* sure, there was some heavy shit back then. *Si quieres los cuentos, primero quiero mucho dinero.* Then maybe I'll tell you about it, eh?"

"I'll pay you, Juan, and pay you well. But I need to understand the truth."

What San Isidro told Armstrong over the next half-hour consisted of a meandering monologue, mostly in Spanish, of a brilliant young *gringo* who had come to Mexico in the 1940s to study Mesoamerican anthropology. This man, Robert Hayward Barlow, had been Lovecraft's literary executor. Armstrong had heard the name before, but what little he knew did not prepare him for San Isidro's increasingly bizarre account of events.

It began plausibly enough. Barlow, he said, had taken possession of Lovecraft's papers after his death in 1937. He had gone through them thereafter and donated the bulk of them to the John Hay Library in Providence, in order to establish a permanent archival resource. However, he was ostracised by the Lovecraft circle, a campaign driven by Donald Wandrei and August Derleth, on the basis that he had supposedly stolen the materials in the first place from under the nose of the Providence author's surviving aunt.

However, what was not known then, San Isidro claimed, was that Barlow had kept some items back, the most important of which was the "Dream-Diary of the Arkham Cycle," a notebook in longhand of approximately thirty or so pages and akin to Lovecraft's commonplace book. It contained, so San Isidro claimed, dozens of entries from 1923 to 1936 that appeared to contradict the assertion that Lovecraft's mythos was solely a fictional construct. These entries are not suggestive by themselves *at the time they were supposedly written,* for the content was confined to the description of dreams in which elements from his myth-cycle had manifested themselves. These could be accepted as having no basis in reality had it not been for their supposedly *prophetic* nature. One such entry San Isidro quoted from memory. By this stage his voice was thick and the marijuana he'd been smoking made him giggle in a disquieting, paranoid fashion:

> A dream of the bony fingers of Azathoth reaching down to touch two cities in Imperial Japan and laying them waste. Mushroom clouds portending the arrival of the Fungi from Yuggoth.

To Armstrong, this drivel seemed only a poor attempt to turn Lovecraft into some latter-day Nostradamus, but San Isidro clearly thought otherwise. Armstrong wondered what López had to do with all this, and whether he would repudiate the so-called "prophecies" by sharing Lovecraft's trust in indefatigable rationalism. That would be ironic.

"How does all this tie in with López?" Armstrong said.

"In 1948," San Isidro slurred, "there were *unos brujos, se llamaban La Sociedad del Sol Oscuro,* and cheap *gringo* paperbacks of Love-

craft were their inspiration. They were interested in revival of worship for the old Aztec gods before they incorporated Cthulhu my-
thology. The gods of the two are much alike, no? *Sangre, muerte, y la
onda cósmica.* They tormented Barlow, suspected that's why he came
to Mexico, because of the connection. Barlow was a *puto,* he loved
to give it to boys, and soon they found out about the dream-diary.
That was the end. Blackmail. He killed himself in 1951, took a
whole bottle of Seconal."

"But what about López?"

"They had to wait *cincuenta años para que se alinearan las estrellas.*
Blood sacrifices, so much blood, the police paid off over decades.
But it was prophesied in his own dream-diary: *el espléndido regreso.*
Even the exact date was written in there. López was the chosen
vessel."

"How do you know all this, Juan?"

"I chose him from amongst us, but I betrayed them, the secret
was passed down to me, and now I need to get out of this *pinche*
country *rápido,* before *mis hermanos* come for me. López, he wants
to go back to Providence one last time"—San Isidro giggled again
at this point—"though I reckon it's changed a lot since he last saw
it, eh? But me, I don't care."

He's as insane as López, Armstrong thought. This is just an
elaborate scheme cooked up by the two of them to get money out
of someone they think of as simply another stupid, rich foreigner.
After all, what evidence was there that any of this nonsense had a
grain of truth in it? Like most occultists, they'd cobbled together a
mass of pseudo-facts and assertions and dressed it up as secret
knowledge known only to the "initiated." Christ, he wouldn't have
been surprised if, at this point, San Isidro produced a "Dream-
Diary of the Arkham Cycle," some artificially aged notebook written in the 1960s by a drugged-up kook who'd forged Lovecraft's
handwriting and stuffed it full of allusions to events after his death
in 1937. They'd managed to pull off a pretty fair imitation of his
stories between themselves and whoever else was involved in the
scam. The results were certainly no worse than August Derleth's
galling attempts at "posthumous collaboration" with Lovecraft.

At last, as if San Isidro had reached a stage where he had drunk
and smoked himself back to relative sobriety, he lurched up from
the easy chair in which he'd been sitting. He ran his fingers

through his beard, stared hard at Armstrong, and said:

"We need to talk business. How much are you going to give me?"

"I'll give you enough to get out of Mexico, for the sake of our friendship, but I can't pay for the stories, Juan. Anyway, someone has stolen them."

Probably you or López, he thought cynically.

The only reaction from San Isidro was that he raised his eyebrows a fraction. Without saying a word he went into the kitchen next door, and Armstrong could hear him rattling around in some drawers.

"If you're going to try to fleece me," Armstrong said, raising his voice so that he could be heard in the adjacent room, "then you and López will have to do better than all this Barlow and the 'Sodality of the Black Sun' crap."

When San Isidro came back into the room, his teeth were bared like those of a hungry wolf. In his right hand he was clutching a small-calibre pistol, which he raised and aimed directly at Armstrong's head.

"Cabrón, hijo de puta, di tus últimas oraciones, porque te voy a matar."

Sweat broke out on Armstrong's forehead. His thoughts raced. Was the gun loaded or was this only bravado? Another means of extorting money from him? Could he take the chance?

Just as Armstrong was about to cry out, everything went black. Despite the fact that it was the middle of the afternoon, with brilliant sunshine outside, the room was immediately swallowed up by total darkness. Armstrong could not believe what was happening. He thought, at first, that he had gone blind. Only when he stumbled around in the inky void and came right up against the window did he see the sunlight still outside, but not penetrating at all beyond the glass and into the room. Outside, the world went on as normal. He began to scream—

"Juan! Juan!"

Armstrong bumped into the sofa in a panic before he finally located the exit. From behind him came the sound of six shots, fired one after the other, deafeningly loud, and then nothing but a hideous silence more terrible than any sound. He staggered into the hallway and into the light, turned back once to look at the impenetrable darkness behind him, and then hurtled down the stairs.

He now gave no thought, as he had done when coming up, as to how precarious they were. He did, however, even in the grip of terror, recall that the building was deserted and that no one could swear to his having been there.

*

After what had happened to him, Armstrong expected to feel a sense of catastrophic psychological disorientation. Whatever had attacked San Isidro, he thought, carrying darkness along with it so as to hide its deeds, was proof of something, even if it did not prove that everything San Isidro had claimed was in fact true. At the very least it meant that the "Sodality of the Black Sun" had somehow called a psychic force into existence through their half-century of meddling with rituals and sacrifices. Armstrong had no choice but to discount the alternative rational explanation. At the time when day had become night in San Isidro's apartment he had been afraid, but nothing more; otherwise he was clear-headed and not prone to any type of hysterical interlude or hallucinatory fugue. Rather than feeling that his worldview had been turned upside-down, however, he instead felt a sense of profound loneliness. What had happened had really happened, but he knew that if he tried to tell anyone about it, they would scoff or, worse, pity him, as he himself would have done were he in their position.

Enrique and María returned to their apartment on schedule, and Armstrong told them of his intention to remain in Mexico City a while longer. They noticed the curious melancholy in him, but did not question him about it in any detail. Nor would he have told them, even if prompted. Armstrong moved out the next day, transferring his meagre belongings to a room in a seedy hotel overlooking La Calle de Bucareli. From there he was able to gaze out of a fifth-floor window in his *cuartito* and keep watch on the Café la Habana opposite. His remaining connection to the affair was with Felipe López, the man who had the mind of Lovecraft, and he could not leave without seeing him one last time. He had no idea whether San Isidro were alive or dead. What was certain was that it was inconceivable that he make contact with him. Were San Isidro dead, it would arouse suspicion that Armstrong had been connected with his demise, and were he alive, then Armstrong had little doubt that he'd want to exact revenge.

Days passed, and Armstrong's vigil yielded no results. There was no sign of López and he had no way of contacting him directly, no phone number, and no address. He was fearful that the Mexican police might call upon him at any instant, and he scanned the newspapers daily in order to see if there were any reports mentioning San Isidro. He found nothing at all relating to him and recalled what he'd been told about the authorities having been paid off with blood money over decades. When Armstrong left his room it was only to visit the local Oxxo convenience store in order to stock up on *tortas de jamón y queso, Faros, y tequila barato*. The last of these items was most important to him. He spent most of the time pouring the tequila into a tumbler and knocking it back, while sitting at his pigeon-shit stained window, hoping to see López finally enter the Café la Habana in search of him. All he saw was the endless mass of frenzied traffic, drivers going from nowhere to anywhere and back in a hurry, oblivious to the revelation that separated him from such commonplace concerns, and which had taken him out of the predictable track of everyday existence.

And then, twelve days after he'd rented the room in the hotel, he finally saw a slightly stooped figure in a grey suit making his way towards the Café la Habana. It was López—there could be no doubt about it.

*

López was seated in a table in the corner of the café, reading a paperback book and sipping at a cup of coffee. As Armstrong approached he saw that the book was a grubby second-hand copy of *Los Mitos de Cthulhu por H. P. Lovecraft y Otros*. The edition had a strange green photographic cover, depicting, it appeared, a close-up of a fossil. López immediately put down the volume once he caught sight of Armstrong.

"San Isidro seems to have disappeared off the face of the earth," he said. "I've been endeavouring to contact him for the last two weeks, but to no avail. I admit to feeling not a little concern in the matter. Have you crossed paths with him of late?"

Armstrong could not take his eyes off the man. Could "The Sodality of the Black Sun" have succeeded? Was the creature that conversed with him now actually the mind of Lovecraft housed in the body of some Mexican occultist called López? God, what a disappointment it must have been for them, he thought. What irony! To go to all that trouble to reincarnate the consciousness of the great H. P. Lovecraft, only to find that after his return he denied his own posthumous existence! But why keep such a survival alive, why allow the existence of the last word on the subject if it contradicted their aims? It made no sense.

"I'm afraid," said Armstrong, "that San Isidro has vanished."

"I don't see—" said López.

"Not all of Lovecraft came back, did it?" Armstrong said, interrupting. "I don't think they salvaged the essence, only a fragment. A thing with his memories, but not the actual man himself. Some sort of failed experiment. You're the one who's been leaving me those warning notes, aren't you?"

"You presume too much, Mr. Armstrong, and forget," replied López, "that I have not, at any stage, asserted that I believe myself to be anything other than the misguided individual called Felipe López."

"That's just part of the deception!" Armstrong said, getting to his feet and jabbing his finger at López. "That's what you *know* Lovecraft would have said himself!"

"How on earth could I be of benefit to the designs of an occult organisation such as 'The Sodality of the Black Sun' if I deny the very existence of supernatural phenomena? You make no sense, sir."

López's lips had narrowed to a thin cruel line upon his face, and he was pale with indignation. His voice had dropped to a threatening whisper.

Everyone in the Café la Habana had turned around to stare, stopped dreaming over their pipes, newspapers, and games of chess, and paused, their attention drawn by the confrontation being played out in English before them.

"The Old Ones are only now being born, emerging from your fiction into our world," Armstrong said. "The black magicians of 'The Sodality of the Black Sun' literally want to become them. Once they do, the Old Ones will finally exist, independent of their creator, with the power to turn back time, re-creating history to their own design as they go along."

"You, sir," said López, "are clearly more deranged than am I."

"Tell me about the notebook, Lovecraft! Tell me about your 'Dream-Diary of the Arkham Cycle'!" Armstrong shouted.

"There is no record of such a thing," López replied. "There are no indications that such an item ever existed amongst Lovecraft's papers, no mention of anything like it in his letters or other writings, no evidence for—"

"Tell me whether history is already beginning to change, whether the first of the Old Ones has begun manipulating the events of the past?"

As Armstrong finished asking his question he saw a shocking change come over López's features. Two forces seemed to war within the Mexican's body, and a flash of pain distorted his face. At that moment the whites of his eyes vanished, as if the darkness of night looked out through them. But then he blinked heavily, shook his head from side to side, and finally regained his composure. As he did so, his usual aspect returned. The change and its reversal had been so sudden that, despite its vividness, Armstrong could have just imagined it. After all, his nerves were already shredded, and he jumped at shadows.

"I can tell you nothing. What you are suggesting is madness," López said, getting to his feet and picking up the copy of the book he'd placed on the table. He left without looking back.

*

Armstrong did not return to London. He acquired a certain notoriety over the years as the irredeemably drunk English bum who could be found hanging around in the Café la Habana, talking to anyone who would listen to his broken Spanish. However, he was never to be found there after nightfall or during an overcast and dark afternoon. At chess, he insisted on playing white and could not bear to handle the black pieces, asking his opponent to remove them from the board on his behalf.

THE BLACK MOULD

The mould first appeared in a crater on a dead world at the rim of the universe. This world, with a thin atmosphere and a surface that comets and meteors had battered for millions of years, spun in a void of sunless dark. Perhaps it had been one of those comet collisions that had brought the mould into existence, some unique arrangement of molecules mutated by radiation and lying dormant in the comet's slushy ice, something waiting to awaken and grow. The mould may have taken aeons to reach maturity and begin the process of reproduction. But when it did so, it grew rapidly and spread unchecked over the surface of that dead world, across its valleys and craters and mountains, across the equator and from pole to pole.

Once it had conquered that first world the mould became conscious, such was its size and complexity. The billions upon billions of simple cells formed a network that developed into a debased, gigantic hive-mind. The mould experienced a progressively horrible sequence of nightmares, a spiral of nameless dread without a centre. Its form of consciousness did not include the faculty of reason, but was a unique faculty—that of derangement. And its monstrous visions grew more intense as it spread, ever more profound in their ineffable malignity.

When it had conquered that dead and distant world, after everything lay under its ghastly black embrace, its nightmares demanded that it reach out across the void. And so trillions of spores were ejected into space.

In the end it brought ghastly, complete darkness to that unknown quarter of cosmic space, for it learnt how to suffocate stars.

It was terror, deepening without cessation, that bore aloft the spores of the mould on their voyage through interstellar space. Nightmarish ecstasy was the soul of the mould. It hungered and sought to consume the universe itself. Its dread was of a nameless horror, a stark madness beyond imagination; an ultimate horror that lurked somewhere in the universe but which it could not yet identify.

The mould had no means of recognising any other form of consciousness apart from its own. As it reproduced, the nameless dread that assailed it became exponentially complex. It existed only in order to experience the ultimate nightmare, the heart of horror, the petrifying vision that ends only in oblivion. It was in the attempt to destroy itself that the mould consumed everything around it, and it dimly looked forward to a time when there was nothing left to consume, when the entire universe was laid waste, and it would wither and die for want of sustenance. It was one entity, eventually separated by the inconceivable vastness of the intergalactic void, and with each spore exhaled between worlds still a component of the whole. Its nightmares were communicated telepathically and were not slowed by the immensity of the cosmos. Dreams are swifter than light.

When the spores found a world, be it asteroid, moon, or planet, they would drift to its surface like soft rain and begin the process of assimilating whatever was found there. Where once there was a mighty empire with towers that reached to the heavens, soon after there were only ruins, and the black mould consumed the creatures of that world. Only husks remained as evidence that they had ever existed at all.

The ravages of the mould increased as it multiplied. As immeasurable time passed, countless galaxies bore the evidence of its all-conquering reign. Where there had been a multitude of worlds of differing aspects, of arid yellow deserts, of misty and scarred blue ice, of airless grey dust, now all were identical. All were blackened, their surfaces entirely smothered by the mould: canyons and mountains, plateaux and craters, cities and forests, ice and sand, even oceans (choked by a miasmal slime that conquered all incalculable depths). The mould flourished everywhere and anywhere. It mattered not if its habitat were a world of liquid methane or water, or a world roasting close to a star, or a world far flung out in space and frozen at absolute zero.

Astronomers on distant worlds looked on with dread at the development. Those that perceived it not, perished all the same. Multiform were the species of the universe, following different paths of evolution and modes of thought, though none were as the mould. But all those that looked outward at the universe felt wonder and terror, whether they were taloned crustaceans in a fungous jungle, cognisant machines of incredible technological complexity, or peace-loving sea mammals that gazed with dark eyes at the stars above the waters of an alien world. All knew the end was near and their kind would, ere centuries had passed, be consumed and then participate in the cosmic corruption of the mould.

One insignificant species amongst the many millions in the universe succumbed to the mould after vain attempts to resist its advance. This species, a nearly hairless race of anthropoids, habited the third planet orbiting an undistinguished star. The mould consumed the outer gas giants and the satellites of this solar system one by one. The simians watched with mounting terror as the spores drew inexorably nearer, moving unaccountably against the solar wind and turning the red desert planet in fourth orbit as black as the other outer worlds.

By the time the mould had reached the third planet's only satellite the hairless apes were in turmoil. Their civilisation was on the brink of anarchy, and they were close to destroying themselves. The light cast by the world's moon at night was no longer white but a deathly grey, shading to black, and becoming dim. It bore the same affliction that had reigned throughout all those galactic regions the mould had conquered. There were morbid ape poets who wrote verses to the contagion and seemed to welcome the insidious nightmares that foretold complete assimilation. But other apes, vainglorious followers of science, who fired rockets into the heavens, watched the explosions that took place on their moon with desperate hope. The satellite bore a hellish aspect, utterly unfamiliar to them. The mould had rendered it terrifying: like decay in a corpse.

And when the spores finally filtered down onto their own world, there were many more explosions and scenes of horror amongst the hairless apes as they turned on themselves, blaming one another for the failure to resist what was, after all, inevitable.

And it was not long before the streets of their cities were thick with the mould, not long before black slime ran in the water, not long before the anthropoids found the first patches of black ichors on their skins. And then the endless dreams came, just before the mould completely consumed the helpless simians.

As soon as the star of that solar system was overrun and suffocated, the spores progressed onwards, their numbers always swelled by the exhalations of the solar systems consumed before. Across the unknown stellar gulfs spread the contagion, never once halted in its expansion. There were other civilisations that tried to resist its advance, but all perished in the end. The most advanced ones, who had cunning and the available means, elected to flee before the mould's arrival. But even these were caught up with and consumed in the end. After aeons, all those who fled found that there was no longer anywhere left to hide.

The mould and its spores became omnipresent throughout the universe. The gas clouds and the gulfs of space were choked with spores. And yet, the mould had not achieved its goal. Although the entire universe had been laid waste and neither life nor thought existed, except for the mould and its exponential nameless dread, still it had not achieved the final petrifying vision that could terrify it into self-extinction.

And so the spores poured into those stars that had reached the final point of collapse, into the black holes scattered throughout the cosmos. The mould appeared in other universes and in every epoch across those other dimensions. It spread and adapted as voraciously as it had ever done, unchecked and irresistible, from the beginning until the end of all existence.

But the ultimate, petrifying vision could still not be glimpsed and the mould, now the supreme conqueror, dreamed on and on in its hideous majesty, doomed to re-experience its nameless dread forever; for it was the mould itself that was the ultimate horror, and of itself it had never dreamed.

It groped futilely, as one in darkness gropes for the light, backwards and forwards throughout all space and time, until all that had been, and all that was to be, fell under its dominion.

And there was to be no release from the nightmare.

THYXXOLQU

Owen Barclay's first encounter with the mystery occurred on the top deck of a number 134 bus as he travelled into work. He had been looking over one of the free London morning tabloids with mounting disgust, when the bus turned a corner and he caught sight of a roadside advertising hoarding opposite. He glanced up from the paper's photograph of pop star Julia Carnage falling out of a limousine drunk at four in the morning, and saw, through the rain-scarred window, the ad for a new brand of canned beans. It depicted a smiling young woman with a well-toned physique holding up a tin. There was nothing out of the ordinary about this, but what puzzled Barclay were the logo and the words above the image. They were in some foreign language, but the characters were not in Roman, Arabic, Cyrillic, Mandarin, Japanese, nor any other type of alphabet that he recognised. He supposed that it was some new kind of marketing gimmick, but the script intrigued him. Although he didn't recognise the language, it seemed somehow distantly familiar, and he had a strong sense of déjà vu, as if he'd once known it and had forgotten it until now.

The recollection bothered him during the day, and he thought of the ad when he should have been concentrating on the emails arriving from clients on his office computer. He stared at the screen in a dead fashion, not absorbing the information in front of him, his eyes glazing over, until he brought on a headache. He tried to clear the backlog of filing that had built up on his desk, but the sight of all the correspondence and having to go through it carefully made him nauseous. Something about the sight of words written in English was making him ill. It was only later in the day that he discovered the effect was not confined to English. A French client had sent him an email and, although Barclay was fluent in French (as well as in German, Spanish, and Russian), he could scarcely bring himself to go through the whole communication, even though it was a matter of contractual importance to the company.

Somehow, by shuffling papers aimlessly around his desk, Barclay got through the day, and he left the building harbouring a sense of resentment at the canned beans ad for having succeeded in embedding itself in his mind.

On the bus home, he took a window seat and readied his mobile phone to take a photo of the ad as he passed it by. He was determined to try and find some clue as to the meaning of the words in the unknown language. The bus slowed down in rush-hour traffic as it passed the roadside hoarding, and he captured a clear, crisp image. He scrutinised it during the whole of the journey, almost missing his stop.

Barclay prepared himself a light dinner and ate idly as he transcribed the words from the image stored in his mobile phone onto paper, and then rifled through his reference books in order to identify the language and decipher the meaning. He could find no trace of information about it.

After three hours of fruitless labour he was so angry at himself for dedicating time to what he now considered a worthless hoax and a definite marketing gimmick that he deleted the image from the phone, tore up the paper upon which he'd written down the mysterious characters, and gave up on the whole investigation. He couldn't bear to read any more of the novel he'd started a week before, since he suffered from a sudden return of the same word-sickness he'd experienced earlier in the day, and instead watched television until sleep crept up on him.

*

Travelling into work on the same bus route the next day, Barclay again scanned the tacky tabloid newspaper that was provided free of charge each morning. He told himself that he would only complete the crossword and would not, on this journey, allow himself to be annoyed by the celebrity gossip that infested its pages. But as he leafed through it, in search of the crossword, he stopped at an article that caught his eye. Unusually, it had no accompanying photo of a drunken reality TV star, a scantily clad footballer's wife, or even a pop singer with telltale traces of a white powder around their nostrils. But more unusually, it was written in an obscure language. Barclay could not be entirely certain, but he strongly suspected that it was the language of the billboard advertisement he'd seen yesterday. He carefully tore around the article and put the piece of paper into his pocket. He had no wish to carry the whole tabloid around with him for the rest of the day and run the risk of being mistaken for someone who had an interest in its drivelling contents. He wished, however, to retain a copy of the article itself, since he realised that the significance of this new language's appearance was not confined to a cheap marketing gimmick. Now that he had more than half a dozen words from which to make a comparison, he might even be able to find out more about it.

When the bus reached the corner where stood the billboard advertisement for canned beans, he saw that the one adjacent to it now sported a new ad for a brand of pills, delivering its message in the same mysterious language. Was it aimed, he thought, at some freshly arrived wave of immigrant workers from a cryptic corner of the European Union? During the last thirty years Barclay had seen the steady increase, from almost zero, of Turkish, Bangladeshi, Ethiopian, Polish, Jordanian, and many other shop signs in London. But ads in a foreign language were rarer. He recalled a few in Spanish and French, but those had been for imported beers.

He had no luck with the crossword. The clues appeared to make no sense to him, and he could scarcely comprehend what answers they were supposed to suggest. It was the first time that he had been defeated by one of them.

Later that day, in the office, as Barclay again tried to avoid looking at his computer screen, and during which gradually all correspondence on paper filled him with nausea, he noticed the T-shirt of one of his work colleagues as he passed by Barclay's desk. This employee, James Monck, had recently been on holiday abroad, but had come back pale and sickly as if he'd actually spent a few weeks in a windowless room shooting up heroin. The garment he wore was an ill-fitting brown T-shirt, about a size too small, and it clung to his emaciated torso like a tight second skin. But it was the circular blue lettering at the centre of the T-shirt that drew Barclay's attention. It wound around the silhouette of a town with a clustered multitude of steeples and domes. The lettering was in the obscure language that was appearing in his life on all sides.

"You picked that up on your holiday, did you?" Barclay asked him, pointing to his chest.

"That's right," Monck replied. "I hated to come back."

"Where did you go?" Barclay said.

"Just over the edge."

"Where did you buy the souvenir T-shirt? I don't recognise the language or the silhouette of the town."

"What, this?" Monck said. "Oh I got it in Qxwthyyothl."

Barclay's expression turned quizzical at the last word. "Which is where?" he asked.

"Qxwthyyothl is the capital city of Thyxxolqu."

Barclay took the article from his pocket that he'd torn out of the tabloid newspaper. He flattened out its crumpled surface and passed it over to Monck.

"Do you recognise this language?" he said, waiting as Monck examined the text.

"This is uxwqol in Thyxxolqus," Monck finally replied.

Barclay stared at him blankly.

"I said," Monck repeated, "this is written in Thyxxolqus, which is the language spoken in Thyxxolqu."

"What type of script is this? I've not seen anything like it before. It doesn't even look Indo-European in origin."

"I'm not an expert, and I wouldn't know."

Monck handed back the fragment from the newspaper.

"Are there many people from this country you visited in London, do you know?"

Monck grinned at the remark. His teeth appeared to be in the first stages of rot.

"Thyxxolqu yho quoxlu," he said, in a strangely guttural tone before abruptly turning on his heels and walking away.

Barclay wrote down the words he'd heard from Monck in phonetics, and managed to conquer his revulsion with the computer screen long enough to punch the characters into an Internet search engine. He tried as many different combinations of the rendering he'd made as he could think of, but none yielded results. The article itself, written in the Thyxxolqus script, was of no assistance to him, since it could not be rendered by any of the keyboard language options available on the computer.

*

After he had finished doing nothing in the office, Barclay stopped off at the British Library. He did not care much for the hard-angled building on the Euston Road that had replaced the old reading room beneath the mighty dome in the British Museum. His objections were not only architectural, for students who regarded it with, in Barclay's view, much less reverence than the former space constantly filled the new one. They treated it like a café or meeting place, and he was concerned that proper research had given way to its being used to spend time searching online via laptop computers or else to improve one's social circle on cyberspace. Barclay's reader pass was of long standing, and he was known by sight amongst the assistants and the security personnel, who waved him through with no more than a token glance at his card.

He consulted with the staff as to the correct volumes that might enable him to identify the script used in the article from the tabloid newspaper and was grateful for their assistance in seeking references to the language that Monck referred to phonetically as "Thyxxolqus." However, they were only able to suggest a number of indices from antique and almost-forgotten encyclopaedias that proved, after consultation, to be of no value. There was a single reference to Thyxxolqus (rendered as "Tyxxollqus") in a cross-reference to an obscure article reprinted in the 1862 edition of *The Collected Works of Thomas De Quincey*. It came from the October 1821 edition of the *London Magazine* and was written under the pseudonym "XYZ." The book contained this article (which was entitled "Voices from the Grave") but was kept off-site and could only be delivered the next day. Barclay requested the item anyway and resolved to return.

On the bus back home from the British Library, Barclay noticed a new development. Above the windows, on the curved angle of the wall before the ceiling, it was usual for the bus company to display advertisements. On this particular bus, they were all in what appeared to be Thyxxolqus. Moreover, someone sitting directly in front of Barclay was conducting, via his mobile phone, a staccato buzzing conversation in the same language. Once the conversation was over, Barclay could not refrain from lightly tapping the passenger on the shoulder and enquiring whether he could translate the advertisements, since he appeared to be a speaker of Thyxxolqus.

The man appeared a little confused by Barclay's interest and gaped at him momentarily as if he did not quite comprehend the request made to him in English.

Finally he responded.

"Do you mean to say huxxkl nyzzzt for yourself? Are you krhjxjk?"

"Where did you learn this language? Are you English?" Barclay replied, conscious that the two of them had drawn the surreptitious attention of all the other silent passengers.

"English? Of course I'm ghxcllu English! Hxchxc joke nyzzzt hythxxu off," he barked back.

An elderly Indian lady, dressed in a patterned sari, sitting alongside the passenger in front then joined in the conversation.

"Please," she said, "let's not jhjkzz, there's no juxxchu fzzzghal and I'm running chjuzzcu yho fghgrxx."

Behind him, Barclay heard more words spoken in Thyxxolqus and turned to see a teenage Spanish couple chattering to one another.

"Qué divertido mi amor. Nxhzzz uglaghk no habla jkgqixx."

Someone else said something in Thyxxolqus. Pure, undiluted Thyxxolqus. It was a small Japanese man clad in a pinstriped business suit. His beetling eyebrows were raised and a look of loathing crossed his face.

As Barclay watched his mouth open and close, forming the strange, guttural words, he saw that the Easterner's teeth were blackened stumps housed in yellow, rotting gums. This Japanese man with a decayed mouth then got to his feet and appeared intent on grabbing hold of Barclay. But after his first unsuccessful lunge, Barclay was already on his feet and hurtling down the steps to the ground floor of the bus. He pushed the emergency exit release button above the doors and jumped clear of the vehicle. Barclay had planned to take to his heels, losing himself in the crowds in the ticket hall of nearby Camden Town Underground Station. But he landed awkwardly, his head thumped against the cold concrete of the pavement, and he blacked out.

*

Barclay had a splitting headache, and his vision was slightly distorted. He rose swiftly into consciousness, adrenaline surging into his veins as the memory of what had happened flooded over him. He was lying on a trolley in what seemed to be a small room that smelt of antiseptic. Someone in a white coat was leaning over him and taking his pulse.

"No sudden movements, please," he said. "You've taken a nasty bump to the head. Concussion is quite likely."

Barclay's mind raced. He wanted to believe that the horrific images that assailed him were a nightmare brought on by the injury he'd sustained. He longed to believe that none of what he'd seen had been real. His blurred vision denied him a clear view of the face of the doctor who was close at hand. He could not make out the man's mouth as being anything but vague black smear, too indistinct to be discerned as either normal or monstrously decayed.

"I'm Doctor Pearce," he said. "You're in University College Hospital. Can you see how many fingers I'm holding up?"

Barclay squinted. It looked like three to him. The fingers swam in and out of focus. Three, well, maybe four.

"Swallow these tablets," the doctor said, "they'll put you to sleep for a while and we'll talk again in the morning. I want you to stay in overnight for observation. Just to be on the safe side."

He lifted Barclay's head, put a couple of pills into his mouth, and then brought a paper cup half full of water with which to wash them down.

Barclay gurgled, swallowed the tablets, and fell into a deep sleep shortly afterwards.

*

When he awoke, his head felt better and his vision had cleared substantially. He found himself in a deserted hospital ward. The beds were unmade and had been slept in and then abandoned only recently. He got up, clutched the white gown in which he was clad tightly to his body, and wandered barefoot across the cold linoleum on the floor. There was no one behind the nurse's desk in the middle of the ward. The only noise he could hear was coming from the corridor. As he approached the source, he recognised it as the sound of a television programme, and it seeped through the windowed door of a patients' recreation room. He opened the door and found himself inside a dingy space with several chairs and their occupants, all facing a television set mounted two-thirds of the way up the far wall.

The occupants, all patients in hospital gowns, were staring at the screen and miming along to the words being spoken by a news-reader. This broadcaster was talking, Barclay was certain, in Thyxxolqus. His mouth was deformed as if eaten away by decay. Moreover, the mouths of the patients listening were the same, like a soggy hole in a crumpled sheet of paper. Now he realised what the Thyxxolqu language reminded him of, as he listened to the swarm of people speaking it all at once. It was like the buzzing of infuriated bluebottle flies.

Barclay felt a hand grasp his shoulder. He turned around, and the man in the white coat who stood behind him leant forward and whispered into his ear. It was Dr. Pearce.

"Let's get out of here and find somewhere where we can talk."

They exited, took a couple of turns, and then Pearce let Barclay into an office. Once they were inside, he locked the door after him and slumped down into a wing-backed chair behind a desk. He drew out a packet of cigarettes from a drawer, offered Barclay one (who refused it), and then lit up. His hands were trembling and he coughed after the first drag. It looked as if he'd not smoked for a very long time.

"What do you think is going on?" the doctor said.

"What do *I* think is going on?" Barclay replied, suddenly feeling, given the circumstances, ridiculously self-conscious in his patient's gown. He was arrested by the thought that this might be an examination of his own mental state. Had the doctor seen what he had seen?

"I've known nothing like it," Pearce said. "The disease, or whatever it is, appears to be airborne, attacks orally, and causes rapid and massive cellular degeneration."

Barclay exhaled, letting out an audible sigh of relief.

"I'm not even sure," Pearce continued, "that it's a disease at all. I've been up all night, taking blood samples from patients afflicted with it. There's no trace of invading bacteria, no trace of a virus. And yet, the symptoms point towards leprosy or something of that ilk. It's like the ghost of a disease possessing people."

"The unearthly language they're speaking," Barclay replied— "that seems to be the key."

"Do you know," said Pearce, "I believe that the corruption allows the infected to articulate the language more clearly than uncorrupted mouths. I wonder if it doesn't go right down into the throat, affecting the larynx and the voice box. What if the language is the disease itself?"

"I can't follow what you're saying. How can a disease be a ghost, how can language affect the material world?" Barclay, having felt a surge of relief at the fact that Pearce was able to share his comprehension that something had gone horribly wrong with the world, now felt disoriented at the bizarre explanation Pearce had formulated.

"I think the process begins in the mind. And then it goes on to alter the brain. You see? If one is able to recognise what's happening, it is the first sign xxghixh of one's having been infected. One is first only aware that the language exists, and only later does one begin to comprehend its meaning. You and I must be in the first stages of the disease."

"But what of Thyxxolqu and Qxwthyyothl?"

"They are the xxtghzz names for death and disease. Xxguxxh familiar, we are on the edge of a great revelation one that dfgxx immaterialism in an insane mind gzzzh . . ."

Pearce's mouth hung open. His tongue bubbled with a mixture of saliva and blood. One side of his mouth then drooped fantastically, all the way to his jawline. His lower teeth and gums were visible and had become brownish fragments set in rotting flesh. He put his hand up and rested it over the deformity, covering the awful sight, in an act of denial and self-consciousness. He tried to smoke from the other side of his mouth and carry on as if nothing were amiss. Barclay was pained by the horror and absurdity of it.

Pearce got up from behind the desk, walked past Barclay, unlocked the door, and opened it wide. He acted silently, and his eyes flashed towards the aperture, indicating that Barclay should leave.

Once Barclay had returned to the still-deserted ward, he took his clothes from the locker adjacent to the bed he had occupied, dressed, and made his way out of the hospital.

*

It was not far from University College Hospital to the British Library, just a six-minute walk along the Euston Road. Barclay tried hard to retain his composure as he set off for his destination, clinging to the idea that if he acted normally, then he might keep absolute terror at bay. He told himself it was vital that he consult the article by De Quincey as he had planned.

All around him, however, the evidence of unearthly intrusion intensified. The adverts on the side of taxis and buses, the road signs, the foreign restaurants, and the language that people spoke into their mobile phones was undiluted Thyxxolqus. It had completely replaced all other languages. He tried to avoid looking at the faces of people, but despite this he was conscious, out of the corner of his eye, that nine in ten of them suffered from deformed mouths.

He crossed the plaza outside the British Library, with its titanic statue modelled upon William Blake's drawing of Newton, and entered through the heavy glass doors. He took the escalator up to the first-floor humanities reading rooms and went inside. The attendants at the desk, with mouths like caves, waved him through as usual, casting the merest glance at his pass, and it was only as he returned it to his wallet that Barclay noticed that its lettering was no longer in English.

He collected the book, volume four of *The Collected Works of Thomas De Quincey* that he'd ordered, and took his place at one of the long rows of the readers' desks. He looked left and right over the shoulders of the other readers between whom he sat and saw that the volumes they were consulting were written in Thyxxolqus. The language had spread into the books, transforming the texts, working its way like a virus through them all.

Barclay turned to the section of the De Quincey tome containing the article "Voices from the Grave" and read the following passage:

> Of the origins of language itself we can give no authoritative account, for speech predates writing and is lost in the period antediluvian. The academies are silent on the matter. And yet, is not language the most incredible aspect of humanity? Is it not the most suggestive of a great mystery? The written forms of antiquity do not suffer in comparison with modernity. They are in no wise inferior, even unto the earliest. They sprang, fully formed and with equal complexity, from the mysterious source whereof I

assert. Words, then, savour of the ineffable and are proof that this cosmos is not easily explained. In this instance we, all benighted, continually regard what is miraculous as merely commonplace by virtue of its extreme familiarity.

Language is the foundation of reality. Without it we would, like the beasts, exist wholly in a world of sensation. We should not be articulate, but be cast adrift from the essence of creation, unable to fathom its infinite depths. And in considering this matter, I cannot refrain from expressing a philosophic speculation that has arisen from out of gazing into that abyss. In what language do the dead converse? Are they freed from the multitude of tongues to which the living are shackled? Do they speak a language (let us call it Txxyollqus) whose meaning contains all possible meanings since their mode of being is outside space and time?

Barclay finished the sentence and closed the book. He left the reading room and went outside in order to gurgle and spit some water from one of the loo washbasins. His mouth was suddenly suffused with a coppery taste.

The sound of conversation amongst people milling around in the first-floor area was in stark contrast to the silence of the reading room. He caught snatches of talk as people passed by and was astonished to find that he could now understand every word perfectly. Moreover, they were conversing of matters fantastically complex and yet rendered lucid by the words they used. Barclay delighted in the awful play of meanings within meanings revealed. He pulled open the door to the men's loo, turned a corner, and came face to face with his reflection in a mirror above the washbasins. His mouth, unsurprisingly, was now quite as deformed as everyone else's.

He had left the book by De Quincey at the desk and could not wait to return to it. He would sit all day in the library staring at it, if need be, until such time as its text was rendered into Thyxxolqus and yielded up even greater revelations.

REGINA VS. ZOSKIA

A blast of cold, damp air outside Chancery Lane Underground Station was sucked down into the depths of the ticket hall and the surrounding passageways. Dunn met its full force as he was carried upwards towards the surface by the escalators. He found the wind refreshing after the sweaty confines of the train and the platforms. However, once he'd emerged onto High Holborn and into the grey morning, all it did was to chill him and increase his dissatisfaction. He glanced at his watch. It was just after ten A.M.

He was already thirty minutes late for the office, despite trying to make up time by catching the tube from Bank instead of walking. At least his boss, Mr Horace Jackson, was rarely in before 10.15 on a Tuesday morning. He was carrying on a relationship with his legal secretary, Miss Jenkins, and usually stayed over at her place on Monday nights, dragging himself into the Gray's Inn chambers in her wake so as not to arouse suspicion. The fact that Dunn obviously knew about the affair anyway seemed not to worry Jackson as much as the need to not acknowledge that such was the case.

He doubted that Jackson would arrive for another ten minutes at least.

The archway next to The Cittie of Yorke pub was dripping wet, and two barristers in periwigs and black gowns sheltered in the short passageway beneath, smoking cigarettes. Both glared at Dunn with inhuman eyes as he passed by, snarling as if they were a couple of Doberman guard-dogs.

He crossed the square, which he could not help associating in his mind with a vast prison courtyard, and passed through a long narrow passageway, until he finally stood beneath the soot-caked tenement that housed 7B Coney Court Chambers. Jackson's offices occupied two small rooms on the top floor, and Dunn's heart sank as he gazed up and saw that the lights above were already lit to ward off the morning's twilight gloom. The old lawyer had arrived before him.

Dunn began to climb the circular flight of stairs that led to the attic chambers. The wooden steps were hollowed over hundreds of years by the tread of visitors, though none wearier than the man who now made the ascent. Doubtless, Dunn thought, Jackson would be sitting behind his desk facing the panelled entrance door, drumming his podgy fingers on the desktop and staring at the clock. A little vein on his right temple, close to one of his bushy eyebrows, would be pulsing with resentment. Emily Jenkins would be sitting in the adjoining office, clad as usual in a tight pinstriped skirt suit, applying makeup, somewhat tired after satisfying Jackson's desires the night before.

Dunn passed the landings and the entrances to the other chambers, F, E, D, C, and then reached the top where A and B faced one another. He paused to catch his breath and put his ear to the door. He heard the muffled sounds of Jackson and Jenkins flirting with each other.

Dunn took a step back and lost his footing, his shoes clattering against the stairs behind him. Almost at once the door flew open and the corpulent figure of the white-haired Jackson appeared. He glared at Dunn ferociously from behind bifocal eyeglasses. The vein on his temple seemed fit to burst.

"Well," he thundered, "Mr Dunn! Good of you to grace us with your presence at last!"

"Sorry," Dunn mumbled. "The trains, Mr Jackson, delays on the Central Line . . ."

Jackson stood back and crooked his finger at Dunn signalling him to enter.

"I'm not interested in your excuses Mr Dunn. As I've told you before, if you left earlier for work you'd be here in plenty of time."

Dunn's desk was situated in the corner of Jackson's office, squeezed into a little nook beneath a sagging shelf weighed down with dozens of dusty legal tomes and briefs bound with red ribbons. It looked as if it might collapse at any moment in an avalanche of pages infested with bookworms and silverfish and crush anyone stupid enough to sit under there.

As Dunn settled himself into his ramshackle chair, Jackson shifted from foot to foot like an ape that was ill-at-ease standing upright for long periods.

"Don't get too comfortable," he said. "While you were idling your way to the office I received a telephone call from our client, Dr Zoskia. We've got to visit the premises and pick up a new series of documents relating to the 'Regina vs. Zoskia' case. I suppose that we'll have to drive there and should leave in about ten minutes or so. They want us by eleven."

Wiping his mouth with the back of his hand so as to disguise a nervous smirk, Dunn nodded his head in agreement. Regina vs. Zoskia was an interminable case that he had only ever heard Mr Jackson mention obliquely, and of which he had scant knowledge. Certainly it had been dragging on for many years and, in an unguarded moment, Miss Jenkins had once hinted to him that it was this case alone which enabled Jackson to continue with his legal practice. Gigantic fees were involved. It had been thus since the time of Jackson's own father, also a solicitor, who had originally taken on the defendant's case on a plea of justification. Dunn thought of it as strangely akin to "Jarndyce vs. Jarndyce."

"I'll need you to navigate," Jackson said, as the effort of standing finally overwhelmed him and he slumped into the leather-upholstered chair. "I too easily get lost in all these stupid modern one-way systems."

Miss Jenkins giggled. It seemed to be a private joke.

*

"I know," Jackson said, changing up from third to fourth gear with a convulsive motion, "that you're probably full of curiosity about the 'Regina vs. Zoskia' case. Well, there's no secret about the thing. It's just a bit confusing, that's all, and it's been going on for a very very long time."

Jackson's battered old motorcar, a Jaguar XJS model that had seen much better days, sped along the dual-carriage way. Its interior was dank with the smell of stale cigars. Dunn looked up from the street-map nestled on his knees.

"I expect," Jackson grumbled, "that the case will finish me off. It did my father. Not that the family hasn't made a pretty penny from it, mind. We certainly have; it's just that—well, it can be easily misunderstood. But it's important. More important than anything else in our files."

There was a weird tone in the old man's voice. It was as if he were opening up to Dunn, cautiously of course, but without any trace of the scorn that had so often characterised his speech.

"Um," said Jackson, "it'll be clearer when we arrive there. I won't be around forever, you know, Dunn. Not getting any younger. Might be better if you did this trip in future."

Dunn's sense of confusion deepened. He looked at Jackson with an expression of complete bafflement.

"I'm really sorry, Mr Jackson, but what you're saying makes no sense to me."

"Not surprised. When I was first told about it I can remember being as confused as you must be."

The car was passing through a particularly desolate part of the city. All the shops were boarded up. Flanking the sides of the road were great expanses of run-down housing estates. Their tenants seemed to have departed some years ago. It looked as if the entire region had nothing to expect from the future except a merciful wave of demolitions.

Jackson's fingers worked along the panel of the car radio, and he adjusted its FM wavelength. His middle digit was adorned by a garish onyx signet ring with his initials inlaid in gold. Dull static issued from the speakers. For some reason Jackson appeared to enjoy listening to this crazy, meaningless noise, and he kept it on in the background during the whole of the trip.

"It's just around this bend," Jackson said, the first words he'd spoken for several minutes. "Up there on the hill. It'll come into view any moment now."

The series of dreary housing estates on either side of the road had begun to thin out, and what few buildings that had been erected (either unfinished or abandoned) were overrun with weeds. The whole area reminded Dunn of those seemingly endless bombsites in the Docklands before the mass redevelopment during the 1980s. Then the hill came into view. It was covered with a profusion of bare trees, their long thin branches swaying in the wind, appearing to rake the leaden sky like claws. At the very summit, above the top of the trees, one could see a domed and weather-beaten clock tower of Byzantine design.

"Impressive, isn't it?" Jackson said. "You know, back in the 1960s, they put the inmates to all sorts of tasks."

"What do you mean, inmates?" said Dunn.

"Well, it started off as an insane asylum and now . . . let's just say it's something else altogether. The director of the place, Dr. Zoskia, believed in collective therapy, in a self-sufficient community formulating its own diagnoses and ethos."

"How did our firm become involved with them?"

"When the inmates decided they no longer wished to be classified as insane. They've been challenging the legal basis on which the definition rests for the last forty-odd years. Dr. Zoskia contends that the hospital is for the sane and that it is the outside world that is occupied by the mentally disturbed. Proving this contention in law became the 'Regina vs. Zoskia' case."

"Surely it's obvious whether or not these people are crazy? If they can't function in society—"

"It's not just that. The thing is that they've trained themselves not to sleep. They're suspicious of those who do. Some of the inmates in that place have been awake, non-stop, for several years. They've been using sleep deprivation to break down the barriers between so-called sanity and madness."

The car exited the dual carriageway at the next junction. The turnoff itself was not signposted, and the pockmarked road the vehicle ascended had vegetation growing out of its cracks and hollows. The banks on either side were not properly maintained, and wild foliage blurred the boundaries between the road and its surroundings. The climb was steep and tortuous, and Jackson had to drive at a crawl in first gear, brake often, and occasionally reverse to avoid the wheels and axles becoming entangled in roots and vines.

The road terminated at the entrance to the Zoskia Establishment. A high lopsided wall crowned with barbed wire enclosed it. Most of the crumbling brickwork was home to a rapacious species of ivy. The entrance gates were rusted and hung at an absurd angle due to uneven subsidence, and were sealed by a huge padlock and chain wound between its central bars. Beyond was a gravel driveway that curved out of sight.

"We're expected. Don't worry, they're all harmless" Jackson mumbled. "We just need to give the right signal to get into the place."

He sounded the car's horn three times in quick succession and then two times in longer bursts. There was silence for a couple of minutes, after which Dunn heard footsteps coming along the path, crunching across the gravel in an uneven, slow rhythm. An aged woman dressed in a patient's gown appeared behind the gates and peered at them with bulging blue eyes that seemed too large for their sockets. Her face was skeletal and fissured by a confusion of deep-set lines. A few strands of stray dark-grey hair hung down across an emaciated cheek; the rest of it was tied back in a ponytail. She was horribly thin and looked more like a scarecrow than a woman. Her feet were bare and filthy. Her arms and legs were little more than skin covering bones.

Jackson waved at the grisly apparition.

"That's Dr Zoskia," he said. "She hasn't changed a bit."

Dunn said nothing by way of response. He sat there staring in dumb astonishment.

Zoskia took out a key from a pouch at the front of her dirty smock and unlocked the chain binding the gates closed. She dragged open one of the huge portals so that Jackson's car could pass through. As the car rolled slowly forward across the gravel drive, Dr Zoskia opened the back door and clambered inside the vehicle, carrying with her the cloying scent of cheap perfume and an under-odour of stale sweat. She mumbled something to Jackson that sounded as if she had said: "You can fuck me later as well if you like." Dunn turned to look at Dr Zoskia and found that her face was a mask of innocent vacancy.

Once they were inside the walls Dunn had his first glimpse of the hidden citadel in its entirety. Between the overgrown foliage that covered the grounds Dunn saw several low buildings in a ruinous state of dilapidation. They seemed to be former chalets, shops, and other outbuildings. There were even deserted tennis courts.

In the centre of these weird holiday camp ruins was an abandoned Olympic-size swimming pool filled with stagnant, weed-choked water. Discarded objects had been dumped there; a few mattresses, a wheelchair, what looked like an old operating table, and a couple of filing cabinets. On the far side, a man sat on the edge of the deep end of the pool, clad in a doctor's white coat. He was kicking his feet back and forth in the swamp, licking his lips and laughing inanely at the splashes he made. He had long black hair and a grizzled beard that grew down to the top of his chest. The man was like some mad Russian mystic from the Tsarist era.

Elsewhere there were the remains of huge pyres, blackened

mounds of vats, drums, and jars. All manner of junk was littered in the spaces between the tall, bare trees: broken chairs and benches, discarded and battered respiratory apparatus, head restraints, and other surgical appliances.

The main building lay straight in front of them. Dunn now saw the whole structure supporting the Byzantine clock tower that had been visible back on the dual carriageway. It was an immense four-storey building at the centre of over fifty acres of land. Parts of the sloping, tiled roof had caved in, and many of the arched windows were either completely broken or riddled with cracks. The white paintwork was peeling away from the outside walls, driven from the brickwork underneath by weathering and an untreated infestation of mould.

The car pulled up beside the steps to the front entrance—a rotting faux-Greek portico whose pillars were strangled by half-dead vines. As the three of them got out of the vehicle Zoskia said, "Let me show you inside."

With Zoskia leading the way, they passed into what had once been a reception area. However, no one manned the admissions desk and the tiled floor was littered with empty tins of food, torn and soiled clothing, used syringes, and broken chairs.

Jackson and Zoskia began to discuss the new documents that the latter had collated as evidence for the interminable court case. Zoskia gestured towards objects on the other side of the hall. A pile of six cardboard boxes sat at the foot of the stairs leading to the upper floors. The advertising logos on the sides showed them to have once contained cans of baked beans. They had since been scrawled over with a black marker pen. The childish handwriting read "INPORTENT LEEGUL PAYPAS FUR RE-JINA/ZOSKIA."

Dunn wandered around the chamber as the other two spoke and was drawn to a huge poster, yellowing with age. Its edges curled away from the wall. It had been displayed up there for decades, no doubt. He could scarcely believe that what he had seen was not an absurd joke:

THE ZOSKIA REFUGE FOR THE TRULY SANE
THE CURSE OF SLEEP DAMNS THE OUTSIDE WORLD

"If you wish to take a look around Dunn, go ahead," Jackson called from the other side of the hall. "We've got one or two details to iron out."

"Try not to get lost, though," Dr Zoskia added.

Dunn nodded back at them as he picked his way around the debris. Although he feared for his own safety, he also felt a sense of irresistible curiosity to see more of this bizarre community. He passed through a double-door with portholes and then entered a long, deserted corridor. This took him deep into the heart of the institution. On both sides of the passageway were cell doors hanging off their hinges, and beyond, in shadow, the inmates' rooms. The doors looked to have been torn open from outside. Dunn peered into the interiors and could make out graffiti scrawled on the walls, all manner of useless junk, and one or two human forms crouching in the corners. These figures chattered away, holding paranoid conversations with themselves in eerie, discordant accents. The stench from these cells was almost overpowering—a mixture of sweat, shit, and urine. Dunn had to cover his mouth and nose with a handkerchief to prevent himself from gagging.

After passing through a series of unlocked doors further along the corridor, he reached some kind of shipping warehouse deep inside the building.

The interior was a mass of activity. Oblong wooden crates lay scattered and piled up on the bare floorboards, and inmates in hospital gowns fussed over the objects. They were too intent upon their work to pay any attention to Dunn as he mingled with them. He was overcome by a mixture of nausea and horror at the scene and felt as if he had stumbled onto the set of an expressionist horror film.

There were dozens of emaciated people working in the chamber. They were all quite obviously mentally disturbed. Their eyes were either dead or manic and surrounded by deep black rings. Yet despite this they laboured as a well-drilled unit. A corner of this vast chamber was filled with banks of manual typewriters. The inmates who worked away on them by candlelight were wholly absorbed in their tasks. In fact, as he drew closer Dunn saw very clearly that the crumpled papers they produced were passed on to the examiners. After glancing at their contents, they raised the crates' lids and inserted the bundles of documents.

Dunn had forgotten about Horace Jackson. Zoskia was, however, now close at hand and looking over a pile of papers covered with a mass of gibberish. The typewriters used here were out of date and rusty, with many missing some of their letter keys. Dunn saw examples of the texts being produced: they were schizophrenic ravings typed upon stacks of old HMSO affidavit forms.

"Listen," Zoskia said, "Jackson told me to tell you he'd arranged for you to take over from him. He was persuaded to retire, to stay and seek refuge from the world."

"To seek refuge from the world? You mean *here*?" Dunn replied. He had to lean a hand against the table to steady himself.

"Yes," Zoskia babbled, sucking at a toothless gap in her gums, "he agreed that he might as well stay. Anyway, we felt he had lost interest in our case. Lack of enthusiasm over time. No good to us outside anymore"

"Look," Dunn said, "I want no part of this, no matter what Mr Jackson's decided. I'm going back."

"You will live in that world of darkness for a myriad of years and no one will know of your existence," she said.

Without responding, he turned away from Dr Zoskia and caught a glimpse of four inmates carrying a heavy crate into the warehouse. Something stuck out of the gap between one of its sides and an ill-fitting, bent lid. Before he had time to think about what he'd seen, an inmate pushed the obtrusion back inside the box. It appeared to have been a lifeless, flabby hand.

"The legal papers are in the boot of Jackson's car. You'll do your job, you'll carry on with our case, and anyway you have no choice. Everyone has to make sacrifices, don't they?"

*

Dunn returned to the offices alone using Jackson's car. He had one of the porters of the Inn assist him in carrying the boxes of legal documents up to the top-floor offices of Coney Court Chambers.

Miss Jenkins expressed no surprise at the sudden transfer of power from Jackson to Dunn. Over the next few days, as he took over the running of his former employers' legal practice, she even began to flirt with him. There was no difficulty in the matter of Dunn now assuming full control over business affairs. Amongst the papers he had brought back from the Zoskia Institution was a codicil signed by Jackson naming him as sole beneficiary.

Despite his horrible experiences, Dunn realised that it was in his own interests to maintain at least the pretence of continuing to pursue the Regina vs. Zoskia case. As well as taking over Jackson's less-than-onerous workload, he was also to benefit from additional income provided by the terms of the codicil, provided he remain. However, the immediate consequence of this was that he had to examine the papers he'd brought back with him from the pseudo-asylum, correlate their contents, and determine how useful they were in relation to previous statements already bearing on the case. So, working at home on the papers until well into the morning, Dunn sat up every night for the next two weeks in his little flat hidden away in a maze of railway arches, renovated warehouses, and alleyways close to Fenchurch Street Station in the City. The gibberish he was forced to read coincided with the onset of a prolonged case of insomnia. At least it spared him from nightmares about the Zoskia Institution.

Dunn's flat, which he had been bequeathed by his uncle Charlie, whom he had met only a few times as a child, was situated within the attic of a mouldy building. Perhaps this had been his late uncle's idea of a joke, for the place was scarcely fit for human habitation. Dunn doubted whether his relation had ever used it during his banking career, though an aunt dropped hints that a prostitute with whom Charlie had become infatuated during his last years had lived there. She'd been forced to vacate the place after his death. Weird, unwelcome legacies seemed to have become a defining feature of Dunn's life. He had no choice when it came to his career and home.

The ceiling of the flat was low and the passageways cramped. From the dusty back window Dunn had a view over the small, hidden churchyard of St. Olaf's. A high brick wall topped with iron spikes hemmed in the burial ground. On a triangular lintel above the gateway there was a bas-relief depicting three horribly grinning skulls. These three were, to Dunn's mind, a most effective reminder of mortality. The churchyard was overrun with weeds and half a dozen stunted trees. Close to the edges of the wall lurked shapeless grave-mounds, eroded by centuries of weathering. The tombstones were lopsided, the names of those whom they commemorated

obliterated by circles of lichen. The buildings that surrounded the
churchyard were all like that one in which Dunn had been forced
to dwell, half-derelict and threatened with demolition and urban
redevelopment. What businesses had operated from the premises
had crept away to healthier environs over the course of the last few
decades. Yet for some unaccountable reason, the tenements still
stood, overlooked monuments to decay and neglect, in defiance of
all the glass and steel skyscrapers in whose shadows they hid.

During one of those long nights, as he laboured into the small
hours of the morning poring over certain of the statements, Dunn
happened to glance out of the smoky window that overlooked the
churchyard. That night was lit by a full moon. Down amongst the
ancient tombstones and the weeds he saw a group of figures digging up a patch of the mouldering soil with spades. Resting against
one of the stunted trees was a ladder that they had doubtless
hauled in after them once they were inside. Somehow the men had
also managed to get a crate over the wall despite the spikes. It
seemed that their purpose was not to disinter one of the graves,
but rather to bury the oblong wooden box.

Dunn watched their activities with a horrified fascination. He
thought of calling the police and was on the verge of getting up to
do so when one of the figures happened to glance upward, giving
Dunn a clear view of his face in the silvery moonlight. His skin was
dead white, the features framed by long black hair and a grizzled
beard that grew down to the top of his chest. It was the man he'd
seen by the swimming pool in the Zoskia Institution, the man with
the appearance of a mad Russian mystic. He was laughing without
making a sound, like an actor in a silent movie. He gestured to one
of his companions, and between them they levered open the lid of
the oblong crate. Dunn knew that, for whatever bizarre reason, this
mummers' play was being performed for his benefit.

Inside the crate was a mass of papers. Dunn could see a ruinous face, protruding like the tip of an iceberg from the turbulent
sea of crumpled pages.

Dunn could not tear his gaze away. He didn't doubt that it was
a warning from his clients. Then a bank of thick cloud passed over
the moon, plunging the churchyard into total darkness.

Later, exhaustion must have overtaken him, for he awoke just
after dawn slumped at his desk and surrounded by papers from the

Regina vs. Zoskia case. As if in a trance, he descended the narrow staircase to the streets, turned the corner, and passed into the churchyard via the gateway from whose lintel leered down the three carved skulls. At the spot where the men had been digging, there was now a small mound of freshly turned soil. Dunn was under no illusion that what he witnessed last night was a dream, or even some hallucination brought on by overwork and lack of sleep. Although there was not a single scrap of paper littering the churchyard, he spied a glinting object nestling in a clump of weeds that confirmed his worst fears. It was a signet ring with a large onyx stone into which were engraved the gilded initials "H. J."

*

A few days later Henry Dunn stood upon the mosaic pavement of the immense central hall of the Royal Courts of Justice in the Strand. Heavy rain lashed at the high windows and cast a funereal gloom over the interior. He was relieved to be inside and out of the downpour, for the great clock tower and arcaded front were so drenched that the whole structure seemed to have lately risen from watery depths. The members of the legal profession who passed by Dunn cast baffled looks at the dishevelled, soaked little man who stood regarding a painting of the Anti-Slavery Convention of June 1840 with a distracted air.

Down the maze-like corridors of that imposing Gothic pile, with more than a thousand rooms and containing over three and a half miles of passageways and stairs, there is an out-of-the-way little chamber with green tiles on its walls. It is unknown to all but a handful of those who use the law courts. Dunn had only learned of its existence since examining the gigantic brief for the Regina vs. Zoskia case. This chamber was part of an almost forgotten division of the law courts, one scarcely used but still forming a tiny, rusty cog in the vast machine of the English legal system. It was to this room that Dunn made his way, clutching his heavy leather bag stuffed with typewritten papers. His boots left sodden footprints in his wake.

Dunn had to consult the hastily scrawled map previously prepared by Jackson when he had been obliged to make the same navigation of the Law Courts' innermost recesses in search of the green chamber. Most of the offices Dunn passed were long aban-

doned, and there were even a number of ghostly Victorian court-
rooms given over to decay; relics from another epoch, their docks,
benches, and galleries occupied solely by shadows. He walked
alone, not having seen another person on similar business for the
last twenty minutes. The lighting was atrocious. Many of the lamps
were broken and those that worked seemed to emit only a dim, often intermittent, glow. The arched ceilings and Gothic niches, the
narrow flights of worn steps, the echoing and serpentine corridors
lined with cracked tiles—they seemed to be endless. Certain passageways even led nowhere, save to darkness. If Dunn had not
been in possession of the map he believed it likely he would never
have been able to retrace his path out of the labyrinth.

The dereliction around him reminded Dunn uncannily of the
Zoskia "Asylum." He realised that here, in the bowels of the Law
Courts, the flip side of the interminable case was revealed: an official legislature as deranged as his clients' and their inner sanctum.
Plaintiff and Defendant were distorted mirror-images of each other, unyielding, forever locked in a grotesque dance, each attempting
to overcome their nemesis whilst in their own death-throes.

Finally, Dunn reached his destination. He stood in front of a
panelled door on which a notice hung. It was written on a foolscap
sheet of aged paper and was held in place by a single nail. Scribbled
on the sheet were the words:

"Regina vs. Zoskia 1964, 7 Q.B. 323. Master of the Rolls, Lord
Justice Hirsig, presiding."

Dunn knocked on the door twice and heard a muffled voice
from within. He supposed it indicated that he was to enter.

It was so gloomy inside the green-tiled room that his vision
took a few moments to adjust. Then he saw the legal briefs everywhere, some piled in towers tottering under their own weight, others massed in scattered heaps. Yet more loose papers littered the
floor, ankle-deep, and Dunn could not avoid trampling through
them as he advanced into the cramped, vaulted chamber. On impulse, he bent down to pick up a random handful of the pages,
scrutinising them as best he could in the appalling light. One passage read:

"—such application of the hidden laws of the universe being
incomprehensible to men even though their strict enforcement is
imperative—"

This is a rubbish-dump, Dunn thought, for all the paperwork connected with the Regina vs. Zoskia case. He stifled a hysterical laugh that bubbled up in his throat.

A faint rustle in the sea of papers to his left made him start. Someone appeared to have been buried underneath a heap of rotting affidavits, summonses, and writs. Dunn saw a shoe and part of a leg sticking out from the bottom of the pile and began clearing away the papers hiding the rest of the body. He uncovered an old man, his face squashed with age, his skull almost turned to jelly. The ancient was toothless and his uncannily bulging eyes were closed. He was dressed in a judge's legal garb, dusty black robes and a periwig. However, a vestige of life still remained in his carcass, for he murmured something and Dunn bent down to catch the words. Drool oozed from the revenant's puckered lips as he spoke in a voice like dried leaves:

"Henry Dunn acting for both the Plaintiff and the Defendant, what have you to say?"

The judge opened his eyes to reveal that the sockets had been hollowed out and then stuffed with crumpled paper balls covered in writing. Perhaps the whole of his cranium had been filled with brittle documents.

Dunn removed a huge brief in a buff folder bound with red ribbon from his bag. He began to present his case—both for and against. He scarcely noticed that he was no longer sane, at least in any recognisable sense of the word.

THE AGE OF DECAYED FUTURITY

Last night I finished work on my fourth novel. It is my greatest achievement, I think.

It was an incredibly untidy business. The results are scattered about all over this room in a hotel by the Baltic Sea, and I really must collate the myriad pages. I have been a victim of that unique mental fever from which only writers suffer. It is a malady brought on by a combination of a retreat into an inner world of the imagination and too much intense concentration. In this state the real world loses substantiality and dreamlike visions from the depths of imagination take over completely.

I really had no idea just how quickly and intensively I would work. My first three novels had each taken at least two years to finish. Yet here I am surrounded by the first draft of my fourth after only two weeks. True, I have slept very little. But, above all, it was inspiration that took hold. Though perhaps *inspiration* is too weak a word for it. Let's say, more precisely, *synchronicity*.

For it was here that I learnt of the Reassembly Cartel.

In six months I had written nothing, and it is upon my literary products that my continued existence is dependent. The reputation I had established floundered, and my agent Leszek Choszcz had almost given up hope that any more worthwhile work would appear from my pen. My past books were out of print and my royalties were drying up. What money I had put aside during the period of my critical and popular acclaim was almost exhausted.

I came to the Grand Hotel in Sopot after he (my agent, that is) recommended the place to me. He said the hotel would provide all the things I was used to in Warsaw, but with none of the distractions. He told me that Marlene Dietrich and Adolf Hitler had both stayed here.

Does one consider a pleasant view a distraction to writing? I suppose it depends on the author. The view from my room afforded a view of the sea, the beach, and the Sopot Pier, the longest in

Europe, its gaunt skeletal structure reaching several hundred metres out to sea. However, with it being midwinter, at least the place would not be overrun with tourists swarming like ants.

What I hadn't known was that Leszek was coming down to stay in the hotel for some of the time, doubtless to monitor my progress and keep me on the straight and narrow.

He fancies himself an expert on the minds of writers.

Do you know the difference between psychiatrists and psychologists? The former are medically trained and are proper doctors. More importantly, they can therefore also issue prescriptions. All one needs to do is to read up on symptoms beforehand, and then it is quite easy to obtain the drugs one requires in order to work, albeit not necessarily what one needs for long term health. I once spoke with a delightful and terribly revealing young male student doctor who told me the consultative aid most at use within the state-funded Health Service is something called the Wikipedia on a computer.

Doctors fear displaying ignorance when it comes to making a diagnosis.

But I have long distrusted all doctors. As most right-minded women do. Doctors are too male and intrusive. Even the female ones. Filled with a sense of self- importance. They can't leave nature alone. They always want to meddle with it.

My name is Joanna Wolski. Perhaps, if you read books (so few nowadays seem to), you might have heard of me. I am a widow, and the author of three novels. Communist science fiction was huge in the 1960s, back in the days of the People's Republic. Even if you *have* heard of me, you *will not* be aware my thighs are dotted with little round burns. Often, when I am smoking and absolutely alone, I turn up my skirt and press the burning tip of my cigarette onto the cold white flesh of my thighs. The pain temporarily distracts me from the anguish I still feel at the loss of my very dear, late husband.

Any honest liar can write acclaimed fiction.

Nowadays the reading public don't care about anything other than a cheap thrill. That's all they've ever wanted.

All that's important is finding the right thrill at the right time for the right audience.

*

When I first learnt of the Reassembly Cartel, I thought that they were just another of those conspiracy theories, such as the faked moon landing, the C.I.A. being behind 9/11, and secret alien—or Nazi—UFOs. Many of my acquaintances had an interest in such monomanias. They have, no doubt, become the new articles of faith for those who reject the orthodox delusions like Christianity.

For my part, I smiled good-naturedly at their follies, feigned interest where required, and popped another pill in order to deal with the problem of existing in an alien universe.

This is how it happened.

It was at a late-night soirée given by Leszek Choszcz in the restaurant of the Sopot Grand Hotel that the conversation around the dinner table turned upon dead literary genres. Waving away the offer of a refill from a bottle of Chateau de Tours that was being passed anti-clockwise from person to person by the waiter, I made a comment about the reactionary appeal of ghost stories, and how the advent of electricity and socialism had largely killed off that genre.

When I made this remark one of our dinner guests, a former U.S. television soap-opera actor called Eugeniusz Kowalski, overturned his wine glass, spilling the dark red liquid onto the white tablecloth.

He was also one of Leszek's clients, but this was the first time I'd met him. Kowalski was not someone you would forget.

He had obviously been in an accident of some kind. His disfigurement was shocking, for his face was a mass of overlapping scar tissue covering a severely misshapen skull. He looked like a gargoyle.

"If you were aware of the Reassembly Cartel," he said, "you would not be so quick to dismiss the idea of revenants."

"Then what, exactly," I replied, "is this 'Reassembly Cartel'?"

"It is a front group of billionaires with absolute power over human society. Their combined wealth is greater than any single nation state. But their names will be unfamiliar to you, because their identities are secret. They have no need of identification when they own whole continents. The greatest power in the world is now located in Los Angeles, U.S.A."

"But the cartel's existence has been reported in the media?" I said.

"They own the media. Nothing is said without their approval. They also control Internet search engines."

He had fallen into my trap.

"Then how do *you* know about the existence of this cartel?" I said, having impaled his ugly little moth of a claim, or so I thought.

"This face is my evidence," he said, waving his hand in front of it. "I am an individual whom they seek to destroy. A gamekeeper turned poacher."

He then told a convoluted and fantastic tale, one that I will attempt to repeat in this narrative with as much impartiality as I can. At the time I believed little of it, but my conviction that he was telling the truth came shortly afterwards.

*

We actors are close to God, I think.

People think of us as superficial, as just playing roles on the stage or screen. But it is a vocation much more significant than that. Actors have to make the attempt to try and *become* people who are not themselves, and to see life through their eyes.

I wanted to be a great actor. A Hollywood star.

In order to do so, talent is not enough, although *without* talent it is impossible. But there are those who will succeed and those who will fail, and the only difference between them is not their talent (a question of degree) but whether they recognise that they do not work in a void.

Charm, contacts (*contacts! contacts! contacts!*), self-assertion, and the seizing of opportunities are crucial. An actor cannot concern himself with anything other than furthering his own career. Why? Simple, and it is the golden rule of success: look out for number one as nobody else will do so. But above all, give praise, praise, praise to those you think may be useful.

Without publicity the actor becomes nothing.

The great actor remains in darkness, a mere nothing on the stage, unless he has the spotlight turned upon him.

Of that I am convinced.

Ludwik Solski Theatre School, a long stint in flea-pit Krakow theatres, Program Three Polskie Radio, and then state television TVP 2.

I eventually appeared in a Polish film with English dialogue that did big box-office in the States, and from then on success seemed assured.

I knew, from the moment I arrived in L.A. and was picked up from the airport by limousine, that the hidden forces had brought me to them, right into the heartland of real power.

I soon secured a lead role in the network syndicated TV series *The Greatest Victory,* in which I portrayed a psychopathic British officer during the American War of Independence. My character, Cecil, the 11th Earl of Worcester, sexually abused children and put rebels into proto–concentration camps where the captives were dissected and then fed, still alive, to the pet pigs of the goose-stepping Redcoats.

I was invited to Hollywood parties in Beverly Hills, where the coke was pure and the women beautiful and filthy. I mingled with porn stars, rock stars, TV stars, and film stars.

But I made a mistake. At the time I thought it little more than a faux pas, but it's the reason my face looks like this.

It was the Polish accent that first caught my attention. Not unusual, of course, in L.A., but nevertheless, one's antennae still go up.

I looked across the ranks of the glitterati, sipping at my dry martini, trying to dodge the cocktail stick skewering an olive, and spotted the source of the voice. It came from a tall, bearded man with a black cloth wrapped around his forehead like a bandana. He was surrounded by a group of bored-looking celebs. He looked rather like an Orthodox Jew, except for one strange detail. His complexion had a green tinge about it, as if he were using some outlandish foundation makeup on his skin.

"I do not mean," the bearded man said, "class war, cultural equality, or the redistribution of wealth. Socialism is dead. This is something else altogether. The New Revolution will be when the unknown masses rise up to destroy the power behind celebrity. This power creates the idiot sports players, cretinous pop stars, and soap opera mannequins who hypnotise the masses. The forces behind the media are more powerful in this world than are politicians. The greatest act of terrorism right now would be for the public to destroy their television sets and mobile phones, burn down the cinemas, and throw their computers out the window. I want to see all commentators, newsreaders, and media moguls dangling from lampposts. They have turned the people of the Western world into gaping-mouthed zombies staring at a screen all their lives. Their goal is to extend their control over as much, too, of the East as they can."

"What about the Internet?" someone interjected. "That's not controlled, is it?"

He scarcely missed a beat.

"Big Business can shut down anything it likes and dictate to governments. On the Internet people think they have freedom of expression. But how can mankind communicate when everyone talks at the same time and, instead of listening, insists upon the *right to talk over* everyone else?"

The man stumbled a little on his feet. He was obviously blotto. But he held the attention of those around him. It was indeed remarkable that this soak felt he had the right to lambaste the very entertainment culture that was providing him with the bourbon he was consuming at a prodigious rate.

Someone nudged my shoulder, and I turned to look straight into the eyes of a person who looked like Humphrey Bogart after half a dozen facelifts.

"Crazy fucking Polack," he drawled, "talking like that. Just because he used to be a big-shot director."

And then I realised who the 'crazy fucking Polack' was—Marek Zapolska. He'd given up on the studio system in the '90s and gone independent after a series of blockbuster movies during the '80s. He'd been married to a string of Hollywood actresses, practically launching them to mega-stardom, all of a type: blonde, slim, stunning, and at least six feet tall.

"The cult of Celebrity is killing our ability to determine our own values. The famous have the aura of magic, of power about them. We hold them in awe because of their appearances on the electronic altar; we worship the manifestations of these gods at the exact same time each day or week as in a ritual. And to see them in the flesh! Why, it is as if they have descended from Olympus to walk amongst mere mortals and grace them with their presence! Snatch their autographs before it is too late! Take a photo to record a brief sojourn on earth before they return to their own electronic dimension!"

It was hard not to laugh at the hypocritical prick. As if anyone would be bothering to listen to him if he were not a product of the very system he now appeared to despise. Perhaps his supply of tall twenty-year blondes had finally dried up.

The plastic-faced Humphrey Bogart at my elbow had wandered off somewhere, perhaps for a smoke outside, and I edged my way closer to the circle of people surrounding Marek Zapolska. I had the feeling he was leading up to something, and I wanted to be there, just in case. The old instinct I had for seeing an opening to my advantage wasn't wrong, either.

"It makes no difference if you are of the right or of the left . . . the cult of Celebrity is in itself apolitical. In the modern world adherents of both political wings cry out for it, for no longer is knowledge power. Knowledge is only that junk which the leaders allow to be revealed to the masses through the mass media. Knowledge can only be increased depending upon the accuracy of the information to which we have access. POWER is knowledge. And power is best achieved through celebrity. Nothing else in this world is of any worth. Fame, notoriety, recognition are everything. That's why my next film will be a satirical exposé of the whole rotten system and the power behind it. It'll be my biggest sensation since *The Evil of Science*. I'm going to call it *Simplicissimus* in honour of my favourite author, Gustav Meyrink."

Like a piranha drawn by blood in the water, I had darted through the weeds separating me from my prey and was now close enough to Zapolska to make direct eye-contact.

"Of course," I said, in Polish, attracting the attention of the legendary director and all those surrounding him, "you'd need the right actor in the lead, someone who's not been corrupted by all the bullshit and treason to self-integrity that Hollywood requires. Perhaps even a fellow countryman!"

What was required to impress Marek Zapolska, in this instance, was a little European cultural snobbery. If that's what it took to get a part in his film, that's the role I'd play. Not much more than a minor detail to someone who'd starred as the psychopathic 11th Earl of Worcester ("The Butcher of Virginia") on cable TV.

"You're that Polish *kurwa* from the television series that portrays the British as a bunch of Nazis during the American War of Independence, aren't you?" Zapolska shot back in English (apart from the expletive). He was known as an ardent Anglophile, having lived in London for ten years during the '60s. His father had fought and died with the RAF during the Second World War.

I was not sure that any of the Americans present understood precisely the meaning of the word "kurwa," but the overall hostility came across clearly enough.

"Then again, maybe you're just what I need to make my point. I like the ironic angle. An aspiring actor who's a part of the corruption, playing the role of a character dedicated to stamping it out," Zapolska said.

And so that's how I got the part.

I wish to God I hadn't. I had no idea what I was up against.

They say all publicity is good publicity. Well, they lie. Sometimes drawing attention to one's self is a bad mistake, especially with revelations that certain powers don't want out in the open. Zapolska's film was poison to the industry. I hitched my star to it simply for the sake of notoriety. I was more than willing to play their game once I was in a position to do so. But I was stupid. I'd crossed the line.

Four weeks later the film *Simplicissimus* went into production. Zapolska had no need to worry about financing. His personal wealth was astronomical. But he had problems getting crew from the start. The project had already attracted negative comments from the trade papers, and people in the industry were warned off by a whispering campaign. Nevertheless, somehow Zapolska got a cast and crew together. It was a combination of loyal veterans and newcomers, people whom Hollywood couldn't control.

You probably all know those stories about Hollywood films that are cursed: *The Omen, Rosemary's Baby,* and *The Exorcist.* Certain events portrayed in those movies subsequently took place in real life and happened to cast and crew members. People struck by lightning or decapitated. The ritual murder of Sharon Tate. Insanity indistinguishable from demonic possession. Our film wasn't supernatural, but it still dealt with a conspiracy of silence, one that would kill in order to keep its secrets.

Well, you won't be surprised to learn that people started dying. At first they'd just disappear. We lost our key grip a week into shooting. He vanished. Just didn't show up on day seven. No one ever heard from him again. The chief hair stylist fell off a tenth-floor balcony in a condo on Playa Vista on day nine. Our first assistant camera was mown down by a hit-and-run driver on Santa Monica Boulevard in broad daylight. The car had mounted the sidewalk. That was on day twelve.

Zapolska was phlegmatic.

"I expected all this shit," he said to me as we going over some changes to my lines in his fourteen-million-dollar mansion off Mulholland Drive. We were sitting out back, by the Olympic-size pool, drinking bourbon and watching the lights of downtown L.A. twinkle in the smog. He'd played a couple of rounds of golf with his neighbour Jack Nicholson earlier in the day, and said he'd taken fifteen grand off the son of a bitch. So he was celebrating.

"One of us has to go," Zapolska said, pushing his glasses up the bridge of his nose, "either me or Hollywood. And it ain't going to be me, sonny boy. Not Marek Zapolska. No way."

I was suddenly aware of the enormity of his ego. Christ, my own was big enough. But only a Hollywood director who had been indulged in his every whim since he was a twenty-three-year-old prodigy, a man who had been isolated from reality for twenty years, cocooned by fabulous wealth and acclaim, could have seriously thought he could take on the whole of Tinseltown and bring it down.

"If need be, I'd gladly sacrifice the life of every bastard working on this picture in order to get it made. I don't care if I have to assemble a cast and crew a dozen times over," he said. And then he told me the true secret behind the Reassembly Cartel—the recondite forces behind the billionaires.

I believed him. And I decided then and there to get out. If I'd made the decision a day earlier, it would have been made in time. But I was too late.

Although Zapolska had no way of knowing, I was going to offer my services to the other side. I'd sell my story to the papers, tell them all that Zapolska was a fraud, get maximum publicity, and get back onside with the Hollywood system.

I drove back towards the intersection with the Valley Circle Boulevard. It was as I approached a sharp bend at sixty miles an hour that I lost control of the vehicle. I pumped the brake pedal, but nothing happened, and the next thing I knew my brand-new Ford Explorer had hit the crash barrier, flipped right over it, and catapulted into the woodland decline on the other side. The last thing I remember, a split second before unconsciousness, was that the air bag on my side didn't inflate.

*

Eugeniusz Kowalski had finished his tale. He didn't bother to add that his disfigurement was the consequence of this accident.

"So there you have it. End of my career," he said. "Six days later and the 'Zapolska Mystery' was born. The butler said he'd come into Zapolska's bedroom to bring him his breakfast on a tray as usual. But all that was left of Zapolska was a huge mass of green vomit all over the bed. No one could explain it. But I believe that he'd puked himself inside out with disgust. Those he sought to oppose had caused him to change form. They made him turn into a symbol of all that he detested."

"But you haven't explained anything at all about the secret of the so-called Reassembly Cartel," I said.

"You really want to know? OK, here's what Zapolska told me."

Kowalski paused and took a deep breath. I noticed his hands were trembling.

"The forces behind the Reassembly Cartel," Kowalski said, dropping his voice to a whisper, "are all dead souls seeking to take over our world for their own purpose. They have no existence aside from electronic media; but they feed on real life. They're broadcast ghouls from an already hideously decayed future. What people think they see in the street, at openings and the like, are manufactured simulacra of humans employed by a worldwide media conspiracy to keep the truth from the masses. The actual celebrities are manufactured in the broadcast factories of the future. The reality is just the same transmissions bouncing around forever.

"You see, this future world is a condition for the persistence of our own world. Its geography is seen in the video recordings of UHF frequencies between TV channels, consisting of immense glaciers of static, the leftover radiation from the Big Bang. The future world is being backwardly projected in time, and it is comprised of anti-matter and controlled by the dead.

"The final goal of the Reassembly Cartel is a world of mental zombies who do nothing but mindlessly regurgitate the poisonous froth of broadcast infotainment.

"The future is already finished. It's over, and what we're getting is advance notice as the nature of time itself begins to rot away."

There was an uncomfortable silence around the table once his final words had been spoken.

Then, shockingly, Eugeniusz Kowalski got to his feet and began screaming. None of us could calm him down. There was a huge rumpus with the waiter in the hotel restaurant, and half the diners were put off their suppers.

Kowalski was finally taken away in an ambulance.

I heard later that he screamed himself to death in the hospital to which he'd been taken. They tried sedatives, but he didn't, or couldn't, stop screaming, and he finally died after bursting a blood vessel in his throat.

Like the death of a character in a cheap horror movie.

*

The following morning I knew that the plot for my next novel had fallen into my lap. The delusions of Eugeniusz Kowalski and Marek Zapolska would form its basis. Except that, rather than its existence being the obvious product of paranoid fantasy, the Reassembly Cartel would be revealed as actually controlling human affairs in secret and moulding reality to its own design.

I did not mention the idea to Leszek, for I hated discussing a work in progress, especially during its formative stage, and thereby giving away any indication as to its theme. Nevertheless, given what had occurred the previous evening with Eugeniusz Kowalski, I wondered whether Leszek did not suspect my intent, when I told him over breakfast that I was now ready to commence work.

His job done, Leszek went back to Warsaw.

All I had to do was turn on the television set in my room.

At first the images were conventional enough; but the more of it I watched, steeling myself to bear talk shows, adverts, soap operas, and all manner of junk, the more I came to recognise the truth of what Eugeniusz Kowalski had claimed. It was necessary to look out for those moments when the person (or rather the dead shell) on the screen was actually trying to communicate directly with me, the viewer. Isolated phrases took on significance, and when one collated these isolated phrases, a pattern emerged.

I discovered, after only two days of continuous viewing, without sleep, and kept awake by amphetamines, that the world of electronic signals is actually the real world and the one outside, *our one*, is a fake.

*

This is the beginning of a new age. I have been busy working on my magnum opus. More than ever I am convinced of its significance.

As it sets the dead sun throws long black shadows across the frozen beach.

I am wrapped in blankets, sitting on the balcony outside my hotel room and looking out over the seafront. My breath is a ghostly vapour. The Promenade is deserted. I haven't seen a soul of late. Everyone appears to have fled the approaching wall of icy static.

I am a last witness to its advance. It rears up now in the middle distance like a titanic cliff-face, blotting out a swathe of the thin blue sky. And there is a deafening roaring and crashing as the electronic glacier bears down inexorably on the land, a sound like millions of television screens exploding, blown apart from within by nightmare images. I see glimpses of invading giant hordes of deformed crabs with gargoyle heads and green faces, revealing the shape we shall assume in hell. The monstrous glacier of static consumes the pier in a grainy haze, obscuring its skeletal iron structure from view.

In my rigid right hand I clutch a pen. On my lap is a pad of paper. My fingers are numb, riddled with black frostbite, but I write on, page after page, consumed by the desire to set down in writing the images flooding into my mind. It is an effortless though frantic undertaking. Sometimes I close my fingers into a fist, digging the nails into the ball of my hand, but still clutching the pen, forcing it across the page time and time again.

I have crossed over. I am now inside the other world. I have become one with the electric cosmos of the dead.

There is nothing to do but write. I must write before I am consumed by outside forces. At all costs I must write. I will write anything to stay alive. To remain alive means to write.

No one is around to recoil at the sight of what I have done to myself.

My lips are chapped with the cold. I can barely move them. My teeth chatter in my mouth.

I stopped feeling sensation in my feet days ago. When I unwrapped the towels wound around the lower parts of my legs, I tore away strips of green and black flesh that had adhered to the fabric. Below the knee my limbs were gangrenous. The same thing is happening to my hands, my nose, and my ears. I crawl around on my belly, like some aimless crab, moving from one sheet of paper to another, writing and writing and writing and writing, until I can finish what I have begun, and before the wall of static obliterates everything in its path.

*

"Joanna Wolski?" Leszek Choszcz snorted and shook his head ruefully. "At my suggestion she took herself off to that flashy northern seaside resort in the Pomerian Voivodeship. The last I saw of the woman was at a hotel dinner party at the Grand Hotel that I threw for her, and where she'd screamed her head off."

"So her fourth novel was not completed?" said the publisher.

"Completed?" he replied. "Why, it wasn't even properly begun. They found the poor woman dead in her hotel room. She'd perished of hypothermia. Forced open all the windows and fallen asleep naked on the tenth floor watching television. It was below freezing that night. As if that were not fantastic enough, apparently there was some talk of self-mutilation too. Quite, quite horrible."

"But what about the book? How do you know it was never begun?"

"I saw the manuscript after her death. Wolski had numbered four hundred and fifteen sheets of blank paper. They were scattered all over the hotel room. There were only a few pages of mystical gibberish—geometrical signs—scrawled on those crumpled, empty pages. Naturally I destroyed them for the sake of her reputation."

MY WORLD HAS NO MEMORIES

When I awoke, it was to the roar of a storm at sea. Gradually, as my senses returned, I became aware of its ceaseless motion all around me, engulfing the world. I was aboard a small vessel, alone, and with no memory of how I came to be there. I struggled out of the single berth in which I lay and my first thought was that I must have suffered a blow to the head, causing concussion and amnesia. My memory was a blank.

The vessel showed signs of occupancy for many weeks. It stank of my unwashed body. The galley was covered with a film of grease, and food supplies in the overhead lockers appeared about half used. I ran some water over my head from the sink and then swallowed a cupful. My throat was very dry, and I assumed I had been unconscious for many hours.

Above the sink was hung a small shaving mirror. A drawn, un-shaven face that I did not recognise stared back at me. My reflection. I guessed that it belonged to someone in his mid-fifties. Eyes blue. White hair shaven close to the scalp. Very thin. Not hand-some, not ugly. Gold wedding ring on the third finger of his left hand. No inscription inside the band.

The cabin was eighteen feet long by eight feet wide. It con-tained all the essentials for a lengthy ocean-going voyage.

By the side of the radio was the ship's logbook, charting the progress of its course, and the last entry gave its position as being unconfirmed. The previous entries were garbled, with notations detailing the difficulties of getting accurate sextant measurements from the sun or stars. The only information it yielded up to me of any satisfaction was the name of the vessel: the *Pulsar* out of Poole, Dorset.

Contact with GPS was gone, as if the damn satellites had simp-ly fallen out of the skies. All compasses aboard were wildly unrelia-ble, their needles pointing in differing directions.

I tried the radio set. Nothing but static on all frequencies.

There was no response to my Mayday requests.

The self-steering mechanism had been operating all the time I had been unconscious. I did not adjust it, since I assumed it was set purposely towards some definite destination, or preferred course, and passed through the cockpit hatch up onto the deck.

A blast of salty wind hit me, making my eyes smart. It was refreshing and clean—a stark contrast to the foul smelling air in the cabin. I gazed across the turbulent sea stretching in all directions, foam and spray sweeping over the monohull yacht. The four sails were up, billowing in the air, driving the vessel through the surging walls of seawater.

The sky above was a sheet of uniform gunmetal grey, featureless and grim, giving no indication of the sun's position. It may have been morning or afternoon.

Retreating back into the cabin, I sought out the *Pulsar*'s emergency flares. Perhaps, I thought, if there were another ship within a reasonable distance I could alert it to my presence. I found the flare gun, but there was no sign of any cartridges. Doubtless I had already exhausted the supply in previous attempts.

How long, then, had I been at sea? Months probably. But to what purpose? Had I set out on the voyage to escape some disaster, or had the disaster struck unexpectedly while I was already at sea? The latter possibility seemed the more probable. Then again, might it not be the case that I had fled in advance of the cataclysm, having been forewarned of its impending approach? That seemed likeliest of all.

It was all so maddeningly vague. I was certain that something terrible must have occurred but had no memory as to its exact nature. My inability to make contact with the outside world—indeed, the very lack of any evidence of there being an outside world with which to make contact—was a strong indication of some worldwide calamity. Had this event in some way affected my brain, impairing my memory to the extent that I could not even remember my own name and history?

What was the cataclysm? Some enormous burst of radiation from the sun, a stupendous solar flare that knocked out the global communications system and also somehow affected the magnetic poles? I could come up with no better solution to fit the facts.

It was either that or madness.

*

I cooked myself a meal in the galley. It consisted of toast, scrambled eggs, and curry powder. My appetite, however, was listless and I picked at the food without enthusiasm. The cabin was insufferably damp, with condensation on the roof, and all around me raged the noise of the sea, an unending primal roar that encompassed two-thirds of the globe.

By now it was getting dark outside. Having finished my meal, I turned on a lamp and wondered how best to pass the night before sleeping. I wandered over to the single shelf of books forming the *Pulsar's* small library. They were mostly navigational and technical books of seafaring, but amongst their number were also a handful of other, more general titles.

Next to them, shoved well back into the recess of the shelf, was a large glass jar. I could not see clearly what it contained, masked as it was by shadows, and so I adjusted its position, drawing the jar towards me. But when my fingertips touched the glass object I almost recoiled. It felt warm, wet, and sticky, as if containing something alive and radiating heat. Repulsed, I slipped on a pair of rubber gloves lying close by on the worktop I utilised for repair of my electrical devices.

Suspended in a transparent fluid was a monstrous flower the size of a grapefruit. It must have been preserved, not for its aesthetic quality, for it was hideously ugly, but instead as a specimen of abnormality. Perhaps it most resembled a rose in its shape, but a rose that had suffered some hideous malformation or disease.

Firstly, its multitude of petals, filaments, and stamens were a leprous white colour. Secondly, across the whole of the surface of them there ran a series of tiny circular suckers, as are found on the skin of Cephalopoda.

I randomly opened the stopper on the jar a fraction. A fishy odour, like that of something washed up from the sea and left to rot in the sun, wafted over me.

I felt nausea, as if drugged. Then there flashed into my mind's eye a nightmare vision.

I saw a succession of such decomposed flowers rising from a watery abyss, their filaments oozing black ink and forming incomprehensible sentences in a spidery script on the surface of the ocean. The symbols intersected one another in spirals and whorls like fingerprints, forming a non-successive narrative that was being constantly dissolved in the foaming spume, only to be reproduced all over again.

Suddenly I was gripped by a sense of hideous panic, as if I were on the verge of passing out. I knew, with a terrifying certainty I could not account for, that the diseased rose of the depths had sought to communicate with me telepathically. But to submit to its intent would be an act of suicide; and *only by being driven insane could I possibly comprehend its meaning.*

I stoppered up the jar with a tremor of revulsion and then gazed at it stupidly for several moments.

There could surely be no doubt now; my reason was in danger of tottering. I was suffering from some form of mental illness. Still, there was one thing I could do to alleviate a symptom, if not the cause.

I went up to the deck, clutching the jar, and then hurled it as far as I could into the depths of the roaring sea and the black night.

A ferocious headache assailed me, almost making me lose my balance and tumble overboard, but I managed to grope my way back into the cabin and collapsed, insensible, into my berth.

*

When I awoke hours later it was still dark outside. My headache had passed, and the sea was calm. The *Pulsar* scarcely moved, and there was no sound of wind or waves. I went up on deck and saw a sky full of brilliant stars, crystal clear in their intensity but strangely unfamiliar. Perhaps I was now in the Southern Hemisphere, and this accounted for the lack of recognition on my part, or else the appropriate part of my memory was a lacuna, obliterated by the damage done to my mind. Nevertheless, with a clear sky it might be possible for me finally to get a fix on my position.

I hurried back below deck to retrieve my sextant and star charts, but stood dumbfounded when I discovered that there, on the small bookshelf, rested the same jar I had recently tossed overboard.

Moreover, the flower inside had grown, filling the jar and displacing the stopper until it had wrapped its filaments around the adjacent item—a book. I thought of hacking away the threads and throwing the whole thing overboard again, or else burning it on deck, but turned my attention to the more pressing matter, retrieving my star atlas and sextant and going back on deck.

After more than an hour of effort I was no closer to determining my position. The stars in the night sky corresponded to none of the charts contained in the atlas. Consequently, my sextant was useless. There was no sign at all of the moon. All I could hope for was that the sky remained clear until dawn, when I could get a rough fix with the sextant from the rising sun.

At least I could be sure of one thing: I was neither in the tropics nor close to either of the polar regions. The temperature was too moderate.

I was about to make my way below deck to the cabin in order to destroy that maddening flower when I spotted a series of objects floating about a hundred and fifty yards off the starboard bow. They were pale, grouped together, and floating aimlessly in the currents like a shoal of jellyfish. The faltering breath of wind in the air was scarcely sufficient even to pilot my vessel across the short distance, but eventually I coaxed the *Pulsar* alongside them.

Looking over the side, I saw that they were all human corpses, more than a dozen of them, bloated by the gases of decomposition; doubtless these gases had brought them to the surface from the depths of their watery graves. As I gazed at the sight, more and more began to bob up on the surface, their numbers increasing with each passing moment as if some Atlantean necropolis were giving up all its dead.

I was now surrounded by bodies on all sides, and the charnel stench was appalling.

Then I noticed something that had been partially obscured by the various states of decomposition the corpses displayed. They were all alike, with closely cropped white hair, males of the same age, as alike as a series of dead clones. I then suspected the monstrous truth about them and lowered a grappling hook over the side to haul one of the cadavers on deck in order to confirm my fears.

I managed to snag a body after a few tries and hauled it on board. It did not seem as badly decayed as some of the others and must have perished quite recently. It was not bloated with gases as were the others, and I was glad of it, for I did not think I could have brought myself to handle some of the foulest specimens.

As I turned the body over so it was facing upwards, the truth was evident. My own features confronted me.

I was about to toss my double back over the side when, to my amazement, his eyes flickered open and revealed leprous white roses blossoming in the sockets. A mixture of blood and seawater bubbled from his mouth. He was not yet dead after all. His hands grabbed my shoulders in a feeble grip and he drew me down closer to him. A watery gasp issued from his throat as he choked out his dying words.

". . . flowers sing in the gardens of madness . . ." was all that I could make out of the sentence he uttered before he expired. Doubtless he had swum up from the depths and, if not a death by drowning, then the nitrogen bubbles forming in his bloodstream during the ascent had finally finished him off.

He was not breathing, and there was no sign of a pulse, so I rolled the body over the side of the deck back into the sea, where it floated.

Again that damnable flower! It was the key to this nightmare series of events and, I thought, only by its certain destruction might I bring an end to the horror.

I went below deck and found that the thing had grown during my absence. Its filaments and stamen had now spread over the whole of the bookshelf, whilst its bloated central mass had burst from the confines of the shattered jar.

It pulsed with an obscene life, oozing filthy spume from its puckered white surface. I hacked at it with a serrated knife, cutting through its pulpy form until I was covered with its black nectar, and then gathered together all the fragments and dumped them into an empty oil drum. I carried it up on deck, poured petrol into the container, and set the contents alight. As the flames consumed the mass of diseased pulp inside, I heard it sizzling in its death throes, its nectar spitting and splattering against the interior of the metal drum.

And then I was seized again by a recurrence of that ferocious blinding headache, blotting out the world entirely, and I stumbled and fell at the foot of the mainsail, grasping at it for support.

*

When I awoke and had recovered my senses sufficiently, I found I was still clutching the mainsail. The drum had vanished, but now there were titanic flowers all over the deck and toppling over the sides into the ocean.

They had entirely expelled all the cabin's contents and forced them overboard, so that the waters around the *Pulsar* were full of shattered debris, now mingled with all the decomposed bodies floating around the vessel.

The wind had picked up and, as I turned my face in the direction of the breeze, the glare on the horizon told me that it was just before dawn. I saw an unearthly motley of intensifying colours as the minutes passed before the disc of a sun began to rise above the rim of the earth.

My eyes were now itching horribly, and I thought that they were deceiving me, for the object I saw was of such a vast extent that its visible radius encompassed a full quarter of the horizon.

Inexorably, the totality of that gigantic *multi-coloured* sun rose into view, its sickly rays casting a spectral reflection on the ocean.

As I watched, hypnotised by the impossible vision, with black ink dribbling down my cheeks, I heard dead laughter—and realised it issued from myself.

It was, again, time to flower.

OUTSIDE INTERFERENCE

Most of the staff had already been transferred out of the old Bloy Building. Only a handful of the company's employees remained, located in a single office on one floor, amidst the thirty other storeys that were now vacant except for the dusty debris left behind in the course of the removal of the building's contents. Constructed in the early 1960s, in the then-fashionable Brutalist style of architecture, it had now decayed to a point past the possibility of further renovation. Just to look at it was to suffer the feeling of gazing upon a corpse in steel, glass, and concrete. One instinctively wished for a controlled explosive charge to blot out the sight of it for good, as one would wish for the cremation of a badly decomposed body discovered by accident.

Those of us left inside were engaged in the last rites of the transfer to the new premises on the other side of the country. All the old company paper records (housed in rusting filing cabinets) were being made digital, and it was our task to transcribe and then forward them electronically. It was tedious, mind-numbing drudgery, and only the most unfortunate and ill-regarded of the Bloy Company's staff, of which I was one, had been assigned the duty.

Each of us resented having been singled out in this manner and having been left behind as our fellow employees departed; and the dissatisfaction manifested itself in our general listlessness, absenteeism, and slow rate of progress. There was also a widespread suspicion that, once our task was finally completed, forced redundancy, at the minimum legal rate allowed, awaited us.

Moreover, to compound our misery, we were trapped not only in the prison house of the old Bloy Building but also in the middle of the coldest winter snap for a century or more. Although the leaden skies and arctic temperature continually threatened heavy snowfall and the happy chance of our remote work location being cut off from the outside world, preventing our attendance, the expected blizzard did not materialise. Daytime consisted of a few

197

hours of murky twilight, followed by the onset of a mid-afternoon darkness, without sight of stars or even of the moon. A freezing and bitter gale continually battered at the Bloy Building, whistling through its structural cracks and running in swirling draughts along the abandoned stairways and corridors. It almost seemed as if the dying edifice was gasping in the icy air.

The heating had been cut off when the central boiler had been decommissioned, and we sat around in our scarves, hats, and overcoats, with only a few emergency and ineffectual electric bar heaters dotted around the remaining functioning office. All the smaller surrounding buildings in the industrial park having been deserted months ago, we were left in a tenantless wasteland and even had to bring in our own meagre pre-prepared meals for lunch, what with the shops and cafés (as well as the Bloy Building's own internal staff canteen, of course) all now closed.

And so the grim routine went on, day after day, with the company minibus picking us up in the mornings at 8 A.M. from the nearest railway station forty miles away before depositing us at the Bloy Building and then dropping us off back at the station in the evening at 7 P.M. Olek, the driver, was a taciturn and bald old man with a drooping moustache who we all knew was a secret toper. He would often put to his lips a tarnished hip-flask, even while at the wheel, and though he claimed it contained nothing stronger than an indigestion remedy, his breath and glazed expression told the true tale. Thankfully, however, there was an almost complete absence of traffic on the route to and from the station to the industrial park, and Olek seemed incapable of driving the company vehicle even minutely in excess of a top speed of thirty miles an hour.

*

I had been desultorily chewing on a cheese sandwich and inputting the contents of a folder twenty years old into my computer when I glanced up and saw the first flakes of snow outside the window. Within minutes it had become a blizzard of frenzied intensity. It was Popov who first voiced all our fears, Popov who, amongst us all—we adepts of slacking and daydreaming—was the undisputed master of work-evasion and idleness. His ability to turn what was normally a few hours' typing into a task of Sisyphean magnitude was legendary.

"Unless we get out of here now," he cried, "we're going to be stranded! Perhaps for days!"

"We need to find the driver Olek and quickly," I replied, "before the roads are completely impassable."

A general murmur of agreement passed between the half-dozen of us in the office.

Just then we heard the ping of the lift door opening in the corridor outside as the machine announced its arrival on our floor. As one we rushed towards it.

Slumped in the corner of the cage was Olek. A thrill of horror passed through us all like an electric shock. He presented a hideous sight. Although his crumpled grey suit was untouched, it appeared that he had recently passed through a searing inferno. His face and hands were monstrously burnt, the skin blackened and peeling away from the flesh. His formerly bushy moustache was charred and patchy on his upper lip. It seemed impossible that he could be alive. We managed to drag his body into the office and propped him up in a chair.

As I fumbled for a pulse, however, a tremor ran through his frame and his eyelids popped open.

His eyes were blank white, as if boiled in their sockets.

And then, slowly, with a nightmarish air, his features composed themselves into an expression I can only describe as a fusion of insanity and mockery.

He turned his head from side to side, regarding us with those dead eyes, before getting to his feet.

Despite the horror of the thing, Popov boldly took a step forward and said,

"Olek, what has happened to you? In God's name! We must get you to a hospital, we must all . . ."

In a voice whose words were like the rustling of dry, dead leaves Olek cut in.

"Leave me alone!"

With a sudden motion he darted past us, gained the corridor, and was within the lift, the doors closing before any of us could catch up with him.

"The stairs! Quickly, we can't let him get away. He must be making for the minibus," Fodot, the office junior, said, his high-pitched wail echoing along the corridor as he took the lead.

We took the stairs down as quickly as we were able, with Popov puffing away some distance behind us, his vast bulk uncertain on the steps. After a few minutes we emerged into the raging blizzard outside and were almost knocked off our feet by the force of the wind. The snow stung our faces with icy barbs, and it was difficult to make out anything in the whiteout. But we heard the noise of the minibus engine starting up and the low grumble as Olek put it into gear.

And then, from the sound of its approach, we realised that it was being driven directly towards us, and Olek intended to mow us down in cold blood. But the poor visibility worked in our favour, not his, for he careened wildly, having finally accelerated some considerable margin beyond his customary limit of thirty miles an hour and crashing with a deafening impact into the side of the Bloy Building, turning the front of the minibus into a crushed wreckage of metal and glass.

*

Popov was the first to try his mobile phone to contact the emergency services, but all he got was a blast of unending static on the connection. We all tried in turn on our own phones, having retreated to the lobby of the building, but with the same result. Any number that we tried to reach was dead except for the sound of loud static.

Fodot was shaking and pale with fear, Irena Krug (the sole female in our party, an unmarried woman of sixty) had begun sobbing out prayers, Popov seemed to be in shock, and the two other men, Kartaly and Leszno, were conducting a fierce argument between themselves as to the next best course of action, whether to flee into the snowstorm or return to the office and await assistance. My own mind was racing, and I tried to put together the pieces of the unearthly jigsaw in which we had been enmeshed.

Obviously, the first question was how it was that Olek had come to be so horribly burnt and yet apparently alive. Could he have set fire to himself in a fit of madness? And yet, why was his clothing untouched? It made no sense. And did his behaviour relate to the fact that our phones had ceased to function properly?

Leszno, meanwhile, after nearly having come to blows with Kartaly, dashed into the lift.

"The landlines upstairs may still be working," he said, "if we try . . ."

His words were cut off by the automatic doors closing themselves. We waited a moment, expecting him to push the button to re-open them manually, but instead the lift began moving. We watched with bewilderment, for the floor level indicator showed that it was descending to the basement rather than ascending to the seventeenth floor where our office was located. Despite frenziedly pushing the call button to return the lift to the lobby, it was unresponsive, and the floor indicator winked out, showing nothing at all after remaining fixed on the basement sign for a short while.

Miss Krug suggested we take the stairs down to the basement and force open the lift doors, thereby freeing Leszno.

Accordingly, we descended via the flight of steps down to the basement level. After banging on the lift doors and receiving no reply from Leszno, we managed to lever them apart via a combination of forcing open a gap using the blade of an emergency fire axe and then pulling from both sides at once.

Beyond the doors we saw nothing but the lift shaft itself. The cage was not on this level. I put my head into the gap while the others held the doors apart. Looking up, I could see nothing but darkness, but from the unfurling movement of the cables close at hand it seemed that the lift cage was still descending and had reached a considerable depth below the ground. Then, faintly but unmistakably, I could hear the distant and muffled sound of frantic screams issuing from deep down in the vertical shaft.

My thoughts inevitably returned to the fact that we had found poor Olek in the lift after he had suffered his hideous burning, and I could not help but speculate that a similar torture was now being experienced by Leszno leagues below.

The horrified looks on the faces of my companions told me that they, too, had heard what I had heard, and it was a grim mercy when the sounds were completely silenced once the lift doors were released and tightly shut.

"I had no idea that there were sub-basements below," Miss Krug said.

"None that I know of," Popov replied, with a tremor in his voice.

There was nothing else to do but for us to make our way up the stairway to the seventeenth floor on foot and try to communicate with the outside world via the telephones and computers in our office.

We had only reached the ground floor when I heard the noise, from the stairway, of something knocking at the glass doors to the lobby. Telling the others to stay where they were, I quit the stairs and entered the lobby alone. Some secret sense told me what it might be that was making the sound, and I was not mistaken.

Behind the glass, half obscured by the swirling snow outside, was the mangled corpse of Olek. It had returned to the building, crawling on its belly, despite its horrific injuries. Most of his head was smashed in on one side, both arms and legs were broken in several places, and when I looked at him I was reminded of a crushed bug that still wriggled its limbs in its death spasms. He was slapping the palms of both hands against the glass over and over again. All the fingers were missing.

One other thing: when he first saw me he grinned mirthlessly, as if we were sharing a private joke, and black blood drooled over the broken teeth—exposed where the whole of his lower lip had been torn off.

I forced my gaze away from the sight, stifling the scream bubbling up from my lungs, and went back to the stairway, slamming the door to the lobby behind me.

"What was it?" Popov asked.

"I couldn't make it out. The snow's falling too heavily," I lied.

He snorted, his hand reaching for the door handle. I grabbed his wrist, sharply pulling it away.

"Don't," I said.

He stared at me blankly, an angry retort forming on the tip of his tongue.

"For your own good, don't," I said.

*

The climb up to the seventeenth floor took a long time. Popov's unfit bulk and Miss Krug's aged limbs slowed us down, and although Fodot wanted to dash ahead, I insisted that we all ascend at the same pace and were not separated by more than a few yards at any time.

When finally we reached our office, the hope that our ordeal was beginning its end and we would be able to summon help from the authorities was dashed. The landlines carried the same impenetrable static signal as our mobiles, and all the computers, too, displayed only a snowy electronic fuzz on their screens. Nothing could be done with them. It was as if they had been infected by the blizzard roaring outside.

Miss Krug kept tapping away at the keyboard of her own machine, repeatedly re-booting it in the desperate hope it would miraculously return to normal.

Popov slumped to the floor and ran a none-too-clean handkerchief across the cold sweat sticking to his brow.

"We have to wait until the snow eases up," Kartaly said, his eyes blinking repeatedly behind the lenses of his horn-rimmed spectacles, "and then one of us needs to go for help. There's nothing else for it."

Fodot was leaning against a wall and smoking a cigarette, his eyes as dead as the stub of ash at its tip. I was worried he would crack first, being the youngest and most highly strung of us.

"This isn't natural!" Popov cried. "Going for help? Pah! You fool! This isn't just a snowstorm, that's not all that's going on. What the hell happened to Olek, burnt to a crisp and still alive? No answer! And what of Leszno? Descending into floors that don't exist . . . it's impossible! I tell you, I believe we're all going stark raving mad!"

I was glad, then, that I had prevented him from seeing the even more fantastic sight of what remained of Olek banging away at the glass doors in the lobby. As this thought crossed my mind, the lift pinged in the corridor outside, indicating its arrival on our floor.

I spun round, expecting to see the grisly remnants of Olek crawling towards us, as if summoned up by my thinking of him. But it was not Olek who appeared in the office doorway; it was Leszno. He was clutching at the frame for support, having staggered from the lift across the width of the corridor.

The visible flesh was charred and blackened, the remaining clumps of hair on his head still smouldering. Though his clothes were untouched by the heat, his eyes had been boiled all-white. Exactly like Olek as we had first discovered him.

But this time, no one rushed to his aid. We merely stood there, dumbfounded and horror-stricken.

Leszno coughed raspingly several times, as if trying to clear his throat and lungs of smoke, and then he tottered across the room until he half collapsed onto the seat directly in front of his computer terminal. He then slumped forward over the desk and stared fixedly with those white eyes into the chaotic burst of static on the screen. His black, almost skeletal fingers began to roam all over the computer keyboard like twin spiders.

Our terror partly conquered by curiosity, we crowded around Leszno in order to see what he was doing.

Popov poked him in the shoulder.

"What's going on Leszno, eh?" he said. "What happened to you, eh?"

Momentarily, Leszno turned to him and drew back his leathery lips in a snarl, baring his teeth. A hollow, mechanical growl sounded in his throat before he turned his full attention once more to the screen.

Was it just an optical illusion, or did the static alter its form according to some rhythm or pattern Leszno was typing out on the keyboard? It seemed almost as if vague images were on the verge of being manifested via the fuzzy interference, and that his tapping of the keys was an attempt to bring them into focus. But always, despite his frantic efforts, the images proved too unstable and kept slipping back into an overpowering chaos.

"His eyes!" Fodot hissed, "Look at his eyes now!"

The eyes that had previously been wholly marble-white were now completely riddled with static, and it shifted and re-formed in sync with the static on the computer screen. Leszno had ceased to blink. It was no mere reflection that we saw there, but an occupying force.

"I read somewhere once," said Kartaly, "of a narcoleptic whose eyelids were pulled back as he slept and whose dreams could be seen passing across his pupils, one after the other."

Miss Krug crossed herself.

"Enough! Enough!" Popov shrieked. He took hold of Leszno by the shoulder and hurled him off the chair with great force. As the charred man lay sprawled on the carpet, Popov grabbed the heavy fire extinguisher from its socket on the nearby wall and held it aloft, ready to smash it down on Leszno's skull.

"Kill it! Kill the thing!" Kartaly cried.

Popov quickly looked at each of us in turn, and only Miss Krug turned away.

Leszno tried to regain his position on the chair, but Popov kicked him back onto the floor. And then he hammered the base of the heavy fire extinguisher cylinder into the upturned face again and again, with a frenzy born of pure adrenaline and terror. After several blows the skull of his victim was completely crushed. And what we saw thereafter only filled us all with a greater sense of horror, for the gore splattered mass of brain tissue was suffused with electronic radiance, and the stream of Leszno's dark red lifeblood that pooled across the floor pulsed with individual bubbles of black and white static.

Popov staggered backwards, dropping the fire extinguisher as if it were red hot, and leant against a desk for support. A deadly silence enveloped us all, leaving us to our own dark thoughts, and the only sound was that of the rampaging wind of the snowstorm outside as it continued to batter against the Bloy Building.

Whoever had gone into the lift since the blizzard struck, I reasoned, had been horribly transformed during the journey. Certainly the lift was the key to the whole mystery. Both Leszno and Olek had gone down into depths of the structure that did not previously exist. In order to discover the nature of the secret that was now spawning horror all around us, it was necessary to find out what was down there in the hidden subterranean levels. But there was no way of doing so without, presumably, becoming a burnt, insane fiend.

It was madness, but there was no other way to know.

I picked up the fire extinguisher that Popov had dropped and wiped off the blood from its base with my handkerchief. I then removed the locking pin and tested it by pressing down momentarily on the handle. A short white burst of freezing carbon dioxide scattered some papers lying on a nearby desk.

"What the hell are you doing?" Kartaly asked.

"I'm going down in the lift. What's down there is the key to all that's happening," I said, "and this extinguisher may just prevent me from ending up like Olek and Leszno."

"Don't be a bloody fool," Popov said. "That won't protect you! They weren't burnt by any *natural* fire. Their clothes were untouched. There's no scorching that I could see inside the lift cage. You go down in that lift and you'll end up exactly like them."

"I'm going with him," Fodot blurted out. "Perhaps two of us will have a better shot than just one at finding out exactly what this is all about."

"I'd rather take my chances out in the blizzard," Kartaly said, shaking his head.

Miss Krug said nothing and was standing at one of the huge windows, looking out at the storm as if hypnotised.

"Well, that's that settled," I murmured. "Come on Fodot, let's go."

The two of us went into the corridor, and I pushed the call button for the lift. We watched the indicator board charting the ascent from the lower floors, one by one.

Popov stuck his head outside the office doorway into the corridor.

"Come back! Don't chance it!" he cried.

The lift arrived, and the doors opened with a ping. There was nothing inside.

Fodot hesitated for a moment, looking back over his shoulder at Popov, who was beckoning him to return to the office.

I stepped inside the lift cage and put the fire extinguisher down on the floor. My hand hesitated over the numbers on the control board.

"Are you coming, Fodot?" I asked him. "You don't have to. It's up to you."

"I'm coming," he replied, stepping in alongside me.

"Let's try the lowest button, then." I pushed the one marked B for basement.

The doors slid shut with another metallic ping, and we began our descent.

*

We watched the floors passing by through the little glass windows on both sections of the lift doors. The panel above the door frame flashed up each number in turn as the lift cage slid smoothly downwards in the shaft. Then we reached the ground floor and the last stop that was marked, the basement.

The lift came to a halt, but the doors did not open. I pressed the B button one more time, but nothing happened. Perhaps the trip switch that set off the door mechanism on this level was jammed, I thought.

"Well," I said to Fodot, shrugging my shoulders, "that's that. We might as well return to the others."

He nodded, and just as my hand sought the number seventeen on the control panel, all the lights on it went dead.

With a shudder and then a jerk, the lift began to move again, continuing its descent.

"Here we go," I said. "Who knows what we're in for."

Fodot grinned bravely, but there was a nervous twitch at the corner of his mouth.

I peered through one of the little glass windows of the lift cage, but saw no sign of any other floors passing by. It appeared that we were in a sheer vertical shaft with nothing but solid concrete all around.

"I wonder how deep this thing can go," I murmured. "Surely there has to be a limit?"

"I don't know," said Fodot. "Perhaps it depends on the length of the supporting cables."

It seemed a sensible assumption.

After several more minutes had elapsed, I tried pushing the buttons on the control panel at random. They were still useless. The panel above the door frame told us nothing.

"I can't see how a cable long enough to reach all the way down here could be attached to the lift. It would weigh tons, and the coils would take up a gigantic amount of roof space."

"Maybe we switched onto some sort of traction rails built into the sides of the shaft," Fodot mused, "straight after reaching the basement."

I recalled the jarring interruption the lift experienced when reaching the basement level and agreed with his theory. It fitted what facts we had.

He pulled out a pack of cigarettes from his jacket pocket and stuck one in his mouth.

"You?" he asked.

I wondered if we'd both suffocate in the confined space, but took one anyway, and he lit it for me. Both of us sat down and puffed away in silence, watching the smoke curling around the confines of the enclosed space before disappearing through the slim gaps between the doors, drawn out by the upward draught caused by our passage through the shaft.

Down and down we went, further and further.

An hour passed. Then maybe two.

All the while Fodot and I made desultory conversation, talking of our pasts, and he particularly of a sweetheart. But it was a strange, unnatural dialogue, for we were constantly on edge, aware that at any moment the lift might halt, the doors open, and an un-known horror fall upon us.

"Duval," Fodot said, finally expressing the thought that had been preying on my mind for some time, "you do realise that we must now be over ten miles below ground?"

I was about to answer, when abruptly the fluorescent overhead lights in the ceiling went out and we were engulfed by utter black-ness.

At the same instant the lift came to a shuddering stop.

I fumbled for the fire extinguisher I'd placed close at hand, and leant on it as I scrambled to my feet.

"Quickly, Fodot," I said in the darkness, "get behind me!"

I heard the doors open with a ping, and we were instantly en-gulfed by an incoming wall of electronic static, which poured into the confines of the lift cage like a huge wave. It carried with it an overpowering stench of burning flesh. My whole body tingled with the shock, and I could scarcely see at all, my senses overwhelmed by the radiance. My eyes felt as if they were on fire and would ex-plode in their sockets.

I collapsed into a corner of the lift cage, crouched foetal, and then heard Fodot's screams as he was drawn over the threshold by the pull of the withdrawing static as it seeped back into the greater void. There was another ping, the doors slid shut, and the lights flashed back on.

I was entirely alone, and the lift was slowly ascending the shaft. Despite my frantic efforts the buttons on the control panel still re-fused to work, and I could not stop its progress.

There was no trace remaining of my fellow passenger except

for a half-empty, crumpled pack of smokes and some cigarette butts littering the floor.

*

Hours later I arrived back at the seventeenth floor. I staggered out of the lift to see Popov leaning casually against the doorframe of the office.

"Changed your mind, eh?" he said with an offensive wink.

Quite what he meant by this, I had no idea, except that he must have been making a joke in bad taste at my expense.

He was gazing over my shoulder, as if waiting for poor Fodot to emerge in my wake. Finally he brushed past me and saw into the empty lift cage for himself before the doors slid shut.

"Where is he, eh? Where's young Fodot?" Popov asked, looking genuinely surprised. By now the others had joined him in the corridor, looking as puzzled as him.

"Gone. Absorbed. Hours and hours ago. My God." I managed to croak out the words.

"Hours? What are you talking about? You've been in the lift for only a couple of minutes!" Popov replied, looking to Miss Krug and Kartaly for confirmation. They both nodded solemnly, as they helped me into the office and sat me down in a chair.

"He's right, Duval," Kartaly said. "You left us to go to the lower floors less than five minutes ago."

I glanced at my watch. There was a difference of over four hours between it and the time shown by the clock that hung on the wall. Unable to fathom the anomaly, I gratefully accepted the cup of hot coffee laced with sugar that Miss Krug brought me. I sipped at it and noticed that my hands were trembling. My gaze roved about the room and I saw that the body of Leszno had been covered with his own coat, blotting out the sight of his crushed head and the crazy bloodstain. I shivered involuntarily.

"Well," Popov said, standing over me, his brow furrowed, "what happened to the kid? Absorbed, you said. What does that mean?"

"Can't you see he's not well?" Miss Krug chimed in. "Won't you leave him alone until he's got his strength back?"

"I recall reading once about a famous case in Versailles,"

Kartaly began to explain, apparently thinking out loud to himself, "of two ladies who found themselves transported into an earlier century . . ."

"Will you please shut up talking nonsense!" Popov screamed at him.

Kartaly's fists clenched and he was on the verge of assailing Popov when we all heard the ping of the lift doors opening in the corridor outside.

Then Fodot staggered into the office.

I dropped the coffee cup.

He was just like Olek and Leszno.

White, blank eyes and blackened, burnt flesh.

Without seeming to notice our presence, Fodot went to the nearest computer terminal, switched it on, and began his attempts to manipulate the static on the screen by tapping at the keyboard.

His eyes rapidly began to take on the appearance of the electrical interference.

"For God's sake," Kartaly blurted out, breaking the spell the sight exerted over us all, "let's get out of here!"

Now no one protested, and even I, despite my weakened condition, acquiesced. I was sick to my soul of it all, and there seemed no alternative to Kartaly's suggestion. To remain in the building would entail certain madness or death. We filed out of the office, making for the stairs, in order to take our chances on foot in the still-raging blizzard outside. I wondered if Olek was still banging his hand against the glass of the lobby door.

*

On the way down, we heard movement through all the doors connected to the other storeys, as if heavy objects were being shifted by an army of unknown visitors who could only have travelled up from the depths. We heard, too, the pinging sound of the lift. It seemed to be much in use, although we did not stop to investigate. Certainly Fodot appeared to be engrossed when we had quit the seventeenth-floor office, so it was unlikely to be him travelling up and down the shaft. It had to be more of the unknown visitors arriving. In any case, our descent was undertaken in complete silence, for we feared alerting those strangers to our presence.

We reached the ground floor, and Kartaly cautiously opened the door to the lobby.

"There are half a dozen burnt men with white eyes out there, blocking the exit," he said.

"Do you recognise them? Did they work here?" I said in a low voice.

"Hard to tell. Their features are pretty ravaged, but I don't think so," he replied.

I peered over his shoulder.

Would they try and stop us or be indifferent to our attempts to leave?

Popov didn't wait for the answer, but pushed past the both of us, his great bulk rushing across the lobby towards the glass exit doors, trying to take them by surprise. In doing so, he had not only revealed his presence to them, but also our own.

He didn't make it very far. Two of the things bore down on him, their lips pulled back in hideous grimaces, while the others sluggishly began to approach us. I just had time to glimpse the first two dragging Popov towards the lift door, and briefly caught sight of the mangled remains of Olek on his knees, trying to assist the assailants by thumping the call button with the stump of his left hand.

Kartaly slammed the lobby door shut. Miss Krug tugged at my arm.

"There's a fire door just around the corner, remember?" she said.

We set off for it, the possibility of escape not yet remote.

Our hopes were dashed, however, when we rounded the corner to discover another three of the things stationed at that exit too. They had completely taken over the building.

Miss Krug's mind snapped. She began laughing manically, backed up against the nearest wall, and then slid down it, refusing to budge despite the advancing forms of the three burnt men with white eyes.

"Let's go," Kartaly cried, "before it's too late."

"We can't leave her here!" I shouted back.

"No choice! She's cracked up! She's already gone, man!"

He pulled me away, and I didn't look back.

We gained the stairs and hurtled up them. The shuffling sounds of our pursuers were not far behind.

"There's another way to get out," Kartaly said. "We smash one of the first-floor office windows and jump for it. It'll be a short drop."

"How do you know the first floor isn't crawling with them?" I replied.

*

We entered cautiously. The first-floor corridor was deserted, and I managed to jam shut the access door behind us by pushing a table right up underneath the handle. I was just in time, for no sooner had I done so than heavy blows began to rain down on the other side.

Kartaly was in the doorway to the office. I came up alongside him.

Inside was a complex range of machines, the likes of which I had never before seen. It looked as if someone had turned a huge series of mainframe computers and televisions inside out and mixed them up with engine spare parts from a motor vehicle repair shop. Snaking tubes and wires ran from the ceiling to the floor, and, amidst all the chaos, several of the burnt corpses manned work stations. A few were pulling levers or making adjustments to wiring, but the majority were in front of static-ridden display screens, tapping away in the same bizarre fashion at their key-boards as we had previously seen with Leszno and Fodot. Like them, their eyes positively glowed with living static interference.

The lift doors pinged on this floor and three more operatives advanced, carrying strange equipment up from the depths below. They took no notice of us, but I shook Kartaly by the shoulder. The jammed door to the first floor was giving way. The burnt men who had pursued us would be breaking through any second.

Kartaly sprang into action. He crossed the floor of the office, picked up a heavy engine part that was lying around, and lifted it over his head. He stood directly in front of the wall window on this storey, ready to hurl it through the plate glass.

A couple of the burnt men turned their heads in his direction, distracted momentarily from their tasks.

Kartaly dropped the engine part and sank to his knees, burying his head in his hands. Our pursuers were upon us and dragged us towards the lift. I did not resist them. There was no point in struggling anymore.

For outside, instead of the blizzard that had been raging around the Bloy Building, there now rolled a seething ocean of living static, stretching into the distance as far as the eye could see.

And it was only when I returned to the surface and saw it through new eyes that I appreciated its incomparable beauty.

THE CRIMSON FOG

Prologue

How far does reality extend? That's the question I keep asking myself.

Across billions of light-years to the mysterious point where the cosmos curves back on itself and the laws of time and space cease to apply? Only just as far as that visible universe mankind can detect and analyse with his instruments? Or is it confined solely within the limits of the skull of each and every isolated person who asks the question?

I think back to the half-ruined temple and its cryptic banners riddled with mandalas. A temple hidden high up on the mountain peak above the jungles of Chang-Yi province, right in the middle of the outland where wreathes the crimson fog and wherein dwell all the fiends with their rites of silent horror. I think of Major Qersh, his deadly revelations, his corpse-eyes, and that same message from him that I heard over the chopper's radio headset. I wonder where Mayhew and Koszalski are now. I try not to look at Yian-Ho.

The final events of my life play themselves out over and over again in my mind as I try to decide just what to do next.

My thoughts are like a maelstrom.

I think I hear the sound of thunder coming from far off.

The past, the present and the future merge into a singularity.

1

You know, like everyone else, how it began. There was nothing of any interest in that region before. The whole area, a thousand square miles of it, had been a wasteland of parched earth and scrubs. Only the wind and the occasional band of nomadic tribesmen ever crossed it—that was all. And then from out of nowhere the crimson fog had appeared. The satellite images made it look as if a pool of blood had formed on the far side of the Asian continent in the territorially disputed Chang-Yi province. And inside the wreath-like folds of the fog there appeared a brand new terrain: jungles, mountains, and the monstrous things that lived in that landscape. And the really damnable thing was this: the fog had a height equivalent to our atmosphere. It made no sense, but there it was. All this and a maximum visibility inside it of ten yards.

Of course we investigated. Firstly teams of Chinese went in, but they never came back. Then the Russians sent men in and they didn't reappear either. They were all swallowed up in the crimson fog. Some fragmentary reports made it out, all crazy and unbelievable. Accounts of fantastic jungles consisting of slimy creepers and giant twisted, deformed trees. No fauna of any kind in the vegetation except for the killers. Those diabolical things must have consumed all the other flesh in the jungle long before they got a taste for men.

You'll remember, I'm sure, the furore that erupted when it was revealed to the world in a photographic exclusive by some American journalist that the fiends could not be caught on camera. You'll also recall, of course, the disgust it engendered in everyone that the only proof of their existence was a physical aftermath. When one of them dissolved into a shapeless mass of bloody slime, being unable to exist outside of the crimson fog for more than a few minutes, someone had used the word "fiends," and it had stuck.

Of course we'd have been better off, in my opinion, to have gone along with the suggestion that we nuke the whole territory and turn the land and everything in it to ashes. But the scientists wanted to study the new landscape and, naturally, the Chinese and the Russians didn't want a cloud of radioactive ash drifting across their countries. Me? Knowing what I do now, I'd rather see a thousand mushroom clouds than that endless crimson fog.

In any case, it was agreed that a multinational force should "pacify any resistance" and then take control of the province so that it could be properly studied.

In the first phase of attack our forces had pushed deep into the territory, waves of helicopter gunships tearing immense chasms in the jungle, followed by the fire of artillery and foot-soldiers, driving back the fiends. And then, like all the previous endeavours, communications were lost and our forces simply vanished. The unimaginably complex expanse of landmass that constituted Chang-Yi province, with its endless jungles from which rose titanic mountain peaks dotted with strange temples to the unknown gods of the fiends, had to be conquered or else there would be no end to the war. Eventually, we supposed, the enemy would pour forth from their strongholds after regrouping in ever greater numbers.

Only one man did not vanish altogether. Major Qersh alone had sent back his last transmission via shortwave radio from deep inside Chang-Yi province two weeks ago. He was trapped, completely surrounded by the fiends on all sides, but bravely holding them off in a ruined temple high upon a nameless mountain peak. He had the secret that could end the struggle. He alone knew how to gain victory over the entities of the crimson fog and even how to dissipate the fog itself. Some cynics said it was propaganda. But those who did so secretly hoped not, even as they said it.

*

Four of us had been chosen to undertake the rescue mission. Koszalski and Mayhew were the others. They were slightly older than I was, but I had seen more combat service. Lieutenant Yian-Ho was to be our guide. The Chinese was the only person who had been to the heart of occupied territory and returned alive.

There were a lot of peaceniks whose opinions grew loud in the media and said we should simply leave the enemy territory alone altogether. We had gained nothing from military action except the loss of good young men and the squandering of hundreds of millions of dollars in a conflict we could not win. After all, they said, the so-called "fiends" had never ventured beyond Chang-Yi province.

Yes, the things were disgusting, but why were they regarded as our enemies? The land they occupied was unpopulated and had been useless anyway. Why not just leave them alone and let them stew in their damn crimson fog? Better non-aggression than the continued futile loss of life on our side. This point of view rapidly gained huge popularity, its logic was impeccable and, just when it seemed on the verge of becoming policy, a startling new fact emerged.

Since its initial appearance, the crimson fog had been expanding at the steady rate of just over a mile each day. It was slowly swallowing up all the land around it and creating more jungle, more dizzying mountains, and more carnivorous fiends. Within two years, to the south, it would flow over the Great Wall of China, and in a further couple of months would totally engulf Beijing. And then of course, someone calculated that, if the crimson fog continued to spread unchecked at its present rate, our entire planet would be transformed in a couple of decades.

Major Qersh became the hope of the world. And we had to get in and then get him out alive.

2

They dropped us six hundred and ninety miles inside the crimson fog, about another ten short of the foot of the nameless mountain. Not even the upper reaches of the mountain were, of course, clear of the fog, so a direct aerial approach was impossible.

It was nothing short of a miracle that we had made it this far inside Chang-Yi province. The six previous attempts had all crashed into mountain peaks obscured by the crimson fog. They had managed to radio back their last positions via shortwave radio, and intelligence had charted a revised safe route based on those six failed previous attempts. We all knew it was only a "safe route" if there wasn't another unknown peak between the one the sixth mission hit and our own target drop.

We bailed out, the four of us, into the billowing crimson mist at four thousand feet and disappeared from one another's sight. I pulled my chute and drifted down towards a jungle I couldn't even see until it rushed up towards my feet when I was nearly on top of it.

Mayhew got tangled in the branches and creepers of a tree forty feet up, but I managed to get him down safely. Koszalski had a touch of panic and worried he'd turned his ankle when he'd hit the ground, but he managed to walk it off pretty soon. It took the three of us several minutes to locate Yian-Ho, who had probably pulled his chute earlier than the rest of us. During that period when he was missing, I wondered if the mission was over before it had begun. Without Yian-Ho there was no way we'd have been able to cross ten miles of unmapped jungle inside a nightmarish fog with visibility down to ten yards, and that made any compass direction as reliable as a mad dog chasing its own tail.

We hadn't gone more than a mile when Mayhew began to grumble about the effect the permanent fog was having on his eyes—like a red myopia. He was right, I knew, but it didn't do any good to voice the thought aloud.

"This voodoo shit," he said, "it's like there's blood inside my eyeballs."

I grunted and shot him a nasty look. We were none of us more than five feet apart and moving forward together in a diamond shape. Yian-Ho was at point, Mayhew and Koszalski either side, and I was bringing up the rear.

The very existence of the crimson fog forced you to think about the big questions in life. Nothing like it had ever happened before.

From what I knew thus far, Koszalski was a Catholic nut, a bead rattler who also kept a little picture of the Virgin Mary in his wallet, rather than one of a wife, girlfriend, or even some fantasy squeeze. I suspected that bugged Mayhew even more than it did me, since Mayhew was one of those modern black guys who were spectacularly secular. With me—my dislike for religion, I mean—it was misanthropy, plain and simple. Nothing profound, and I wouldn't apologise for it, not after what I'd seen and been through in the psych ward. My gut instinct was that my being born was a mistake. But Mayhew liked to read books of philosophy, and I suppose he thought humans at their best were rational beings, not mystical idiots.

As for Yian-Ho, he was a complete mystery. Moreover, his English wasn't exactly great. I put him down as a Buddhist. Or something. Maybe he was Taoist.

Koszalski had a tendency to mutter prayers under his breath as he smoked. And he smoked a lot. I suppose it was a substitute for incense. He was painfully thin.

As we trekked through the jungle he started up again.

"Cut it out, Koszalski," Mayhew finally said. "Concentrate on the job at hand. Jesus ain't coming."

"Both of you keep it down," I whispered forcefully through my gritted teeth.

Yian-Ho turned back and nodded to emphasise my remark.

"Many fiends around here before," he murmured, almost inaudibly.

It was true that the fog muffled most sounds anyway and a fiend would have had to have been within twenty yards to hear any of our voices, short of someone screaming, but there was no point in wasting our breath talking.

Ten miles through this rough, nearly impenetrable terrain took four or five times longer than covering the same distance across clear ground. The advance was exhausting and slow. At times we had to hack our way forward through walls of dank vegetation with our machetes, over hillocks and down hollows.

And the realisation was growing on us that we were bound to encounter one or more of the fiends eventually. We'd just been lucky so far, but it would be a chance in a million that we wouldn't do so before reaching the ruined temple where Major Qersh had holed up and was surrounded.

When I was a kid, growing up during the 1970s, I used to read a lot of horror and science fiction. I graduated from comic books to paperbacks around the time I entered my teens. And I want to say that what 99% of that stuff tells you about supposed encounters with the unknown is a formulaic convention. No one faints like a chicken-shit or else reaches for a weapon like Arnie Schwarzenegger in the face of something so utterly terrifying there isn't even a name for it. What those writers don't know is that what happens in an encounter with the outside is this: the moment slows down to such an extent that time itself simply stands still in your head. I suppose that fact doesn't make for good characterisation. It's incommunicable. I think they call it the numinous.

I once did a semester in creative writing after graduating, around the decade King was outselling every other author on the planet, but could never make the grade. Still, I read a lot of the best attempts. Maybe that's why someone like Lovecraft, or Machen, or one of the old-school writers of that stuff I used to read had almost pulled it off. They were no good at characterisation and tended to use ciphers, presenting the phenomenon itself as the main protagonist, because it was the way things are when you encounter it. The thing empties you, draining out any semblance of normalcy, no matter what your history is or what you think you're all about. Real horror consists not of the worst thing in the world you can imagine happening, but in encountering some abomination you cannot possibly imagine, something even worse than fear: a shard of absolute outsideness. Human characters become shadows, just shadows.

I think Yian-Ho knew it, though he didn't let on. I never did find out what it was that made him come back into the crimson fog. Maybe he'd been drugged up to the eyeballs, maybe his family were being held hostage, but I do know this: no one sane would be dropped back in the middle of the crimson fog a second time unless he had no choice. No one who has ever been up close to a fiend in its native habitat would want to repeat the experience.

We were exhausted when it happened.

For four hours straight we had been hacking our way through the dense vegetation, crawling like bugs sometimes, inching our way up an incline. Our clothes and bodies were soaked with sweat, our limbs were like dead weights, and finally, when we reached the top, Koszalski just sat down and refused to go any further without five minutes' rest. Neither I nor Mayhew were disposed to argue with him, so we dropped our machetes, pulled out water bottles, and started chugging at them. Yian-Ho, however, was still on his feet. He was alternately looking down at us and scanning the impenetrable red gloom, as if he had X-ray vision.

"No stop now," he said. "Better no stop now."

I soon realised he wasn't acting that way due to anything his eyes might have told him, but rather what his nose did. He must have caught a whiff of it long before any of the rest of us. And when that odour finally wafted into my nostrils, I, like Mayhew and Koszalski, got to my feet at once and we all had our rifles in our hands.

It was the stench of something atrociously *wrong*. I am not sure I can put it any other way. The actual smell was itself indescribable. It was not pungent at all, in fact it was rather subtle, but I am sure it bore no relation to anything in the history of the world, not animal, mineral, or vegetable. But when that scent got inside your nostrils it made all the hairs on your neck feel as if they were standing on end, your breath came in little gasps, just like the onset of a high fever; the first symptom of some horrendous infection.

We all felt it. We all looked back and forth at one another with the same expression in our eyes.

For five minutes nothing happened.

No one said a thing. We just watched and waited, guns ready.

The crimson fog drifted all around us, muffling everything.

I thought the unearthly odour had faded somewhat, but perhaps that was my imagination, or perhaps the first unendurable shock of it was already starting to wear off.

And then a twig snapped somewhere to my left. Under normal circumstances it would have been barely perceptible; but in the dead silence and with our heightened sense of dread, the sound was like a crack of thunder.

The chambers of our four AK-47 assault rifles were emptied by us into the depths of red gloom. The noise was deafening, and bits and pieces of mutilated vegetation scattered into the air like wedding confetti. After three or four more bursts we ceased firing.

"See anything?" I said.

"Nothing," Mayhew replied.

"Think we got the bastard?" Koszalski said.

The smell of cordite masked everything else.

We examined the spot we'd devastated. There was no body there. I don't know if I was relieved or not. It was a toss-up between the relief at seeing one dead and not seeing one at all.

No one seemed quite certain of what to do next.

"We go now," Yian-Ho said finally, taking the initiative. He reminded me of a seasoned dope fiend guiding college freshmen through their first bad acid trip.

3

Three hours later the sun went down. We pitched camp in a small clearing and built a fire. It could not possibly give away our position, of course, due to the omnipresent crimson fog. The wood we chopped from the trees did not burn easily, but we got a fire going eventually, though the flames coughed and spat in protest at their source. We cooked our rations and ate in silence.

The jungle was so quiet it was increasingly oppressive, now that we were surrounded by the darkness. Jungles are never quiet places, especially not at night. There was not even a breeze to rustle the treetops. Nothing that moved of its own accord lived and breathed here, no insect, no bird, no animal of any kind, except for the fiends. Except for us.

Mayhew set up the shortwave radio. He relayed our status and position back to H.Q. and was advised that we were to make our first attempt to try and contact Major Qersh. Communications from him had ceased two weeks ago and no one knew if he were alive or dead, something we, of course, had been dropped into the middle of Chang-Yi province to ascertain—and then to extract (if he were alive) the secret to killing the fiends and dispersing the crimson fog. No one knew if Qersh was dead, if his transmitter was destroyed or damaged, or whether even shortwave was beginning to fail to penetrate the crimson fog as its diameter inexorably expanded. Mayhew was a stickler for protocol and, I thought, was being absurd in keeping up with the use of military code when it was unnecessary.

"Blue Tiger Leader, this is Orange Tiger Pick Up, due south of your position, come in please. Over."

Nothing but ghostly static came back.

"Are you receiving me, Blue Tiger Leader? Over."

More static.

"Come in, Blue Tiger Leader. Over."

This one-sided exchange went on for around five minutes while the rest of us were sitting around staring dumbly and spooning into our mouths the pork and beans that we'd cooked directly in their cans in the embers at the edge of the fire.

When we finished the chow, Koszalski lit a cigarette, shook the pack in my direction. Even though I'd quit three months ago, I took one anyway. So did Yian-Ho. It's funny, I thought to myself, the prospect of an imminent death being a contributory cause of lung cancer.

Still no response from Qersh. And it must have been over a good seven or eight minutes now of Mayhew trying. He looked about ready to give up and also to finally help himself to Koszalski's supply of Lucky Strikes, when some words burst through the static intermittently. They were difficult to make out.

". . . is Blue Tiger . . . ome . . . derful . . . den. Radio . . . for God's sa . . . hurry . . . ver."

"Repeat last message, Blue Tiger Leader. Over."

More ghostly static. Mayhew kept on trying for an hour, but there was nothing more than what we'd already received coming back. He quit the fruitless task.

And sure enough those few words through the ether were all we heard. But it was Qersh all right. There was no one else it could have been.

I can't say our spirits were lifted. Mayhew relayed the information to H.Q. and they, of course, were enthused by this new development. We were to press on at dawn tomorrow to complete our mission objective.

We stared at one another around the campfire. It was our first time as a group with no immediate orders to carry out. We'd been thrown together only for this three-day mission and, truth be told, the chances of our carrying it out successfully were slim. We were a trial run for the real thing, expected to get to the mountain perhaps, but not to make it as far as Qersh. We'd been dropped in primarily to make sure he was still alive. Our job was to reconnoitre and if we got incredibly lucky, then it was all a bonus. But far more likely was that the next multinational team would piggy-back on our efforts and take all the plaudits and glory.

"You know about Apollo 10, right?"

"Sure," Mayhew replied. "The mission before the actual moon landing. Full dress rehearsal."

"That abandoned lunar module must still be out there, somewhere in space, drifting in orbit around the sun."

"What are you talking about, Sloane?" Koszalski said.

"Nothing, forget it."

I think everyone, Koszalski included, knew what I was getting at. But Mayhew spelled it out anyway.

"Crew of Apollo 10 were told there wasn't enough fuel for a landing. But there was. The tanks were all full. NASA lied out of their asses to them. Couldn't take the chance the astronauts would flip and risk landing anyway," Mayhew said.

"Not true story. In fact, Chinese were first on the moon, 1962," Yian-Ho said, with a wry grin.

"Communists," Koszalski said, "will believe anything."

"So you believe in all that other stuff instead, hey Koszalski? Heaven, Hell, the whole Jesus fairy tale? And the Devil too?" I said.

"I don't want a debate about it right now. For a start, we won't agree on basic definitions. Secondly, we won't agree on the burden of proof. Thirdly—"

"Looks to me like Hell is all around us now," Mayhew cut in, "looks to me like Hell has come to stay. Ain't no magic involved, only science this time. This is real."

"Read some Aquinas," Koszalski said, passing around his cigarettes.

"Maya. Illusion," Yian-Ho murmured.

Maybe he was a Buddhist *and* a communist. You could couple Buddhism with anything. It wasn't a judgemental deal. Atheism, Christianity, Shinto, even Devil-Worship. Nazism too, probably. Real tolerant.

We smoked and looked at one another blankly. But the moment didn't last long. Any conversation was better than the gaunt silence of the fog. So we discussed movies, and sports, and women, and anything else that came into our heads until we ran out of small talk and finally needed some shut-eye. Strange how quickly men become stereotypical cyphers in the face of fear and the unknown. I suppose my misanthropy was kicking in again.

Yian-Ho took first watch, I was to take the second, Koszalski the third, and Mayhew the fourth. Whether the fiends were more active during the night I couldn't say. Since some scientists claimed that the things never slept at all, unlike all other animals we know of, I suppose it was something of a moot point.

*

Inside the confines of the tent Mayhew and Koszalski were both as restless as I was, despite our shared exhaustion, and we kept shifting position and muttering indistinctly. It was like a psych ward at night, when the effects of sedatives and painkillers are beginning to wane and the final drug trolley isn't due for another hour. When I did finally manage to drop off, I slept badly, dreamlessly, and it seemed only moments later that Yian-Ho woke me up for me to take my shift. I could tell he was eager to get back into the tent alongside the others, rather than being left all alone out there, and I accused him, falsely, of shaving off a good half hour from the duration of his turn at watch.

When I was outside I realised there are worse places than psych wards.

The silence was the worst of it. The only faint background noise came from the crackling embers of the campfire. Tentacles of red mist crept across its dim, twelve-foot circle of light, and I occupied my time drinking acrid black coffee, poking at the low flames with a branch, and tossing in more strips of wood to keep the fire alive.

There was no point in trying to spot something in the fog and darkness.

For all I knew there could have been a hundred of those evil fiends out there in a circle around me, staring blankly, their dreadful protoplasmic eyes and bodies bubbling with insane hunger, and I would have had no way of telling.

I tried to think about something else, *anything* else, because once a thought like that got hold of you it was the beginning of the end.

I checked my wristwatch. It indicated I had been alone outside for twenty minutes. It seemed more like twenty hours. Then, stupidly, I was convinced the thing was broken and I held it up to my ear. I didn't want to hear the ticking of the mechanism, but there it was nevertheless. Had it stopped I would have had an excuse to go back inside the tent and rouse one of the others.

My mind wandered again. Creeping fear. Nice phrase. Or "The Creeping Fear." Must have been the title of one of those Lovecraft stories I read back on that useless creative writing course. A fat lot of good those classes ever did for anybody. I never managed to sell a thing, just wasted a lot of time and effort and watched our big shot teacher (whose one claim to fame was having sold a script to the final series of that syndicated TV show, *The Dusk Domain*, back in the 1960s) as he worked his phony charm on his female students one after the other. I bet he never suffered from the creeping fear, only the creeping STD itch.

But *The Dusk Domain*—now that was a good show. Old school. They don't make them like that anymore. Nowadays it's all maggot-riddled zombies. Or serial killer neighbours. What was that great episode of *The Dusk Domain*, the one with a manic Leonard Nimoy on an airplane, and he's the only one who can see that the flight crew are all demons, or something, and the passengers' destination is Hell? Or the other one about the radio that's tuned into tomorrow, and the guy (must have been a young Dennis Hopper) who bought it from a junkshop and who makes a fortune at the racetrack until he hears nothing but static? And it turns out the next day the U.S.A. and the Soviets went to war and both sides have dropped the bomb, wiping out the entire planet. Nothing but static. It was the noise of that static that was the sucker punch. Just like the static punctuating Qersh's indistinct words.

". . . is Blue Tiger . . . ome . . . derful . . . den. Radio . . . for God's sa . . . hurry . . . ver."

Maybe Qersh had cracked up there all alone in the crimson fog. He was probably so crazy by now it was a waste of time trying to get to him. Twenty minutes—was it still only twenty minutes? Qersh had to be insane by now. No one could not be under such circumstances. All those fiends out there in the jungle, hiding away and just staring in the darkness, in the fog, thousands of sunken eyes like currants in gingerbread men, staring and waiting for the right moment to strike, waiting in silence, waiting until a man has completely lost his mind. I bet there's something savoury about a meaty brain that's cooked in its own juices . . .

"Sloane? Sloane! Answer me!"

A voice. Someone was shaking my shoulder.

"Time for me to take over."

It was Koszalski. The bead-rattling Papist.

I checked my watch. My shift was finished. Somehow I'd lost track of time altogether.

"Hey," he said. "Are you OK? You were really out of it."

I didn't reply; I just went back into the tent and tried to get to sleep. Eventually I thought I heard Koszalski outside muttering words to himself over and over again. It sounded like the Lord's Prayer but it could have been the Hail Mary, or maybe it was both mixed up. But even as I noticed it, I was losing consciousness.

*

Mayhew woke me this time.

"Koszalski's gone," he said.

"What do you mean, *gone*?" I replied. "Has he run off?"

I knew he wouldn't have run off; no one would willingly take their chances alone in the crimson fog, even in daylight. But I didn't want to frame the only alternative I could think of.

"You'd better see for yourself," Mayhew said.

We woke up Yian-Ho and went outside.

The fire was still burning, at a low ebb, and the electric lantern was doing most of the work in keeping the darkness back. A few things had been turned over in what looked like a brief, one-sided struggle. Koszalski's assault rifle, pack, and helmet were lying there like discarded mementoes.

"Look," Yian-Ho said, pointing to something else.

At a spot close to the edge of the fire there was an empty camouflage uniform and two boots in a crumpled heap. From the pile issued a trail of stomach-churning malodorous red slime or excreta, leading right off into the depths of the fog and the jungle. That fever smell was unmistakable and repugnant; it reeked of the fiends' presence. One of them had probably got Koszalski while he was gazing into the fire. It must have jumped him from behind and then fastened onto him; covering his mouth with its own so he could not scream and then drawing up all his flesh and blood and bone into itself, dissolving him silently, like a python. And the damn fiend, all fat and loathsome, then excreted, leaving that sickening trail of human jam behind it.

So much for the efficacy of Koszalski's prayers. His rosary beads were right in the middle of the red trail of excreta, and it seemed the thing didn't much care for the taste of them.

We kitted up, weapons ready, and followed the bloody trail for about five hundred yards into the gloom. It appeared to terminate at the base of a huge tree, but then we noticed that the trail actually continued vertically up the trunk and into the obscured branches high overhead. I thought of firing off a few rounds up into the distance; but there was no telling where the bullets might come down, and we knew those fiends moved from tree to tree like monkeys anyway. The overwhelming probability was that it was long gone rather than staring down at us with a satisfied grin on its ugly face. There was no point in wasting ammo.

We made our way back to camp. No one felt like sleeping, and in any case the sun was up in less than an hour.

"We need to bury him," I said.

Mayhew laughed. It wasn't a pleasant laugh: there was too much sarcasm in it.

"I'm serious," I said, gritting my teeth.

Yian-Ho didn't seem inclined to join in the debate and began cleaning his machete with a rag.

"Look," Mayhew said, "there's nothing of him left to bury. You want to waste energy on making a grave for a couple of boots and a stinking uniform? Forget it."

"It's the right thing to do. I don't give a shit for his beliefs, but it's a mark of respect for him as a soldier. We have a duty."

"Forget that foolishness. You want to waste your own time, you go right ahead, Sloane, but count me out," he said.

"Fine, I'll do that."

I began to dig a shallow grave. Yian-Ho helped at some stage, but not with much enthusiasm. When it was finished I put Koszalski's clothes and boots into the hole, kept the pack of cigarettes I found, and then went and retrieved his rosary from the sticky red trail. I threw it on top of the heap and covered the whole mess with a layer of soil. I tried to remember the words of a prayer, any prayer, but couldn't manage it.

"So long," Yian-Ho finally said.

Mayhew had watched us working for a little while, but soon occupied himself with the radio and attempted to get through to H.Q. and report, I suppose, that we were now down to three men.

He couldn't get through.

There was only static this time. Louder than before.

We ate breakfast without saying a word. As the sun came up, the darkness all around us gave way to the crimson of the fog in daylight.

I would have given all I had for the sound of a dawn chorus.

4

We pressed on through the jungle in a line, Yian-Ho at point, me in the middle, and Mayhew bringing up the rear. The masses of vegetation that had slowed us down and forced us to hack our way through with machetes had thinned out, and there were now long stretches of clearing where our passage was relatively unhindered. I was amazed at Yian-Ho's navigational skill. It seemed to me incredible that he could accurately chart any sort of route to the base of the mountain. Our course was serpentine, not direct. There were not even any landmarks to give him his bearings. Perhaps he had one of those almost psychic senses of direction some rare people seem to possess.

Maybe it was just my imagination, but it seemed to me the stench of the fiends was more often close at hand than before. At first I thought it must have clung to me after I'd handled Koszalski's slime-covered apparel, but the smell was not constant—it came and went in degrees of intensity. And after that business with the thing having left its bloody trail vertically up a tree, I spent as much time desperately squinting into the crimson gloom above my head as I did squinting into the vegetation on the ground. I imagined troupes of the things swinging from treetop to treetop, alongside the hordes of them creeping through the bushes alongside us.

I didn't voice the thought aloud, but a part of me wanted the fiends to come out into the open and attack us. It would mean an end to the unbearable suspense and the chance to take down some of them with our weapons. I wanted to know for sure they could be killed, that a hail of bullets could tear right through their stinking hides, and I wanted to hear one of them scream in agony as it died. What I couldn't stand was the idea of them appearing and disappearing into the crimson fog, picking us off one by one, as elusive and impervious to physical damage as phantoms.

We made good progress during the afternoon, after we'd stopped briefly to eat and to try to radio H.Q. We couldn't get through again. And, although we were closer to Qersh's position than before, when we had been partially successful, we couldn't establish contact with him either.

After several hours of extreme physical exertion coupled with a continued thinning out of the obstructive vegetation that had slowed us down before, we found ourselves steadily ascending new terrain.

"The foot of the mountain," said Yian-Ho as we pressed on with redoubled effort.

The ground became rocky and we gradually left the trees behind. It was a tremendous relief, because now I knew that the fiends had no cover for their activities. Although the crimson fog still hid them from direct sight, our line of fire would now be completely clear without any obstacles.

"Let's rest here for a short while and then set up camp for the night slightly further up," I said.

Yian-Ho paused and turned back. The smile he had on his face froze.

"Where Mayhew?" he said.

There was a muffled sound of gunfire coming from about five hundred yards back along the route we'd taken. Only the firecracker racket of shots fired could penetrate across that distance. It was coming from right at the edge of the tree line. I don't know whether Mayhew had stopped to tie a bootlace, had turned his ankle, or what had caused him to fall behind, but it had occurred. Nevertheless, he was still alive, and he had the radio. We had to go back for him.

Yian-Ho and I retraced our steps in the fog with our guns blazing, and I think it was this that caused the enemy to retreat before it had finished entirely with Mayhew. Such had not been the case with Koszalski, where it had time to linger over its activity, slowly ingesting him and hauling itself off into the jungle.

We found Mayhew, all right. Perhaps as much as half of him was left. The fiend or fiends (I had no idea how many it would take to do that to a fully grown man) had retreated into the combination of cordite smoke and red fog entirely leaving behind no trace of their presence, save for the lingering alien stench.

Mayhew was spread-eagled like a puppet whose strings had been cut mid-performance. Two of his limbs, a whole arm and leg, were gone completely, dissolved, and so too with the torso and head, as if acid had been poured over his body. What remained twitched in spastic fashion, and from the corner of its ruined mouth there issued a steady drool of black liquid.

I think the remaining half of his face was the worst.

Mayhew was not a man likely to succumb to spiritual mayhem. Even in pain and impending death I imagined that cold logic and scientific reason would be his guiding lights. He was ever the stoic. But the expression in that remaining half-face was like a vortex. Unfathomable, insane ecstasy stared out from its depths, not horror. The destruction of his physical form could not account for that aspect.

And he was murmuring something. Words he wanted to impart to me.

Yian-Ho aimed his weapon so as to put a bullet through Mayhew's brain before I had the chance to hear what he said, but I knocked aside the barrel of Yian-Ho's rifle, and his shot went wide.

I bent down over Mayhew's body to catch the words he was saying.

"Go away," he said, "and let me alone. Let them come to me. To feed and be fed. Oh, there is such beauty in the enemy. Such beauty. If you only knew . . ."

I drew my sidearm from its holster, pressed the business end of the pistol to his temple, and squeezed the trigger before he could finish the sentence. The sharp recoil as it discharged reminded me of the last time I'd jerked off.

Blood and brains fountained onto the grass. More red and grey. Less green. Synaptic convolutions cooked in creeping fear.

"Come away now," Yian-Ho said, taking me by the arm, and so we started back up the slope taking the shortwave radio with us, leaving the tree line behind, and then . . . and then . . . well, there was just the two of us left in the crimson fog.

I thought of burying Mayhew. But it wouldn't have been a mark of respect.

5

We set up camp after about fifteen minutes of trekking up the side of the mountain, slightly further than I had originally intended to go, but I wanted to put some distance between us and the spot they'd got Mayhew. Most of the light had gone by the time we got a campfire going using the branches Yian-Ho had thought to collect in his backpack before we had quit the forest. We cooked something in their cans, though I could scarcely tell what it was. Some kind of stew, I supposed. Even my sense of taste and smell seemed to be deadening, like my sense of sight, in the omnipresent crimson fog. After we'd eaten I took out Koszsolski's pack of cigarettes. There were only four left. I lit one and passed one to Yian-Ho.

I decided to ask him the question I'd been wanting to ask for a long time.

"What made you come back?" I said suddenly, without leading up to it.

He looked at me steadily as he puffed on his smoke and took so long before answering I thought either he hadn't heard me or didn't want to speak.

"Qersh," he finally replied.

So that was it. The old motto of never leaving a comrade behind. As simple as that. I hadn't realised they'd served together. Of course it made sense, but then . . .

"I came back to kill that sonofabitch," he added.

Then, over the course of half an hour, Lieutenant Yian-Ho

told me what had happened before. In the previous mission led by Major Qersh the group had consisted of six at the start. Somehow Qersh had got lost on the first day after their drop into the crimson fog. On the evening of the second day he wandered into camp and claimed to have caught up with and followed the company's trail. But the odd thing was that he had the unmistakable stench of the enemy on his skin and clothes. He reeked of it. This fact he attempted to explain away by claiming he'd had a close run-in with the enemy, fired at several of them, and was lucky to get away with his life.

As the group halved in numbers over three nights, Yian-Ho had realised that it was always the man on last watch who disappeared in a trail of red slime. Qersh organised the rota, and this confirmed—or so it seemed to Yian-Ho—he was somehow in league with the enemy. Indeed, there had been something not quite right about Qersh since he had returned, and it wasn't just the stench of him. Even if the matter of the order of the overnight watches was a coincidence and the fiends preferred to strike just before dawn, sometimes Major Qersh looked at a man in a strangely sadistic way. Rather like the way, so Yian-Ho said, cats finally, gleefully, look at mice when they've got them trapped in a corner and know the deadly game is almost over.

With only three men left now, Yian-Ho had tried to persuade the other Lieutenant, Li-Hung, that they had to kill their commanding officer or they were done for. It helped that the two were very old friends and had served together for the past five years. Both agreed that they would shoot Qersh while he slept, for he invariably took the second watch. He would know nothing about it and would scarcely suffer any pain. It would be a mercy.

That night, just after two in the morning, Yian-Ho crept into the tent and silently awoke Li-Hung, and after a moment or two both men trained their rifles on the recumbent form of Major Qersh in his sleeping bag.

At a signal from Yian-Ho both men would open fire at the same instant so the killing act would be shared equally.

Yian-Ho duly nodded to Li-Hung, and they both pulled their triggers.

Nothing happened except for dual clicks.

The ammunition cartridges had been emptied.

Slowly Qersh rolled over and sat up. Th0ere was a mirthless smile on his face.

At almost the same instant, as if on cue, the tent was torn apart and the stench of the fiends was everywhere as they bore down on the men.

Somehow, in the ensuing chaos, Yian-Ho managed to get away, plunging alone into the depths of the night, the fog, and the labyrinthine jungle, the screams of Li-Hung ringing in his ears and all the devils of hell in pursuit of him.

A week later he stumbled, bloodied, famished, and exhausted, into the fortified camp of the last scientific mission to be overrun just before its occupants had all been evacuated.

Yian-Ho had finished his account and threw the butt of his cigarette into the flames of the campfire.

"This raises more questions than answers," I said.

"How so?" he replied.

"Why would our C.O. send you back in on a mission to rescue Qersh after you'd been debriefed and told him what you've told me?"

"I not tell him. I say I want to come back and help rescue great hero Major Qersh, hope of the world. But I keep secret he is son-ofabitch."

*

There was no attack that night, and what with there now being only two of us to keep watch neither Yian-Ho or I got enough sleep. I wondered if our being outside of the forest as well as some way further down that part of the mountain where Qersh was supposedly encircled by hordes of the fiends meant this area was relatively free of them. Certainly the stench appeared to be have receded.

Before we broke camp I tried the shortwave radio again, but without success. It seemed a useless, heavy burden; the thought crossed my mind to leave it behind here, but I dismissed the suggestion. Who knows what might have happened by now to Qersh's own shortwave radio and whether it was still even functional?

Yian-Ho led the way up the rocky approach route towards the higher reaches of the mountain, and I was hard-pressed to keep up with him. His agility, balance, and surefootedness in the ascent were far superior to my clumsy abilities.

We hadn't said much since he had told me his tale about Major Qersh; naturally, I couldn't tell how much of it was true. I didn't doubt that Yian-Ho had come back to kill Qersh, but whether or not events had transpired exactly as the lieutenant had related them to me I had no way of knowing. I didn't doubt that I would only gain some measure of an insight into the truth when the two men came face-to-face. But, in any case, I knew I could not simply stand back and allow Yian-Ho to gun down Qersh in cold blood at first sight. My orders had been to rescue the man, not to let Yian-Ho to destroy him.

There was also the question of my own safety to be considered. If Yian-Ho planned to assassinate Qersh, he had put me in a position of being forced either to be an accomplice or else to oppose his scheme and make myself an obstacle.

I read in Yian-Ho's eyes that he knew what I was thinking. And doubtless vice versa. I still wasn't sure he was even sane. Nothing, not even revenge and loyalty to fallen comrades, could have made me travel into the crimson fog a second time.

As we climbed the ascent became ever more perilous, and I couldn't help but wonder if he was choosing the most difficult path upwards. I lost my footing several times, once or twice even coming close to taking a fall of—I imagined—several hundred feet. It would not have been so damnable were it not for the crimson fog. I could neither tell how far we had come nor how far there was to go. For all my senses told me we could have been climbing a mountain that had no beginning or end but stretched from one side of infinity to the other.

While I brooded over these thoughts, my eyes peering desperately at the ground a few feet in front for suitable footholds, I hadn't noticed that Yian-Ho had stopped ahead of me and turned around, waiting until I was less than a few yards behind him and it was too late for me to react.

He had drawn his pistol and was pointing it at my chest. His expression was deadly serious. There wasn't anything like fear or anger mixed in with it, just a steely determination. Normally, of course, in such situations one's focus tends to be on the firearm that threatens to blank out one's earthly existence with a loud bang.

But I had expected something like this, for I had been at the wrong end of a gun before, and I knew the routine.

"Take it easy, Lieutenant," I said, raising my arms without being asked to do so. "We're on the same side, remember. There's no need for this."

The sound of my voice comforted me. If he'd intended to gun me down without listening to what I had to say I'd already be riddled with bullets.

"I can't take the chance," Yian-Ho said. "You try to stop me when I get to Qersh."

"So you're going to kill me, is that it? Just as Qersh did to your friend Li-Hung and the others?"

"No. I give you a choice. Either let me do what I must do or go back now, the way we came. I let you decide. This you must swear."

"All right," I said.

"Throw down your weapons," he ordered.

I complied with machete, rifle, pistol, and even the jackknife I kept hidden in my boot. He kicked them all off the path and they fell into the tentacles of red mist, all except for the pistol, which he had stowed in his pack.

"You take the lead now," he said, waving me past him. "Sorry for any inconvenience."

His sense of decorum rather touched me.

"I don't know the route."

"One route only possible. Straight up, please."

6

It was worse being at the front. As I've said, I'm no climber and my sense of balance and my agility aren't exceptional. Our progress was even slower than before with me leading the way. I couldn't see any further than ten yards ahead of me; but at least when I'd been at the rear, gazing at Yian-Ho's back and following his lead, the fact didn't seem as dangerous. He was taking most of the risk. Now I was, and it had more than doubled now, for both of us. I heard him swear a few times, in Mandarin, cursing my ineptitude after I stumbled—or staggered—and he would then almost be on top of me.

Of course the other danger, for me at least, was that I now didn't have a weapon with which to defend myself. If one or more of those fiends suddenly decided to lope out of the fog ahead and take hold of me I'd have to rely on Yian-Ho to get me out of trouble. And he'd have to shoot through me in order to hit the enemy. Either way I'd have had it.

How far does reality extend? That was the question that kept running through my mind.

Here I was trapped up on the side of a mountain in some crimson fog that reached all the way up into outer space before dissipating, with no scientific explanation to account for its properties.

How far does reality extend? Only to the limits of our senses? Or the limits of thought and the imagination? Beyond it is the vast unknown. You open the creaking door and enter *The Dusk Domain* . . .

I'd read something once about supposed boundary conditions as the universe expands, and it turned out there was no real edge, only a limit to our observational ability. In fact, anywhere in the universe is the centre of the Big Bang event. The far side of the universe is billions of years in the past only by virtue of its being on the far side from our own perspective.

I don't know about that; I'm no mystic or astrophysicist. But what I did know was Major J. Qersh was at the centre of this particular foggy red cosmos. Maybe he had all the answers about the phenomenon, as he claimed to have, or maybe he was just a mad "sonofabitch" as Yian-Ho thought. Or maybe it didn't matter a damn either way and all reality was finally tearing itself apart at the seams as the cosmos expanded.

*

The stench was back. The fiends couldn't be far away now. The smell had been getting stronger for the last half hour. At first I caught a vague impression of it, but as we ascended there could be no doubt. We were climbing up into another area where they swarmed, invisible, like flies in fog.

Yian-Ho must have noticed it too, but he didn't comment on the thing. We hadn't said a word to each other since he'd taken control of the situation. He must have realised how defenceless I was and I expected him, sooner rather than later, at least to offer me back the use of my pistol for my own protection. My reserve reached breaking point. I knew it would be better to wait for him to make the offer, but I could no longer go on pressing into the depths of the fog ahead without a weapon. It was suicide. I was right on the verge of turning around in protest and making my plea when I heard muffled shots behind me. A bullet whistled past my left ear with a sickening whine like a mosquito. I instinctively dropped to the ground, rolling onto my side and looking back.

How far the bullet had travelled I could not tell.

Yian-Ho was nowhere to be seen.

I wondered whether he had screamed at the last when he was taken and if the fiends and the fog had blotted out the sound entirely.

At least, I thought, they would be occupied with him for some time. The fool should have given me the pistol back. There was no way I could tackle those fiends with my bare hands.

And so there was nothing else for me to do except to go on.

7

I reached the outer part of the ruined temple half an hour before dusk. The path upwards became flights of steps carved into the rock until finally they terminated and I found myself traversing the flagstones of a courtyard. The structure was not level and was tilted over at about ten degrees or so. I almost felt drunk as I made my way across it. Broken columns and a profusion of deep wells dotted the surface. I was terrified that I might stumble into one inadvertently, and when I paused to look down inside I heard something silent throwing itself around in the darkness below, and an all-too-familiar stench wafted up from the inky depths.

Eventually, after inching my way forward with the utmost care—for dusk gave way to night quickly—and with only my flashlight to pick out the wells that lay ahead in my path, I reached the inner temple.

A flight of crumbling steps, hollowed by the tread of centuries of feet, led up to a pair of rotten wooden doors that were ajar. I passed through them and entered into the interior of the structure.

For the first time since I had been dropped into Chang-Yi province I could see further than ten yards. The crimson fog did not penetrate into the confines of the temple, and my eyes took time to adjust both to seeing objects in the middle distance again and to the illumination within.

Thousands of candles burned inside, and my gaze was drawn up towards the lofty dome above my head by the array of hangings that fluttered in the warm air. These hangings all bore cryptic designs, ciphers I can only describe as curiously horrible mandalas. There was something vertiginous in their aspect and something fascinating too. It was difficult to tear one's gaze from them.

When I did so I saw ahead of me what must have once been the altar. Situated there was a couch fashioned from branches and vegetation, and there was a figure dressed in khaki reclining on it. As I approached, the figure got to his feet and I had my first good look at Major J. Qersh.

He was a heavy-set man in his early fifties, just under middle height, balding, wearing horn-rimmed eyeglasses, with a salt-and-pepper goatee and unchecked stubble elsewhere on his jaw. He was smiling, but the smile seemed artificial, as if he were putting it on only for my benefit. His left hand hovered over the pistol holster on his hip while in his right he held a long-stemmed pipe he had lately been smoking.

I should have saluted him, but somehow the gesture seemed absurd.

"You're Major Qersh," I said.

"That's what they called me, I reckon," he replied in an accent marking him out as someone from the deep South.

When I was within a few feet I saw the dead expression in his ink-black irises. His eyes were utterly vacant and seemed to stare without any rationality lurking behind them. They gave his whole visage a disconcerting, mask-like aspect. The odd smile he wore seemed frozen on his features as if, having once adopted that expression, he had forgotten how to easily replace it with another.

"You're the rescue party, I take it," he said, sliding back onto the couch, his left hand drifting away from his holster and occupying itself with finding a lighter which he used to relight the contents in the bowl of his pipe.

"What's left of it," I said. "I'm Captain Thomas Sloane."

"And how, uh—exactly—do you propose to get me out of here? Doesn't look exactly like a well-organised mission."

"We were sent in to bring you back to the position where we were dropped off. They're probably already levelling the forest there so they can land a chopper."

"I'm not going anywhere, son. I like it here."

Qersh was drawing heavily on the pipe, sucking some foul-smelling smoke—the colour of the fog outside—into his lungs and slowly expelling it with a sickening rasping noise. I watched it eddy and whirl in tentacles around his head, before drifting upwards in the air.

"But your last transmission—it seemed to indicate you were under attack and needed to be evacuated."

"Things aren't always what they seem."

I wondered if Qersh hadn't made his broadcast simply in order to lure others to their deaths in the crimson fog. I wanted to make the accusation, but I knew I had to play the situation carefully. He was armed and I was not, and the cards were stacked in his favour. Right now, all he seemed to want was an audience to watch him perform.

"Those things in the fog aren't monsters, you know," he said in that drawl of his. "We could learn a lot from them. I have learnt much from them already."

"Those *things* have killed the rest of the men who came to rescue you. They're not human."

"You know so little. They only came here to trade. Our world for their superior wisdom. Our flesh for their secret glory. They exchange all their thoughts with one another, sharing everything. Each one is part of a greater whole. Absolute equality. We can become a part of that whole, either willingly or unwillingly. Don't you want to be part of something greater than yourself? Something real, something physical, something that will last for generation after generation and not some absurd ideal?"

The man was insane. I realised I should have listened to Yian-Ho all along. And now it was too late. It seemed obvious that once Qersh was tired of me he would put a bullet through my head and feed me to the fiends. As if reading my mind, and in answer to my thoughts, he spoke again.

"They consume one another too, you know. Not very often, but it's the way they reproduce. It's their sexual cycle. For each one that's eaten they eventually excrete the nuclei of two more—

newborns of red slime. They want to interbreed with us, with humanity I mean. We must not fear the Other. We must become one with it. They are so much more tolerant than the human race, so much more open-minded. What do we have to lose?"

"Only that which makes us human."

"What makes us human? You think our miserable species worth saving? Mankind, the scum of the universe. Mankind, the bad joke. Mankind, his own worst enemy."

He grinned, his dead eyes, magnified by the lenses of his spectacles, hanging over his smile like those of some enormous, hungry shark.

"And these things," I said, "these cannibal fiends, what are they and where do they come from? What makes them better than, as you put it, human scum?"

My voice had taken on an accusatory tone. I felt, in that strange temple high in the crimson fog, that I had taken on the role of defending counsel for my species. I knew I was going to die here, and I wanted the scene to be played out with my having at least registered my contempt for Qersh and his betrayal of his fellow man.

"Since you ask," he said, "and have come all this way into the new order in search of answers, I had better tell you. That first night when I was amongst them, when they gladly welcomed me, I participated in their secret rites of consummation."

"You mean you copulated with the fiends and then fed them your comrades."

"In the end," he said, "my former comrades welcomed their destiny. As will you."

I thought of Mayhew and his final words.

"You haven't answered my question," I said.

"Haven't you realised? These things are not fiends. They are the final stage of human evolution. They haven't arrived from some other planet or dimension. There are no aliens anywhere. We are all the sentient life there is in this useless void. They are the gods we are to become. And now, inevitably, the future has caught up with the past. They're what we've been working towards as a species, what we've always been working towards. They have come to invade their own history."

And thoughts I had thought before, not long ago, came back

to me. Reality tearing itself apart at the seams as the cosmos expands. What lies beyond the edge of the visible universe cannot be known. The distance is greater than what light itself, or any other form of radiation, can reveal. The crimson fog—existence itself is bleeding to death.

Qersh had set aside his pipe on the couch and rose to his feet.

The final reckoning was at hand.

I somehow knew it lay within Qersh's power to call forth hordes of the fiends—from the pits littered around the temple, from the jungle, from the endless clouds of the crimson fog—and that they would fall upon me at his bidding. All that I thought constituted my notions of humanity would cease.

"Sonofabitch!"

It was the voice of Yian-Ho. He had crept into the temple while Qersh and I were speaking and had only revealed himself at the last moment, waiting for his opportunity to strike.

His cry was followed by several rifle shots and, as I rolled onto my side, I saw Qersh collapse under the impact of the bullets fired. His expression did not alter one iota as the lead tore into his body, staining his khaki with red blotches. Even as he fell, like some marionette whose strings have been severed, those dead eyes continued to stare vacantly.

Yian-Ho and I got out of there as quickly as we could.

8

We didn't encounter a single fiend on our way back to the pick-up point. Perhaps most of those in the vicinity had accumulated at the temple in order to pay their respects to the fallen Qersh and were preoccupied.

Of course it was much easier going back, retracing our route down the mountain and across the jungle, following the paths we'd hewn through the dense vegetation, and we made good time.

I asked Yian-Ho how he had escaped their clutches, but he told me he had simply been lucky and that the fog could be a help as well as a hindrance.

By the time we were close to the pick-up point I had a horrible sense of foreboding that the jungle wouldn't have been cleared with aerial firepower and the chopper would not be there to pick us up. But some little time before we reached the rendezvous area I caught the aroma of burnt vegetation filtering through the fog, and my hopes were raised. At least I was sure the first part of attempt to pick us up had been made, even if we did not yet know if the helicopter had successfully landed and was awaiting our arrival. The fires raised by incendiaries wouldn't burn for very long. Most of the vegetation was too pulpy, and the air too thick and damp with the fog, for total conflagration.

During the confusion back at the temple I had left behind the portable shortwave radio and we had no way of communicating ahead to the chopper, to headquarters, or to anyone else. The suspense was terrible. Yian-Ho and I had exhausted all conversation long ago, and we had exchanged no words since he had passed my pistol back to me after we had fled the temple.

Finally we reached our destination and found scorched earth and blackened dead trees. The noise of huge blades slowly slicing through the air, churning up the fog like a maelstrom, prefigured the sight of the chopper itself.

Our relief turned to fear when we discovered no sign of the crew and saw three trails of red slime leading out of its interior. The rescue team could only have been taken within the last hour or so, perhaps immediately after landing. Blasting the forest must have drawn dozens of the fiends to wait for the flames to die out. Even now, it was likely they were consuming the air-force men.

I could fly the chopper sure enough, but my first concern was about fuel. The gauge showed the tank two-thirds full, so we had enough for a few hours' flying time. Enough to carry us several hundred miles and just clear of Chang-Yi province.

I did a quick, very basic instrument test and then Yian-Ho and I buckled up, the blades increased speed, and we hurtled straight up. I waited until reaching a reasonably safe altitude, to overfly any mountains, before heading in the direction of the eastern edge of the crimson fog.

9

When I tried the chopper's radio all I heard through the headset were bursts of static. Sometimes I thought I heard ghostly voices like Raudive phenomena. I don't know whether it was my imagination or not, but one of them that came through was eerily familiar:

". . . is Blue Tiger . . . ome . . . derful . . . den. Radio . . . for God's sa . . . hurry . . . ver."

I didn't mention it to Yian-Ho.

We have been in the air for more than three hours now and there is no end to the crimson fog. I haven't altered course and we have been following the same dead east heading. I believe that the fog has suddenly expanded exponentially, has crossed the Chinese border, flowing over the Great Wall, and transformed all it encounters into alien, occupied territory.

Yian-Ho started to look at me suspiciously an hour into the flight, and three times now he has accused me of deliberately flying around in circles. He doesn't know what he's talking about and has become dangerously unhinged.

Once, I'm sure, I heard him mutter under his breath the word "sonofabitch."

He knows, now that I have my pistol back, that he needs to think twice about making a hasty move, but he's just crazy enough to try it. Even though it would mean both our deaths.

I figured out his shooting Qersh could be a way of setting himself up as the new go-between between mankind and the fiends.

And Qersh said they can get inside your brain, sharing thoughts, making you think the strange things they want you to think.

Yian-Ho's under their spell all right.

More than that, even, there's something dead and Qersh-like about his gaze now.

I think his eyes must be full of either blood or fog.

There's thunder rolling in from far off in the distance.

I calculate, from the gauge, there are fifteen minutes of fuel to go before the chopper's tanks are empty.

Another ten minutes and, if he keeps on staring at me, I'm going to put a bullet through his occupied red brain.

Then I'll try to set the chopper down.

How far does reality itself extend?

Nowhere near as far as what's going to replace it.

COURT OF MIDNIGHT

I had been wandering aimlessly for months around the dark corners of conquered Europe seeking respite from the tyranny of dreams when I finally found myself a resident of the Court of Midnight. Much of the city surrounding it was reduced to ruins and rubble after the war. The actual name of the city I could never discover, for every single map had been subject to the recent censorship, and all references to its existence in books had been purged after the final victory of our foes. The original populace had been cleared out altogether, and what few newcomers there were could tell nothing more of its history. That it had once been a metropolis of great import seemed apparent, despite its now derelict character. The empty façades of its once-mighty boulevards and the innumerable spires and bell-towers of its close-packed churches told a tale of vanquished glory.

I was sick, having recently been stricken with the lunar fever that was raging across the continent, and further exposure to the night sky and the ghastly light of the moon would have been fatal. The last episode had been nightmarish and had left me in a state of incoherency.

After being examined by an official of the region with minimal medical skills, I was advised that all hospitals in the city had been either been destroyed or else were in a state of dilapidation. The only immediate treatment he could provide was a course of pills to prevent dreaming. These would ward off certain death, but a long-term cure required the ministrations of a specialist doctor called Prozess.

I was further advised by the bureaucrat that the best course of action for my health in the interim was to rent lodgings in the Court of Midnight. He could make the arrangements here and now. There was a cheap attic room available I could occupy at once, provided I possessed the requisite stamped forms. Furthermore, a request that Dr Prozess attend to my case would be dispatched by letter immediately. After I had filled out the forms and paid the official of the region with banknotes he wrote down directions to the place and handed over a small bottle of pills, my residency documents, and house keys. I thanked him, picked up my valise, and set off on foot.

I tramped across two miles of cobbled streets at dusk, lined with peak-roofed houses in varying stages of decay. All was vacancy and desolation. No sight or sound of pedestrians or horse-cabs broke the sense of loneliness; only the scurrying rats glimpsed from the corners of my eyes provided evidence of activity.

And then the initial fever symptoms began to rise inside me, a warning that the moon lay just below the rim of the horizon and would appear in the sky within the next ten minutes or so. My skin was already beginning to develop the first traces of small, white, leprous patches, and a sheen of sweat moistened my brow. I gritted my teeth and pressed on with more pace and urgency. Finally, after turning a sharp corner, I found myself in front of the entrance to my destination. Pushing through a rusted trellised gate in front of a low arch, I entered into a narrow brick passageway that opened out into a square and I finally stood in the Court of Midnight.

I saw why this place was a refuge for those stricken with lunar fever. On all four sides the court was enclosed by six-storey edifices, but they were each acutely crooked and had tipped together at roof height, blocking out entirely the sky above. No ray of moonlight could penetrate within the confines of the court. A single streetlamp, mounted on a tottering iron pillar, fought against total blackness, its gaslight casting a sickly glow that only accentuated the appalling state of neglect into which the court had been allowed to fall. A tenacious ivy, the colour of ash, had run riot along the walls (and the overhanging balconies of the buildings), and in the few spaces it did not conceal there was revealed rotten stucco, peeling away like dead skin. There were circular windows, dozens of them, that made me think of the fixed stare of eyeless sockets in the long-dead.

Nothing truly human could live here, only things verminous.

But my fever had stabilised, held in abeyance since my arrival.

Checking my watch, I saw that the moon was now up. Were I to go back the way I had come I would be a delirious wreck within a few minutes of exposure, my body ravaged by the pockmarks that would later develop into deep craters, while my brain would give way to an impulse to voice aloud the mad laughter—the black laughter, with screams mingled in it, the laughter of no purpose, the laughter that bubbles and seethes and rolls on and on and on like an endless river of blood. I knew I could not stand another episode like the last.

There was no time to find an alternative refuge, at least not tonight.

I pulled out the paper with the directions the official had scrawled on it in pencil, and the house keys.

I unlocked the outer door to one of the residences and fumbled my way up a crazily angled stairwell whose steps protested at each tread. The interior was musty and unlit, and several tiny feathery wings brushed across my face—belonging to moths, I supposed. My left hand guided me along worm-eaten panelled walls during my ascent to the top flight. Gaining the landing, I fumbled for a match and struck it into life. Before me appeared a narrow door, coffin-like, upon which the number five had been chalked. The second of the keys fitted the lock, and I crossed the threshold.

The attic room was sparsely furnished. A bed with an iron frame, a desk and chair facing one of the circular windows I had seen from outside, a wash-basin and mirrored cabinet, a small primus stove, a single wardrobe, a few shelves, and a gas-lamp affixed to a wall formed the sole contents. The floor was bare boards. All the walls were unpainted.

The ceiling sloped acutely from the inner wall to the outer wall, and the roof itself was therefore directly overhead.

I lit the gas and put my valise on the bed. I then unpacked its contents, a spare suit, change of underwear, toiletries, my writing materials, and two bottles of English gin.

I found a dusty tumbler glass in the cabinet, washed it clean, and then poured a large measure of the liquid into it. I took the glass and the bottle over to the desk and sat down, lit a cigarette, and began to drink. The sharp icy edges of fugue-state that always accompanied the lunar fever were only bearable when dulled by alcohol. I did not wish to write, but the horrible compulsion was upon me. When it took possession of my brain I was no longer myself but some terrible Other, and the only thing to do was to drink and drink until the possessing force was conquered and I could fall, stupefied, into the relief of complete unconsciousness.

So I drank.

Then, unable to resist the lure of the old crime, I wrote.

And finally, after swallowing two of the aoneiric pills, there came a dreamless sleep.

*

When I awoke, many hours later, I was slumped over the desk. The evidence of my crime lay before me.

A few legible lines survived on the page amidst the labyrinth of scored-out doggerel. It was the wreckage of a poem.

> *the fear of masks removed*
> *as black lightning illumines*
> *new quests for nothing*
> *the amnesiac thoughts*
> *of dying brains*
> *repeated but forgotten*

I washed away the fur in my mouth with water from the sink. Looking out of the circular window, I could see that the court beyond was in semi-darkness. I thought again of vermin, their souls crepuscular, scuttling abroad, who, like me, went in search of welcoming shadows. I felt a smile, without mirth, creep over my face and turned away from the window.

The gas-lamp still flickered and I burnt the poem, lighting a cigarette from its flame, and then heated some strong black acrid coffee on the stove.

Another day stretched out before me. The prospect of it was like grief. Each one seemed more interminable than the last.

*

The next day I received a communication from the doctor named Prozess. It was in the form of a telegram and had been pushed under my door whilst I was absent from my room, having gone out to replenish my supply of English gin and cigarettes. This is what it said:

EXPECT TO ATTEND PERSONALLY TO YOUR CASE
MONDAY STOP

DR PROZESS END

I screwed up the piece of paper on which the words had been printed and tossed it across the room. Reading it had provoked in me a sense of acute anxiety and I slumped onto the bed, rolled onto my back, and tried to think things out. How had I come to this terrible pass? Before the war I had enjoyed a position of great respect and status in society, but now all writers, musicians, and artists were dying off one by one, their very creativity making them more susceptible than the mass of the general populace to the lunar fever. Some had suffered destruction at their own hands, some had been lynched by mobs, and those few who remained—the last of our kind—suffered from disordered thoughts, were drugged into vacancy, or else herded together into leper colonies, into such dreamless ghettos as this one: the Court of Midnight.

*

Later that day I caught my first sight of one of my fellow dwellers in these half-abandoned and grim tenements. I had been sat staring aimlessly out of one of the circular windows when I heard the slam of a door and a limping figure came into view below. He began to circle around the confines of the court, like a prisoner taking his daily exercise in a yard, and I watched him with a growing sense of despair. He was far gone in the final throes of lunar fever. His movements were erratic, like those of a bug partially crippled, and when he turned his face upwards in a random gesture—one born, I suspected, of desire for natural rather than artificial light—I almost recoiled at the sight. His face was a travesty of the human. Fully half was corroded away by craters, revealing the skull beneath. Never before have I seen such white, leprous skin, colourless like alabaster. How terrible were the depths of his wholly black eyes! They stared, devoid of all intelligence, like holes pressed into putty.

And yet, even in what remained of those ruined features, I suddenly recognised all that was left of a old friend of mine, the poet Santon. I shouted out his name, and he seemed to recognise it, for he stopped his aimless perambulations, tilting his head this way and that as if to discern the source of words he had not heard in ages.

"Santon," I cried, "stay where you are! I am coming down to fetch you! It is your old friend, Melchior."

And so I descended, took him by the arm, and led him up into my chambers, seating him on the bed and pouring out a large measure of English gin.

He drank thirstily, spilling a good deal of the alcohol down his white chin. I tried not to stare directly into his eyes, but it seemed that, black as they were, he had not lost his sight. Although he did not look at me directly, I nonetheless felt they were upon me the whole time, as if he saw as clearly at the peripheral edges of vision as he did when his gaze was fixed intently upon an object.

Santon had been, before the advent of the lunar fever, a man of action, someone whose poetry rang true and clear in his deeds as well as his thoughts. He had fought in wars, brawled with his rivals in taverns, and invariably sought to win the secret of words for life rather than death. Not for him the secluded life of the cenobite I had sought. Indeed, he had claimed to despise me for it. And yet there had been a strange respect between us two, I from the old country, and he from the new lands to the west. He had written that I was the past and he the future; but now as imagination itself warped in the rays of the moon, past and future had merged into a single moment of the dying present. Memories and hopes alike were now diseased and unreliable.

"Melchior," he said, in a rasping, sepulchral voice, "I can dream now only of darkness!"

We sat and talked together for hours thereafter, consuming my supply of gin, but as we did so I noted the discrepancy in our recollections of the events that had brought us to this pass. His own explanation for the reasons the foes had come to isolate poets and dreamers to prevent them from contaminating society differed markedly from my own interpretation. I saw it as a consequence of some unnatural outside force acting upon our minds, but Santon insisted that the affliction had germinated within certain sections of mankind, blossoming from the depths of the unconscious and noxiously flowering into reality.

"We were too weak to master our dreams," he mumbled. "What you call the lunar fever is only a mask to hide the truth. The lunar fever is a symptom, not the cause. I know now what that face is staring back at us from the moon. The Death's Head. The doctor. We have been found wanting."

He laughed bitterly and gulped back another slug of neat gin.

I was glad when he finally closed his eyes and drifted off into a deep sleep, for I hated to look at them.

It must have been later than I realised, for gradually, one by one, as if gathering in collective force, the multitudes of bells in the church steeples dotting the skyline around the Court of Midnight began to toll.

I passed over to the window again and saw, as if summoned by the crescendo of bell-ringing, a parade begin in the courtyard below. All the ruinous denizens of the tenements started to spill out of their dwellings, sometimes individually, sometimes in groups, and when they were all collected together the ritual began. It took every last effort of my will to stop myself from joining in with them. Even Santon, who was insensible with catatonic inebriation, turned restlessly to and fro on the bed, as if desirous of participation in the gathering.

Beneath that single flickering gas-lamp in the courtyard below, there were enacted grotesque horrors, all played out in a mocking attitude of jest, as if the participants were staging some grand comedy; the stylised, twisted shapes they formed, in combination and recombination, plumbed the depths of uttermost despair. As I have said, the desire to join in with them was almost overpowering, but though I resisted, still I could not prevent myself from grinning mirthlessly at the spectacle, as if in sympathy with the ends the ritual was performed to celebrate. I can think of no more appropriate analogy than that they had become human mandalas, enacting some terrifying display signifying desolation and idiocy. A terrible sound of laughter rose up from the actors as they struck their distorted poses. As the awful rite reached its culmination, it became one with the tolling of the bells, surging and falling, and it was only when it ceased altogether and a deafening silence terminated the nightmare that I realised I too had been laughing with misery. It was the black laughter of no purpose, the laughter that threatens always to bubble and seethe and roll on and on and on like an endless river of blood.

With the ceremony concluded its participants drifted back into their dwellings, dispersing like the fog of a half-remembered nightmare.

*

I turned back to look over at Santon. He was groaning now, and twisting and turning upon the bed as if in mortal agony. His deathly white skin was covered with a sheen of sweat and ravaged by deep craters. I tried to wake him, but as I grabbed his shoulders, to shake him into consciousness, my fingers sank into the soft flesh beneath his clothes as if moulding wet clay. Perhaps, I thought, if I could open his eyes . . . but the purchase my fingers gained caused first the lids and then the blackened eyes beneath to smear off like ink. And I saw that the eye-sockets were not vacant but provided direct visual access to the phantasmagoria of cryptic images that raged like an aurora inside his empty skull. His dreams flared and finally consumed his consciousness, like flames feeding on a book, leaving behind no meaning in the ashes.

I wrapped his body in blankets and later hauled it downstairs, leaving it at the entrance to the Court of Midnight where it would be collected at some point before dawn, along with the rest of the human debris on the streets. No investigation would be undertaken. The telltale signs of the lunar fever on his corpse would see to that. He would be burnt on one of the funeral pyres erected nightly. If he were recognised his name and photograph would feature on a poster amongst those other artists who had lately perished. Each list naming the dead was welcome; it reduced the number still able to infect the general populace.

*

That night I slept and dreamt of darkness. When I awoke I found my own body riddled with the stigmata of lunar fever. Craters pockmarked my body, and between the hollows ran black veins close to the surface of my white near-pellucid skin. Thoughts, over which I had little control, ran riot through my mind, and I did not believe them to be the product of my own consciousness. I was fully dressed and had obviously ventured abroad during the night—a somnambulist drawn by the allure of the moon. And I kept chattering to myself, repeating over and over again the lines of doggerel I had destroyed previously.

*

Time passed and strange thoughts that are not my own demanded expression, and the only thing left to do was release them whence they were confined.

And so I wrote down this account.

Now the bottle is empty and, I assure you, I am not in the least drunk.

The moon has risen.

I have an appointment for my own good that cannot be put off.

The bells in the endless multitude of church steeples are all tolling in unison with black laughter.

If I go to the window I know I will see the denizens of the Court of Midnight performing the great spectacle once again.

We shall all laugh and dance and dream together.

Another telegram had been pushed under my door. This one read:

ARRIVING TONIGHT AT MIDNIGHT STOP
EXPECT GREAT REVELATIONS STOP
DR. PROZESS END

IN THE COMPLEX

The trains are more frequent than ever. Their rumbling approach makes the room shake and causes the single, bare lightbulb overhead to chart a tiny circle on its short cable. I make a small line on the wall in pencil as each train passes. I have not recorded fewer than five hundred a day. Each time the orderly enters the room with my daily ration of food he scrubs away the marks I have previously made. Whether he allows me to keep possession of the pencil through indifference or via an official order, I cannot say. He refuses to speak a single word. For a long time I wished for a window to see outside, even one that was barred, tiny and high, as in a prisoner's cell. But no longer. I am not, after all, entitled to the rights of a prisoner. Dr Prozess has finally explained the facts to me: I am a symptom of a disease; he is the antidote to it.

When they brought me here, by ambulance, in the dead of night, I first insisted I felt perfectly well and saw no need. But the orderlies calmly showed me the documents that confirmed my health was potentially in serious danger, explained sagely that an attack could occur at any moment, and ended by insisting that the peril not only was confined to myself but could also affect others around me. I had a responsibility to be reasonable in the matter. If my condition worsened, as it was likely to do, then they would be obliged to confine me involuntarily anyway. To demonstrate compliance at this stage would be the first step on my road to recovery.

Lying in the back of the ambulance, they strapped me down and administered a sedative by injection, and I slipped in and out of full awareness as the vehicle raced through the streets. I could not doubt, due to the length of the journey, that I had been taken out of the brightly lit metropolitan area altogether and into the depths of the utterly dark countryside. When the ambulance reached its destination I was still groggy and they carried me across a driveway. The sound of shoes crunching gravel underfoot was accompanied by the rumbling of the trains nearby as the engine-cars hauled carriages over the tracks. I tried to gain some idea of my surroundings, but thick cloud covered the night sky. No outside light emanated from the building into which I was delivered. Only when we had passed through a set of huge metal doors was it possible to see again; and my eyes smarted at the sudden, brilliant white-blue glare caused by endless overhead strip lighting.

When my vision adjusted I saw that the shadows were all wrong, like those of vast insects. They were cast upon the tiled walls, not the floors. They were the type of grotesque, distorted shapes that are thrown up by searchlights. I called out to be unstrapped from the stretcher but was told, with a hiss, to be quiet.

On and on they carried me, deep into the labyrinth of what appeared to be a vast, level complex. As I turned my head from side to side I saw no sign of any other persons roaming inside the structure.

I could, however, still detect the sounds of the trains passing in the distance.

At last the orderlies carried me into a room with a single overhead bulb, gave me a different injection, and left me there as I sank into unconsciousness.

*

Pain accompanied my awakening. My upper front teeth were broken. My lips were swollen and encrusted with blood. I could not see clearly through my right eye, which had half closed up. I tried to call out but could make only a gurgling noise in the back of my throat. I was strapped to the bed in an unfamiliar grey smock. My possessions had been taken away, including my phone and watch, so I could not determine how much time had passed.

Was it morning?

The trains were still running. I could hear them. Perhaps they were freight trains—which often run through the whole night.

Hours later the orderly made his first appearance. It was very brief. I think he simply wanted to make sure I was still alive. He would not reply to any of my questions, but when he returned for a second visit, hours later, he tossed onto my bed a crumpled note upon which were a few words scrawled in pencil:

"You did this to yourself."

When he departed, I heard the sound of bubbling laughter piped into my cell via what I presumed were hidden speakers. The sound must have been looped—a recording—because its intensity did not vary, and it went on and on and on until I actually began screaming to try and block it out. Gradually, almost imperceptibly, the volume faded to zero and I became aware once more of that omnipresent, dim rumble of trains in the background.

I think I passed days in this fashion. The orderly, though, must have entered the room on the few occasions I slept, for the jug of brackish water was replenished and two dollops of congealed muck, mostly rice, were left for me to eat from a round plastic plate. The bedpan was much less frequently replaced, and its stench permeated the interior of the cell.

They had removed the bonds that had kept me immobile, but I scarcely had the strength even to make a circuit of the room in search of its hidden speakers. When the noise of laughter returned it seemed to emanate from all directions at once, as if mocking my attempts to isolate the source.

It was, however, during one of these circuits, that I discovered the stub of pencil left behind by the orderly. The thing must have fallen from his pocket and rolled out of sight, concealed underneath the bed. Then again, perhaps it had been placed there deliberately, as part of some test—or experiment—which I could not fathom. I knew that it formed some sort of link with the reason for my being confined in the first instance, and that the use I made of it would be of significant import. Whether or not they anticipated my first impulse I cannot say; but it was to drive the point into the artery below my left ear, push deep, and put an end to everything.

Instead, I began marking on the wall the passage of each train as it passed by. Quite why I began to do so it is difficult to explain; but to keep a strictly accurate record became an obsession with me. I felt, in some profound yet irrational way, that the rhythm of my own existence was intimately connected with their continued, regular motion. Some long delay between one and the next wrought panic in me, like that overwhelming sense of doom that prefigures impending heart failure.

And so further days passed.

*

Although the marks on the wall were regularly erased, I was allowed to keep the pencil. Perhaps I had done something that was expected of me, and regarded as the correct behaviour, for the orderly handed me another note, one that this time read:

"You are to be taken on a visit tomorrow."

I had no idea exactly what this meant. Was I to be taken around the confines of the building or permitted to leave it (presumably accompanied by my captors)? I found it hard to believe that the latter could be the case. They surely would anticipate that the first thought to spring into my mind—as indeed it had done—was to consider an attempt to get away from their clutches altogether.

I turned the question over and over again in my head during the waiting period. Moreover, as I did so I gradually realised that a new consideration bubbled up therein. I became increasingly anxious that, due to this turn of events, trains would pass without my being able to keep up-to-date my record of their existence. I seriously considered making a protest about being taken on this "visit," but then considered that the manner in which the note was phrased was more in the nature of an instruction, or an order, than a request. To make any objection might well mean the privileges I had gained since my arrival might be revoked. As a consequence, I might even damage myself, as I had been assured I had done previously, and I had no desire to reopen wounds that had only just begun to heal properly.

But I need not have concerned myself.

Before being taken on the visit, while being tied into a wheelchair for that purpose, the kindly orderly sat on the edge of my bed and continued to detail the passage of the trains on my behalf with the stub of pencil, since I could not do so.

I was ferried about the structure by another orderly I had not previously seen, an individual as silent and inscrutable as his fellow employee.

We passed down narrow corridors illuminated by the overhead strip lighting I recalled from my last trip, and I saw again the crazily distorted shadows on the tiled walls. They disturbed me more than ever. I had thought them to be drug-hallucinations or faulty memories on my part. Now there could be no doubt that they were as real as all the other objects I saw here in the complex. My mind, you see, was remarkably clear and focused, without any of the mental turmoil that had dogged my arrival.

At last the journey terminated at the entrance to another cell. The orderly slid open the metal cover of a spyhole, glanced within, turned on the light, unlocked the steel door, and wheeled me into deepest darkness.

He then walked out and relocked the door behind him, with me still tied to the wheelchair.

I could see nothing. The blind void inside that cell almost seemed tangible, as if I had been plunged bodily into a huge tank of thick black ink. I even struggled for breath, such was the shock of the transition. And then my hearing and smell began to gain in alertness, in reaction to the sudden sensory cessation from my eyesight. I detected a low moaning whisper, gradually getting closer and closer, accompanied by the rank smell of a long-unwashed body. Something flopped towards me awkwardly in the darkness, half crawling and half dragging itself across the short distance between us. The stench increased.

I struggled in the wheelchair, but my bonds prevented any movement away from the approaching entity that sniffed the air around me greedily.

It got hold of my legs, pulling itself up onto me. I turned my head away, but my chin was gripped by a claw-like hand, more bone than flesh. The stench now made me gag; a wet, curiously hollow mouth closed over my own and then slithered a wet path across my cheeks and neck. An inanity punctuated the assault, words in a language from the back of its throat. Words I seemed to know but could not understand, and definitely not foreign—"ereh fo tuo em teg"—something grossly reversed in its form.

I struggled as best I could in the total darkness, resisting the clamour of the creature, shouting out for the orderly, nauseous with terror and repulsion.

The door was unlocked.

The thing that had latched onto me slipped away, crawling back to the corner whence it came.

A shaft of vivid blue light invaded the room as the door was thrust open.

My eyes smarted at the flash, powerful as a lightning burst. The scene was doubtless rendered stark and clear to the orderly; he must have seen a tableau wrought from nightmare-made-life.

But I was stunned by the intensity of the illumination and, before my pupils could make the adjustment, was turned around and wheeled out of the cell, back towards my own.

*

When I had the opportunity to examine it again, shortly after the visit I have described, I had the distinct impression that the orderly had not kept up my accurate record of the passing of the trains. Some of his pencil marks were scarcely visible, as if he were unsure whether a train had really passed by or not. His attempt to substitute for me was slovenly, even if kindly in intent. Also, the number he set down in my absence appeared insufficient for the time that had passed. The trains kept to a regular schedule, of this I was certain; even though I could not confirm the fact by reference to the likes of a clock or stopwatch. (I would have given anything to obtain such a device.) It seemed to me that I had to try and impress upon the power running the complex that to cause my absence from my work was neither in their best interests or mine.

During a lull in the passage of the trains back and forth, I found time to write a single sentence of complaint amidst the myriad of the day's small straight lines.

"I request not to be taken again from my cell," I wrote.

The following morning when I awoke the message was gone, with all my lines (which was usual). They had obviously reacted badly to my impetuous request, however, since my feet had been crudely amputated at the ankles during the night. The stumps were wrapped in blood-caked bandages. Written multiple times on the bandages, although somewhat obscured by deep red stains, was the reply:

"You brought this upon yourself."

The speakers were on full blast for the whole day.

Thoughtfully, though, they still allowed me use of the pencil.

*

I refrained (as I am sure you will appreciate) from making any other requests during the weeks that followed, and duly suffered no further, self-responsible, mutilation. I had the business of the trains to occupy me, after all, and did not care for any distraction from that all-important task. Although I had been corrected, I had also been left to concentrate on my work and had not been taken away again from my cell, which was quite in accordance with the request I had written down. The loss of my feet proved less of a punishment than I first imagined. For I had nowhere to go in any case, and no desire to be elsewhere. In fact, I even felt gratitude that they had been so considerate in their chastisement. I don't doubt that the power behind the complex knew that the removal of my hands instead of my feet would have been for me truly intolerable.

The wheelchair now stood as a fixture in the corner of my cell, and I would periodically sit in it and navigate around the room for my own amusement, especially when the speakers were on full blast. Of course I kept a mental account of trains passing whilst occupied in this diversion and then added them to the daily record on the wall once I had completed my circular navigations.

You may wonder whether I ever thought of the outside world or of my past life, but I can honestly state that it is of little importance to me and a subject upon which I did not much dwell—except in one regard. After all, it was my actions therein that had led to my present state of affairs, and to this making amends for it, an extraction as much for my own benefit as for society's. My disease would infect others and my quarantine was only right. Communicable disease of my type is a form of violence when those afflicted by it refuse treatment. It is even more dangerous because it manifests itself unseen, with no physical symptoms.

*

One afternoon I found my cell unlocked. The door was left ever so slightly ajar. I thought at first that the crack between the jamb and frame was an illusion. Wheeling myself over to it, however, I discovered my eyes were not deceiving me.

This, of course, presented me with a dilemma.

Had it been purposefully left unlocked or not? Was it a test of some kind?

I could scarcely neglect my work of recording the trains passing by and satisfy my curiosity on some unauthorised jaunt along the outside corridors. In any case, I had already advised them I did not wish to leave the cell. But what if I were meant to leave the cell? Removal of my feet had been a consequence of my expressing that desire to remain inside. And I was not leaving the confines of the whole complex itself, after all, just venturing beyond this tiny sub-section of it.

Perhaps there was a solution.

I wheeled myself back to the wall and rapidly filled in enough pencil marks in advance to cover the period of my absence. Provided I returned to my cell within an hour or so, it was impossible for me to have fallen behind in the tally. Recall, too, that I was very likely to encounter no one else wandering the corridors at this time. The orderlies made their rounds only in the morning.

Having satisfied myself that the marks I had made were sufficient, I returned to the door and slowly opened it wider, ensuring that I made as little noise as possible.

The corridor was deserted and stretched out ahead of me in both directions. I decided to turn right, though I had no idea whether this would lead me deeper into the complex or out towards its edge. There were no crazily angled shadows on the walls, an absence that seemed to me to be significant, though I could not say why.

I wheeled myself along for several minutes, passing locked cells. No sounds came from within them, so I imagined they were either empty or else occupied by the silent. If the force running the complex felt it necessary to remove limbs then it was entirely possible that tongues, too, might be extracted.

The unaccustomed exertion took its toll on my body, and I had to pause in order to recuperate. My arms ached and my breathing was laboured. While I sat there, marooned in the labyrinth, I caught the noise of the trains passing—their dim rumble muffled, and thus reaching me from further off in the distance than from my own cell. I therefore deduced I had travelled deeper into the complex.

And then I detected another sound, not mechanical but, rather, insect-like. Long, drawn-out, and chitinous in nature. It went on and on, rising and falling in tone. I continued to sit there. Should I seek out the source or avoid it altogether? There was no guarantee that I would not be putting myself in danger by satisfying my curiosity.

However, while I was debating the point in my own mind, I felt someone take hold of the back of my wheelchair and shove me forwards. An orderly had crept up behind me unawares, probably just exiting from one of the cells I had passed. I had not heard his footfalls and turned back and down to see he was wearing rubber-soled, white canvas shoes. My head still twisted back, I glanced up at his face. It was a mask of benign indifference.

He ignored all my attempts to impede our progress towards the source of the disturbance—my cries of protests, reasoning, apologies—and even put me in a headlock when I physically tried to resist by clambering out of the wheelchair.

Had I, then, been observed all along? Had my cell door been left ajar not through oversight but on purpose? I could reach no other conclusion. It seemed important to them to impress upon me the fact that each punishment they inflicted upon me was a direct consequence of exercising my own free will. They were not, in and of themselves, directly to blame.

The noise like insects massing grew even louder, and the orderly wheeled me through a series of double doors, straight into the heart of the commotion.

I was in a former library of vast proportions. It was circular in design, the interior architecture baroque and built across four open-plan floors. The place was in total chaos. Columns of high, carved wooden shelves and antique bookcases had either been denuded of their contents or else overturned and left in a state of wreckage. Most of the books had been stripped of their essence; innumerable torn pages littered the floors and the remains had been tossed down into the central well at the core of the structure. Scattered amidst the library were hordes of mutilated inmates each dressed, as I was, in a grey smock. They were the source of the chitinous noise. It rose and fell in unison as they worked, pulling volumes from the shelves and tearing them to pieces. Some lacked hands for the task and used their teeth.

They had all been blinded—eyes extracted at the root with the surrounding skin sewn back.

Black holes gaped sightlessly—abominable flowers in the stark blue-white electric glare.

The orderly bent down to my right ear and whispered into it, ever so softly, some lines of doggerel.

the fear of masks removed
as black lightning illumines
new quests for nothing
the amnesiac thoughts
of dying brains
repeated but forgotten

I thought, then, he might reach for my eyes in order to pluck them out with his long bony fingers, but instead he turned me around and wheeled me along the winding length of corridors back to my cell.

I noticed that the shadows had returned.

On the bed was another note for me. It read:

"You left too many marks."

*

The next time I awoke I found they had severed my left hand.

Throughout the same day the familiar orderly began ferrying piles of books into my cell. He brought them in cardboard boxes, dumped the contents on the floor, and then returned with more. This went on for the several hours. While he was absent I arranged them into free-standing columns as best I could whilst I sat amongst them and with only one hand now remaining to me. I did not take much note of their actual contents or titles, although I was aware that they were a mixture of old and new volumes, paperbacks and hardbacks, and all rather battered (although not torn apart). I did note, however, since the fact was so remarkable, they were all written under the same byline: Dr Prozess.

I also neglected to keep up with my record of the trains passing while I was engaged in this new activity. I was immediately tormented by the question of what exactly constituted the appropriate response to this fresh development concerning the arrival of all these books.

Was I meant to read them or destroy them?

Even doing neither might be interpreted as an act of sedition.

I opened one at random. The first words I encountered were: "You are not to read this book."

I closed it and picked up another. This time the first words were: "Forget about this book."

I decided to open just one more and no others. The words my gaze fell upon were:

"You are the book."

Then they turned on the speakers again and I couldn't hear the trains at all.

*

The next thing I was aware of was being wheeled along the corridors. I knew I had greatly offended the rules of the complex this time and that I was at last going to meet Dr Prozess face-to-face. What revelations he had in store for me would be more interesting than the mediocre threat of removing my right hand or my eyes. Perhaps it would be necessary to slice into my brain, so that only the parts that registered the appropriately infinite degree of pain and terror would be left intact. The drooling sutures crisscrossing my shaven skull told me that they had probably already monkeyed around with my memory.

They were taking me outside of the complex. We passed several signs with arrows pointing the way to the exit. I tried to ignore the gleefully dancing insectoid shadows upon the walls.

At last there was a familiar set of titanic metal doors up ahead. On their inside was scrawled the legend:

"Exit and Prozess."

Then I saw the outside world for myself.

A television-sky receiving a broadcast of a close-up of the death's-head moon. Brilliant, dazzling blacks and whites, combining and recombining; maddening in intensity; a heaven of unendurably nightmarish static. Sublunary shadows stretched in all directions over a landscape of hills and vales, crisscrossed by motorway flyovers and surface-level railway lines. Endless automated freight trains, all riven by rust and corrosion, rumbled along the tracks, back and forth, while huge self-driving lorries, caked in soot, their combustion engines groaning, rolled arduously above them. And in between the railway lines and the roads there was a dull grey carpet of motion, a countryside of refuse and ashes teeming with a sea of deformed locusts pockmocked by the reductionism of lunar fever, things that might once—before the strange revelations of Dr Prozess, that is—have been human beings.

I covered my eyes, but my skin tingled and then began to peel as the seeping corrosion of inevitable futurity worked its backward effect upon me.

*

After I was taken back to my cell, the overhead light had been turned off for good and I was left to stew forever in total darkness. The speakers were left on continuously, at full volume, and I slipped in and out of consciousness, unable to think coherently due to chronic sleep deprivation. My existence became an indistinguishable monotony of exhaustion and of horror.

Other parts of my body were removed on a weekly basis; even certain internal organs.

Eventually I ceased to notice the noise from the speakers. I tried to detect the noise of the trains, but the depthless silence was as absolute as the darkness.

Then, one time, an incalculable period later, I dreamt I had a visitor.

The door to my cell was unlocked. Another inmate from elsewhere in the complex was wheeled inside, but I could not hear what he said, having no ears.

Instead I sniffed the air, located a strangely familiar scent, and hauled my rotten, mutilated carcass towards its source, trying desperately to communicate my misery.

I could see nothing through the hollow craters where my eyes should have been.

I found the footless legs of my visitor, clambered up onto its lap, and held it in an embrace, desperate for any human contact, and managed to gargle out the words "ereh fo tuo em teg" from the back of my throat.

But they swiftly took my visitor away.

Now they have finally loaded me onto one of the trains whose destination is nowhere, along with all the others of my ilk from the complex—we who had brought this fate upon ourselves.

And thus, of necessity, to be utterly forgotten, as futurity must redact the past.

ACKNOWLEDGMENTS

"The Age of Decayed Futurity," first published in *Cinnabar's Gnosis*, edited by Dan Ghetu (Ex Occidente Press, 2009).

"Apartment 205," first published in *The White Hands and Other Weird Tales* (Tartarus Press, 2003).

"The Black Mould," first published in *The Man Who Collected Machen* (Ex Occidente Press, 2010).

"Cesare Thodol: Some Lines Written on a Wall," first published in *Strange Attractor Journal* #2 (2005).

"Court of Midnight," first published in *Uncertainties II,* edited by Brian Showers (Swan River Press, 2015).

"The Crimson Fog," first published in *The Red Brain: Great Tales of the Cthulhu Mythos,* edited by S. T. Joshi (Dark Regions, 2017).

"A Gentleman from Mexico," first published in *Summer Chills,* edited by Stephen Jones (Carroll & Graf, 2007).

"Ghorla," first published in *Inferno,* edited by Ellen Datlow (Tor, 2007).

"In the Complex," first published in *The Prozess Manifestations* (Zagava Press, 2017).

"Mannequins in Aspects of Terror," first published in *The White Hands and Other Weird Tales* (Tartarus Press, 2003).

"My World Has No Memories," first published in *Written in Darkness* (Egaeus Press, 2014).

"Outside Interference," first published in *Written in Darkness* (Egaeus Press, 2014).

"Regina vs. Zoskia," first published in *The First Black Book of Horror,* edited by Charles Black (Mortbury Press, 2007).

"Sentinels," first published in *Alone on the Darkside,* edited by John Pelan (Penguin/Roc, 2006).

"Thyxxolqu," first published in *Shades of Darkness,* edited by Barbara & Christopher Roden (Ash-Tree Press, 2008).

"Vrolyck," first published in *The White Hands and Other Weird Tales* (Tartarus Press, 2003).

"The White Hands," first published in *The White Hands and Other Weird Tales* (Tartarus Press, 2003); current longer version first published in *The Mammoth Book of Best New Horror #15,* edited by Stephen Jones (Robinson/Carroll & Graf, 2004).

Mark Samuels lives in Kings Langley, England. He is the author of six previous short story collections—*The White Hands and Other Weird Tales* (2003), *Black Altars* (2003), *Glyphotech & Other Macabre Processes* (2008), *The Man Who Collected Machen* (2010), *Written in Darkness* (2014), and *The Prozess Manifestations* (2017)—and two novels: *The Face of Twilight* (2006) and *A Pilgrim Stranger* (2017). His latest book is a compilation of recondite essays on some classic authors of weird fiction under the title *Prophecies and Dooms* (2018).

Michael Dirda, who received the Pulitzer Prize for his essays and book reviews in *The Washington Post*, is the author, most recently, of the Edgar Award-winning *On Conan Doyle* and the essay collection, *Browsings: A Year of Reading, Collecting, and Living with Books*. He is currently at work on an appreciation of late 19th and early 20th-century genre fiction in Britain.